WHEN WE *Burn*

New York Times and *USA Today* Bestselling Author

KRISTEN PROBY

&
AMPERSAND
PUBLISHING, INC.

When We Burn

THE BLACKWELLS OF MONTANA
BOOK ONE

KRISTEN PROBY

&
AMPERSAND
PUBLISHING, INC.

WHEN WE BURN

A Blackwells of Montana Novel

Kristen Proby

For every girl who thinks she's too broken for love.
You're not.
This one's for you.

Spicy Girls Book Club

TBR

Reading List:

Beyond the Thistles by Samantha Young
Nero by SJ Tilly
Forbidden Hearts by Corinne Michaels
Tattered by Devney Perry
Runaway Love by Melanie Harlow
The Secret by Lulu Moore
Stay by Willow Aster
Bourbon & Lies by Victoria Wilder
Just This Once by Lena Hendrix
Bull Rush by Maggie Rawdon

Content Warnings

You can find a comprehensive content warning list at the following link:

https://www.kristenprobyauthor.com/potential-trigger-content-warnings

Kristen

Prologue

DANI

Twelve Years Old

"**D**ANI!"

Oh, no. No, no, no.

I made him mad. *Again.*

My heart is pounding in my ears, and I think I'm going to throw up.

Hide, Dani.

No, I can't hide. It'll only make things way worse if he has to look for me.

I poke my head around the side of the living room, looking into the kitchen, and swallow hard when Dad's eyes narrow on me.

"You didn't do your chores this morning."

"I d-d-did. I just forgot the eggs." By the time I utter

the last word, it's hardly audible, and he's stomping toward me. Oh, God. *Please don't do this, Dad.*

I cringe when he takes me by the shoulders and gives me a shake. How I wish Holden was here.

"You're worthless," Dad spits into my face. I can smell beer on him, even though it's before nine in the morning. "You're *nothing*. I should kill you, just like I did your fucking whore of a mother."

I can't stop the sob that comes out of my throat, and that only makes him madder.

"Oh, are you going to *cry*? Of course, you are, you stupid bitch. Well, then I'll give you something to cry about."

"No!"

He stops, and I cringe. Talking back is the absolute worst thing to do. He tugs me even closer, his nose almost touching mine.

"You think you can fucking sass me, you little cunt?"

I whimper, and that horrible smile slithers over his face. *I might die today.* I almost wish I would because then this wouldn't happen to me again.

"Guess it's time to teach you a lesson."

I want to plead, to beg for him not to do this. But it wouldn't do any good because my father is a monster. He's worse than anything that could be thought up in movies or books.

He's the devil.

With something between a snarl and a laugh, he grabs my hair and yanks me, striding fast through the kitchen.

He's not going to just run the faucet over my face this time?

Oh, God. Mom, if you're in heaven, I think I'm coming to see you today.

He busts through the back door, still dragging me. I can vaguely hear my sisters crying. I don't know where they came from. My eyes are wild as I try to see, to look around us. I think that's Darby running toward the barn, and I hope with all my might that Dad doesn't see her because she'll get it next.

We're not allowed to go to the barn.

Dad's yelling, but I don't understand the words through the rushing of blood in my ears. I can see the pond now. The pond that's so dirty, so filthy and full of snakes and bugs that none of us will go near it. But right now, my choice has been taken away. Again.

The next thing I know, my head is being held under the water, and all I can hear is the bubbles in my ears. I hold my breath as long as I can, and just when I think I have to take a breath, I'm pulled out, and Dad's face is in mine again.

"You stupid little fucking *bitch*!" I'm gasping, struggling to pull in enough air because I know I'm about to go back into that water.

But suddenly, I hear the horse, and then Holden has punched Dad, knocking him on his butt, and I'm being gently urged away from the water as Holden punches Dad again.

"No!" I scream, reaching for my brother. "He'll kill you!"

Oh, God, what have I done? Dad will kill my brother. *We can't lose him.* We'd never survive.

I hear the crunch of bones, and my heart drops in terror.

"You fucking rat—"

Whack!

"You'll never lay another fucking hand on them, you hear me?" Holden yells.

And then there's a terrifying thump, and I'm too scared to look. But Dad's knocked out, and then Holden's in front of me, holding my face in his hands. "Are you okay, baby?"

I nod, and then I wrap myself around my brother. Oh, God, what if he killed Dad? What would we do if Holden went to jail? As much as I hate him, *please don't let him be dead.*

My sisters are with us now, all crying. Darby's the oldest, and she's trying to comfort us. I feel horrible because I'm so wet, and I don't want them to get wet, too. But no one seems to care about that.

Clinging to each other, Holden herds us to the truck, grabs a towel out of the back seat, and wraps me in it, before getting us settled. There aren't enough seats for all of us to have belts, and we have to sit on laps, but he's driving away from our ranch and over to the Blackwells'.

We always go to the Blackwells' ranch when we need to escape.

I don't know why, but Dad never follows us here. It's the place that we feel the safest.

Someone must have called ahead because Brooks,

Beckett, and Bridger are there to greet us. I wonder when Holden told them we were coming. I'm both mortified and relieved, though, and so thankful that we're here. We're led inside, and it's then that I lose the fragile hold on my strength.

The tears start.

My father tried to kill me.

And then as I replay the last twenty minutes, they won't stop, and it only makes it harder for me to breathe.

"You should take her up to the shower," Brooks says to Darby, who's holding my hand. "Get her cleaned up. You don't want to get sick from that pond water, Dani."

"I don't want a shower," I say, instinctively pulling away from Darby, but then Bridger's there, and he takes my hand.

"It's okay, kitten," he says, and my heart pounds as I look up at him. He's smiling, but his eyes look hard, like he might be mad. I don't think he's mad at me, though. "Just a shower, not a bath."

"That's right," Darby says as she leads me upstairs and into a bathroom. "I promise, you're safe in this water, Dani. I promise."

I take a deep breath and look back at Bridger. He's three years older than me, and he's always been my friend.

He nods and steps back. "I'll wait right out here. It's okay."

I sigh, and then Darby murmurs something to him and closes the door.

"Come on, baby girl. Let's get you cleaned up."

The shower wasn't so bad, even though we had to wash my hair and my face, and now I'm sitting out on the porch with all of the siblings. Not just mine, but Bridger's, too. There are ten of us kids, so it's a good thing the porch is big.

Their mom came home—not surprised to see us all there—and gave us ice cream. Vanilla fudge ripple.

It's my favorite.

"How are you doing?" Bridger's sitting on one side of me, and his sister, Billie, is on the other. My twin sister, Alex, is sitting on the floor between my knees, and I'm running my fingers through her hair, soothing us both. It's what Mama used to do when we'd sit at her feet.

"Better." I smile up at him. All of the Blackwells are cute, but Bridger? I've started to notice things about him lately. Things that I'd never tell him because I would be mortified. He's just my friend, but he's my brother's best friend, and I know those two things will never change. "You don't have to stay with me. I'm okay."

"I'm happy here," he says and then looks over my head to his sister. "You happy here, Billie?"

"Yep," she says and licks her cone. "Why did he do it, Dani?"

I blow out a breath, still not altogether steady. *It.* No one wants to say out loud what he just tried to do to me.

"I-I-I forgot to get the eggs this morning, and when he said he was going to hurt me, I said *n-n-no.*"

They're quiet for a long minute, both of them forgetting all about their ice cream. Alex tips her head against my leg. She's so quiet, and I know we'll huddle together under the blankets later and cry.

"He's a monster," Billie whispers, repeating what I thought myself earlier. She leans her head on my shoulder.

But Bridger still hasn't said anything at all, so I take a peek up at him, and the look on his handsome face almost scares me.

He's *mad.*

"Bridge?"

"Fuck, Dani." He shakes his head and tosses his cone into a trash can before he wraps his arms around me and hugs me close. "I'm sorry. I'm so fucking sorry."

I let him hold me, because Bridger gives really good hugs. Billie's rubbing circles on my back. I look around the porch and notice that everyone is quiet, watching us.

They heard.

Holden's breathing hard, his eyes narrowed. I know he wants to kill Dad, but he can't because then he'd go to jail, and he won't leave us.

So we're just stuck. Charlie, my baby sister at just two years younger than me, crawls into Holden's lap, crying. She's ten, but she still clings to our older brother as if she's a baby, and he holds on to her but never looks away from me.

I feel loved here. Protected. But I have no idea how long this feeling will last. *If it will at all.* Because the monster will never stop.

Chapter One

BRIDGER

Her skin is velvet. Pure sin. Pure fucking everything. Her big blue eyes shine as she bites that lower lip and spreads her legs, welcoming me to rest my pelvis between them. I'm so fucking hard, I can barely breathe as I rub my length through her already wet pussy, and she arches her neck back on a moan.

"Bridger. Yes. Oh, God, yes."

Her fingers fist in my hair, but I grab her wrists, kiss them, and pin them over her head before I lick and suck on her already hard nipples.

"You like this, Dani? You want me to lick your delectable little body?"

She purrs, her hips lift, and her mouth makes a perfect O as I rear my hips back and rest the crown of my cock against her entrance.

"Yes. Please, Bridger."

I nip her jaw, lick my way over to her ear, and whisper, "I'm going to fuck you so good, sweetheart."

"Yes!"

I've wanted her for my entire adult life. She's a siren that I can't walk away from, and with her spread out, so hot and wet and needy for me, I can't resist her. I nudge just the tip inside of her, and she moans, and I can't hold back.

I slam into her. Her eyes go wide and glassy, and her legs lift, already begging for more. Her walls clench around me, as if she's already right there, on the edge of falling apart.

"Jesus Christ," I growl against her lips, licking along the seam of her lips, and she opens for me, giving me back as good as I give. "You're a goddamn temptress, you know that?"

She's so damn beautiful.

So perfect.

"Oh, Daddy!"

"Daddy!"

Oh, fuck.

I turn onto my side to hide my morning wood, courtesy of that sexy-as-fuck dream about a woman I've wanted for-fucking-ever, but a woman that I'll never have.

"Good morning, peanut."

Birdie, my five-year-old, giggles behind me. "You have to wake up, Daddy. We have to go shopping."

I reach over to tap my phone and scowl. "It's only eight, baby. The stores don't open for a while yet."

"You need breakfast."

I grin. That's code for *I want breakfast.*

"You're right. We need to eat. How about if I take a quick shower and then get started on the French toast, okay?"

She leans over so she can look at my face and pats my cheek. Now that my nether regions have calmed down a bit, I roll to her and pull her in for a big hug.

"On second thought, never mind. We're not going shopping. You're not big enough to go to school. You're just a baby."

I bury my face in her neck and blow raspberries, making her giggle. She smells like her baby shampoo, and she's so sweet and small in her cute *Tangled* nightgown.

"I'm five." More giggles as I continue to kiss her cheeks. "I'm a big girl."

"No way. You're my baby." I hug her tight, and she wraps her little arm around my neck and hugs me back. "My tiny peanut."

She was *so small* when she was born. So little and sweet. But never fragile. Not my girl. Even with the medical challenges we've had over the past year, she's never been weak.

"I love you, Daddy."

I grin sleepily at her and kiss her cheek. "I love you, too, baby bird. Do you *really* have to grow up and go to school?"

"Yep. And I need clothes and shoes and notebooks. There's a list."

"Ah, yes, the list." I bop her on the nose. "You go get dressed and watch something on your tablet for a little while, okay? I'll get ready, too. We won't forget your list."

11

"Okay." She launches herself off my bed and runs for her bedroom, just down the hall from mine.

I sigh and drag my hands down my face. I came off a three-day stretch last night, and when I got home, Dani was outside, wearing fuck-me short shorts and looking like a walking wet dream. No wonder I dreamed about fucking her.

The woman is gorgeous, with all that dark hair and blue eyes, and don't even get me started on her curves. Breasts and hips that would fit perfectly in my hands.

And there goes my dick again.

With a sigh, I get out of bed and pad into my attached bathroom, resigned to fucking my hand to get rid of this hard-on that only seems to happen when I see my sexy neighbor. Or even *think* about her.

I've known Dani Lexington since we were little kids. She's a few years younger than I am, and she and her siblings were staples at our ranch growing up. Her brother, Holden, the eldest of the siblings, is one of my best friends. I know that they had a rough childhood that fucked with all five of them. What they went through... well, their father should have been in prison. He was fucked up.

I'm sure that if I talked with Holden and told him that I wanted to date his sister, he'd be pretty cool about it. After he punched me, just for good measure.

I'd expect nothing less.

But Dani and I have been good friends through a lot of shit in her childhood. Then, when she became a teenager, I noticed that I didn't actually have *brotherly* feelings toward her, but I was eighteen, and she was a minor.

No way I was going to dick around with that. Literally.

So, I kept a healthy distance. She graduated and went to college in Bozeman, and I stayed here to be a firefighter.

And I met my ex-wife. And the rest, as they say, is history.

But now she's back, and although she's still put me squarely in the friend zone, I'm going to do my damnedest to make her see that we could be so much more than friends. I know I want her. I've wanted her for a long time.

But she's also been gone for a while, and I need to get to know her again. I'm not stupid. I can't just flash a smile, tell her she's fucking gorgeous—even though she *is* —and expect her to spread those pretty legs and tell me she can't live another minute without me.

It's going to take some time. And given her traumatic past, I don't want to scare her. I don't even know if I *would* scare her if I told her how much I want her.

Again, I need to get to know her better.

With the water running, I strip out of my T-shirt and boxers and get into the spray, my hand immediately wrapping around the base of my cock and moving up, with thoughts from my dream in the forefront of my imagination as I slide my fist up and down my length, until I come hard against the tile, then grab the handheld and wash it all away.

Jesus, this is ridiculous.

"Daddy, I'm hungry."

"Coming, peanut."

Between Birdie and a *very* full-time job of being fire chief of Bitterroot Valley, I have enough on my plate already, but ever since Dani returned to town, it's highlighted that something was missing from my life. I'm not lonely, per se—my life doesn't allow that if I'm honest—but on the quiet nights when Birdie is asleep in bed, there's been a noticeable absence of someone to spend that time with. I want to cuddle up with someone, feel them against me, talk about my day, and listen about hers. And I know that the only woman who appeals to me is Dani.

In some respects, it's always been her.

"If we're going to the pool party later, we need to go now." I'm holding the door open for Birdie, waiting for her to shimmy into her sneakers. The shoes I bought her at the beginning of summer are way too small now.

It's a good thing we're going shopping.

"Okay," she says after grabbing her sunglasses, which always makes me grin. She decided that because I wear them, she should, too, and hers are pink with green polka dots. "I'm ready."

I hear the lawn mower going as we walk out to my

truck, and suddenly, Birdie is waving like mad. The lawn mower cuts off, and I follow my daughter's gaze.

There's Dani, standing behind the now-quiet mower, in cutoff denim shorts that barely hide her ass, a white tank that leaves absolutely fucking *nothing* to the imagination, her hair up on her head, and a sheen of sweat covering her dewy skin.

Fuck me.

"Hi, Dani," Birdie yells, still waving.

"Hi, Birdie," Dani replies with a sweet smile for my daughter. Then her gorgeous blue eyes shift to mine. "Hi, Bridger."

"Dani." I nod at her the way I always do and nudge Birdie toward the truck. "Let's go, peanut."

"We're going shopping for school," Birdie informs Dani. "'Cause it starts next week."

"I know," Dani says with a chuckle. "I'm going to be your teacher."

My heart stops. *What?* I knew that Dani would be teaching at the elementary school this year, but I didn't know that meant that she would be my daughter's teacher, which means I'll see her often, and *that* is a very good thing.

"You are?" Birdie asks, almost screeching with excitement. "Yay!"

Dani laughs now and nods. "I am. Your dad should have received that information in an email." Her gaze turns to mine again, with more humor in it now. "Along with the supplies list."

I take a deep breath and let it out slowly, willing my

galloping heart to slow the fuck down. "I must have missed that part."

"Have fun shopping," she says and turns to start the mower again. It only takes her two pulls on the string before it fires up, waves, and then walks behind it, her hips and ass moving with every step, and I have to pry my eyes away.

Get a grip, Blackwell.

"Come on, peanut. We have a full day today."

"If you spent all day school shopping, you need a beer." Blake, one of my brothers, passes me a cold bottle, and I flip off the cap and take a pull. Yeah, I could use a drink, and not because of the shopping spree that I took my daughter on today. No, I need it because I just discovered that Dani is also at this pool party.

Which makes sense because it's being held at a friend's ranch, Ryan Wild, who Dani is now related to by marriage.

Of course, she's here. I should have realized that she would be. But I didn't think of it, and now here I am, sitting with a few of my brothers, Dani's brother, Holden, and a couple of the Wilds, watching as kids run around, swim, and play while a whole bunch of people drift around.

It's three families, and yet, it's chaos.

Because apparently in Bitterroot Valley, no one

knows the meaning of having just a couple of kids and getting on with it. No, we're overachievers here in this town. Someday, I'd like to have more kids. Maybe not five, though. That's a lot.

"It actually wasn't that bad," I say to Blake. "I ended up getting her more shit than she needs, and we found everything on the supply list the school sent. She'll be set for a few months at least. Until she has another growth spurt, and I have to replace it all again."

"It's good that she's growing so well," Blake, the doctor in the family, says. "It means she's healthy, Bridge."

"I know. I'm not complaining at all. Hell, I'll buy her a new wardrobe every week if it means we keep her healthy."

I glance over to where Birdie is playing with a few other kids just a couple of years older than she is. She's laughing and running, and it wasn't that long ago that we didn't know if she'd be doing something so simple again.

No, I'm absolutely not complaining.

"How are things at the hospital?" I ask him. Blake is a doctor, splitting his time between the family practice clinic and the hospital. I always figured he'd move to a city and start a practice, but he came back to Bitterroot Valley, and I'm glad. He's a damn valuable asset to this town. I'm close to all of my brothers, but since Blake is only two years older than me, we've always been tight, not to mention that, given our career choices, we're like-minded, too.

"Busy. Always busy." He sighs and sips his own beer,

which tells me that he's not on call today. And neither am I.

That never happens.

"Any good stories to share?" Brooks, our eldest brother, asks. "Anything particularly fucked up you've seen lately?"

Blake laughs and sits back, thinking. "Aside from a guy who almost tore off his face with a garbage can? Not really."

"That's disgusting," I say with a scowl. But I know exactly who that was. I was on that ambulance call.

"Dinner's ready," someone calls from the outdoor kitchen area. I get Birdie's plate made first and situate her with her friends at a little picnic table just for the kids at the side of the patio. She's thrilled with a hotdog, chips, and some watermelon, and then I go back to fill my own plate and sit back where I was before. I can see Birdie from where I'm sitting and can keep an eye on her.

Not that there aren't dozens of eyes on all the kids at all times, but I like being able to see her.

I also happen to notice that Dani's sitting with Charlie, her youngest sister, in one of the lounge chairs by the pool. They're eating, and Charlie's obviously talking Dani's ear off because Dani's just smiling that beautiful smile as she listens. She's in a different outfit this evening, some flowy white pants and a matching white button-down top that's open over a cropped pink tank. One side of the white top falls over a shoulder, showing off golden skin. Her hair is still up, with loose pieces hanging down around her face, and she isn't wearing any makeup.

She doesn't fucking need makeup. It's one of the things I like most about her. She's naturally beautiful.

It makes sense that she's not in a bathing suit. Who would want to be near the water after what she was put through? Fuck, it still affects me, remembering that summer when we were kids.

I-I-I forgot to get the eggs this morning, and when he said he was going to hurt me, I said n-n-no."

I've never felt so fucking enraged. *What sort of monster could do that to his little girl?*

Mentally shaking my head, I take a pull of my beer and turn my attention back to the conversation going on around me.

"Are you guys going to the hootenanny tomorrow?" Beckett asks. "I'll have a booth set up with milk and stuff for sale. Ice cream, too."

"Fuck no," Holden replies, shaking his head. "There are people there. I'll just come get your ice cream from your house."

"You're so social," Blake says with a chuckle. "It's for a good cause, you know. Several, actually."

"I'll donate money. I don't have to go there," Holden replies, his eyes scouting the area for his wife. When he finds her, his shoulders relax.

He married one of my best friends, Millie, months ago. They're stupidly in love, and it's mildly nauseating.

"I have to go," I reply. "I have to man a booth, too."

"In your firefighter gear?" Blake asks.

"Yeah, why?" My brother just grins at me, and I glare back at him. "Fuck off."

"You know you get more donations when you're in uniform," Blake says with a laugh. "Are you going to wear a shirt this year, or go without?"

"Are you jealous?" I tip up an eyebrow, and Blake only laughs harder.

"Fuck no. I think it's hilarious that you're a sex symbol. Women have no taste."

"He's so pretty," Holden adds, enjoying flinging me shit.

"Who is?" Millie asks as she joins us and sits in her husband's lap.

"Bridger," Holden replies.

"Beautiful," Millie agrees, and I flip her off.

"Now, don't make me kick your ass for disrespecting my wife." Holden's voice has no heat in it, and Millie's giggling.

"You're all a bunch of assholes. I'll be keeping my shirt on, thank you very much."

Suddenly, there's a splash, a scream, and my heart thuds as I kick into action. There's a second splash, and I run to the pool and take in what's happening.

Birdie—God, *Birdie*—is in the deep end, flapping around, and Dani has her, pulling her to the side of the pool. I meet her there and pull Birdie out and into my arms. She clings to me, wrapping her arms around my neck.

"Hey, are you okay? What happened?"

"I wanted to swim where it's deep." Her voice is small, and I can tell that it scared her, but she's not hurt.

I turn back to the water and see that Dani's having a

hard time, her clothes now soaked and heavy, and her eyes are wide in terror. Before I can pass Birdie off, several of the guys—Blake, Ryan, and Holden—have jumped into the water and are helping Dani stay above water, leading her to the shallow end of the pool and then out of the water entirely.

She sheds the sopping white shirt and lets it fall, but then her teeth are chattering, her eyes dilated.

Fuck. She's going into shock.

Or having a panic attack.

Maybe both.

Why did she jump in? She's terrified of water.

"Hey," Blake says as he takes a towel from Ryan and wraps it around Dani's shoulders, rubbing her arms briskly. We all know. We all saw what *he* did to her. It strikes me, again, that the way that bastard died was too good for him. "You're okay, sweetheart. I know you don't like the water."

Jesus, she's *terrified* of the water, and she jumped in to help my daughter.

"Can I swim some more?" Birdie asks me, and I kiss her cheek and then set her down, not taking my eyes off Dani.

"No, baby bird. Go wrap up in a towel and play with the other kids."

"But—"

"I said no."

She doesn't argue, and I'm thankful she's mostly so compliant. Yes, she loves to push my buttons—often—but she doesn't fight me when she knows I won't budge.

Considering her mom's selfishness, Birdie's sweetness frequently amazes me.

My daughter runs off, and I cross to where Blake is consoling Dani.

Oh, kitten. I hate this for you.

"In through your nose," he says perfectly calmly, doctor mode obviously kicking in. "Out through your mouth."

"Sorry," she mutters and closes her eyes, her teeth chattering. "I d-don't like water."

"I know," Blake says grimly, and then his eyes find mine. He raises an eyebrow but doesn't say anything as he passes her to me.

I immediately wrap my arms around her and hug her close.

"Thank you, kitten," I murmur into her wet hair. God, I haven't hugged Dani in years, always careful to keep a safe distance, and I'm not sure that it's a good idea right now, but she's so scared, and she helped my girl. "Thank you for jumping in for her."

"It was too deep," she manages as she clings to me. "She scared the heck out of me."

I grin. Dani's always refused to swear. It's probably a good quality to have in a kindergarten teacher.

"Me, too." I rub my hands up and down her back. "You okay?"

She nods, and I look over her head to the crowd gathered around. "She's okay."

Holden's eyes catch mine. Hands on his hips, his face is grim. He shakes his head, and I can read his thoughts.

This will be bad for her.

So, despite the fact that I want nothing more than to keep her with me, I let him hold her. Holden raised his sisters, kept them safe from a fucking tyrant, and she's *his* baby girl.

She's not mine.

Everyone resumes what they were doing before the fall into the pool. Birdie's completely fine, laughing with some of the Wild kids as she warms up in a big pool towel and they eat ice cream from Beckett's ranch.

About an hour later, when I'm about to get Birdie ready to go home, I spot Dani watching me from that same lounge chair as earlier. Someone gave her different clothes to change into, and her hair is mostly dry now. She doesn't look away when I meet her gaze like she usually would.

I have to know that she's okay.

So, I cross through the yard to where she's sitting by the pool and tap her lightly on the shoulder.

"Can we talk somewhere private?"

Chapter Two

DANI

Holy moly, my heart's pounding, and my hands feel shaky. Not just because I willingly jumped into that godforsaken pool.

But because Bridger wants to chat.

Bridger, the man I've had a crush on since I was a kid, but who firmly told me when I was fifteen that nothing could ever happen between us. Because I was a kid, and he was an adult, and we were just friends.

I can respect that, but it totally broke my poor little teenage heart at the time.

The hardest part about moving back home, moving into the house right across the street from him, was that I'd have to see him and his adorable daughter all the time and keep my hormones in check.

I don't want to flirt with him and make it all uncomfortable again. I've known Bridger forever, and our families are tight. He's always going to be a part of my life, and I just have to deal with it.

I *can* deal with it.

Maybe I'll download a dating app or something to distract myself from my hot neighbor.

Bridger leads me into the house, which is perfectly quiet. Everyone is outside, so we're all alone when he turns back to me and shoves his hands into his pockets.

"Are you okay?" he asks.

"I'm going to be fine."

His eyes narrow. "That doesn't answer my question."

"I'm okay," I confirm softly. Jeez, he makes me nervous. I really just want to go home. "Listen, if it's weird for you that Birdie's in my class, since we know each other and stuff, I can have her transferred to another class."

He scowls, and I'm so nervous that I just keep talking.

"That might be for the best, right? I don't want to make you uncomfortable or anything. Yeah, I'll do that. Okay, I have a date, so I'd better go."

"Who the fuck—"

But I'm already out the door and saying goodbye to my hosts. I want to run away, but I also don't want to be rude, and I absolutely do *not* want to make a scene.

When my goodbyes are said, I climb into my car and drive away. I see Bridger gathering Birdie and also saying his goodbyes, and I want to get home and inside before he does so I don't have to see him.

God, I don't want to see him. I've worked hard for years with a therapist to build up my self-confidence and to feel like I can speak up for myself. To overcome all the horrific shit my father put me through, not to mention the bullies in school.

The bully that Bridger ended up marrying and having a kid with.

Yeah, that's a mind mess all on its own.

After pulling into my driveway, I hurry inside and close and lock my door. Less than ten minutes later, I hear Bridger get home, but I stay in. I don't want to see him. My feelings are too raw where he's concerned, and he hasn't given me any indication that he feels any differently about me than he did when I was fifteen.

I totally lied about having a date. I just said the first thing that came to mind to get me out of there, which is stupid, and my therapist would tell me that I just need to be honest and say, *I feel uncomfortable, and I want to leave.*

But did I? No. I lied. To Bridger.

My friend.

Maybe it's time for another therapy session.

Summer is hanging on to Montana by her fingernails this year, making it extra warm during the day, and I love the balmy evenings. I make sure to keep my driveway swept because on hot days like this, I like to lie down on the warm concrete and look at the stars, when the neighborhood is quiet, and the only sounds are the crickets and my own thoughts.

It's my favorite time of day to meditate and do my affirmations.

So, while I wait for the rest of the world to go to bed, I clean my cozy house and get ready for school next week.

I'm a night owl by nature, so when it's finally late, I slip outside—barefoot in my shorts and a tank, because I want to feel as much of that warm concrete as I can—and lie down in the middle of it.

There's no moon tonight, so the sky is dark and full of sparkling stars, and I begin my affirmations.

I am enough.

I am proud of myself.

I am a great teacher.

My family loves me.

I am in charge of my life.

I can do new things.

I am healing.

I keep going through my list, whispering them to the stars as I breathe and relax into the warmth beneath me.

And then I hear them—footsteps—but I don't jerk up or run away. I heard his door a second ago, and even though my heart is knocking in my chest, I've managed to stay calm.

"Dani? Jesus, are you okay? Did you fall?"

"I'm fine." I keep my voice quiet. "I do this almost every night."

Suddenly, his face is above me, frowning down at me and blocking my view.

"You're in my way," I say, proud of myself for sounding so unperturbed. I wish I didn't react to Bridger's presence like I do. My whole body's suddenly tingling. Can he see how my nipples have hardened through the tank top?

"What are you doing?"

27

I take a long, deep breath. "I'm enjoying this warm concrete, staring at the stars, and meditating, if you must know. It's nice."

"You're—"

"Try it." I gesture with my hand to the spot beside me. I don't know why exactly I did that because now he's going to stay here, with me, and I'll just be awkward, but my mouth ran away from me. "Lie down and look up."

He pauses, but then he actually does what I say. He lies down next to me, maybe a foot away.

"It *is* warm."

"Mm-hmm. Is Birdie sleeping?"

"Yeah, and I have her monitor on my phone. She's fine."

We lie in silence for a few minutes, taking in the night noises and looking at the stars.

"How was your date?" he asks at last. He doesn't sound happy with his question at all, and I wish he'd forgotten I'd said anything.

"I didn't have a date." I feel my cheeks heat, but I steady my breathing. "That was a lie."

"Why did you lie?"

I swallow hard. "Because I wanted out of there, and that was the first thing that popped into my head. I'm a horrible liar. You should have seen through me."

"I used to be able to see through you," he says quietly. "But I don't really know you all that well anymore."

"True." I lick my lips. "I have a question. You don't

have to answer it if you don't want to, but I have to ask."

Good grief, Dani, why are you asking this now?

"Shoot."

I still can't look at him. If I look at him, I'll get tongue-tied and awkward again, so I just keep staring up at the stars. He doesn't owe me an explanation, but this has stuck with me for the last five years. *How could he have liked her? Wanted her?* I may never get this chance again, so I decide to be brave and ask.

"Why Angela?"

I feel his head whip to the side to stare at me, but I keep my eyes up.

"That's the question?"

"Yeah. That's the question. Why her?"

He's quiet for a minute. "Look at me."

"Nope. And if you're not going to answer, just say it's none of my business."

He curses under his breath.

Angela was in my class, which means we're the same age. She was horrible, and she stayed in Bitterroot Valley after high school to work in her dad's store. From what I heard, when I was a senior in college, Bridger hooked up with her, she got pregnant, and they got married.

And I wanted to die.

"Jesus, Dani."

"Never mind. I told you that you didn't have to answer."

He pulls his hand down his face. "It was a one-night stand. I'd been at the bar one night after a particularly brutal fire where one of my guys was badly injured, and I needed a drink. Angela was at the same bar, I got drunk, and we hooked up. She got pregnant, and when she found me, I did the right thing and married her."

In shock, I look at him now and see his jaw tense. Well, that was a fast explanation. At least, it sounds like he didn't love her.

"Turned out, after Birdie was born, she didn't want to be a mom, so she fucked around with some tourist from New York and followed him out of here, leaving us behind."

"Oh, my God." I look back up at the sky and feel like shit for asking. "I'm sort of sorry, Bridger."

That makes him chuckle, and it's a sound I love because he doesn't do it often. "You're *sort of* sorry?"

"Yeah. I mean, no one deserves to be left like that, and cheaters are just jerks, but I didn't like her, so I'm not *all the way* sorry."

"You didn't like her?"

"No. Not at all. Aside from...*him*, she was my biggest tormentor."

He sits up now and frowns down at me. "*What?*"

"Look, you don't come from the horrible home life I came from without having bullies in school because kids suck. My dad didn't buy us new clothes. We weren't poor, but he didn't spend his money on us girls. And I was always super shy and meek. A book nerd. I'm *still* a book nerd, actually, but you know what I mean. I didn't talk back to anyone because I was taught that you *never* talked back."

I have to swallow hard as memories flood through

me, and Bridger's hand is suddenly in mine, squeezing my fingers, grounding me, and giving me the courage to continue.

"Anyway, she was such a mean girl. Like, just a grade-A witch. She always told me I was too fat. *No one likes a fat girl*, she'd say. She called me Miss Piggy."

"The fuck? You're absolutely not fat, Dani." Perhaps it's petty, but I do like his angry response to Angela's teasing.

"I'm curvy now, and back then, I was definitely a bigger girl, thanks to awkward teenage hormones. My body was figuring itself out, and after a lot of years of therapy, I understand that. My body's gotten me through a lot, so I cut it some slack."

"You're fucking beautiful." He's gritting his teeth, glaring over at me, and I have to swallow hard before I continue.

"Um, thanks? Anyway, I went away to college to get away from her as much as to get away from my dad."

"I had no idea."

"It doesn't matter. I just didn't know why you chose her, and I've always wondered, but now I know."

I swallow hard and look away, but suddenly, his fingers are on my chin, making me look at him.

His brown eyes narrow.

"One time"—I just can't stop talking when he makes me nervous—"she was looking over my shoulder, and I didn't know it. I was reading a text from you. I don't remember what you said, but I must have had a dopey grin on my face or something, and she saw it, and she—"

I bite my lip, not wanting to say more.

"She what?"

I shake my head, but his grip on my chin firms.

"She fucking what, Dani?"

"She laughed at me," I whisper and let my eyes close. "Said that I was pathetic, that Bridger Blackwell would *never* like someone as stupid as me, and you were just being nice to me. And we'd already had the conversation where you said I was way too young for you, and we were just friends, and I knew that. I was a kid. But boy, did she drive it home that someone as hot as you would *never*—"

I shake my head and clear my throat.

"Anyway, it was a long time ago."

And I feel so stupid. So ashamed. So foolish.

"I probably shouldn't tell you all this."

"You should have told me this years ago."

I shake my head mournfully. I can still hear my father's words. Even after so much work with my psychologist, some of his words still creep in. *"You're worthless. You're nothing. No one gives a shit about you."*

"I had no self-esteem, Bridger. I had no confidence in myself, and I believed her. *Of course*, you wouldn't like me back. I was just...me."

"I did like you." His voice is still quiet, and my eyes fly to his. Tense. He seems so tense, and it's scary how handsome he looks, even when he's broody. "Why do you think that, even though I knew you were too young for me, and if I started something with you I could get into a lot of trouble, I still talked to you?"

He was interested. In me?

"Oh, that's really sad." It's the only thing I can think to say, because it's the absolute truth. "But then I left. And you met her, and she got pregnant."

"Yeah, she did, and I knew right away that she was absolutely not the woman I'd want to spend my life with, but she was pregnant, and we did the right thing. Almost immediately after Birdie was born, she started staying out all night, shut me down completely, and hardly paid Birdie any attention. I've pretty much been a single father since day one."

"That really sucks."

He pulls in a deep breath.

"I'm sorry, Dani. For all of it." His voice is so quiet, and his words are a balm to my heart that I didn't know I needed.

I rest my palms on the concrete, grounding myself, and stare up at the stars. "Me, too. I'm glad she's gone from your life, and I won't apologize for that. She was horrible, and she would have been a really crappy mom, and Birdie deserves so much more than that."

"I know." He turns onto his side, facing me, and links his other hand with mine, lacing our fingers, and now my heart speeds up all over again. "She gave up her rights, and we haven't heard from her since the day she left. That doesn't mean she hasn't come to town; we just don't hear from her."

I give his fingers a squeeze. "Birdie's amazing, you know."

"I know." I'm still not facing him, and I don't look

his way because now I'm out of my element, and I don't know what to do. "Look at me."

"I'd rather not."

"Why?"

"Because."

He chuckles and squeezes my hand. "Because why?"

I press my lips together. Finally, I turn my head and meet his gaze.

"I feel like a piece of shit."

"You didn't do anything wrong, Bridger. Do you still want me to have Birdie's class changed?"

"I never wanted you to do that."

I nod as relief rushes through me. "Good. I like her. She'll be fun in class."

"Dani, about today." He frowns, and his fingertips brush over my cheek, and it sends a shiver down my whole body, waking up the nipples that had just calmed down. "You jumped into the water."

I swallow hard as the terror from those few seconds settles around me again. "Don't remind me."

"Thank you for that."

"You already thanked me."

"Yeah, but I know how fucking hard that was for you, and I don't want you to have nightmares from it, sweetheart."

I lick my lips and swallow again, because he just called me *sweetheart,* but then plaster on a brave smile.

"Don't do that."

"Do what?"

"Don't fake the smile with me. I know better."

"What do you want me to say? That I'm afraid to go to sleep tonight? That having my head under the water, even for those few seconds, took ten years off my life? All of that is true. But, I survived it. I'm right here, lying under the stars with you, and I didn't die today. And, most importantly, nothing happened to Birdie, that little daredevil."

He grins, just like I'd hoped, and then he sighs, and I can't help but smile back at him.

"Dani?"

"Yeah?"

His eyes dart down to my lips, and I instinctively lick them again.

"I want to kiss you."

"You do?"

His brown orbs come back up to my own, and he nods as he sobers once more. "Yeah, I fucking do. So, if that's a problem for you, I need you to say so."

I lift my eyebrows, but I don't say anything at all because the idea of Bridger's lips on mine is absolutely *not* a problem for me.

But before he can press his lips to mine, his phone rings, and he winces.

"I'm sorry, this is work."

"Then you'd better answer it."

He sits up again, fishes his phone out of his pocket, and answers. "Blackwell. Shit, okay. I need to contact one of my family members to stay with Birdie." He looks down at his watch, and I can see the internal war taking place.

"Bridger, go. I'll watch her," I whisper. He looks at me, and there's indecision in his eyes.

"One moment," he says. Man, does he sound sexy when he's in fireman mode. My ovaries are doing the hula. "You sure, sweetheart? I can call one of my brothers or—"

"Happy to."

He turns back to the call and says, "ETA is twenty minutes."

He hangs up and then shoves his hands through his hair. I push myself to my feet and then brush my hands together. "Go ahead and go. I'll head over to your place and watch her. She'll just sleep anyway."

"You don't have to—"

"We can stand in the driveway and argue about it, or you can go to work. It's fine. I know my way around a kid, and Birdie knows me."

Bridger blows out a breath. "Thank you. Go grab whatever you need, and I'll meet you over there."

"Deal."

I rush inside and gather my pillow and a throw blanket, and then decide that's really all I need and hurry across the street. The door opens before I have the chance to knock.

"She's out cold," he says. He's already changed into his uniform, and it makes me salivate.

Good God, Bridger's hot in uniform.

"Dani?"

"Huh? Sorry. Don't worry about us. You'll be home before she even wakes up."

"I should be," he replies grimly. Just when I think he's going to leave, he pulls me to him and hugs me tightly, and my whole body is on high alert. Bridger gives the *best* hugs. I hope he can't feel my nipples harden through my shirt. Again. "This was really shitty timing."

I grin against his chest and shrug a shoulder as I pull back. "Oh, are you under the assumption that I'd put out on the first stargazing night?" I smirk. "No way, Chief."

He blanches at that and cups my chin in his hand. "Did you just call me *Chief*?"

"Yeah. I did."

"No." He shakes his head.

"No? I can't call you chief?"

"Fuck no, Dani. My guys call me that. Not you."

I laugh and then shrug again. I shrug a lot when I'm nervous. "Okay, fine. So, what's going on here, anyway?"

"I don't know." His face is sober as he brushes the backs of his knuckles down my face, and holy moly, my nipples take notice, puckering up again, and Bridger's eyes drop down. "But it's not nothing."

"That's...not helpful."

He grins, then pulls away.

"No nightmares tonight." It's not a request, it's an order, so I nod once.

"No, sir."

His eyes narrow on me. "You've gotten sassy, Dani."

"I'm working on it. That's the goal."

With a grin, he presses his lips to my forehead. "Good night."

He turns to leave, and I feel chilly without him

pressed against me. *He wanted to kiss me.* Just the thought still has chills running down my spine. How did we get here so fast?

"Good night, Bridger."

The door closes behind him, and I glance around his house. It's bigger than mine, and it's definitely been maintained better. His kitchen is open to the living room, separated by an island. The sectional couch looks cozy, and I'll be perfectly comfortable sleeping there until Bridger gets home.

But, suddenly, I hear a cry coming from down a hallway, so I jog down and open the door and find Birdie sitting up in bed, crying.

"Birdie, it's Dani. I'm here with you, baby girl."

"Where's Daddy?"

"I'm sorry, he had to go to work, but I said that I'd come hang out with you while you sleep. Did you have a bad dream?"

She hiccups and knuckles the tears in her eyes as she nods her sweet little head.

"I'm sorry, love. Don't worry, everything's okay. There's nothing to be afraid of."

She sighs and then holds her arms out to me, and I sit on the side of her bed and fold her to me, breathing her in. She smells like bubble gum—probably her baby shampoo—and sweetness, and I love having her in my arms.

"It's okay, sweetie. Do you need to use the bathroom before you go back to sleep?"

"Yeah." Her voice is so small, and she scurries out of

the bed and pads to the bathroom in the hallway. A few seconds later, she rushes back and jumps into her twin-sized bed, pulls her blankets up to her chin, and sighs.

"Better?"

"Better."

I brush her hair back from her face and smile down at her. She really is the cutest, sweetest little thing. And she looks just like her daddy.

"Will you stay with me? In here?"

"Of course, I will." I lean over and press my lips to her forehead, and it's not long before the little girl is sleeping soundly again.

I creep out to the living room to fetch my pillow and blanket, and when I return to Birdie's room, I lie down on the floor.

It's where I'm most comfortable most of the time anyway.

I curl up on my side and pull the blanket over me, but realize that in my tank and shorts, I'm too chilly, even with the blanket. I should have changed my clothes before I came over here, but I was in too much of a hurry, and I didn't feel cold at the time.

Now, I do.

I stand and quietly return to the living room and spy a hoodie hanging by the front door. Bridger's hoodie. Without overthinking it, I snatch it off the wall and push my arms inside, wrapping it around me, and I can't help but tug it up to my nose so I can breathe him in.

He smells so *good*. Like citrus and a little woodsy and that unmistakable *man*ness that makes me go all gooey.

I can already tell that I won't want to give this up tomorrow morning, but I shrug and pad back into Birdie's room and lie on my makeshift bed, snuggled up in Bridger's hoodie. It's wild to me how different the dynamic between Bridger and me is after one day. After just two conversations, he went from restrained to wanting to *kiss me*.

He's still broody and a little quiet. But he's always been that way.

This feels fast.

It also feels so dang good.

I sigh, snuggling down, and let my eyes close.

Chapter Three

BRIDGER

Tonight was *brutal.*

I wasn't supposed to be on call, but this fire was so big, it was all hands on deck. It's a good thing I never even finished that one beer at the pool party, because I had to have all of my wits about me as we fought that motherfucker.

The Campbells are a young family of six, with four kids under the age of five, and now, they're homeless, and it makes my chest ache for them.

It also pisses me the fuck off.

I know that they have family to stay with, and it's not my responsibility to prevent every single house fire in Bitterroot Valley, but it always makes me fucking sad because nine times out of ten, it was preventable.

But tonight's fire was different.

Because someone set that shit ablaze on purpose.

With just a couple of hours before the sun is due to come up, I plan to take a shower and sleep until it's time to get up with Birdie, but first, I have to check in with my sexy babysitter. If she's sacked out on the couch, I won't wake her. She can stay.

I'd much rather have her in bed with me, but having her here in my house is a good place to start. Now that the fire is out, and I've had time to think, I feel horrible that, of all the women for me to have gotten tangled up with, no matter how briefly, it was Dani's high school bully.

What are the odds of that? And a niggling part of my mind now wonders if Angela orchestrated the one-night stand because she knew Dani had a crush on me in high school, and she was vindictive enough to sleep with me to get one over on my friend.

Honestly, knowing what I do now, I wouldn't be surprised if that was exactly what happened. Angela just didn't plan to get pregnant. Neither of us did.

But Birdie's mine, that I know for sure. As soon as Angela found me and told me she was expecting, I had testing done to confirm that the baby was mine.

And I can't regret it because Birdie's the best thing that ever happened to me. I love her more than anything.

I just hate that the whole situation hurt Dani, even a little bit. Because damn it, I *am* attracted to her, and not just physically. She's fucking smart and sweet, and I've always loved being around her.

Lying on her driveway, as crazy as it sounds, was the most peaceful I've felt in years.

I want more of that. I *crave* it.

And damn it, I'm going to have it. I know I have

some work to do to earn her trust, to mend our friend-ship and build from there, but I've never been afraid of hard work.

Silently, I let myself into the house. The lights in the living room are on, but Dani's not asleep on the couch.

With a frown, I walk down the hallway and peek into Birdie's room, and my heart stumbles.

Birdie's sleeping peacefully in her bed, and on the floor beside my daughter, lying on her side with her hands folded under her chin, is Dani.

Fuck, she didn't have to sleep in the same room as Birdie. And definitely not on the goddamn floor. I never want her to sleep on the floor.

After checking on Birdie, I squat down and wedge my arms beneath Dani, then lift her easily in my arms, cradling her to me.

"I'm sorry," she whispers without opening her eyes as she loops her arms around my shoulders. "She had a bad dream."

"Shh." I press my lips to her forehead and breathe her in. Fuck, she's sweet and smells like apples. I lay her gently on my bed and tuck her in, and she burrows down, buries her face in my pillow, and is already asleep again.

She's in my hoodie, and the sight of it surprises me.

I like it.

I like it a lot.

With a sigh, I close the door behind me and head for Birdie's bathroom for that shower, and then I fall asleep on the sofa with thoughts of the sexy woman in my bed.

The sun had just barely started to lighten the night sky, and I couldn't sleep on the couch any longer. It's big enough for me, but it's lumpy, and I kept dreaming about Dani.

Dreams that might have had me returning to my bed so I could have my way with her, and while she may have been game for a kiss in her driveway, I know for certain that she's not ready for me to fuck her.

Not quite yet.

I'm leaning against the counter, sipping on black coffee, when I hear footsteps coming lightly down the hallway. They're not my daughter's footsteps, I know that for sure.

And within seconds, it's confirmed when Dani stops, her eyes widening when she sees me, and I don't miss the way she drinks me in, from head to fucking toe.

"Good morning." I sip the coffee and tuck my free hand into my pocket. Fuck, I want to touch her. Her hair is messed up, and her eyes are sleepy. She's still in those tiny shorts and my hoodie, which is zipped all the way up to her neck.

"Um, good morning," she replies and scratches her nose. "I woke up in your bed."

I nod, watching her. "Yeah. I found you on Birdie's floor."

"She asked me to stay in her room. Bad dream." She shuffles forward and leans on my island, watching me with her wide, blue eyes. "I was fine on the floor. You didn't have to give up your comfortable bed."

"I don't want you sleeping on the floor, Dani. It wasn't a problem to carry you to my room."

She swallows in that way she does when she's nervous. She's fucking adorable, and it makes my lips twitch. "You *carried* me?"

"How do you think you got there?"

Dani tugs on her bottom lip, and that makes my dick come to attention.

I want to bite that lip. I want to sink my teeth into it as I push inside of her and make her moan.

"I'm sorry I missed that," she admits out loud and then flushes beautifully. Fuck, she's not making me want her any less. "I should go home."

I'm not ready for her to leave yet. I like having her here in my house. "Do you want some coffee first?"

She scrunches up her nose and shakes her head. "No thanks, I don't drink coffee."

I blink at her. "I'm sorry, what?"

"I just never acquired a taste for it."

"How do you start your day, then?"

"With water? Oatmeal? Sometimes, if I go out for breakfast, I'll splurge on an orange juice. I will do an iced coffee every once in a while, but that's because they're sweet, and I have a sugar addiction, as evidenced by my hips."

I narrow my eyes on her, not finding that funny at all. "What the fuck is wrong with your hips, kitten?"

She blinks and bites that lip again. "Uh, maybe I'm

still tired. Or nervous. Probably nervous. I'll just go home and get out of your way."

"Why are you nervous, Dani?"

She blows out a breath and then looks at me like, *really?*

"You don't ever need to be nervous with me. It's just me."

She chuckles at that and turns to go, but then stops and unzips the hoodie and starts to take it off. "Sorry, I got cold and borrowed this."

"Take it with you." Her eyes whip up to mine as I sip my coffee. "It's chilly out this morning. Just take it."

I love seeing it on her. It's sexy as fuck, knowing that something of mine is wrapped around her.

"Okay," she murmurs, pulling the front up to her nose. "Thanks. I'll wash it and bring it back."

I don't give a shit about getting it back, so I don't reply to that. "Thank you for staying with Birdie. I'll return the favor."

"You don't owe me anything. She's the sweetest little thing, and I was happy to help." She rubs her hands down her face. "And I don't mind sleeping on the floor. I actually like it."

"Why?"

Her gaze finds mine again. "Why do I like the floor?"

"Yeah."

"Oh, no reason. I'd better go—"

I cross the room in three strides and tip her chin up to look at me. "Why do you prefer the floor, Dani?"

Her lips part, and her gorgeous eyes jerk down to my lips.

"I slept on the floor most of my childhood." The admission is a whisper. "We couldn't all fit in Holden's bed with him."

The reminder of what Dani and her siblings went through as children is an arrow straight to my heart, and I pull her in for a hug, gently rocking her back and forth. I know all too well that their father terrorized all five of them, having witnessed the aftermath too often. I also know, thanks to a conversation I had with Holden earlier this year, that their father killed their mother when Dani was roughly four years old. Holden was the one who raised his sisters, and it would make sense that when things were extra horrible, they'd seek comfort in their big brother's bed at night.

"I'm okay," she says against my chest as she pats my back. "I really am, Bridge. I'm doing a lot better, especially now that he's gone."

"You're not okay," I murmur as I rub my lips over the top of her hair, enjoying this moment with her. "You're fucking incredible."

I grin down at her as she pulls out of my arms.

"I really do have to go," she says, but she doesn't pull away when I hold her hand in mine, and I take that as a damn good sign. "School starts in just a couple of days, and I have a lot to do."

"I understand. I have to get Birdie ready, too. Go get ready for the swarm of rug rats."

She chuckles and pulls away, walking toward the door. "Have a good weekend, Bridger."

"You, too, Dani."

The last few days have flown by. I've managed to get Birdie all ready for school, finishing up with a trip to the grocery store so we could get all kinds of things for her lunches. We spent Sunday at my family's ranch, riding horses and hanging out with most of my siblings. My brother Beckett runs the ranch now, and he's slowly adding on a guest ranch, having just finished building beautiful cabins on the property. He'll continue his dairy operations, but we have a big property, and he'd like to start capitalizing on the tourists that come to Bitterroot Valley by the thousands every year.

Beck's a damn smart man.

He's also busy with a litter of puppies that Birdie couldn't get enough of—she begged and pleaded for us to take one home—but I had to explain that not only aren't the puppies old enough to leave their mama, but we're not home enough to train a dog.

She didn't like that answer.

But now it's the first day of school, and Birdie's forgotten about the little black-and-white puppy and is currently agonizing over which dress to wear.

"I thought you wanted to wear the blue one?" I frown down at the top of her head as I make my way through a French braid. My sister, Billie, finally gave me enough lessons for me to muddle my way through it by myself.

Mostly.

My fingers are too big and clumsy for Birdie's soft, fine hair, but she insists that she wants braids for her first day, so damn it, she'll have the fucking braids.

"But what if it's not the right one?"

"Why are you agonizing over your fashion choices at five years old?" I ask her in return. "It's kindergarten, sweetheart, not a fashion show."

"I want to be *cute*," she emphasizes.

"You would be adorable in a burlap sack," I inform her, and she turns to scrunch her nose at me.

"What's that?"

"Never mind. The point is, no matter what you wear, you'll look great. So, you should be comfortable because you're going to be gone all day. You understand that, right? I'm going to drop you off at your class with Miss Lexington, and then I have to leave, and you'll be there with her and the other kids until later this afternoon."

"Yeah." Her voice is kind of small, and it makes my stomach jitter. "I know."

"It's going to be a lot of fun," I rush to remind her. "And you'll make so many friends by the end of the day."

"Maybe."

I tie off the second braid, and then I turn her to me and take her shoulders in my hands. "It *is* going to be fun. You're such a great kid, peanut. You don't have any problems making friends, and you already know Miss Lexington."

"Why can't I call her Dani?"

"Because it's school, and you have to be respectful and call her Miss Lexington, unless she says otherwise."

"That's weird. Okay, I'll wear the blue dress." But before she runs to her room, she hugs me. "What will you do without me, Daddy?"

I grin and fold my arms around her, holding her close. My girl has the biggest heart, and I don't want her worrying about me. "I'll be just fine, and I'll see you this afternoon and you can tell me all about it. I'll want to hear every detail, so take lots of notes."

"I can't write yet."

"Oh, right. Well, then just remember everything and tell me later, okay?"

She grins and nods and then seems happy to go get dressed.

What will I do? I'll be stressing the fuck out, that's what.

My baby is going to school, and I'm *not okay*. What if someone's mean to her? What if some kid makes her feel like shit? What if she has an asthma attack or gets suddenly tired the way she used to? I hate that I won't be there to watch over her and keep her safe.

But, less than thirty minutes later, we're in my truck, parking in the elementary school lot. For the first day, I get to escort Birdie to her classroom, but after today, I'll drop her off in the drop-off line.

"I'll carry it," Birdie says when I pull her backpack

out of the truck, and I help her put it on her shoulders before taking her hand and walking into the building with her.

This elementary school hasn't changed much since I went here a million years ago. Before long, we step inside Dani's classroom, and Birdie gasps with happiness.

Dani's gone with a unicorn theme this year, and it's bright and cheerful and as welcoming as the woman herself.

"Birdie." Dani crosses to us and accepts Birdie's hug, then smiles up at me. "Welcome to your first day. Are you excited?"

"Yes. Do I really have to call you Miss Lexinson?"

Dani laughs and tugs lightly at the end of my daughter's braid. God, her smile lights me up inside. "No, you can call me Miss Dani. Lexington is a mouthful, isn't it?"

"Kind of," Birdie says with a giggle.

"Okay, I'm going to show you where to stow your stuff and where your desk is." Dani turns to me. "Do you have any questions, Dad?"

"Her medications and stuff."

"I've read her case file, and I know that everything is on hand for her at the office," Dani assures me. "I have her rescue inhaler locked in my desk, just in case, and I know to call you if she has to use it so you can decide if you'd like to come get her."

I nod, relieved that Dani read everything thoroughly. "Thanks."

I shuffle my feet, not wanting to leave my baby, and Dani's face softens as she squats by my daughter. She looks hot as hell in her black pencil skirt and white blouse. She's not even trying to look like a seductress, and yet, she does.

"Birdie, your desk is right there, next to Callie. Why don't you go ahead and have a seat, okay?"

"Okay." First, Birdie throws her arms around my legs. "Bye, Daddy!"

And then she's off, and I suddenly feel...*emotional.*

"Hey," Dani says softly. She doesn't touch me, but I can tell that she wants to, and damn it, I want her to. "She's going to be great, Bridger. I'm right here, and I won't let anything happen to her. I have your baby. Now, you go so she can settle in and get comfortable without you."

I blow out a breath, grateful for her words. "Yeah, okay. Seriously, call me if you need anything."

"Of course." But I can tell by the smile on her beautiful face that she knows that she won't need me. "Have a good day, Bridger."

"Yeah, thanks." Reluctantly, I leave the classroom and walk out to my truck and decide that even though it's my day off, I'm going to go to the firehouse and work out. We have a state-of-the-art gym, and I need to sweat some nervous energy out of my system.

There are a few of my guys working out, lifting weights, and running on the treadmills. After changing at my locker, I decide to work on my back and shoulders today, so I cross to the pull-up bar and start with twenty pull-ups. By the time I'm done, the burn in my back is satisfying, and I make my way to free weights.

52

"Hey, Chief," Diego Martinez, one of our younger guys, says. "I didn't think you were on today."

"I'm not, just here to work out," I reply, grabbing dumbbells for arm raises. "I dropped Birdie off for her first day of school today, and I'm not excited about it. She did preschool last year, but that's not the same."

"I get it," Diego says with a nod much wiser than I'd expect from a man his age. He's a big guy, taller than my six-foot-three, muscular, with a lot of tattoos, and he's always fending off female attention, but Diego's a happily married man. "Our oldest started kindergarten last year, and I was shaking like a leaf when I left him there."

I frown at him. "How fucking old are you?"

"Twenty-four," he replies with a shrug before doing a deadlift. "Shandy and I had him right out of high school. Anyway, the first day is the worst. For you, not for her. She'll have a fucking blast, and then it'll break your heart that she didn't miss you at all today."

I grin at him, feeling marginally better than I did when I walked in here. "Thanks, man."

"Sure thing."

We go our separate ways, concentrating on our own workouts. When my muscles are screaming for mercy, I pack it in and check some emails—happily deleting the one from Evans, a disgruntled applicant who won't give up—before heading home.

I spend the rest of the day cutting the grass, and then I cut Dani's, too, since she's at work and doesn't have as much free time anymore. It'll cool down soon, and we won't have to mow the lawn for long, but until then, I'll do hers when I do my own. I edge, take care of weeds, and generally try to keep myself busy, and then take a shower to wash off the workout and the yard work.

When I get out of the shower, there's a text from Dani, and my heart stops but then picks up again when I see it's just a photo of Birdie, sitting at a short table with a bunch of other little girls, giggling over her PB&J.

Dani: She's having a great day!

I'm going to kiss the hell out of her, just for that.

When there are only thirty minutes left before school is out, I pack Birdie a snack and head over to the school, where I wait in my truck until the bell rings.

Kids come pouring out of the doors, most of them smiling, excited to see their parents and go home for the day.

Finally, I see my daughter, holding Dani's hand, as they both walk outside. They're grinning at each other, and Birdie's talking about something that makes Dani laugh, and my heart catches again.

Shit, she looks good with my kid.

I'm so fucked.

I should not be so hot for the teacher look, yet it seems a new kink has been unlocked because all I can think about is bending her over, pulling that tight skirt up around her waist, and taking her from behind, making her scream my name. Making her forget her own.

"Daddy!"

I shake my head and grin at my daughter, who comes skipping to me.

"Hey, peanut. Did you have a good day?"

"Yes! We learned math, and I drew a picture, and we had a snack, and Jacob was smelly, but that's okay because not everybody has learned self-control."

My surprised gaze jumps up to Dani, who just smiles and shrugs a shoulder. "It was a big day, but Birdie did fabulous. It's going to be a great year."

"I'm happy to hear that." Birdie slips her hand into mine, and I give her a little squeeze. "Should we get pizza for dinner to celebrate?"

"Pepperoni," she says with an enthusiastic nod.

"Join us," I say to Dani. It's not a question, but she's already shaking her head.

"Oh, thank you, but I'm going to Holden and Millie's for dinner tonight. You guys enjoy your pizza. I have to go talk to this parent. Thank you for a great first day, Birdie."

She gives me a little wave, and then she's off, and Birdie is already dragging me toward the truck.

"I'm *starving*, Daddy. We might need two pizzas."

Chapter Four

DANI

The first week of school went off without too many hitches. There are always going to be a few minor obstacles to hurdle, especially early on in the year. These kiddos are new to all-day school, so some will get homesick, some will get tired and throw mini tantrums, and some even have accidents.

Poor Jacob had a rough week, but I have a whole bin of clean clothes for him, just in case. I think he's simply nervous.

I also keep a cabinet full of healthy snacks and even nonperishable meals for those kids who might need extra calories or aren't getting enough food at home.

I was once that kid. I don't want any of my students to feel they are unable to participate in class simply because they're hungry. That's something I can help with.

I've just finished organizing the fresh snacks and

meals that I bought on my way home from school. It's Friday evening, and I know without a doubt that once I'm home for the weekend, I'm not going to want to go far.

Exhaustion has set in, but that's okay. It means that I'm spending my days with about twenty excited, energetic five-year-olds, and there's nothing else I'd rather do.

My front porch is in the shade, and it's been a particularly hot late-summer day, so I step out and sit in the simple Ikea chair I bought for myself and breathe in the fresh air. Putting my bare feet up on the ottoman in front of me, I scoot down so I can lean my head back against the cushion and get cozy. There's a light breeze blowing through that feels great after being inside most of the week.

I have so many projects to do around the house over the next couple of days. I knew when I rented this house that it was a total fixer-upper. The original owners had passed away, and their kids don't live here anymore and wanted to rent it out. I got it for a steal, and in exchange for the cheap rent, I'm doing some minor cosmetic surgery on the place. Mostly just some paint here and there or replace a light fixture or two.

That sort of thing.

My brother threw a fit when he saw the inside of this place. But it's clean, it's cheap, and I can make it look great with some elbow grease.

And I'll get to it, as soon as I'm finished enjoying my porch.

Meow.

My eyes pop open, and I listen, and then suddenly, there's a calico cat on my lap, staring at me with wide, gold eyes.

Meow.

"Hey there. Who do you belong to?" I tentatively hold my hand out, and she leans into my touch, rubbing her cheek against my fingers. Her motor immediately kicks into gear, and she's a tiny purring machine. "You're sweet. You're a baby, aren't you?"

I don't know much about pets. By the time I was thirteen, Holden made Dad stop bringing home animals that weren't either horses or cattle, and my sisters and I were so grateful. *Not that we ever said that out loud.* After all these years, I can still hear Charlie's and Alex's cries after what *he* did to a tiny kitten. My sobs into Holden's chest as my dad laughed with glee at our torment. *Why did he torture those poor animals*? How did he become so ... barbaric? It was horrible. Okay, that's an understatement.

So, I've never really taken care of a pet before. Not that I'm about to start now.

"You should go on home," I inform her, but she just turns in a circle and begins to wash her paw. "You're going to take a bath on me? Really?"

A minute later, Bridger and Birdie get home.

"I have to use the bathroom," Birdie announces loud enough for the whole neighborhood to hear after she climbs out of the truck, slams the door, and runs inside the house.

Bridger, on the other hand, looks over at me, then proceeds to walk my way.

He's in jeans and a tight white T-shirt that molds over his broad shoulders and bulky biceps in the best way ever, and the short sleeves show off his tattoos. He has sleeves on both arms, colorful and sexy as all get-out. He's lean of hip, with a flat stomach, that razor-sharp jawline, and lips that a girl could probably lose herself in.

I mean, I would assume.

"Hey," he says with a crooked smile as he approaches, and then his eyebrows climb when he sees the cat. "New friend?"

"Help me," I whisper loudly. "She just jumped up here, and I don't know what to do."

His eyes soften as he approaches, squats next to us, and runs his hand down the back of the cat, making her purr even louder.

And who can blame her? I'd purr, too, if his hands were on me.

"You could try petting her," he says.

"She has to go home."

He frowns down at the cat. "She's really young. Probably just a couple of months old. Might be a stray."

"She can't stay here. You take her."

Bridger drags the backs of his knuckles over my cheek, and I want to melt right into his touch. "I can't. Besides, she really likes you. Looks like she's claimed you as her human."

I feel my eyes go wide as panic sets in. "I can't." I

swallow hard and stare down at the cat. "I can't keep this kitten. I don't even want to touch it."

"She isn't a snake or a spider. It's just a kitten, sweetheart."

He chuckles, but this isn't funny.

"Bridger. I can't—I don't know how—" I shake my head, and then he blinks as though it dawns on him as to why I'm freaking out.

"Whoa. Okay, I get it. I'm sorry, Dani. She's just a kitten. A baby. It doesn't look to me like anyone's missing her. She's pretty skinny, sort of dirty, but no fleas or anything like that."

I swallow hard, and the kitten looks up at me and blinks, as if she's totally content here in my lap.

"Hi," I whisper to her.

Meow.

"She likes you," Bridger says with a soft voice. "Of course, what's not to like?"

"Duh," I reply, without taking my eyes off the cat.

"Daddy!"

"Let me grab Birdie," he says, disappearing from our side. I lift my gaze enough to see him run across the street, take Birdie by the hand, and guide her over to my house. "Dani found a kitten."

"Oh, she's so cute," Birdie says, approaching carefully. She reaches up and gently strokes the cat's back, letting out a sweet, tinkly laugh. "So soft. Are you keeping her? What's her name?"

"I..." I shake my head, but then the darn cat lies down on her back, exposing her belly, still purring, and

60

proceeds to reach for my chin with her tiny front paws. "Oh, darn. It looks like I'm keeping her."

I hear Bridger chuckle, and Birdie jumps in excitement.

"But I don't have anything for her."

"We can go together to get supplies," Bridger offers. "While we're gone, just put her in the bathroom, in case she has an accident."

He lifts the kitten off my lap, and I exhale in relief. Then, an hour later, we're back with a cat box, litter, bowls, food, and toys. I even bought the cutest bed for her to sleep in, and Bridger bought her a tree thing for her to climb on and look outside from.

"What's all that?" Bridger gestures to the totes full of food that I have on my dining room table as Birdie plays with the kitten.

"Oh, that's the snacks and meals that I keep on hand for the kids at school."

I fill the water and food bowls and set them on a mat in the kitchen, then pour litter into the pan and show the kitten where that is in the mud room.

She uses it right away, and I'm convinced that she's the smartest cat in the world. And I'm still terrified about keeping her. *What if I don't know what to do and accidentally hurt her?*

When I turn back to smile at Bridger, he's watching me with a frown. "What? What did I do?"

"Why do you keep snacks and meals in your classroom, and why do you buy them yourself?"

"Because sometimes the kids are hungry. Sometimes

they don't get enough food at home, Bridger. No kid of mine is going to suffer through a full day of class on an empty stomach. And I pay for it because the school never would. It's fine, I can afford to—"

I'm cut off when he crosses to me, cradles my face in his hands, and stares at me intently.

"Are you kidding me right now?" His voice is hard and rough and ... *angry?*

"Why are you mad at me over this?" I hate how apprehensive my voice sounds, and he tips his forehead against mine. He's never touched me like this. It's intimate *and* intense.

"Not angry. Definitely not that. Tell me the next time you go, and I'll help."

"The kitten loves the cat tree," Birdie announces, running into the kitchen. Bridger casually pulls back and smiles down at his daughter.

"Is that right?"

"Miss Dani, what are you going to name her?"

"Oh, I don't know. Maybe you can help me name her."

"Pickles." Birdie's voice is as sure as it can be. "Definitely Pickles. I've been giving it a lot of thought."

I laugh and brush my hand over the sweet girl's soft hair. "Pickles it is, then."

The weekend went by too fast. I didn't get nearly enough done because I was too busy watching the cat, in case she needed something, and now, here I am, on Monday morning at the drop-off line, yawning.

"You need a nap."

I turn at the familiar deep voice and grin. Holy heck, he's wearing his baseball hat backward, and I'm pretty sure my ovaries are singing the "Hallelujah Chorus." "Good morning."

"Have I told you how beautiful you look in your teacher gear?"

I wrinkle my nose at that and glance down at my gray slacks and simple pink blouse. "This is as boring as it gets."

"That is absolutely false," Bridger replies and hugs Birdie back when she wraps her arms around his legs.

"I'm going in," Birdie announces and runs off.

Bridger sidles up next to me and brushes the back of his hand over mine. His minimal touches here and there get my blood pumping.

"I should *not* be flirting with a dad when I'm at work," I whisper to him, making him grin.

"I disagree, as long as I'm the dad. Otherwise, you're in big trouble, kitten."

"I'm not kidding, Bridger." I take a deep breath and let it out slowly when he takes a tiny step away from me.

"You're coming to dinner tonight." He arches an eyebrow when my gaze whips up to his. "No excuses this time. I want to flirt with you without prying eyes."

"Your daughter will be there."

"I don't care if *she* sees me flirt with you." His answer is so easy, his smile so dang smug. "Say you'll be there, Dani."

"What are you planning to feed me?"

His lips twitch. "Burgers on the grill."

I narrow my eyes at him. "You know I love a good burger."

"I'm glad to hear that hasn't changed. So, say yes."

"Okay, yes, I'll come." My eyes widen, and when he snorts, I shake my head. "Not like *that.*"

"Oh, yeah." He leans in a bit, still not touching me, but whispering in my ear so only I can hear him. "Like that. Maybe not tonight, but soon."

His beautiful face splits into a grin when I don't have a comeback for him. "I'll see you tonight. Have a good Monday, Miss Dani."

He winks and then saunters over to his truck and drives away, and it takes at least another two minutes before my heart slows down. Why did he have to break out the backward hat? Is he trying to kill me?

Now I have to get through the day while thinking about dinner at his house. I should have asked him if I could bring something, and I would have, if I wasn't so befuddled by him.

I glance at my watch. The bell rings in five minutes, so I make my way inside to start the day.

"I brought brownies," I announce as I walk into Bridger's house. "I got them from The Sugar Studio downtown."

"Yum," Birdie says with a smile.

"You didn't have to bring anything," Bridger says when he takes the plate from me, then presses his lips to my temple. "I'm just glad you're here."

He's ridiculously swoony, in a broody, grumpy sort of way. I read a lot of spicy romance novels, and Bridger ranks up there with some of the hottest book boyfriends I've ever read. Like, he shouldn't be real.

But his lips are on my skin, and his free hand is pressing against my lower back as he leads me toward the kitchen, and he *feels real.*

"We're grilling burgers," Birdie informs me.

"I heard. Thank you for inviting me."

"You didn't bring Pickles," she says, her brown eyes concerned.

"No, she has to stay at home, but you can come see her soon."

"Okay. Daddy, can I go watch TV?"

"Until dinner," Bridger confirms.

"What can I do to help? I can press out patties or cut vegetables or whatever you need."

"You," he says, pointing to me with the business end of a knife, "sit your gorgeous ass on that stool and talk to me while I work."

"You're quite complimentary." *The hottest man I've ever seen just called me gorgeous.* I inch up onto the stool and lean on the countertop, watching him, not sure what else to say.

"I call 'em like I see 'em." He winks at me and pops a piece of cheese into his mouth, then passes one to me, which I accept.

I'm starving. My post-school snack seems so long ago right now.

What also feels like so long ago is when Bridger made it clear we'd never be more than friends. And despite usually being clueless about these things, even I can feel the shift. He wanted to kiss me in my driveway. He touches me, flirts with me. All I can conclude is that Bridger has changed his mind about being just friends. What it's going to lead to, I have no idea, but I'm interested to find out because grown-up Bridger is way better than he was when I had a crush on him when I was a teenager.

However, I'm also nervous because I wasn't lying to him this morning when I told him that I shouldn't be messing around with a student's parent. There's no explicit rule against it, but surely it's frowned upon from an ethical point of view.

"You got quiet," he says and gestures for me to follow him out onto the deck in the backyard so he can put the burgers on the grill that's already fired up.

I watch him put the patties over the fire and close the lid, and then he turns his attention over to me.

"Talk to me, sweetheart."

"I was just thinking that what I said to you this

morning isn't wrong. I really shouldn't be doing... *anything* with a student's dad."

He narrows his eyes and crosses his arms over his chest, making his biceps bulge, and I salivate.

"Could you get fired?" he asks.

"No, there's nothing explicitly written in my contract."

His body relaxes with my answer, and he reaches out to take my hand, links his fingers with mine, and brings it up to his lips, where he presses a kiss to my knuckles.

"Then we're not doing anything wrong," he says. "This is a small town, Dani. People have relationships all the time. And it's not like I'm fucking you on your desk, although when I saw you in that black pencil skirt last week, that quickly became my number-one fantasy."

Stunned, my mouth opens and closes, but no sound comes out. Finally, I squeak, "What?"

"You heard me. In case I haven't made myself crystal clear, I think you're gorgeous, and I plan to spend a *lot* more time with you. If you think that I can stay away from you now that you're back in Bitterroot Valley, and we're both single, and we have this chemistry between us, you're crazy. We're not hurting anyone."

Did I fall and hit my head? Am I in a coma? Is this an alternate reality?

"Breathe, kitten."

I pull in a breath. "You're not kidding."

"I'm dead fucking serious." He reaches up with his free hand and tucks my hair behind my ear, then he skims those magical knuckles down my cheek. "The timing was never right before. You were too young for me, and then when you weren't, you were gone. The time is right now, and I'm not stupid enough to walk away from you. However, if this isn't what you want, I need you to spell it out for me so I don't waste any more of your time."

I frown. "You would do that? You'd walk away if I told you to?"

"It would fucking suck, but yeah, I would. Because you deserve everything good in this life, and that includes being with someone that *you* choose to be with."

Holy. Swoon.

"So, no more friend zone."

"I fucking hate the goddamn friend zone."

His dark eyes are on mine, taking in every expression on my face, in that serious way he's always had that makes my toes curl.

"I'm not going to tell you that I don't want to see more of you."

He blows out a breath, as if he's immensely relieved.

"Just no big displays of affection at my job, okay?"

"I can do that." He nods and releases me long enough to flip the patties. "You know, I still haven't kissed you."

"You just kissed my hand."

"I haven't nibbled on those plump lips or tasted your mouth. I haven't gripped your hair while I kiss the hell out of you. I haven't heard the noises you make or felt you shiver in my hands."

Cue the wet panties.

Bridger is a dirty talker. Holy crap, who knew? Not me. I might have fought harder back in the day if I had.

Who am I kidding? No, I wouldn't have. I wouldn't have known what to do with him, and my shyness would have gotten the best of me.

I'm not feeling shy now.

He slips cheese on the patties and closes the lid, then looks my way. He's not touching me at all, but his words are imprinted on my skin, and I have goose bumps all over my body.

"Keep looking at me like that, sweetheart, and I'll forget that my daughter is ten yards away and wide awake."

"How am I looking at you?"

"Like you want me." It's such a simple statement, but holds so much weight. He runs his tongue over his lower lip and then swears under his breath as he pulls the patties off the grill and turns it off. "Come on, trouble, let's go eat." *Trouble.* If anyone is trouble here it's this sexy-as-heck man in front of me.

In case I haven't made myself crystal clear, I think you're gorgeous, and I plan to spend a lot more time with you. The timing was never right before. You were too young for me, and then when you weren't, you were gone. The time is right now, and I'm not stupid enough to walk away from you.

From what my friends suggested, other guys flirted with me during college, but I never took them seriously. Too much baggage to believe them, and when I did participate in flirting, and tried to date or have a relationship, it was sorely lacking. But this is Bridger, and I know and trust him. I always have. He's definitely given me something to think about. After dinner. *Or maybe tomorrow.*

Thankfully, Birdie's infectious laugh and hearing her tell stories from her day diffuses the sexual tension between us, and we settle into a nice dinner. The burgers are delicious, and after we've eaten the brownies, the two of them escort me back to my house so Birdie can look in on Pickles.

"Thanks for dinner," I murmur. We're standing on the porch, and Birdie's inside, playing with the cat. "I had a really nice time with both of you."

"You're welcome. I'm really glad you came over." He takes a tiny step toward me and skims his fingertips down my cheek. "God, you're soft."

Feeling brave, I brace my hands on his hips, just over his waistband and under his shirt, feeling his skin.

"And you're warm."

His eyes sharpen and fall to my lips, and I lick them in anticipation. Just as he's lowering his face to mine, the door flings open, and Birdie's crying.

"Shit," Bridger mutters and turns to his daughter. "What's wrong, peanut?"

"Pickles scratched me." She holds her arm up, and there's a tiny pink line on her forearm. "I just pinched her back foot a little so I could look at her toe beans."

"You don't pinch anyone's anything," Bridger says with a sigh. "You're fine, but we'll go give it a wash. Tell Miss Dani good night."

She knuckles the tears in her eyes and scowls. "Good night."

"'Night, sweetie."

Bridger picks her up, and she leans her head on his shoulder. She's tired. But before he walks away, he leans down and kisses my forehead.

"Sleep well, sweetheart."

"You, too."

Chapter Five

BRIDGER

My baby sister is a badass.

We've always known it. Bee, as most of us call her, has the kind of personality that says *I don't give a fuck*. If she wants it, she's going to figure out a way to get it.

And the woman isn't even twenty-five yet.

A couple of years ago, she decided that she wanted to open a bookstore here in Bitterroot Valley, but the space she wanted, right next to the coffee shop, wasn't available. The owner made noises about selling, but then they would change their mind. Did Bee buy or rent something else instead?

No. That firecracker waited them out because no other space would do, and now, Billie's Books is close to opening.

It's Thursday, I've just dropped Birdie off at school, and I've decided to grab some coffee before I see how the progress is going at the new bookstore.

Millie Wild-Lexington, owns Bitterroot Valley Coffee Co, and she's another badass woman in my life.

I'm surrounded by them.

"Hey," Millie says when I approach the counter. "Your usual?"

I don't know how she's managed to memorize every customer's usual, but she has.

"Yeah. How's it going?" I side-eye the plastic that's covering the big hole that was cut between the two stores so customers will be able to get coffee and reading material. "Not too much dust over here?"

"Nah, the plastic helps," she says with a smile, sliding my mug of hot, black coffee my way. "She's almost done over there, Bridge. It's *so* great. Have you popped over?"

"That's my next stop. I needed a caffeine hit first."

"And I appreciate your patronage." She grins at me but then scowls when I don't smile back. "Why are you always so grumpy?"

"I'm not."

She rolls her eyes. "You have been lately. Cheer up, Chief. Nothing's that serious. How's Birdie?"

"She's been feeling pretty good." I frown, not wanting to jinx it. "Loving school. She's in Dani's class."

"Yeah?" Her eyes sparkle as she watches me. "And how is that going?"

"Birdie loves it." I take a sip of coffee.

"And how is it having my sister-in-law across the street?"

"No complaints from me."

Millie exhales and rolls her eyes. "Are you flirting

73

with her? Dating her? Come on, I saw the way you looked at her. You like her."

"Sure, I like her. I've known her forever."

I laugh when Millie narrows her eyes at me.

"I'm attempting to date her, okay?"

"That's better." She grins. "Is that why you're grumpy? Because you haven't been dating her enough? What dates have you been on, anyway?"

"You're a pain in my ass. She came to my place for dinner on Monday."

She blinks at me. "That's it?"

"I have a job. She has a job. I have a kid. She has a cat."

"Wait, she has a cat?"

"Yeah, it was a stray. Not that Pickles is any excuse." I shake my head, and Millie frowns.

"Who's Pickles?"

"The cat."

"Back up." She leans on the counter and crosses her arms over her chest. "You haven't even taken her on a real date?"

"You're not listening. She came to my house for dinner." I say the words slowly so she can comprehend them.

"Was Birdie home?"

I lift a brow at her. My best friend is starting to piss me off.

"Then it wasn't a date, Bridger. Did you walk her home and kiss her?"

I wince. "I walked her home, but before I could kiss

her, Birdie interrupted. That seems to be happening a lot. Getting interrupted."

"Interrupted doing what?"

I turn at the sound of my sister's voice and wince again.

"Nothing."

"He's trying to date Dani, but he's a single dad, and his kid is always around," Millie informs her, giving her the bare version of the story.

"Oh, I wanted to talk to you," Billie says, and then pauses. "Well, now I want to talk to you about a couple of things, but the first is, I want Birdie for the weekend."

"Convenient," Millie says with a toothy smile, waggling her eyebrows. "Say you have the weekend off, Bridge."

"I have the weekend off." I turn to my sister. "Why do you want my kid?"

"Because I'm less than two weeks from opening my supremely fabulous bookstore, and I want to celebrate with my best girl. I'm going to spoil the shit out of her. Auntie time is important, and I've been too busy to take her much. I'll pick her up from school tomorrow and bring her home on Sunday."

I blink in surprise, thankful once again that my kid has such an incredible network loving on her. It's not the first time she's spent the weekend with Bee—one of the necessities of being a fire chief and a single dad. But then a plan begins to form. "Okay. What was the other thing you wanted to talk about?"

"You're dating Dani? Our friend Dani? My *best* friend, Dani Lexington?"

"I don't know any others."

Billie frowns and looks down at the coffee that Millie just passed her. "But it's Dani."

"Do you have a problem with her?" I cross my arms over my chest, waiting. "Like you just said, she's one of your best friends, Bee."

"I know. I love her to pieces, but...I'm surprised, that's all."

"Why?"

My sister sighs, side-eyes Millie, and chews on her lip.

"It's okay," Millie says. "Say it."

"She's just not your usual type. And I say that with all the love in my heart for Dani. She's the best. But with her past, and—" She blows out a breath. "You know what? Never mind. It's none of my business."

"She's stronger than you give her credit for." My voice is low but not soft, and Billie winces. "Don't tell me you think she's damaged goods or something fucking stupid."

"Jesus, no." She looks horrified, and that makes me feel marginally better. "I'm simply surprised, that's all. But she's awesome, so I hope it works out. Now, come see my fabulous store."

She takes my hand and leads me out of the coffee shop and next door, and it takes me a moment to snap out of my sudden mood. *"She's just not your usual type."* She's always been my fucking type, but I've had to steer clear.

Shake it off.

When we step inside, I'm surprised to find that most of the bookshelves are already full.

"Wow, you've done a lot of work in here, Bee."

"I know. My back is killing me, and I need to find a massage therapist. But I love it so much. I need Birdie's help this weekend buying children's books for the kids' corner over there. I want to do a story hour once a month, and I want it to be a fun spot for kids to sit and read while their parents browse."

"I hate to burst your bubble, but you'll probably end up with some ripped books and stuff. Kids aren't usually careful."

"I'll have some out that the kids can read and damage, and the brand-new ones will be in cellophane if they're within reach."

"Good idea."

She shows me around each section. I notice the romance section takes up more than half of the store, and when I point that out, Bee grins.

"As it should be," she says. "It's the best-selling genre out there."

"You're the expert. Are you sure you want Birdie for the whole weekend?"

"Yes. I was about to call you, actually, so don't even worry about us. I have extra meds for her at my place, just in case, remember? Not that she'll need them."

"I really would like to spend some alone time with Dani." And I'm completely floored that Bee's offer aligns with my weekend off. That never happens, but it's something I've tried to implement across all of my team. Rotating weekends off. *Myself included.*

"Done. Do it. Enjoy." She grins at me. "Wrap it before you tap it."

"Jesus fucking Christ, Billie."

"Hey, it's good advice."

After I left the bookstore yesterday, I got called to a fire and didn't get home until late. Birdie ended up spending the afternoon and evening with Merilee, a retired teacher that Brady Wild recommended, and I have to admit, she's a lifesaver. She even came to my house, so Birdie was at home.

I never had the chance to call or even run over to see Dani, but I'll see her this morning when I drop Birdie off at school.

"Now, don't forget, Aunt Bee is picking you up, and you're spending the weekend at her house."

"I *know*," Birdie says with a little shimmy in her seat. "We're going to have so much fun."

"And I'll see you on Sunday."

"Okay." She's not concerned at all, and I love that my girl doesn't get separation anxiety when it comes to being away from me.

After parking in the lot, I walk Birdie over to the sidewalk where teachers are greeting kids.

"I'll see you Sunday," I say as I squat down to hug my daughter. "Be good and have fun, okay?"

"Okay." She kisses my cheek. "Bye, Daddy."

And with that, she rushes inside of the school, and as I stand, my eyes lock on Dani.

She's in khaki pants today that hug her curves, and a navy blue button-down top that shouldn't be provocative at all, yet, I want to strip her out of it and have my way with her.

"Good morning," she says as I approach.

"Good morning." I reach out and tuck her hair behind her ear. I want to kiss her and pull her in for a hug, but she already set the boundary of no affection at work, and I won't cross it. "So, Bee is picking Birdie up from school today. I wanted to give you a heads-up. She's already listed with the office."

"Oh, thanks for letting me know. You must have to work?" She chews on her lip and frowns. "Not that it's any of my business."

"No work," I reply easily. "I have a date."

She blinks, and hurt moves into her eyes, and I feel like a giant asshole.

"Oh, how nice. Have fun."

"No." I step closer to her. "Sorry, that was a really bad way of saying, I'd like to take *you* out on a date."

She swallows, licks her lips, and then glances up at me. I hate that she still gets so nervous around me, so apprehensive.

I want her to trust me.

"What time were you thinking?" she asks, trying to keep her voice casual.

"Seven. I'd like to take you to dinner."

"You would?"

I can't help but feel a mixture of humor and frustration. "Why wouldn't I, Dani?"

"For a whole host of reasons." She blows out a breath. "Yeah, dinner at seven sounds good. Casual?"

"I was thinking pizza or BBQ. Are you craving anything?"

"Pizza sounds good, actually."

"Pizza at seven, then."

"We can just order it in, if that's easier for you."

God, I want to touch her. We're going to have to talk about this rule of hers. "No. It's not easier for me. I want to take you out to dinner, Dani. Seven o'clock."

"See you later."

I wink at her and then return to my truck. I have flowers to buy, and I need to make a phone call.

The phone rings through my speakers, and Holden answers on the second ring.

"Hey, man," he says.

"Hey, are you busy right now?"

"I'm just working on some paperwork in my office. What's up?"

I clear my throat. "The office at your barn at the ranch? Can I pop out there?"

"Sure. Door's open."

He ends the call, and I head out of town, toward the Lexington ranch. Holden inherited it after their dad died earlier this year. One of the first things he did was have me and my guys come out and burn every building to the ground to purge the property of his bastard of a father. It was a great training exercise for my guys, and as the flames destroyed everything, I could almost see the weight lift off my friend's shoulders.

I'm glad that I could be there for him and help with that.

I also wonder if Dani's been out to her family's property since she and her sisters collected whatever they wanted from the farmhouse.

It's a twenty-minute drive to the turnoff that leads me to the barn, and I park next to Holden's truck, then hop out and walk inside, finding my friend in his office.

"Hey." I grin and lean against the wall opposite him since he's in the only chair in the room. "How's Millie?"

"Fucking gorgeous and perfect in every way," he answers and then narrows his eyes at me. "What's going on? Is someone dead?"

I might be, if this goes poorly.

"I need to have a conversation with you about Dani."

Holden stands and crosses his arms over his chest. "What about her?"

"I'm taking her out on a date tonight."

A muscle clenches in his jaw. "Why?"

"Why?" I scoff at that and push my hands through my hair. "Because she's amazing. Because she's funny and beautiful, and I want to see her. I want to date her, actually."

Holden's sigh is loud and full of frustration. "What else do you plan to do to my sister?"

"I don't think you want me to answer that question, man."

"Fucking hell." Holden paces away, hands on his hips, and then turns back to me. "You hurt her, I end you."

"Obviously."

"No, that's not an idle threat. My girls have been to hell and back, and nothing is ever going to hurt them again. So if you so much as *look at her* sideways, I'm coming for you, and I don't give a rat's ass if you're my best fucking friend."

"I will *never* intentionally hurt that woman, and you know it. For fuck's sake, Holden, I know what you all went through. I'm not dicking around with her for shits and giggles."

He swallows, watching me, and then nods. "As long as we understand each other."

"We do."

At 6:57, I walk across the street, with flowers in hand. I ring the bell and Dani answers, and her whole face fucking lights up when she sees the yellow roses in my hand.

"For you."

She takes them and buries her nose in them in that way that women do that I find so fucking adorable.

"Thanks."

"You're gorgeous, Dani." It's true. She's in a red-and-white dress that buttons down the entire front and falls just above her knees.

When my eyes find her face again, she's looking at my arms, and it makes me feel smug. I've caught her looking at my arms and shoulders before. I work out a lot—I need to be strong for my job—and I'm glad that she likes what she sees.

"I'm just going to set these in some water."

I follow her inside and see that Pickles is curled up on the couch, napping.

"How's it going with the cat?"

I can hear the water running in the kitchen, and then Dani returns, carrying a vase with the flowers in it.

"She's sweet," Dani says, smiling softly at the kitten. "She sleeps with me, and she always greets me at the door when I come home from work."

"So, you're glad you kept her?"

"Yeah, I am. Okay, I'm ready to go when you are."

"Let's do it." I hold my hand out, and without hesitating, she slides her palm against my own, and I link our fingers, guiding her across the street to my truck.

The drive to Old Town Pizza is quick, and the owner, Heather, winks at me when we walk inside. I called ahead and asked if she could reserve us a table on her rooftop, since it always fills up quickly, especially on a Friday night.

"Well, hello, you two. I have your table ready. Follow me."

Dani frowns up at me, but I just shrug, and we follow Heather up a set of stairs to the open-air rooftop. There's a bar up here and umbrellas over the tables, but we have an unobstructed view of the ski mountain and most of downtown.

"It's pretty up here," Dani says once we're seated.

"I think so, too."

She looks my way and then chuckles when she finds me just staring at her. "You're just trying to be charming."

"Me? No way. What do you like on your pizza, sweetheart?"

"Oh, I'll eat anything." She pushes the menu away and looks back at the mountain, so I reach over and take her hand in mine, getting her attention.

"But what do *you* like? If you're home alone and you order pizza, what do you get?"

"We can get whatever you want. Really, I like anything."

"That's not what I asked you." I narrow my eyes and lean forward. "Dani, I'm trying to get to know you. I'm learning you. I sincerely, from the bottom of my heart, want to know how you order your freaking pizza."

She presses her lips together in a line and then says, "I like pepperoni with pickled jalapeños, pineapple, and mushrooms. It's weird. So when I eat pizza with anyone else, we just get something normal, like pepperoni or Hawaiian."

The waitress arrives, setting down the drinks we ordered when we got here, and says, "Are you ready to order?"

"Yeah," I begin, watching Dani. "We'll take a large pepperoni with pickled jalapenos, pineapple, and mushrooms."

Dani's eyes have widened and her jaw drops in surprise. Jesus, has no one ever ordered her pizza the way she likes it?

"Do you want hand-tossed or deep-dish?" Sandy, the waitress, asks.

I lift an eyebrow at Dani.

"Hand-tossed," she says, and I nod at Sandy.

"What else?" Sandy asks.

"I think we need more carbs," I add, "so let's do some cheesy breadsticks."

"With ranch," Dani chimes in, earning a smile from me.

Good girl, I mouth to her, and her cheeks redden.

Fuck, I want to see her blush *everywhere.*

When we're alone again, Dani says in a small voice, "You didn't have to do that."

"It sounds delicious."

She snorts out a laugh, but when I don't laugh with her, she looks at me like I'm not telling the truth, and I don't like that.

"There's nothing on that pizza that doesn't sound good to me."

"Okay," she replies, but I can tell she doesn't believe me.

That's fine. I'll prove it to her.

"How long have you lived in your house?" she asks me, changing the conversation.

"About three years. I bought it because I liked the backyard and that it backs up to the woods, so it's a little more private."

"You do have a good backyard," she says with a nod. "Holden hated that I moved into my place. Hated it."

"Why?" I sip my iced tea, watching her.

"Because it's old and shabby, but it's cheap, and it's clean, and I have some projects planned for it. Some paint and stuff, nothing too crazy. But I like the neighborhood, and I'm not too far from work. In fact, I usually walk."

I blink at her. "Wait, you *walk*? Dani, that's more than a mile each way."

"I won't do it after it gets cold, but it's been nice out lately." She shrugs and sips her Coke. "I like to be outside, in case you hadn't noticed."

That's true. I find her outside often.

"Any particular reason for that?"

She sighs. "You know we don't have to talk about my crappy childhood all the time."

"I didn't ask about your shitty childhood."

"No, but most of my quirks circle back to that. The house I grew up in was horrible, so I liked to be outside, and I still do." She shrugs. "It's not a sad thing; it's just a thing."

"You don't look sad to me," I admit, shaking my head as I watch her. "I don't see you that way."

"Good. Because it would suck if you were only hanging out with me because you felt sorry for me." She frowns and presses her lips together, as if she didn't mean to say that, and I decide to put that shit out of her head *right now* and reach for her hand, linking our fingers.

"I don't see anything to feel sorry for, Dani. You're beautiful, a successful teacher, you have your own place, and you've carved out a life for yourself that you love. I admire that you take such good care of your students, especially since my daughter is one of them. She has nothing but amazing things to say about you and being in your classroom. Yeah, you came from a pretty shitty situation, but you're thriving *despite* it, and you're absolutely someone that I want to spend a lot of time with. Not because I think I *should*, but because staying away from you isn't a fucking option for me."

"Here you go," Sandy says as she places our food on the table, and I have to pull back, releasing Dani's hand. When we've confirmed that we don't need anything else, Sandy bustles away.

"Okay," Dani says, obviously in response to what I said before the food arrived.

"So, why are *you* here?" I ask her as I slide a slice onto her plate. "My good looks? My charm? My cool truck?"

She doesn't laugh the way I expect her to. Her eyes widen, and then she licks her lips. "Bridger, I don't know if anyone has ever told you this before, and if they haven't, well, shame on them, but you're hot."

I bust up laughing, and that makes her laugh, immediately lightening the mood.

"You're just here because I'm a piece of meat?"

"No. I don't just mean physically, although, yeah." She waves her hand around, indicating all of me, and I can't help but grin at her because she's adorable, and my dick has decided to join in on this conversation. "You have that going for you, but it's in the things you say and the way you just are. You're...yeah. You do it for me."

Now I'm fascinated, and I lean in, ignoring the food on my plate.

"I do *what* for you, sweetheart?"

She blushes again and pulls a piece of pineapple off her pizza, popping it into her mouth.

"I am not having this conversation here." She glances around nervously, looking shy. "We know half the people in this restaurant, Bridger."

"I don't give a fuck. Let them see."

She laughs and shakes her head. "This conversation is to be continued, Chief."

My stomach jolts the same way it did the first time she called me that.

"No."

Her eyes are full of mischief as she takes a bite of her pizza. "No?"

"Absolutely fucking not."

"Hmm." She licks at some sauce on her mouth, but she doesn't get it all, so I reach over and wipe it away with my thumb, then lick it off myself, and her eyes dilate. "I want to call you a nickname. You call me stuff."

"Not chief." I shake my head and bite half of a breadstick. "Pick something else."

"Daddy?"

I choke and reach for my tea as she laughs across from me.

Jesus fucking Christ, she's going to be the death of me.

I'm hard as fucking stone. This whole conversation has turned me the fuck on. When I've got my breath back, I stand and circle the table, sit next to her, and lean in so I can whisper in her ear. I brace one arm on the back of her chair and the other on the table, caging her in.

She's already breathing hard.

"You want to call me *daddy*, kitten?" My voice is a whisper against her ear, and I love the way she visibly shivers.

I'm going to make her squirm later.

She licks her lips. "It was a joke, Bridger. Obviously, I read too many spicy books."

That has my eyebrows climbing. "We have so many things to talk about when I get you alone."

She smiles at me, her lips mere inches from mine. "I can't wait."

Chapter Six

DANI

I don't think I've ever had a better time on a date in my whole life. Granted, between the trauma from Angela's bullying and my dad's abuse, studying, and working to support myself through college—trying to heal with a therapist—I didn't date much. I'm no virgin, but no one has ever made me feel like everything I say is important, or that they're happy just to be with me. The conversation has never flowed so easily. I've never felt so valued. Valuable.

No one has ever made me feel so...*good*.

I loved teasing Bridger at dinner, and when I made the joke about calling him *daddy*, well, I'll be laughing about that for a long time. The shock on his face was just hilarious. But then he made it sexy by coming around the table to whisper in my ear, and every nerve ending in my body sat up and took notice.

Holy crap, the things that Bridger does to me.

And he stayed there. He didn't go back across the

table. He pulled his plate over and sat by my side for the rest of the meal. He'd steal a touch or a quick kiss to my cheek, and I ignored the other people there, whether I knew them or not, and simply enjoyed him.

I don't know why I suddenly felt unsure and self-conscious again earlier today, especially after we had such a nice dinner on Monday, but Bridger put any lingering doubts out of my mind.

And it feels amazing, if not surreal, given I never thought we'd get here.

Bridger pulls into his driveway and turns to me. "Wait for me."

Happily, I nod and stay in my seat as he walks around the truck and opens my door, leans across me to unbuckle my belt, pressing a kiss to my cheek in the process, and then he takes my hand and guides me out of the vehicle.

I move to walk toward my own house, but he gives my hand a little tug, and I glance up at him.

"Come inside with me, sweetheart." His gaze is intense, his hand firm around mine, and I absolutely, without a doubt, am not ready to go home.

"Sure."

He unlocks the front door and then leads me inside his house, and once the door is closed, he crowds me against it. One hand moves up to my cheek and the other leans on the door, and his face is so close to mine, I can feel the heat of his skin.

Finally, this man is going to kiss me.

"You're so fucking beautiful," he whispers before

those lips are on mine, and I can't help the moan that escapes my throat as my hands cling to his back and his tongue urges my mouth open. He tastes like tea and the ice cream we shared after dinner, and I just want to climb him.

I feel like I've waited my whole life for this moment. To be here with this man.

His five o'clock shadow feels delicious against my skin, and I just can't get enough of him.

But he pulls back, his dark eyes bright with lust, and he's as out of breath as I am. "Holy shit."

"Yeah." I lick my lower lip, still tasting him there, and my eyes fall to his lips. "Wow."

"Sweetheart, if you don't—"

"I do." I grin up at him as his hands glide down my back and grip my rear, lifting me so I can wrap my legs around his waist. My fingers plunge into his thick, dark hair, and there's really nothing I've ever wanted more in this life than Bridger. "I really do."

"Thank Christ."

I'm vaguely aware of him carrying me through the house, but I'm too busy kissing him. My arms are locked around his neck, and his fingertips are digging into my butt, so close to that extra sensitive place between my legs.

Bridger lowers me to my feet, and one of his hands fists in my hair at the nape, holding me where he wants me as his mouth continues to plunder mine, as if I'm the feast that he can't get enough of.

We may have been interrupted all week when it came

to getting our lips on each other, but he's making up for it now, and it's so much more than what I could have imagined.

My hands are under his shirt, on his smooth, warm skin. His stomach is hard, his abs defined, and I can't wait to see them, so I nudge his shirt up, and I feel him smile against my lips.

"In a hurry?" He's kissing down my jawline, making me shiver.

"No hurry." I swallow thickly, his tongue making me lightheaded. "Just needy."

"What do you need, kitten?"

I need things that I do *not* feel comfortable articulating out loud. I love that Bridger seems to be a dirty talker, but I am not good with words. I learned at an early age that speaking up led to pain. *This* is not that, but old habits die hard. Still, I give him the words he needs to hear.

"You."

He smiles against my skin, and his hands have moved to the buttons of my dress, slowly pulling them free.

"And?"

I don't reply. I just tug on his shirt, and finally, he reaches over his head and pulls it off, tossing it aside.

"Better?"

"Yeah." Holy mother of God. I feel my eyes go wide as they travel down the length of his long torso. He's got muscles for days. My fingers reach out to brush lightly over the hills and valleys of those muscles, and my entire body tightens with need. "Did you sell your soul to the devil to look like this?"

His chuckle is low and full of satisfaction as he kisses my forehead. "You're good for my ego, kitten."

Shaking my head, I let my fingertips drift over his chest, over the light dusting of hair there and down to each nipple, circling them softly.

"Fuuuck," he mutters as his head falls back. My fingertips move up his neck, over his Adam's apple.

My eyes flick up to his when he lowers his chin, and he's watching me. His jaw is tense, the sexy muscle there twitching.

And when my hand drifts to the button of his jeans, he circles my wrist and brings it to his lips, kissing the tender flesh over my pulse point.

"Not yet," he murmurs. "Take off your dress."

I've never done the striptease thing. Typically, if I was getting it on with someone, it was dark, and we just got naked and did the deed.

Quick and efficient.

There was no teasing, no flirting—no revealing my larger body—just get to the point. I wouldn't know how to be...I don't know...*alluring*, if a million dollars was on the line.

Bridger's eyebrows raise, and his hands return to my buttons. "Do you want me to help?"

"Yes, please." I lick my lips, and he goes back to work, slowly releasing each of the plastic disks, until my dress is open like a robe.

His big hands push it apart and over my shoulders,

and then it's pooled at my feet, and I'm standing before him in my pretty, matching sage green bra and panties.

"Jesus. Christ," he whispers. His fingers aren't quite steady as he reaches out and brushes a fingertip over my skin, just above the cup of my bra. "I'm about to lose control, Dani."

"It's about time."

His eyes flare before he lifts me as if I'm weightless. "Wrap those legs around me, baby."

I do as I'm told, and then he's crawling onto the bed, and my back is pressed into the mattress. He lowers to his elbows and cradles my head in his hands as he continues to devour my mouth. Bridger is an excellent kisser.

Like, if it were an Olympic sport, Bridger would not only be a gold medal winner, he'd hold all the world records for all time.

His back is hard and broad and is just begging for my hands, and when they move down to his butt, I'm frustrated when I find denim.

"Not fair," I whisper in his ear.

"What isn't?" He brushes his nose over mine.

"Your pants."

"You want them off?"

I nod, and he smiles.

"Tell me you want me to take my pants off, kitten."

I bite my lip, and his thumb tugs it free.

"Tell me," he says again.

"I want your pants off. Please."

"I love it when you ask nicely."

With a smug smile, he shimmies out of the jeans,

leaving him in black boxer briefs that do *nothing* to hide his erection.

I can't help it, I gasp.

"Don't worry," he murmurs, returning to me, kissing me softly as he brushes his fingers through my hair. "I'm going to get you good and ready for me."

I'm not worried at all.

I'm freaking *excited*.

His hand has drifted to one of my breasts, and he teases my already hard nipple through the lace. Finally, he urges me to arch up so he can unclasp my bra and then tosses it aside, and his mouth closes around one nipple, tugging so hard my pussy clenches.

He growls as his hands roam farther down, gripping my hips and my thighs.

"I could worship your breasts all night."

I moan at his sexy words, and then he's kissing down my stomach, and I immediately clam up.

"No."

His head shoots up, his eyes narrow, and then he's over me once again, cradling my face in his hands, gently brushing his thumbs over my cheeks.

"Why?"

I bite my lip, suddenly nervous, and he lowers his lips to mine and kisses me long and slow, calming me once more.

"You just don't have to do that," I whisper against his lips.

"Why not, baby?" I love that he's whispering back to me.

I narrow my eyes at him, but he just gives me a half smile, and it's so sexy, I can't help but rock my hips up just a bit, making him groan.

"I want to bury my face in you, sweetheart. It's a fucking honor and a privilege to taste you, and I've been thinking about it for weeks. So, if you don't like that, I just want to know why."

"Because it's gross and a chore, and not...*fun*?" The last word is said on a whisper and a question because his eyes have widened, and he looks horrified.

"Who the fuck...you know what? Don't answer that. Because I'll want to kill any bastard that made you feel that way. Are you telling me that no one has had their mouth on you?"

I lick my lips and shake my head.

"Oh, baby, that's about to change." He nips at my lips. "I'm going to make you come the fuck apart. I want you to come all over my mouth. I want you to soak me as you're screaming out my name."

"I don't even know what that means."

I can't believe I said that out loud. I turn my head to the side and hide my face in his bulging biceps. *This is so embarrassing.* Looking like he does, Bridger has probably had so many partners over the years. More than I want to know about. He might say he wants me, but surely, he'll hate how insecure I am. *How inexperienced.*

And then I feel his lips next to my ear.

"Do you trust me?"

I nod.

"Use your words."

"Yes." It's muffled against his skin.

"Then why are you hiding, kitten?"

"Because I'm mortified. Should I just go home?"

I feel him smile against me, and then his fingers are under my chin, and he turns my face up again, but my eyes are closed.

"Open those gorgeous blue eyes for me."

I open *one* eye and see that he's smiling so widely, he could light up the room.

"Both of them."

When I've complied, he brushes his nose against mine again, and that makes me sigh with happiness.

"Tell me you're not a virgin, Dani."

I snort at that, and he seems to visibly relax in relief. "No. Not for a long time."

It's true, I'm *not* a virgin, but I've only had two forgettable partners. I know with absolute certainty that tonight is not going to be forgettable.

Now his eyes narrow like he's jealous.

"You asked, you know."

"I'd like to kiss your pussy. I want to lick you and fuck you with my tongue and make you crazy."

My eyes have grown with each word. "You do?"

"Hell yes. Tell me I can. I promise, you'll fucking *love it*. I'm going to make you addicted to it, sweetheart. You'll be begging me to eat you out at every opportunity, and I'll happily do it. I'll spend the rest of my life on my knees for you, if that's what you want."

Wow, I might let him do *anything* right now. "Okay."

"If you don't like it, just tell me to stop." He kisses

my chin and then smiles up at me as he starts his descent down my torso, dragging his lips over my skin, his eyes full of sexy promises. "But I guarantee that you're going to like it."

I smile back, and then his shoulders nudge my legs wider, and I have to close my eyes because no one has been that up close and personal to that part of my anatomy.

I'm still wearing my panties, but he doesn't seem to care. He kisses me, right over the fabric, and my hips move of their own volition, wanting more friction *right there.*

"You're already so fucking wet," he says, dragging a fingertip up and down my slit, over the cotton of my panties. "You're so damn ready for me, Dani. Open your pretty eyes, baby."

I take a steadying breath and then comply, and holy cow, if he isn't a sight, his face so close to my core, his eyes bright with lust, and his tan finger moving over my underwear.

Can a girl come like this? Because I might be able to.

"You smell like sex," he says, and I feel my cheeks flame, and my knees want to close, but he holds me open. "Oh, I like that. I like it when you blush, and now I know that you blush everywhere."

One hand returns to my breast, and he rolls the nipple between his fingers as he lowers his face and presses a kiss over my slit.

"I'm going to pull your panties off." He hooks his hands into the sides of my underwear, and I lift my hips so he can pull them down my legs. Instead of just flicking them aside, he buries his nose in them and *smells them*— oh, my God!—and sets them carefully aside. "I'm keeping those."

"What?" It's a squeak, and it makes him chuckle. "Why?"

"I'll replace them." It's not an answer, but I don't ask again because he's lowered his face and has started licking me, and I've never felt anything like this in my life. I can't help but reach out and bury my fingers in his hair, holding on for dear life as he glides that tongue through my folds, and every nerve ending in my body is on fire. It's a good thing I have a firefighter at my disposal. "Fuck, you're wet, sweetheart. You taste so damn good. So fucking sweet."

His words are just so sexy. So rough and hot, and I know without a doubt that he's about to ruin me for all other men.

He pushes a finger over my lips, through the tender and sensitive folds of my most intimate skin, before it slips inside of me, and I swear I'm about to come apart.

"Oh, God. Bridger, I'm going to come."

"That's it, let go." His lips brush over my clit, and then he sucks on it, and that's it. I couldn't stop the tsunami of pure sensation that moves through me if I tried. "Fuck yes, baby."

My hips buck, my head thrashes, and I have no idea what the words are that are coming out of my mouth as I come so hard and so long that I don't even remember my own name.

I'm vaguely aware of Bridger kissing my inner thighs, my hip, my stomach, and up the center of my chest, before he kisses my lips, and holy Moses, I can taste myself on him.

It's not at all unpleasant.

And that one guy from my past who told me that eating out a woman was a chore or gross should be beheaded, right here and now.

At the very least, I hope he runs out of gas a lot.

Bridger leans over and fishes a condom out of his bedside table. I like that it's a new box that he has to break into. But before he can roll it on, I cup his face in my hands.

"I have an implant," I tell him softly. "And I haven't had sex in…a long time. I'm clean."

He tosses the condom away, making me chuckle.

"Are you telling me that I can take you bare?" He brushes a piece of my hair off my cheek. "Are you sure?"

"Trust, remember?"

And then he's kissing me again, and he pulls one leg up higher against his side, and his crown is *right there,* nudging its way inside of me.

"Ah, baby." His teeth are gritted, as if he's in pain as he touches his forehead to mine. "Fuck, you're so tight."

I take a deep breath and relax my muscles, and his free hand cups my cheek as he pushes the rest of the way inside of me, and *oh, my God.*

"Breathe," he says, and I do, making him smile. "Jesus, you're so incredible. So fucking amazing, sweetheart."

And then this man starts to move.

He groans as he lowers his forehead to mine again, twines his fingers with my fingers, and holds my hands above my head, moving in and out of me in long, intense movements that are pushing me right back up that glorious hill to a climax that I already know will be unlike anything else I've ever experienced in my life.

He looks down at where we're joined, and I follow his gaze and feel my breath catch.

He's so *big*, and he's glistening with my wetness as he moves in and out, and it's the sexiest thing I've ever seen.

"Holy fuck," he growls and starts to move faster, and I know he's almost ready to let go, and I'm right there with him. "Go over, baby."

"Go with me."

He groans, and then he pushes hard, buried balls deep, and we're shuddering together as wave after wave of the tsunami pulls us farther out to sea.

After we've had a minute to catch our breath, I'm the first to roll away. "Bathroom?"

Bridger can't breathe yet, so he points to the door, making me grin, and I snag up my dress before I wobble my way into the en suite and close the door behind me.

Wow.

First, I look at myself in the mirror, and my hair is a tangled mess. My lips are swollen, and the skin around them is a little pink from his scruff. My eyes are glassy.

I look ... sexed.

I grin at myself and then do my business and clean up

the best that I can before I wrap my dress around me and button it up. I can't walk home naked.

When I walk out of the bathroom, Bridger's returning from the hallway, where I assume he was using the other bathroom, and his eyes narrow when he sees that I'm dressed.

"You have a tub big enough to swim in. Anyway, this was fun." I smile and retrieve my bra, but leave the panties because he said he wants to keep them. "Thanks for dinner."

He's standing there, impressively naked, and crosses his arms over his chest, frowning at me. "Where do you think you're going?"

I frown back. "Home?"

"Why?"

Now I cross my own arms over *my* chest, mirroring him. "Because I live there? And I have a cat."

He abruptly turns away, steps into a pair of gray sweatpants, and then turns back to me. "Can I have your keys?"

"Why?"

"Because I asked for them."

I blink at him. "It's a keypad. The code is one-one-four-six."

He nods, and then he's gone. The front door opens and closes, and I'm not sure what I'm supposed to be doing, so I walk out to the living room and watch through the window as he slips into my house. Five minutes later, he walks out of my house with my cat in one arm and her bed in another.

I open the door for him, and he passes me Pickles, drops the bed on the floor, then kisses me hard and backs away.

"I'll be right back."

I cover my lips with my fingers as he takes off again, still barefoot and only in those sweats, and disappears inside my house, but just a few minutes later, he comes back out again. He locks my door behind him, and then he crosses the street and walks into his own house with a litter pan and her food dish, full of food.

"There. She's here. If you need to go home because of your cat, I just solved that problem. Birdie's gone until Sunday afternoon, and I'm not wasting a minute of this weekend without you."

Well then.

What can I really say to that? It's not as if I *wanted* to leave Bridger. Tonight has been the best night of my life. I've felt valued, listened to, and he freaking worshipped every inch of my body. I've never stayed for round two—never believed I was wanted that badly, and honestly, no one has ever invited me to stay. And yet, he still wants more. Not going to lie, that makes me feel incredible. This stunning, kind, sexy god in front of me, who I've crushed on for years, wants me.

I set Pickles on the couch and turn to see him watching me, as if he's waiting for me to make the next move.

The ball is in my court.

"I could use a shower."

His lips tip up in a relieved smile. "We can make that happen."

Chapter Seven

BRIDGER

I don't remember the last time I felt this content. This relaxed. Or, I admit, this damn smug.

Dani's curled up around me, draped over me with bare skin, sleeping soundly. And she should be. I woke her up just two hours ago to fuck her again because she was in my arms, just like this, and I couldn't resist her.

How could anyone resist her?

And how is it possible that anyone lucky enough to be in Dani's bed never had their mouth on her? Don't get me wrong, the thought of another fucker's hands or mouth anywhere near this woman makes me feral, but what a bunch of absolute idiots. She's so fucking amazing she takes my breath away. Soft, warm skin, breasts that beg for my hands, and a pussy so damn delicious, I know that I'll never get my fill of her. The noises she makes, the way she clutches my hair in her fists, Jesus, everything about her is just...*fuck*.

Even now, the mere feel of her, skin on skin, has my cock thickening, but I drag my hand down my face and mentally tell it to calm the fuck down. She needs to rest, and I need coffee.

Gently, I slide out from under her and nudge my pillow against her, smiling when she hugs it close and nuzzles that gorgeous face into it, sighing back into sleep.

Dani Lexington is every fucking fantasy I've ever had in my life, and she's finally in my bed.

I plan to keep her there as much as possible, which won't be nearly enough, given that I have a five-year-old, but we'll figure it out. I wasn't kidding when I told her that staying away from her isn't a damn option for me.

After tugging on some sweats and a tank, I pad out to the kitchen and get a pot of coffee going. Pickles is curled up, sleeping on the couch as if she's lived here all her life. When I walk over to pet her, she stretches, blinks at me, and then turns in a circle to go back to sleep.

"Get used to this," I whisper to her before returning to the kitchen. I usually drink my coffee on the deck, on the rare days that Birdie and I aren't rushing to get out the door, and I wonder if Dani would like to have breakfast out there today. I have stuff for pancakes and bacon, and I even have some fresh fruit that I picked up the other day.

I'll give her a while to sleep, and then I'll ask her. The great thing about today is, there's no agenda. Neither of us has anywhere to be, my daughter is well taken care of by my sister, and Dani and I can just *be*.

I've just poured myself some coffee when I hear bare

feet on the hardwood, and when I turn, my tongue glues itself to the roof of my mouth.

Holy fucking Christ.

Dani's rubbing her sleepy eyes, and her dark hair falls around her shoulders, messy from my fingers and bed. Those pouty lips are swollen, and I can't wait to taste them again.

But that's not what's rendered me speechless.

She's in my fucking Bitterroot Valley Fire Department T-shirt. The arms fall to her elbows, and the hem to mid-thigh. Her legs and feet are bare, and fuck me if my heart doesn't kick into overdrive and my cock isn't instantly begging for her.

"Good morning," she says, her voice raspy.

She blinks at me, and I can't speak yet.

"Bridge? Are you okay?"

"Yeah." I clear my throat and set my mug aside. "Sorry. You're in my shirt."

She looks down at herself and bites her lip. "I found it in your drawer. It's comfy. Really soft. Is it old?"

"Yeah." I swallow hard and step toward her. "And I didn't say you could borrow it."

Let's be honest, I'll give her anything she wants, but first, I'm going to fuck her here in my kitchen.

Her gaze whips up to mine, and she frowns. "Uh—"

Before she can say any more, I frame her face in my hands and kiss her. She moans, leaning against me, her hands immediately going for my ass, and I can't help the grin that slides across my face.

"I guess I should take it off," she whispers.

"Let me." Gathering the hem in my hands, I pull the shirt over her head, and she lifts her arms helpfully. And she's left bare-ass naked. "Fuck, baby."

There's a smile in her cobalt eyes as she bites that lip, and then I lift her onto the counter, and she gasps from the cold marble hitting her skin.

"I'll warm you up," I promise. "Spread your pretty legs for me, kitten."

I step between her legs, and she's at the perfect height for this. Her arms wrap around my shoulders, and she opens her mouth to me, kissing me with a hunger that matches my own.

Who knew that quiet, shy Dani would be absolute *fire* when it comes to sex?

She lowers one arm and presses her hand against my hard-as-steel cock, and I drag my lips down her jaw so I can bury my face in her neck.

"God, baby. Take it out."

She pushes my sweats down my hips, and when my cock bobs free, she grips it.

"Yes, stroke it, just like that." She swipes her thumb over the crown, and I bite her fleshy shoulder.

"You're so big and thick." Her words are a whisper, making me groan against her.

"What is?"

She whimpers and presses her lips to my own shoulder, but I want to hear the words. I want to hear the *dirty* words from her clean mouth.

"What is, Dani?"

"Your ... appendage."

My head jerks up at that, and my eyes narrow on her. "Oh, you can do so much better than that, kitten. Try again."

She frowns. "I don't like to swear."

"I'm going to make all kinds of filthy things come out of your perfect little mouth. Come on, you can do it. When it's just you and me, no one else, you can say it." I kiss her neck and palm her breast, rubbing her nipple between my fingers, and she gasps. "What's big and thick, Dani?"

"Your ..."

"Say cock, baby."

Her aroused gaze finds mine, and as she continues to work me over, she lifts that chin in that way she does when she's being particularly brave, and she says, "Your *cock* is so big and hard, and I want it inside of me, Bridger."

Fuck me sideways.

"Good girl." Wrapping my hands around her ass, she lifts herself up as I drag her closer to the edge of the countertop, and Dani herself guides me to her, burying the crown in her slick wetness. She's so damn wet, so ready for me, that I slide inside of her effortlessly, balls deep. "This thick cock is going to fuck you until you see stars, sweetheart. Lean back."

She moves back to her elbows, and I lift her legs higher, fucking her as if I wasn't inside her four times in the past twelve hours.

But who's counting?

"Bridger."

"Yes, sweetheart?" God, I fucking love it when she rasps my name, when she whimpers and clenches around me.

Her mouth is open, her bright eyes on me, and I can't resist reaching up and resting the pad of my thumb on that lower lip. She sucks me into her mouth, and I'm the one who sees fucking stars.

I'm an animal possessed now, hammering into her, making her body quake with every thrust. I pull my wet thumb out of her mouth and cover her hard clit with it, and she cries out, her head falls back, and her pussy clenches around me like a goddamn vise.

"Oh. My. God!"

"Yes, baby. God, you're so fucking perfect." She's squeezing me, milking my cock, and I can't hold my climax back anymore. I pull her to me, bottoming out, and come so hard I lose my breath.

After taking a few lungfuls of air, I reach over for a towel, rest it under where we're connected, and then pull out of her and use the towel to catch my cum.

"Wow," she whispers, chest still heaving, nipples hard as stone. She sits up, and I grip her jaw and kiss her hard. "Gonna need another shower."

"You do that, and I'll get breakfast going. We can eat on the deck."

She smiles softly. Her cheeks are still so rosy, her lips puffier, and I can't resist pressing my mouth to her once again.

"You're the most beautiful woman I've ever seen."

She blushes harder, which I didn't realize was possible, and I help her down to her feet.

"Breakfast on the deck sounds really nice," she says as she reaches for my T-shirt. "I'm wearing this today, by the way."

"It's way too big for you."

"But it smells like you." She shrugs. "So, I want it."

"Then it's yours."

Before she can walk away, she turns back to me with a frown. "What are we doing today, anyway? We can't just hole up in here and have ... sex."

I cross my arms over my chest and grin at her. God, she's fucking adorable. "Why not?"

She swallows hard.

Okay, sex all day is off the table. Literally and metaphorically.

I do know something that she'd probably love to do. When Millie found out that the Lexington girls had never ridden horses—thanks to that cruel bastard of a father—she was determined to make sure they not only learned to ride, but would love it as much as she did.

So, I think I know what would make my girl happy today. I can give her more orgasms later to put the icing on the proverbial cake.

"I was thinking we could go out to the ranch and ride some horses, if you're up for it."

Her whole face lights up at that. "Oh, I'd love that. Millie's been teaching me, and it's been a couple of weeks since our last ride. I don't want to get rusty."

I reach out and push a strand of her hair behind her ear. "Then we'll go ride. But first, breakfast."

"And a shower."

She turns, stark naked, and I enjoy the view of her ass, the dimples in her low back, and the bruises from my fingers as she walks away.

"I'm impressed."

Dani's just finished buckling the saddle to the horse that I chose for her. Crackers is a sweet girl, easygoing, and I know that she'll love Dani. "I'd never know that you just recently learned how to do this."

My girl grins with pride and runs her hand over the horse's flank, then she gives her a hard pat. "I love it," she confesses. "It's one more reason for me to hate my dad. It still aches, you know? His wickedness. How could I have grown up on a ranch and never learned to ride a horse? Why did he hate us that much?"

Oh, kitten. Fuck, I hate him. I want to tuck her into my side and protect her from the pain in her eyes, but I'm going to keep it positive today.

"He was cold-blooded. But despite his attempts to crush you, you're learning now, and you have a whole lifetime ahead of you to enjoy horses. And that's something he can't take away from you."

She nods and grins, and she doesn't look particularly sad or angry. "You're right. Did you know that Millie and

Holden are going to build a new barn to house rescued horses?"

"Yeah, they told me about that. I think it's pretty cool."

"So do I. I plan to volunteer as much as I can, and I think it would be fun to do a field trip out there once a year with my class."

I wrap my arms around her from behind and kiss the top of her head. She smells like my shampoo, and I like it.

She is good to her word and is wearing my T-shirt, but she's tied it into a knot around her waist so it doesn't look like she's wearing a dress, and she looks adorable in it. She paired it with a pair of jeans that she fetched from her house, along with some boots, and I'd like to fuck her here in this barn.

But I promised her a different kind of ride.

"Need a boost up?" I ask her.

"Nah, I've got it."

I reluctantly let her go and watch as she expertly lifts up into the saddle, settles her feet in the stirrups, and holds on to the reins, smiling down at me as she pats Crackers's neck.

She looks sexy as fuck on a horse.

I boost up onto my own horse, Copper, and then we stride out of the barn.

"You know, aside from the farmhouse and this horse barn, the ranch doesn't look much like it did when I was a kid," Dani says. "And we spent a lot of time out here."

"Beckett's been changing a lot since he took over for Mom and Dad," I agree as we ride, side by side, over to a new path that's been forged this year. "This is a horse trail, but it's also going to be a cross-country ski path in the winter."

"Do you guys do that often?"

"Not really. But Beckett just had eight tiny cabins built back this way, on the other side of this grove of trees, for guest cabins."

"He's making the Double B into a guest ranch?" she asks, surprised.

"He is, yeah. He's keeping the dairy farm, of course. That's the bread and butter of this ranch, and it always will be. But with so many more tourists coming to town every year, he thought it would be worthwhile to add the guest ranch side, and he's already booked up through next summer. He hasn't even officially opened yet."

"That's incredible." She tips her face back and takes a deep breath. "Fall is here. I mean, it's still warm enough, but can you feel the cold on the back side of it? Does that even make sense?"

"Yep, I feel it. The trees will be turning in the next week or two."

"It's my favorite time," she says. "I love all the colors and the more comfortable temps. Also, the bugs die and go back to hell where they belong."

With a laugh, I grin over at her. "All good things, for sure. Can I ask you a question, kitten?"

"Of course." She grins over at me. "Go ahead."

"Since the day that you and your sisters met up with Holden at your ranch and took out what you wanted from the farmhouse, have you been back out there?"

She frowns, staring over the top of the horse's head, and I worry that I've just ruined our day.

"No," she says at last. "There's nothing out there for me except for bad memories, Bridge. The best thing my brother ever did was have you burn it all down. It's like it cleansed the land or something, you know?"

I nod, waiting for her to continue.

"I know that Holden would give me a piece of that property if I wanted to build a house out there or something, but I honestly don't want it. I don't care if I never go back out there, except to the horse rescue when it's finished. I go out to Ryan Wild's ranch for riding lessons with Millie. And we've been out to the Wild ranch for dinners and stuff, which is *so* ironic because my dad would rain down hellfire if he knew that was happening."

I nod, listening, so proud that she's able to talk about this without it upsetting her.

"So, no. I don't have a need to go out there. My sisters and I grabbed the few things of our mom's that we wanted to save, and Charlie has all of that in her garage for some time in the future when we want to go through it. The rest is over."

"I'm so glad he's dead." I swallow hard with that admission, and Dani turns her gaze to me. "I didn't know until this year that he killed your mom. I knew he was an abusive fuck, and I hated that you always had to go back."

"He and the sheriff were best friends when I was

young," she reminds me. "He got away with anything and everything."

"I know. It was just so fucked up that he never paid for what he did." And that fact makes me so goddamn angry. How they're not all screwed up is a testimony to Holden's determination to love them so much. I notice where we are and then say, "The cabins are just around this bend."

A row of eight A-frame cabins come into view, and when we circle around to the front of them, we see that this whole side is nothing but windows, letting in the view of the beautiful mountains ahead.

"Oh, Bridger, these are amazing."

"Come on, I'll show you one."

I hop off Copper and then help her off Crackers, and we secure their reins before I take her hand and lead her to the first cabin. I know that the door isn't locked.

"This is the biggest one and can sleep up to six. The others sleep either two or four."

She nods, and I open the door, and we step inside. They aren't furnished yet, but they're already impressive.

The kitchen and living room are open to each other. There's a loft above, which sleeps four, and there's a tiny bedroom that sleeps another two. There's one bathroom for the whole cabin.

"It's so much bigger inside than it looks from out there," she murmurs, walking around. "And these *windows*. Bridger, someone's going to come in here and never want to leave."

I chuckle and shove my hands into my pockets, nodding.

"I know. I told Beck he'll have people offering him a million dollars to buy one."

"You may joke, but I think you're right."

"It's not really a joke." I stay back and let her wander through, then up the stairs. She leans over the railing, smiling down at me.

"Hey." She waves.

"Hey yourself, beautiful girl."

She laughs and then comes back down the stairs. "Beckett is going to kill it with these. Is he going to offer hunting guides and stuff, too?"

"Yeah, that's the long-term plan." I can't help it. I pull Dani against me, wrap my arms around her shoulders, and plant my lips in her hair, hugging her to me. I need to touch this woman constantly. She's like a drug, and I'm completely addicted to her.

"You're so fucking amazing, sweetheart."

"Gosh, Bridger, you give the *best* hugs. I know others have told you that, but it's so true."

I like to hug. And not any of that half-assed pat-you-on-the-back bullshit, either. If I care enough about someone to hug them, I want to *hug* them.

And I love the way Dani melts into me, her head pressed to my chest in exactly the right spot, her arms wrapped around my torso.

She fits me.

"How are you feeling?" I ask her softly. "Ready to keep going?"

"Yes. I want to see the cows. I've always had a soft spot for them."

"What about the goats?"

She frowns up at me. "You have goats?"

"Yeah, and chickens—" She stiffens at that, and I narrow my eyes at her.

"No chickens, okay?" Her lower lip quivers, but she firms it and raises her chin. "Not today."

"No chickens. Let's go see the cows and goats. How do you feel about puppies?"

"Oh, I am fond of puppies."

"I thought you'd say that."

She's not just *fond* of puppies, I discover when we make our way over to the dairy barn, where Beckett's milking cows and keeping an eye on the little terrors that are almost ready to find homes.

She freaks out over puppies.

Dani sits on her butt, right on the ground, and giggles as all seven of the dogs climb around her, into her lap, and all around, trying to kiss her face.

Beckett and I share a smile, and then Dani climbs to her feet again and scoops one of the pups into her arms.

"Oh, you're just a baby." She kisses its nose and then buries her face in its neck. "You're so sweet. And you smell so good."

"Puppy smell," Beckett agrees. "Someone should figure out how to bottle it. They'd make a fucking fortune. By the way, are you going to say hi to *me*?"

"Hey, Beck," Dani says with a laugh and crosses to my brother, lifting onto her toes to kiss his cheek. "Why do you keep getting more handsome every time I see you?"

"Hey now. No flirting with my brother."

Dani smirks at me and then sets the puppy down so it can run back to join its siblings.

"Wanna learn how to milk a cow?" Beckett asks Dani.

"Heck yes, I wanna learn how to milk a cow. Show me."

We spend a couple of hours with Beckett and his men in the barn, and as he shows Dani how to set the cows up to the machines as well as the process of getting the milk from them, I change the water for the dogs, tidy up their pen, and then go out and water our horses.

When I return inside to gather my girl and take her home, I can hear her laughing with my brother.

This woman can do anything. She's currently helping Beck unhook the machines from a cow's teat, and she's giggling like crazy.

Birdie would love this. I can picture the two of them here, playing with the puppies and harassing Beckett, and I make a mental note to bring them both next time.

"Are you about ready to head back?" I ask Dani when she turns and smiles at me.

"Yeah, I think so. I hope I didn't ruin all this afternoon's milk supply, Beck."

"Only most of it." Beckett winks at her. "It's a good thing you're an excellent teacher because it's safe to say that you're *not* a dairy farmer."

"Well, shucks. That breaks my heart." She giggles

again and walks right to me, wraps her arms around me, and hugs me. "Let's go."

Beck winks at me over the top of her head, and I turn to guide her out to the truck.

"That was so fun," she says with a happy sigh as she settles into her seat, and I maneuver the truck onto the highway to town. "The ranch is so beautiful. Do you ever miss living out here?"

"Nah." I shake my head and reach over to rest my hand on her thigh. "I love going out to spend some time there, but my life is in town, you know?"

"Definitely. But it is fun to visit." She yawns, and we're quiet as we drive the rest of the way into town.

Suddenly, my phone rings, and I answer it on the screen.

"Bob's Pizza."

Tinkling laughter pours out of the speakers, and Dani snickers next to me.

"Dad, you're not Bob's Pizza!"

"What are you up to, peanut?"

"Aunt Bee and I got nachos, and I helped her at her new store. And we saw Millie and Holden, and I got a hot chocolate. And now we're going home so I can have a bath, and then we're going to have pedicures and facials."

"Wow, you're really going all out on the girls' weekend, aren't you?" I smile and slow down when a logging truck pulls onto the highway in front of us. "Are you having fun?"

"Of course, she is," Bee calls out. "She's with me."

"Yeah, of course, I am," Birdie echoes, and now Dani's laugh fills the cab of the truck.

"Do you have a girl with you?" Birdie asks.

"I'm with Miss Dani," I reply easily and take Dani's hand in mine, giving it a squeeze. "We went out to the ranch for a while and rode the horses."

"Did you see the puppies?" Birdie demands.

"We did," Dani replies. "They're so cute. Do you have a favorite puppy?"

"I can't decide. They're all my favorite," Birdie replies. "Okay, I have to go. Love you, Daddy."

"I love you, too, peanut. Have fun."

I end the call, and Dani sighs next to me. "She's so funny. She's like this all day in class. Not afraid to speak up and volunteer information or ask questions. I never know what she's going to say, and it cracks me up."

"I love that you get along with her."

"Who wouldn't get along with that beautiful girl?"

That makes me smile. *Takes one to know one, Miss Lexington.*

When I pull into my driveway, Dani waits for me to cross around to open her door. When she lowers to her feet, I see the wince on her pretty face.

"Hey, what's wrong?"

"Oh, nothing. I'm fine."

I cup her chin and make her look me in the face. "What's wrong, kitten?"

"It's kind of embarrassing."

"No way. Tell me."

She nibbles that lower lip. "I'm sore. My ... nether

regions ... aren't used to this much action. Between last night, this morning, and then spending all day on a horse, yeah. Ouch."

I pick her up and carry her into the house. "Come on. Let's put you into an Epsom salt bath to help relieve some of that pain. I have some ibuprofen for you, too."

"Thanks, that sounds nice, and your bathtub is insane, but I can totally just go home and—"

"No." I tighten my arms around her. "You're staying, and I'll take care of you. No arguing allowed."

"I really do love that tub."

"I know." I kiss her temple as I carry her back to my bedroom and set her gingerly on the bed. "The previous owners did the renovations on this place, and the tub was here when I bought it. You're okay with the bath these days?"

She nods and lets me tug off her shoes and socks, then wiggles her toes as I lean over to kiss the top of her foot. "Tubs are fine. Now, it's mostly just bigger bodies of water and swimming pools that I won't go near. But thank you for asking."

She's fucking incredible. The shit she's overcome, the incredible strength she has to be so amazing slays me.

"Good to know. Hang tight, I'm going to get the water going."

"I'll be right here."

Chapter Eight

DANI

As Bridger saunters away into his ridiculously amazing bathroom, I lie back on the bed and take a deep breath. I love the way his bedroom smells. It's him. A little woodsy, a little spicy. Maybe there's a hint of cinnamon? I don't even know for sure. All I know is that it's heaven, and I love it. I could just bury my nose in it and smell it forever.

Also, *how is this my life?* Because only a few weeks ago, I'd resigned myself to staying in the friend zone with Bridger and being Birdie's teacher, never the lines to blur. Yet, here I am, having experienced one of the best twenty-four hours of my life.

I hear the tap on the tub turn on and then Bridger moving about in the bathroom. In the past, taking a bath would not have been my first choice. Obviously, I have issues with water, but as I've gotten older, even I understand the virtues of soaking sore, tired muscles in hot water. I also might have been downplaying the whole *I'm sore* thing. *I'm in agony.* Everything from the waist down is screaming, so a salt bath sounds amazing. And, I admit, having a sexy Bridger take care of me is exactly what the doctor ordered.

"Did you fall asleep?" I hear from the doorway. His voice is low and rumbly and sexy, and despite the soreness in my body, it makes my core tremble.

"No." I don't move or even open my eyes. "I'm just relaxed."

"Well, come on, you can relax in the bath. The salts will help."

The mattress dips, and I crack an eye open to find Bridger, one knee planted at my hip, grinning down at me.

"You did this to me," I remind him.

"Not sorry," he agrees, and when I smile, he takes my hand, kisses it, and helps me up to standing. "I have to take your clothes off, kitten."

"Isn't this how we got here in the first place?"

His lips tip up into a smirk. A lock of his dark hair has fallen over his forehead, so I reach up to brush it back.

His eyes heat as I drag my fingertips down his cheek. "Come on, baby. I want to get you more comfortable."

I untie the knot at my waist of the T-shirt I stole from him, and he slips it over my head. He helps me out of my jeans and underwear, and then we walk into the bathroom.

I'm not just sore *there*, but my butt, my inner thighs, and even my lower back are all screaming. I won't complain because today has been one of the best days of my life. But I'm glad that I said something to him, because this pampering stuff is the best.

"Here, take this." Bridger passes me two tablets, along with a glass of water to wash them down. When I pass the glass back to him, he sets it aside and then helps me step into his tub.

"I'm pretty sure you could fit about six people in here."

He smiles softly as I sit in the water, and I sigh when the heat wraps around my lower body.

"Oh, that's nice."

"Lie back." He has a small pillow in his hands, and he rests it behind my head against the end of the tub. "Relax. I'll be right back, okay?"

"Trust me, I'm not moving. I may never leave. You'll have to have me evicted."

He turns out the light, and aside from the light coming in from the window, I notice that Bridger lit a candle, which is flickering on the vanity.

He thinks of everything.

Several minutes later, he's back with two glasses of wine, and he sets them on a table at the end of the free-standing tub, then he begins to strip.

I bite my lip, watching with anticipation. He whips his shirt off, and there's that broad chest and those sculpted abs and the inked arms I can't get enough of.

And then his pants are undone, and he pushes them down and off, along with his boxer briefs.

"Lean forward, sweetheart," he says, taking the pillow away.

I do as he asks, and he slips into the tub and sits behind me, his legs on either side of my hips, and loops his arms around me, pulling me back to lie on his chest.

"Okay, if I thought that was good, this is *far* better."

I feel him nuzzle the top of my head, and then he reaches over to grab our wineglasses, passing me one.

"Thanks."

Leisurely, we sip our wine and soak. Bridger's knee comes up out of the water, and I run my fingertips over it, enjoying the way the water sluices through the light spattering of dark hair on his skin.

"Can I ask questions about your job?" I ask him softly.

"You can ask me questions about literally anything."

"If you don't want to answer, just say so."

He sighs and kisses my head again. "Okay, but I won't. Shoot."

"What was the scariest call you've been on?"

He doesn't answer for a minute, so I tip my head back and look up at him.

"I'm thinking. Do you mean scariest in what was happening at the scene, or scariest in what could have happened to *me*?"

I swallow hard and turn back around, leaning against him. I might not want to know.

"Either."

"We got a call for a cat in a tree," he begins. "And it was pretty high up there. Stupid cat. We got the ladder up, and I climbed it, and I almost fell."

I gasp. "What?"

"Boot slipped, I reached wrong, and I thought for sure I was going to fall and break my neck. Scared the hell out of me. The fires don't scare me because we've been trained extensively on how to handle them. We have gear and tools, and we're never careless. Don't ever think that if I walk into a fire I might not walk out."

I have to swallow hard around the lump suddenly in my throat. "Okay."

"It's all the other shit. Car accidents can get sticky because drivers don't slow down to get around us. I had a buddy in Idaho get hit by a car on the scene of an accident, and now he's paralyzed and in a wheelchair."

"That's awful." I take his hand and kiss it, not caring at all that it's wet, and then link his fingers with mine, holding on tightly.

"I've seen some bad shit. I won't lie. We're a small town, so we're ambulance as well as fire, and sometimes we walk into things that are just tragic. Some death, a lot of illness. But there's good stuff, too. Like saving more lives than you don't and helping people."

"I know this is the understatement of the year, but it's not an easy job," I add.

"No, but I really love it."

I tip my head back again, and now he's grinning at me with satisfaction, and I can see the truth in his eyes.

"I know, and I'm glad. Life's so much easier when

you love what you do. I had jobs to get me through college that I was *not* a good fit for."

"Like what?" He kisses my cheek, and his free hand roams under the water to my hip, causing my body to come alive again.

"I was a waitress. A horrible waitress. Back then, I wouldn't say boo to someone, so when customers got mad about stuff, I couldn't stick up for myself, even if it was just to tell them to hang on a minute or to lower their voice. So, yeah, that was not for me. Then I tried working in a call center."

"A call center?"

"Yeah, you know, like phone sex." I press my lips together, and suddenly my shoulders are in his grasp, and he's turning me to look in my face. "Kidding. I couldn't even hardly say c— that word earlier."

"Which word, kitten?"

I roll my eyes and continue my story.

"Anyway, it was just a call center for an electric company. You know, in case there's a power outage or someone's having issues or something?"

"Sure."

"Man, if you thought people in restaurants are grouchy, you've never had to take phone calls where they can't see your face."

"Basically, people are rude," he reminds me, his hand still roaming over me.

"Yeah, they are. I've gotten better at dealing with them. My therapist helps. I love working with kids because most of them aren't rude yet. Now, some of the

129

parents are a different story, but I just keep communication lines open and try not to take too much personally."

"Good. How are you feeling?"

"Better." I scoot forward and then turn over, facing him, and straddle his lap. He's already hard, and I nestle him in my cleft, making his eyes narrow as his hands find my hips and his fingertips dig in, as if he just can't help himself. "A lot better, actually."

"We're not doing this right now, sweetheart."

I raise an eyebrow. "Why not? Feels like we are."

"Because you're hurting."

"I promise, I'm feeling a *lot* better." I rock, and he slips through me, and it feels like heaven. "We can take it easy, right?"

"Whenever I'm near you like this, I don't think about taking it easy." His breathing has sped up, and he licks his lips. "All I can think about is fucking you into next week."

"And that's lovely." His lips twitch at that, and I wrap my arms around his neck as I raise up high enough that I can take him inside of me, and we both groan as I lower onto him. "But this is good, too."

"You set the pace," he says against my lips. "Go easy. I don't want you hurting more, and I mean it."

I brush my nose over his and sigh as I move, rocking a little harder, making the water slosh.

"Feels really good," I say softly, loving the intimacy of the steam around us, his face just inches from mine, being held in his arms while I rock against him.

"What does, baby?"

"You."

He raises an eyebrow, and I know he wants the dirty words. I've always shied away from swearing, but when I'm with him, like this, and I know how much it turns him on, I find myself wanting to say something filthy out loud.

"Use your words."

"Your dick," I whisper against his lips, "feels amazing in my ... pussy."

That last word is hardly audible at all, and I feel so naughty for saying it out loud, but his hands are on me, and his face is full of longing and lust, and I love that my few words can turn him on so much.

"You're fucking incredible," he says as I begin to squeeze him harder. "Ah, fuck, baby. I won't last."

I'm holding on to the back of his neck and head, and although I'm not rocking any harder or faster, my muscles clench, and I'm going to go over with him.

"Bridge." His name is a prayer on my lips, and then I'm falling over the cliff into bliss. He calls out, both hands holding my bottom, as he succumbs to his own climax, and then I rest against him as we catch our breath. "At least we're already in the bath this time."

He chuckles, and I feel it vibrate in my cheek.

"I love that you've gotten sassy."

Four days later, I wonder if it was all a dream.

"Why do you look like you're pouting?" Alex, my twin sister, asks as she scoops a heaping pile of garden salad onto her plate, then does the same to mine.

"I'm not pouting."

Alex pours the dressing on, then licks her finger, sizing me up. "You are. What's wrong? Come on, let's eat these delicious salads and talk it out. Tell sissy everything."

We carry our dinners and drinks into her living room. I sit on the floor with my back against the couch so I can use the coffee table, and she sits in a chair.

"I'm honestly not pouting," I reply and shove salad into my mouth.

"I know you," she reminds me. "I'm your big sister."

"By two minutes."

"Exactly. Does this have anything to do with the fact that I heard that you went out with Bridger Blackwell?"

"Where did you hear that?"

I didn't just go out with him. I spent two glorious days with him, and I did not want to go home on Sunday. Even Pickles didn't want to go home.

The traitor.

"Several people said they saw you with him at Old Town Pizza. You looked cozy, according to my sources."

"Who, exactly, are your sources?"

"I'll never tell." She laughs and pops a crouton into her mouth. "Is it true?"

"Yeah." The salad is good. Alex is an excellent cook. My sister is good at a lot of things. "We actually spent the weekend together. Birdie was with Billie."

Alex's eyes, so much like my own, although we aren't identical twins, widen, and she sets her fork down with a clatter.

"Dani. Lexington. You banged *Bridger Blackwell* and haven't told me? It's *Wednesday,* for fuck's sake."

"I know," I admit and bite my lip. "I haven't seen him since I went home on Sunday when Birdie came home."

"So?" She takes another bite. "It's only Wednesday. He's busy. You're busy."

"I know that," I echo with a shrug. "He does send me good morning texts every day, and that's nice."

"Aw, that's nice. We've known Bridger forever, Dani. He knows all about ... before. You don't have to try to explain anything or worry about issues or anything like that with him."

"That part is nice. Plus, wow."

"Yeah?" She waggles her eyebrows. "How *wow*? Are we talking *well, that was nice,* or are we talking *holy shit, I feel like I've been torn in half*?"

"I had to soak in a hot bath after the first night. Of course, he joined me."

Her jaw drops, and she stares at me for a heartbeat. "You lucky bitch."

"And I know that I'm being needy now, but I went from spending every minute of the day with him for more than forty-eight hours, to just getting a text in the morning, and now I'm feeling insecure."

Alex chews thoughtfully. "I can see that. You get attached, and then real life sets in. It's a pisser."

"I don't have to swear." My voice is as dry as a salt lick. "Because you do enough of it for both of us."

"You're welcome." Alex winks at me, making me chuckle. I missed this when I was away. At college, then living in Bozeman. Missing a sibling is one thing, but missing the person who knows you inside out, who can finish your sentences and thoughts, that's different. "Give him a little time. I've heard that they've been extra busy this week. Two more homes were set on fire, and they think it's an arsonist."

My sister's a reporter for the Bitterroot Valley News, so she keeps her finger on pretty much everything going on in this town.

"You're kidding."

"I wish I was. As the chief, Bridger's probably ready to pull his own hair out."

I blow out a breath, not proud of myself for being relieved that there's an arsonist at large, and the lack of attention from Bridger isn't because he got me out of his system.

Not that the kiss he gave me after walking me home that afternoon gave the impression that he was done.

He almost sucked my face off. In a really nice way, not in a gross way.

"Well, I hope they catch the guy fast. That's actually really scary."

"It is." Alex is somber as she nods. "So far, it's been two residences and a garage."

"Random?" I ask her with a frown.

"As far as they an tell," she confirms. "So, you stay safe, sister."

"You, too. Yike."

"How's schoo going?"

I push my empty plate away and sigh. "It's good, but man, it's exhausting. I know that I'll get used to it and fall into a routine, but it's a lot of work in the beginning. I have back-to-school night tomorrow night."

"How many hours are you putting in right now?" She gives me a knowing look, and I stick my tongue out at her.

"About twelve a day," I admit. "But I'm a new teacher at is school, and I want to make sure that the administration's happy with me. I want my *kids* to be happy."

"That's my sister, always the pleaser." Alex shakes her head, but she's smiling at me with a lot of love in her blue eyes. "I promise you, everyone is going to be more than happy, Dani. You give your heart and soul to your classroom every year. I thought there was going to be a riot in Bozeman when you quit to come here because so many parents wanted to request you for their kids. It'll be that way here, too."

'I hope so. I'm trying to make a good impression on everyone, so yeah, I'm putting in extra time, but I have to make sure that everything's perfect."

"You're so type A," she says with a sigh. "You need to learn to relax a little, my friend."

I think of last weekend and all the relaxing I did. That was fun.

"I can almost hear your thought" Alex says with a laugh. "You pervert."

With a satisfied grin, I shrug a shoulder. "Do you want me to relax or not?"

"Hey, whatever works, babe."

Every morning since my weekend with Bridger, I've woken up to a text from him that simply says, *Good morning, sweetheart.*

I never knew that three words could make my heart erupt in my chest, but they do. Every time.

It's Thursday, and when I check my phone, there's no text waiting for me.

My heart sinks, and I open my messages, bringing up Bridger's thread, just in case my phone glitched or something, but no. No text today. But then I think about his words and take a deep breath.

"The fires don't scare me because we've been trained extensively on how to handle them. We have gear and tools, and we're never careless. Don't ever think that if I walk into a fire I might not walk out."

"He's just sleeping or something," I assure myself as I get out of bed and pad into the bathroom. I know that we're both busy with our lives, but dang it, I miss him.

I miss him a lot.

By the time I leave for work, there's still no message

from him. However, his truck is in his driveway, so hopefully that means that he's safe.

I can't think about the alternative.

Besides, this is a small town. If something had happened, I would have heard about it by now. He's just busy.

And so am I.

Give the man a break, Dani.

Chapter Nine

BRIDGER

"**B**irdie, you're going to be late. Let's go, peanut. School starts in twenty minutes."

It's the first morning I've been home to take my daughter to school all week. Between my sister, Millie, and Merilee, they've handled the drop-off and pickup all week, and I feel guilty as hell about it. I know that I shouldn't. It's not my fucking fault that some asshole has decided to torch my town. We're all on edge and working more than our share of hours.

I finally dragged my ass home at two this morning so I could shower and sleep and be here to take my daughter to school myself.

But she's whiny this morning, and I get it. She's like this when she hasn't spent enough time with me.

"Daddy, I need help."

"Okay." I walk down the hallway and find that she hasn't even gotten dressed yet. "*Birdie Mae.*"

My daughter frowns and crosses her arms. "What?"

"You're not dressed. We have to go. Now."

"You didn't tell me what to wear."

I pinch the bridge of my nose. "I set your clothes out on your bed." I point to them. "Right there."

"I didn't know."

"I'm not arguing with you right now. We don't have time for this. Come on." I tug her to me and help her strip out of her pajamas, then I quickly pull the fresh clothes on.

"I hate this shirt."

"No, you don't. You told me last week that it's your favorite." I sigh, not wanting to lose my temper with my daughter. "What's up with you today, peanut?"

"I'm hungry."

"You ate two poached eggs on toast. Try again."

She doesn't answer me, just glowers as I try to get her into her shoes.

"Honey, I love you." I pull her into my arms and hug her tight, but she doesn't relax against me. "I love you *a lot*. You know that, right?"

She nods, but she doesn't say anything.

"Are you sad because I haven't been home much this week?"

There's a pause, and then she nods again.

"I know. It makes me sad, too. I miss you. But my job has gotten complicated, and I have to pay extra attention to what's going on there. Have you been okay with Bee and Merilee and Millie?"

"Yeah." Her voice is so small, and it makes my heart hurt.

"Listen, I have to go to your back-to-school night tonight, and it's just supposed to be for parents, but how about if I bring you with me, and then we'll get dinner at the diner together?"

She raises her head from my chest and watches me somberly.

"Can I have a milkshake?"

"You can have anything you want, even a milkshake. We'll have a date night. How does that sound?"

"Okay. But what if your work calls you?"

"I'm taking the night off for my best girl." I kiss her cheek. "Now, come on. We really do have to go."

She springs into action with newfound energy, and less than five minutes later, we're driving to the school. I should get her there just in time.

This is when being a single father sucks the most. Yes, my daughter has a whole family who loves on her and loves on her well. But she's my baby girl. Mine to protect. Mine to love. And moments like these are the hardest because I can't be in two places at once.

I've missed the hell out of her this week.

And then there's Dani. I haven't seen Dani since I walked her home on Sunday afternoon. God, I've missed her. I've barely had time to shoot her a text in the mornings, and I know that I owe her a hell of a lot more than that.

I didn't send one today because I know that I'll get to see her in person, as long as she's still outside greeting kids.

Pulling into the parking lot, I see that I'm in luck. I

help Birdie out of the truck, and she runs inside, waving at me over her shoulder as I approach Dani.

"Good morning," I say to her with a smile. God, she's a sight for sore eyes. She's in a brown dress that's cinched at her waist, with brown boots, and I want to pull her to me and kiss her long and hard.

Instead, I have to settle for shoving my hands into my pockets and smiling at her.

And she returns the grin, but I don't like the guarded look in those baby blues.

"Good morning," she replies. "I started to get worried when I didn't get a text this morning."

She bites her lip and frowns at the ground, as if she didn't mean to say that, and I decide to fuck the rules and reach over to tuck her hair behind her ear.

"I knew I'd see you in person, and that's much better. You okay, kitten?"

She smiles up at me now and nods. "Yeah, I'm okay. How are you? I hear things are rough right now."

"Things are a shit show," I confirm, not bothering to censor myself since most of the kids seem to be inside. "I'm sorry I haven't been able to call or see you. But I'll see you tonight at the back-to-school thing."

"Right, yeah. I'll be here." The bell rings, and she glances back at the school. "I better get in there."

I fucking hate that I agreed to the no-touching rule at her job because I think we both could use the reassurance of a hug or a kiss, but instead, I just nod. I feel fucking useless.

"Have a good day."

141

"You, too." She smiles, and then she hurries off, and I'm back to feeling frustrated.

I'm not doing a good job with either of my girls this week, and that pisses me the fuck off.

I should go home and sleep for a solid six hours, but I find myself pulling into a parking space in front of Bitterroot Valley Coffee Co. and my sister's bookstore and cut the engine. The sign in Billie's new store says that she'll open on Saturday, and I'm so damn proud of her. I hope I'll be able to come in that day. I plan to, but if the bastard with a fire kink decides to set something ablaze, I'll be at work.

Walking into the coffee shop, I'm surprised to see that it's quiet inside. I guess now that we're past Labor Day, the tourists are thinning out and we're headed straight for the shoulder season.

I admit, I love the shoulder season.

"Hey," Millie says with a big smile as I approach the counter. "Your usual?"

"Yeah, but make it decaf." She raises an eyebrow. "I'm going to try to go home and sleep."

She nods and gets to work. "Rough week. Any leads?"

"I can't talk about it," I remind her and rub my fingertips into my eyes. No, there aren't any fucking leads.

And that also pisses me off.

"But I feel like I've been isolated from everyone for a few days, and I wanted to stop in to see how you are."

"I'm great," she replies with a grin. "Holden and I are

finishing up the rescue barn, and we're getting our first horses next week."

"That's incredible. It's such a great way to use that land."

"I'm so excited." She passes me the cup and does a little dance. "I know it will be a lot of work, and the poor horses need so much love, but I think it's going to be great. Anyway, did you hear that we're getting a Sidney Sterling concert at the end of the month?"

"Who is?" I ask at the mention of my favorite country artist.

"*We* are. Bitterroot Valley."

I blink at her and then look down at the coffee. "Are you on something, Mill?"

"Ha ha. You're funny. No, the little Campbell girl, one of the kids of the family that lost their home last week?"

"I know them."

"Well, she goes to school with my niece, Holly. And Erin is related to Sidney by marriage."

I'm too tired for this. I need a map or a graph.

"Okay. I think." Erin is married to Millie's oldest brother, Remington. She's originally from Seattle, and her family is huge. And most of them are celebrities.

"Well, Erin mentioned to Sidney that the family lost everything in the fire. I have no idea how the subject came up, but Sid loves it here, and she's been wanting an excuse to visit, so she offered to do a concert to help raise funds for the family. Now, I'll bet it'll be for all the families that have recently lost their homes."

I blink at my best friend. "So, Sidney Sterling, country music megastar, the woman who sold out her last world tour, is going to put on a concert *here*? Where would this happen? We don't have a venue for that. The fire codes would be a nightmare."

"Here you go, making everything not fun. Again."

I narrow my eyes at her, and she sighs.

"The Wild River Ranch has volunteered the space. They'll set up a stage and stuff, and it'll be field seating."

"No." I shake my head, the absolute nightmare of that making my head want to explode.

"Yes. The permits have been secured," she says softly. "But there will be a cap on tickets at ten thousand."

"You think it's safe to pack *ten thousand people* out at the ranch, at once?" I shake my head, wishing I hadn't come in here today. "What if something goes wrong, Millie? We have *two* ambulances. Only two."

"Listen, I don't know anything about the specifics. Talk to Chase."

"Oh, I'll be calling your brother and his boss." I pay for the coffee, but before I can leave, Millie stops me.

"How are things with Dani?"

"I had the best weekend of my life with her." Millie's face lights up. "And I haven't seen her since."

She loses the smile.

"Yeah. I guess I did see her this morning, and I can tell that my being MIA has given her doubts, and I don't have time to reassure her."

"Bullshit. Yes, you do. A text message or a quick call is all she needs, Bridge."

"I've sent texts, but damn it, she deserves more than that."

"It's one week," she reminds me. "It's not like you ghosted her for a month. And she knows you're slammed. We all know."

I nod and sip more coffee.

"I'm going to see her tonight at the school thing."

"Take her flowers," Millie advises me. "Trust me on that."

"Good idea." I can do that. It's not enough, but once again, it's all I can do to hopefully soothe the rough edges that this week has caused for us. I nod and turn to go. "Have a good day, Mill."

"You, too, Bridge."

Dani's presentation for her students' parents starts in about fifteen minutes, and I was hoping to get there early enough to give her these flowers on the down-low.

Thanks to Birdie being motivated by ice cream and french fries after this, we're not late.

Dani's standing by her desk in her empty classroom when we arrive, and when she sees us, she smiles.

This time, it's a genuine smile, and it soothes my raw edges just a bit. It would be better if I could get my hands on her the way I want to, but I'll settle for that stunning grin of hers.

"Hey there," she says.

"Hi. I know it's not a kiddo night, but Birdie and I have a date after this."

Dani waves that off and shakes her head. "Don't you even worry about it. Birdie's always welcome here. Did your day get better, sweetie?"

I frown down at my daughter and then back at Dani. "What happened?"

Birdie sighs and leans into my side.

"Just an off day for this one," Dani replies and pats Birdie on the shoulder. "Nothing to worry about. I hope you're going somewhere fun for your date."

"The diner," Birdie says with a smile, and Dani nods.

"That *will* be fun."

God, she's gorgeous. She hasn't changed since this morning, and her hair is a little messier, and she looks tired, but she's so damn beautiful, it's a hit to the chest.

"If you'd like to join us, you're welcome to."

"Thank you for the invitation," Dani says, eyeing Birdie. "But I suspect that Birdie needs some alone time with her dad."

Birdie doesn't argue, and that tells me that Dani's right.

"These are for you." I pass her the bouquet of sunflowers that Summer, the owner of Paula's Poseys, recommended, and Dani smiles.

"Thank you. You didn't have to bring me anything."

"Yeah." Since no one is here, I reach out and take her hand, linking my fingers with hers. "I really did."

More parents start to filter in, and she pulls her hand

out of mine, and Birdie and I take a couple of seats in the back.

For roughly twenty minutes or so, Dani explains who she is, what her plans are for the school year, and what her curriculum consists of. Her eyes land on mine, and she gives me a half smile before continuing on.

I want her. More than I've ever wanted anyone.

"I'll be staying after for a while, in case any of you have questions or concerns. I'm really looking forward to working with your kids. It's going to be a fun year."

About half of the room leaves, but just as many parents stay to talk with the teacher, so I decide not to hang around any longer, especially since Birdie is clearly ready to go. I don't even catch Dani's eye as we leave.

I need time with her soon.

Birdie bounces in her seat in the back of the truck as we make our way to Kay's Diner. This place opened up not too long ago, and it's outfitted to look like a vintage diner from the 1950s. I have to admit, the burgers here rival the local pub, The Wolf Den, and that's saying a lot.

Once inside, Birdie and I are shown to a booth by the windows. The table is white, and the benches are bright red. The diner is what you'd expect in a place like this with black-and-white tiled floors, a jukebox in the corner, and old-school rock and roll memorabilia all over the walls. There's a long counter with glossy red-topped stools, as well.

"Hey there," Shirley, a waitress that I know, says with a wink. "How are you two this evening?"

"We're doing well. Thanks, Shirley," I reply and smile down at Birdie, who's sitting in the booth next to me. "We're hungry, right?"

"Yes," my daughter agrees. "Starving."

"Well, then you came to the right place. Do you need a minute with the menu?"

I shake my head and order for the both of us. Birdie loves the burger and fries on the kids' menu, and I get the adult version of the same meal, along with a chocolate milkshake for us to share because they come in a giant metal container that is big enough for four people to drink out of.

Birdie is happy to color on her kids menu as we wait for our food, so I shoot Dani a text message.

> Me: You were absolutely gorgeous today, and the hot teacher thing is doing it for me. Don't forget to eat something tonight. Would you like me to bring you something from the diner?

I bite my lip as I see the little dots hopping, signaling that she's replying.

> Dani: You're such a flirt. Thanks for the offer, but I'll heat up some soup. Have fun with your kiddo. I think she needs some extra attention today. xo

Me: I'll call you later.

I sigh and set my phone aside, then turn to my daughter.

"Did you have a rough time at school today, baby girl?"

She doesn't look up from her art project and shrugs a shoulder. "I was just grouchy."

"Even though we said we'd go out for dinner?"

She just shrugs again, and I tip her chin up so she can look at me.

"You know that I have to work a lot and that I have an important job."

"Yeah. I know."

"You can't take it out on everyone else, Birdie. That's not fair." I kiss her forehead and then tap her coloring page.

I glance up and notice that Chase Wild, one of Millie's brothers, just walked into the restaurant. He asks Shirley something, nods, and when he sees me, he walks my way and sits across from me.

"I'm waiting on an order to take home," he says with a grin. "Hey, Miss Birdie."

"Hi," she says with a smile. "I'm on a date with my daddy."

"I see that," Chase replies. "Pretty fun."

"I plan to call your boss tomorrow," I inform my friend, who frowns over at me. "A Sidney Sterling concert at your ranch, man? Seriously?"

Chase lets out a gusty breath and shakes his head

149

before dragging his hand down his face, and I can tell that he doesn't disagree with me.

"I know. I don't like it either."

"Then why is it happening? We don't have the manpower for that, and you know it."

"We'll pull in departments from neighboring towns, and the Montgomery family—*Erin's* family—plans to hire a whole bunch of security, medical staff, you name it. I figure with so many big names in that family, they have people to make sure everyone stays safe."

"I want meetings," I reply, shaking my head. "I want a plan. That's too many people in one place without having a plan."

"Hey, I'm on your side. We'll make it happen. I'll make some calls and be in touch."

Chase's name is called, and Shirley's holding his bag of food.

"Have a fun date, you two," Chase says, winking at Birdie.

When he's out of earshot, Birdie turns to me. "Sidney? Do I get to meet her?"

I laugh and kiss her head as our food is delivered.

"Probably not, but we might get to listen to her sing."

The look on her face is so stunned, so full of absolute *joy*, it makes me laugh again.

"Dad! She's our *favorite!*"

"I know, baby." And I hope that we can make it work. Because it would be an awesome thing for the community.

But damn, it makes me nervous.

Chapter Ten

DANI

Saturday mornings are my favorite. I take time to linger over my coffee before I clean my house and tidy things up, and then I go outside to mow my grass and pull some weeds. I even let Pickles outside on a leash. She loves to nap in the sunshine, all curled up and adorable on the rug on my porch. I was so nervous to keep her, but now I can't imagine my life without the sweet feline.

I've just finished mowing the strip of grass by my driveway when I see Bridger's truck turn onto our street, and he parks in his driveway. When he steps out of the truck, he glances my way, does a double take, and then marches straight for me.

This man is just ... *delicious.*

He's in jeans that mold around his thighs perfectly and a blue T-shirt with sleeves tight over his biceps and chest, making me sigh and my lady bits quiver with happiness. His jaw is set as he walks—no, *strides*, my way, as if he's a man on a mission.

And I do believe that I'm that mission.

Yay me!

"Good morning," I say.

"Come here." He takes my hand in his and doesn't stop walking. He just pulls me with him, straight into my garage, and when we're far enough in so that no one driving past could see us, he frames my face in his hands and kisses me like a man starving for his next breath.

I hear the door closing, and the only light coming in is from the narrow windows along the top of the wide door. He must have pushed the garage door opener. And the next thing I know, Bridger has me pushed against my SUV, one of his legs pressed between my own, rubbing on my already hot cleft, and I can't help the moan that escapes my lips as he sinks into me. Just this, and my body is *alive*. Burning for this man that's so big, so strong, so sexy. He smells so divine that I'm immediately lost to him, and I can't get close enough.

With one hand fisted in my hair, he tugs my head back farther, and those amazing lips slip down to my chin, making me shiver.

"God, I've fucking missed you," he growls against me. His muscles are taut, straining against his shirt, and I could just bite him. "Everything about you. You're all I think about. And you're right here, across the street, but it's too fucking far away."

My hands fist in his shirt, and I tug it up, needing to see his skin, and Bridger leans back long enough to help me get it up and off him. Oh, this man's chest and arms. Those colorful tattoos, the muscles beneath them.

"I never get tired of this view."

"Your turn," he says, reaching for my own T-shirt. I'm wearing the one he let me borrow last week. "I fucking love it when you wear my shit. But it's even more miraculous when I get you out of it. I want to see these amazing fucking curves, kitten."

"Birdie?"

"At a party."

I grin before leaning in to press my lips to his chest, and I can feel the rumble of his moans before he kisses the top of my head. His fingers make quick work of my bra clasp, and then the material is falling down my arms and cast aside.

"In the *garage*?" I ask with a laugh, but I don't want him to stop.

"Too impatient," he replies before his mouth is on mine again. His fingers unclasp my denim shorts, and they pool around my feet. "Christ, I want you. I never stop wanting you."

"I'm right here."

His hot eyes whip up to mine, and I boldly reach out to unfasten his jeans as he toes off his shoes, and I work the denim down his hips until he can step out of them. He's only in his boxer briefs now, his hard length straining against the cotton.

"Your body is *insane*," I inform him, not shy at all about looking my fill in the dim light. "Jeez, Bridge, do you even eat?"

He smirks and drags his fingertips over my clavicle, down my chest to my belly, and steps closer.

"Six days is too fucking long to go without you." He almost sounds angry, and the old me would have apologized, but I just wait to see what he says next. "It's too goddamn long, kitten. Come here."

He steps back into me, kisses me hard, licking and nibbling my mouth, making me hum against his lips, before he turns me around and presses my front against the car. The metal is cool against my skin, but I brace myself on my arms, my butt already popped out for him.

I want him so bad.

"I'm going to fuck you from behind." His hands drag down my back to my butt, and he flexes his fists, gripping me firmly, just the way I love it. "And it has to be hard and fast this time, baby."

I whimper and push back against him again, my body on fire and needing him. Hard and fast sounds amazing right now.

"Tell me you want my cock."

"I want it."

He chuckles and plants his lips by my ear. "Use your filthy words, sweetheart."

I bite my lip, and then the crown of his cock is *right there*, and I've never wanted something so bad in my life.

"I want—" I gasp when he pushes inside, just a tiny bit, and then pulls back out again. "Bridger."

"No, that's not what I want to hear." His lips graze the back of my shoulder, and a hand brushes down my spine, sending shivers through me. "Come on, beautiful girl. Give me your words."

"I want your cock."

He slams into me, so quickly that I see stars and have to brace myself against the car.

"That's right," he growls against my shoulder. "You want *this* cock. Only mine."

"Only yours," I repeat as he pulls out and pushes back in again, harder this time, his hips hitting my butt, and I arch my back further, wanting to feel more of him. "It's so deep."

"What is, baby?"

"Your cock. It's so hard and so deep like this." I moan and rest my forehead on my arm, pushing back against him with every hard thrust. "It's so good. God, I've missed you."

"Fuck." His hands are on my hips now, holding on so tightly that there will be bruises later, and I don't care. I want to see his mark on me. I want to see the evidence of this long after it's over. "You're so damn wet, and I've hardly touched you. Jesus, baby."

"You don't have to touch me." I shake my head, loving the drag of the tip of his cock against my walls, loving the way he's breathing so hard and the feel of his fingertips on my fleshy hips. "You just look at me, and this happens."

"You're so goddamn perfect," he whispers against my shoulder and jerks harder, and then one arm wraps around me, and he presses his fingers to my clit, and my world explodes.

"Oh, fuck." *Was that* me? "Oh, fuck, I'm gonna—"

"Jesus, yes. I love it when you use your words. What? Tell me."

"I'm gonna come." My voice is high and desperate, and suddenly, it's as though Bridger loses control. His hand presses harder on my clit, his hips are moving faster, pumping in and out of me so hard, it steals my breath. I'm consumed by him.

"Let go, baby. Come all over this cock. Soak me, sweetheart."

His filthy words, combined with his big body behind me, his hands and dick all doing such magical things to my body, sends me over.

"God, you're such a good girl."

Oh, that makes me clench again.

"You like that? You're such a good fucking girl, Dani. God, you feel so fucking good, milking me like that."

I *love* his words. I think I could come just from listening to him praise me. It lights me up inside.

"Come inside of me, Bridger."

His voice is rough as he swears incoherently, his hands tighten on my hips, pulling me back even harder, and then I feel him let go, filling me.

I'm panting, pinned between him and my car, but if he lets go of me, I'll fall on my face. My knees are jelly.

Bridger doesn't pull out right away. He guides me back against him and wraps his strong arms around my shoulders, plants his face in my hair, and holds on to me so tightly, as if he never wants to let me go.

"My good girl."

My muscles contract, and I feel him smile against me. "You like that."

"Yeah." I sigh and hug his arms against my chest. "I like that."

"I wish I could stay with you today." His voice is calmer, quieter, as he brushes his lips rhythmically over my hair, back and forth, soothing us both. "But Birdie's at a birthday party, and I have to go get her in a few minutes."

I sigh again, but I nod. I know and respect that Birdie is his priority. If she wasn't, I wouldn't be as attracted to him. I love that he's a good dad to his adorable little girl.

Sure, it adds a layer of difficulty for us. Maybe it means that this isn't going to be a relationship. Maybe sex is all we can do right now, with everything that we both have going on in our lives.

And, honestly, I'd take it. Because there's nothing like this. Absolutely nothing in my life has ever made me feel as amazing as being with Bridger does, and I don't want to let go of it.

"I'm sorry," he whispers, and I can hear the sincerity in his voice, but I can't have him feeling guilty for even one moment.

"No." I let go of his arms, and he pulls out of me, giving me room to turn around so I can plant my hands on his chest as I look up into his dark eyes. "Don't apologize for Birdie, Bridge. Never. *Not ever.*"

He nods and kisses my forehead, sighing almost in relief. "Okay, then. What are your plans for today?"

It feels a little weird to be standing in my garage,

naked, well and truly sexed, talking about my day, but here we are.

"I'm going to finish my yard, and this afternoon, I'm going to check out the new bookstore. Bee wouldn't let me come before this because she wanted it to be a surprise."

He grins down at me and swipes his thumb over my lower lip. "We'll be there a little later, too. Maybe I'll get to see you."

Reluctantly, Bridger turns away to put his clothes on, and the sexy moment is over, which makes me sad. I don't know when I'll see him again, aside from catching glimpses of him coming and going, which is absolutely not good enough now that I've had so much more with him.

But I'm not about to make him feel guilty about that. When he can see me, he will. It's not like he's made me any promises. *Although, today showed me that he wants me as much as I want him.*

Once we're both dressed again, I open the garage door, letting in the breeze. Before leaving, Bridger pulls me in for one of his amazing hugs, and I press my head to his chest, enjoying his warmth and the steady beat of his heart. Then he tips my chin up so he can brush his mouth over mine in that way that makes my toes curl.

"Don't work too hard out here," he murmurs against my lips. "Take some time for yourself today."

"I will."

I want to ask him when I'll see him again, but I don't. I let him walk away, across the street and into his own house before I check on Pickles, pleased to see that she's still snoozing happily on the porch. I hurry inside to quickly clean up enough that I can comfortably finish mowing the lawn.

By the time I go back outside, Bridger's truck is gone again, and I get back to work.

The bookstore is the most beautiful store I've ever seen.

The shelves look old, made out of honey-colored wood that you just want to drag your hand across, and are filled with so many colorful novels that it fills my book-loving heart with pure joy. There are decadent, colorful, deep-stuffed chairs by the windows for someone to curl up in and read, and everything about this store screams cozy.

Welcome.

Sit a while.

Have some coffee and relax.

"Pumpkin spice latte?"

I turn and smile at Millie, who's holding a tray of small cups with lids.

"Don't mind if I do. Wow, this is so great."

"I know," Millie says with a grin. "People have been in and out all day long, going back and forth between our stores, and it's damn awesome."

"I love this so much." I sip my latte and sigh in happiness. "I will spend literally all my spare time here."

Millie eyes me playfully. "Or, you know, with Bridger."

"Did someone say my brother's name?" Bee, dressed in a gorgeous pink dress, her dark hair up in a high pony-tail and her makeup flawless as usual, wraps her arm around my shoulders and squeezes me. "What did he do now?"

I laugh and shake my head. "Nothing."

"*Nothing*?" Millie demands. "I might have to smack my bestie around because he's clearly slacking if he's done nothing to you."

"Well, he didn't do anything bad, is what I should say," I assure her, and then look around to make sure no one is eavesdropping. Thankfully, it looks like the store has hit a lull. I know that both of these women are aware that something has been brewing between Bridger and me.

And I need friendly advice.

"Honestly, I think—" I press my lips together, unsure of how to phrase it.

"Tell us," Bee says gently as she brushes her fingers through my hair. "We can help. Don't get too graphic because it's my *brother*."

"I think it's just going to be a friends-with-benefits thing." The words rush out of me in a whoosh, and then I sip my latte to mask my embarrassment. "I mean, we're both so busy, you guys. I hardly see him."

"Is there no chemistry?" Bee asks. I know that despite the fact that we're discussing her brother, she can be impartial and give me excellent advice.

She's always been good at giving advice.

"Oh, there's chemistry." I bite my lip and then decide to tell them about my garage just a few hours ago, and that has them both wrapping me in a hug. "But, isn't that the definition of ... convenience? We bang when we can, but otherwise, there's not much going on?"

Bee frowns, and Millie's head is cocked to the side, watching me with her lips pursed.

"Mm, I think you should talk to Bridger," she says at last. "Because that's not the impression that I got from him the other day."

"Why? What did he say the other day?"

Millie shakes her head. "He's my best friend, and I can't betray a confidence, but you really do need to talk to him, Dani. Hey, I gotta go. It looks like we have a line."

Millie hurries back to her coffee shop, and Bee links her arm through mine.

"She's right," she says. "I'm *your* bestie, and I'm telling you, you need to talk to him. You've come so far in sticking up for yourself, in speaking up for what you need. Don't stop that now, babe. Bridger's not really the fuck buddy type, so seriously, just have a conversation."

I nod and swallow the lump that just formed in my throat. I needed to talk to her about this because the doubts I've been dealing with have been driving me nuts.

And she's right, the only person who can tell me what he's thinking is the man himself.

"Okay, enough of that. Back to the reason I'm here. The store is amazing, Bee."

She grins. "Right? So far, the response has been so fantastic."

"I love how well-stocked the spicy book section is," I inform her, waggling my eyebrows. "I'll be buying, like, twenty books today."

"Good. I'll let you."

"Excuse me."

We turn at the sound of the voice and smile at the willowy redhead before us. She has the most remarkable green eyes, and her skin is like porcelain.

She's gorgeous. And I might be a little jealous.

"Hello," Bee says. "How can I help?"

"Well, I overheard you discussing spicy books," the stranger says, and I hear an accent in her voice. Irish? Scottish? It's so pretty. "And I also noticed that you have a wonderful selection. Have you read Samantha Young?"

I nod, but Bee shakes her head no.

"Do I need to read her?" Bee asks us, looking back and forth between us.

"I strongly recommend her," the woman says. "I'm Skyla, by the way."

"Bee. And this is my friend, Dani."

We all shake hands, and I tilt my head to the side, watching the newcomer.

"Are you visiting, Skyla?"

"Actually, I recently moved to town," she says with a hesitant smile. "I came from New York, but I'm originally from Galway, Ireland."

"Honestly," Bee says, "I'm a little in love with your accent. Welcome to town. What do you do?"

"Well, I'm about to open a dance studio." She smiles softly, and I think I'm a little in love with her, too. "I was a dancer in New York City, and I'd like to teach children."

"We know about a hundred kids who would *love* that," I assure her. "In fact, I'll bet Birdie would be all over it. My ... friend's daughter. Is five too young to start dance?"

"Not at all," she assures me. "I'd love to have her."

"Well, this is exciting," Bee says. "And now I'm thinking that we should start a spicy book club."

"Sign me up," I reply with a nod.

"Oh, me, too," Skyla agrees.

"Three members already." Bee laughs. "And let's start with a Samantha Young novel."

All in all, it was a good day. I spent a couple of hours at the bookstore, talking more with Skyla, who is just so pretty and sweet, and then other friends who drifted in and out. My sisters all came by. I left before Bridger and Birdie popped in, but I was getting hungry, so I came home.

It's late now, and although we're squarely into September, and it's not warm anymore once that sun goes down, the sky is clear tonight, with a full moon, and I want to lie out on the driveway to do my daily affirmations and meditation.

So, I bundle up in Bridger's hoodie, close the door behind me, and walk down to my spot. Once I'm lying down, I take a long, deep breath, hold it for four seconds, and then let it out slowly, all while keeping my eyes pinned to the stars above.

First, I start with the affirmations for today.

I am smart.

I am a good teacher.

I am worthy of love.

I am a good friend.

I deserve to be in a happy relationship.

I bite my lip on that one.

I can hear Bridger's door open and close softly and then, just a few seconds later, the sound of his footsteps as he makes his way across the street. He doesn't stand over me this time. I notice he's in another hoodie, similar to the one I'm wearing, and he lies down next to me, linking his fingers with mine.

He pulls in a deep breath and lets it out.

"Hi," he says, and just that one syllable has my stomach tightening.

"Hi." I smile, still looking up when his fingers squeeze around my own. "Your sister's store is amazing."

"Yeah. It is. She said you were there."

"I was there."

Our words are soft, meant only for each other, before they're carried away on the crisp early autumn air.

"Bridge?"

"Yeah, kitten?"

I smile at the endearment.

"Can I ask you a question?"

"You can ask me anything. You know that."

"Okay." I press my lips together for a long minute, not sure how I should phrase this, and it reminds me of that first night that we were out here, just a few weeks ago.

Bridger and I have always been honest with each other, so I should just say it.

"Is it a hard question?" He's not mocking me at all. I can hear the curiosity in his voice, and it softens me a bit.

"Kind of, yeah. An uncomfortable one, anyway."

He pulls his hand out of mine, and I feel him roll onto his side, resting his head in his hand so he can look down at me. His other hand glides up my thigh and under the hoodie, resting on my belly, and it feels warm and soothing.

"Look at me."

I rub my lips together, but I don't look his way, and then his fingers are on my chin, turning my head in his direction.

"Talk to me, beautiful. What do you want to ask me?"

"Are we just ... *fuck buddies?*"

Chapter Eleven

BRIDGER

Before I can even process that question, let alone answer it, Dani keeps going, the floodgates open.

"I mean, it's okay if we are. It's totally fine. I just want to make sure we're on the same page because it's been such a confusing week. God, not that that's *your* fault, I just ... we had such a good time last weekend, and then all hell broke loose, and I've hardly heard a peep from you until earlier today when you stormed over here and railed me in the garage, which was totally fun, and I'm a big fan, but I just need to know if we're only going to have sex when we have the opportunity and otherwise I won't hear much from you so I can just prepare my brain and my heart for that because my loins are *in*. As long as it's monogamous, though, because otherwise, gross."

She takes a breath, and I take that opportunity to cover her mouth with my hand, and she frowns at me.

"Stop talking for two seconds, okay?"

She nods, watching me with those expressive eyes that shine like diamonds in the moonlight, and I move my hand back down to her belly, under my hoodie, against warm, soft skin.

"It's *not* okay," I begin, "to just be fuck buddies. Jesus, I can't believe you said that."

"I got nervous."

"So, you swear when I'm inside of you or when you're nervous?"

She starts to say something and then pauses. "I guess that's right, yeah."

"Baby." I brush my thumb back and forth over her skin. "No. We're not *just* anything. This week was a shit show, and that might be the case until we catch the fucker that's decided to play with fire, literally, and there's not much I can do about that."

"I know, I just—"

"My turn, remember?" I lean in and kiss her cheek, nuzzling it with the tip of my nose. "If you need me to keep reassuring you, I will. I have no problem with that. Because eventually, you'll believe me and the doubts won't fuck with you anymore. You are all I see, Dani. Just you. I hate that I had to say goodbye to you on Sunday, and then I barely saw or spoke to you until today. It was fucking torture. Last weekend was a big deal, right?"

"I thought so," she whispers, and that earns her another kiss, this time on the lips.

"Yeah, me, too. This isn't just sex for me. Don't get me wrong, it's the best fucking sex of my life, and I plan to be inside you as much as humanly possible, but that's not all it is. Every minute with you is the best part of my day."

She smiles and reaches up to cup my face. "Aww. Same here, Chief."

"Nope." I roll closer and nip at her chin. "That's still a no-go."

"Come on, it's cute."

"No. It's my job, and you are *not* my job. Not even close."

She sighs, and her eyes are happy, the insecurities I saw earlier wiped away.

"Eventually, I'm going to come up with a nickname for you."

I move my hand up farther on her stomach, ghosting over the skin, and then narrow my eyes at her. "No bra."

"It's late, Bridger. Of course, I'm not wearing a bra. The girls need to breathe a little."

My fingers graze over one nipple, and it's satisfying as fuck when the nub puckers right up for me, making Dani sigh in that sexy way she does that makes my dick twitch.

"If you want labels on what we're doing," I tell her softly, "that's fine with me. I want the world to know that you're mine. You're *mine*, sweetheart. I'll make that perfectly clear, right here and now. You want to call me your boyfriend? Go right ahead."

"Wow, we're really clearing the air." She pushes her hand into my hair and uses her nails to lightly scratch my scalp, and it makes my eyes roll back into my head. "You like that."

"You can do that for a million years. Holy shit."

She giggles, and I pull my hand out from under the hoodie. I like having free rein to touch her, but this isn't the time to get us worked up.

I need to make sure she's okay. All the way okay. I hate that this woman has so many doubts, especially about us. That's unacceptable, and we're going to permanently squash it right now. If I'm honest with myself, I've always considered Dani to be mine. Even when I was living in a nightmare marriage to Angela, she was never far from my mind. *Except back then, I thought I'd never get to kiss her, let alone have her in my arms.* Fuck, I'm not sorry Angela bailed on us either.

"I need to veto one of your rules, by the way," I inform her and roll back a bit.

"Which rule?"

"The no touching you at your job rule."

She shakes her head and starts to talk, but I interrupt her.

"There's no rule with the school that says you can't date a parent. We're both single, consenting adults who aren't doing anything wrong. Jesus, I'm not going to make out with you in front of five hundred students, but I need to be able to cup your cheek or kiss your lips. Simple touches, Dani. I need them, just like you needed to know what's going on with us tonight."

That makes her bite that lip, and she finally nods.

"Yeah?" I rub my nose over hers. "You can live with me stealing a kiss at the drop-off line at school?"

"I can live with it," she confirms. "I want the world to know that you're mine, too, you know. You're a smoke show. See what I did there?"

I can't help it. I bust up laughing and bury my face in her neck, pulling her closer.

"We're going to have to invest in some kind of mat or foam or something for out here because this is not comfortable for long, intimate talks."

Dani chuckles and then sits up, pulling me with her. "I do have chairs on my porch. I don't know if you noticed, but I bought an extra one, just in case you wanted to come out and sit with me."

My head whips to the porch, and there it is. The second chair. And I don't know why, but that makes my heart stutter. And the tiny seat sitting next to it has me leaning in to plant my lips on her cheek.

"You bought me and my daughter our own chairs for your porch?"

"I didn't think you'd fit in my lap." She grins and stands, and I join her as we walk to the porch. "Oh, I need to return this and your T-shirt to you."

She plucks at the hoodie, and I scowl.

"The fuck you do. You're keeping that. I love seeing you in my shit. I don't want it back."

"You didn't let me finish. I need to give them back to you because I've worn them pretty much nonstop for the past week, and they don't smell like you anymore. I need them to smell like you."

Without a word, I march over to my house, quietly let myself in so I don't wake my daughter, and gather up a sweatshirt I wore yesterday, along with two of my T-shirts out of my drawer, then walk back to where Dani's still sitting on the porch and hold them out for her.

"Here. You can have them all. Keep them."

Her eyes bounce from mine to the clothes I'm holding, and then she takes them and buries her nose in them, inhaling deeply.

"Nothing smells better than you," she murmurs, and it makes my heart stutter *again*, and my cock twitch. "Hold on."

She hurries inside and returns ten seconds later with the T-shirt, and passes it to me. Then, she looks around to see if anyone's watching, turns her back to the street, and quickly strips out of my hoodie, shoves it at me, and replaces it with the zip-up I just gave her, pulling the zipper all the way to her neck.

She buries her face in the red material and sighs happily.

"That's so much better."

"You just stripped on your porch, kitten."

"I wanted to trade you." She shrugs while still sniffing my sweatshirt. "No one saw."

"You'd better hope they didn't, because if *anyone* sees what's mine, I'll fucking tear their eyes out of their head. Don't do that again."

She blinks and then walks right into my arms, holding me tightly around the middle, her head pressed to my chest. "Okay."

I kiss the top of her head and brush my fingers through her soft, dark hair. "Come out to the ranch with Birdie and me tomorrow. We're going to spend the day riding some horses and hanging with the family. Come with us."

"Oh." She shakes her head and frowns up at me. "You should spend some time with Birdie, Bridge. I know that if I didn't see much of you this week, neither did she, and—"

"Whoa." I kiss her nose and cup her jaw, my fingers in her hair. "I want you with us. I want Birdie to spend time with you outside of school, when it's the three of us together. I want you out at my family's ranch, and you'll stay for dinner, too. Sundays are usually a big deal out there, and I think even Blake is off from the hospital, so he'll be around, too. Bee's gonna come for dinner after the bookstore closes. Brooks closes down the garage on Sundays. Come be with my family, sweetheart."

I tip her chin up and brush my lips over hers, and her hands fist in my shirt.

"Okay," she whispers against my lips. "What time should I be ready?"

"Come over for breakfast at nine. Hell, come over whenever you want and come cuddle with me in bed."

I waggle my eyebrows at her, and she chuckles.

"Don't look now, but you're sounding a little needy."

"A *little*? I need to up my game. Because when it comes to you, I'm a lot needy."

"Aww, that's cute. I'll see you in the morning."

"For cuddles or for breakfast?"

"Probably both, who am I kidding?"

She came for both, arriving right around eight. I wanted to pull her into my bedroom so we could snuggle in my bed, but I didn't want Birdie to walk in on that and have questions.

I need to talk to Birdie about Dani being around more often.

Instead, we cuddled up on the couch, me lying on my back and Dani curled up on top of me, with a blanket over the both of us.

I could have stayed there all day, but eventually, I heard Birdie stir, so we got up to make breakfast before we got ready to head out to the ranch.

We've been here all day, and it's now mid-afternoon. Time for the three of us to take a ride. Nothing too crazy because Birdie's still learning, but I'd like some time alone with them.

"Daddy, I want my *own* horse today."

"I think that's okay," I reply, eyeing my daughter. "We won't go far."

She just doesn't have the stamina in her tiny body for a long ride yet. But I love that she enjoys the horses. She has no fear where they're concerned.

Dani and I get the horses saddled and ready to go,

and before long, the three of us are wandering down the same path I took Dani on last weekend.

"The trees have already started to change so much in just one week," Dani says with a smile. "It's fun to watch. Pretty soon, it'll be time for pumpkins and apple picking and all kinds of fun things."

"I like to carve punkins," Birdie says. "And I want to be a princess for Halloween."

"Of course, you do," Dani replies. "Because you *are* a princess. Which one do you want to be?"

"Guess!"

I grin, enjoying the two of them. They're so natural with each other. It makes me want things that I never dared want before because I knew that I was never going to make a family with Angela. She wasn't ever going to fit in with us like this.

But Dani? Dani fits in just perfectly.

"Hmm." The woman I'm falling in love with taps her chin, as if in thought. "Snow White?"

"No." Birdie shakes her head, grinning. "Try again."

"Jasmine?"

"Nope."

"Okay, tell me. I'm dying to know."

"Tiana," Birdie says with a little wiggle. "I like green, and her dress is so pretty."

"Her dress is beautiful. You'll be a lovely Tiana. Do you have a frog?"

Birdie laughs. "I have a stuffed one."

"Perfect." Dani winks at me, and then it's time to circle back around to the barn. Once we've put the horses away and have given them treats and rubs, we make our way to the house for dinner.

"Can we see the chickens?" Birdie asks, and my gaze immediately goes to Dani, who's gone pale.

"Are you guys back already?" Blake asks as he comes around the barn. He's with both Brooks and Beckett, and they're all grinning at us.

"I want to see the chickens," Birdie tells him, and Brooks's gaze immediately moves to Dani.

We all know that Dani and her sisters have a difficult past with animals on the ranch because we all experienced the many times when the Lexington girls would arrive at our house looking haunted. *Fucking traumatized by their asshole father.*

"Why don't we take you?" Beckett offers my daughter with a grin. "Let's see if the ol' girls left anything for us, and then we'll go inside and pull dinner together."

"Okay," Birdie says, letting Beck take her hand, and along with Brooks, they set off for the chicken coop behind the house.

Blake stops to brush his hand lightly over Dani's hair. "You okay, gorgeous?"

I growl, but he ignores me. It may be stupid, but I don't want *any* man touching her, even my brother.

"Sure." Her voice is thready, and neither of us believes her.

Blake's eyes turn to mine, and I nod, silently telling him that I have this.

We all love her and want to protect her.

So, my brother follows the others, and I take Dani's hands in my own. Her eyes look glassy, like she's somewhere else, and I press my lips to her forehead.

"Baby, are you really okay?"

"No," she whispers, and I'm relieved that she trusts me enough to tell me the truth.

Without overthinking it, I scoop my girl into my arms and carry her to the house, up the steps of the wraparound porch, and settle her in my lap in one of the rocking chairs, holding her to me.

"You can tell me." I kiss her head, run my hand down her arm, and hold on to her shaking hand. "Talk to me about the chickens, kitten."

It took Holden a while, but somehow, he talked his father into only keeping the larger animals on the ranch.

"Something especially bad must have happened with the birds."

She shivers and wraps her arms around my neck, burying her precious face in my neck, and a sob makes its way out of her that tears my chest wide open.

"Ah, baby." I hug her close, rocking us back and forth, my lips pressed to her. It's like she can't get close enough to me, like she wants to be safe inside of me, and it makes me ache for her. "I'm so sorry, honey. I'm so fucking sorry."

"He would p-p-pluck them"—my eyes close because I can guess where this is going—"while they were still alive. And they would scream so loud. And he would laugh."

Fuck, I want to kill him. I want to raise that mother-fucker from the grave and tear his guts out.

"He liked to make things bleed." She's still clinging to me, pressed as close as she can get, and I hold on tight, not letting her go. God, I'll never let her go. "He liked to make them cry. God, Bridge, he was so damn mean."

"And he liked to make you girls cry the most." My voice is rough, and she nods.

"He never made *me* bleed." It's a whisper, and I have to listen closely to hear her. "But p-p-poor Darby."

I feel my eyes widen. I had no idea that he made his oldest daughter bleed, and I wonder if Holden knows. Christ, I can't imagine it. I can't fathom putting my daughter through that.

I'd kill anyone who even tried to look at Birdie wrong.

"He hurt everything. Everyone," she continues, her voice stronger now. "He got off on it. We had a cat once. I can't go there. I can't talk about the unspeakable things he did to those poor, defenseless animals. But the chickens, Bridge. They were the worst, and they were my chore."

"What do you mean?"

"I was in charge of gathering eggs, and I had to go out there every day, and they were just so sad. And I couldn't help them. If I tried to help them, he'd run the water over my face."

Fuck me.

"I just can't do the chickens, and I'm sorry for it. I wish I could, but I just can't—"

"Hey, you look at me." I cup her face and urge her back so I can look in her pretty eyes. "Baby, you don't ever have to see another chicken as long as you live if you don't want to. Birdie's fine out there with me or my family."

"I wish I could enjoy that with her." She sniffles, and I swipe at the tears on her cheek with my thumb. "But I can't."

"I know, and it's okay. You need to let that guilt go, because it's okay. And it's not your fault. I promise, baby, we only want you to be comfortable here, and if that's the one place that's your hard limit, we'll respect that."

"Thank you." She wipes at her tears and takes a deep breath. "I hope we're not having chicken for dinner."

I can't help but chuckle at that, relieved that she has some color back in her cheeks.

"I think we're having pot roast."

"Yum." She sighs against me and rubs her hand over my chest, as if she's comforting me as much as herself. "I've worked really hard to keep the shit I carry around because of that man away from my everyday life. I did a good job of it when I lived in Bozeman."

"But you're here now, and there are going to be some hard moments."

"I'm sorry if I'm a lot."

I feel my brows pinch together. "I can handle it, kitten. Don't worry about me for a second. And if you have one of those bad moments, you just tell me, and we can do this until it's better."

She swallows hard and then offers me a small smile. "You're pretty good for me, you know?"

"I like to think we're good for each other."

A car pulls in, and we both look over to see Bee parking in front of the house. When she climbs out of her car, she looks tired but *very* happy.

"I'm making a killing at the shop," she says by way of a greeting. "Here's hoping that trend continues. Hey, you okay, D?"

Dani nods but takes Bee's hand when she approaches.

"Chickens," is all Dani has to say.

"Got it. Better now?"

"Yeah."

Bee's gaze finds mine, and I nod.

"Good. Let's go eat before our brothers scarf it all down and we're left with the dregs of mashed potatoes and a sliver of pot roast."

"Let's go eat," I agree.

Chapter Twelve

DANI

I splash some cold water on my face and then stare at my reflection in the mirror. I don't look quite as pale as when I came in here a minute ago. Bridger joined his family in the dining room, and I detoured to the bathroom to calm down the rest of the way.

I've had such a great day with my man and his adorable daughter. Being on the ranch is fun and doesn't bother me at all. I've always loved it out here.

Unless someone mentions those darn chickens, and then I lose it. They're just birds. But the trauma I still carry from them is in the marrow of my bones, and it might be the one thing that I'll never fully recover from. *The screams.* The horrifying noises that the chickens made when my father tortured them. I'll never *un*hear those screams. The stricken expression on my sisters' faces.

I shudder.

I know it could be much worse, and it felt good to

have Bridger hold me through the worst of the panic attack.

I pat my face dry with a towel and take a deep breath.

I'm not going to let bad memories ruin the rest of this day. The house smells delicious, and I'm hungry, so I open the door of the bathroom and am surprised to find Bridger leaning against the opposite wall, waiting for me, his arms crossed over his chest, looking delicious.

"You should be eating," I inform him, taking his offered hand and linking our fingers.

"I'm making sure my girl's okay."

His girl. It never fails to wake up the butterflies in my belly.

"I'm much better, thank you." I boost up on my toes and offer him my lips, and he gives me a quick kiss. "And I'm hungry."

"Well, we can take care of that."

Bridger leads me to the dining room off the kitchen, where everyone's already seated around the table, filling their plates.

"How's the school year going, Dani?" Brooks asks as he passes me a wooden bowlful of fresh rolls from the oven. He smiles at me, and any remaining nerves I have dissipate.

"It's going really well," I reply as I dig in, accepting platters and bowls to add to my dinner plate, and then passing them on. "I was a little nervous about starting at a new school, but all of the staff has been so great. It helps that I already know so many of them, and my kiddos are super fun. Aren't you, Birdie?"

"We're fun," Birdie confirms with a nod as she scoops up some mashed potatoes onto her fork. "Miss Dani has snacks and really pretty unicorns all over the room, and we play outside, too."

Birdie usually calls me Miss Dani, even at home, and I don't correct her. It's probably easier for her.

"Recess was always my favorite," Beck says with a wink. "What did you learn this week?"

"We're writing words that start with C. And we had to take something to class that starts with C. I wanted to take Pickles, but Dad said no."

I blink at Bridger, who just laughs. This is news to me.

"Who's Pickles?" Blake asks.

"My cat," I reply with a chuckle. "Yeah, it was probably for the best that you brought in some carrots. Besides, you brought enough for everyone, and it was a healthy snack, right?"

Birdie nods and eats her salad.

"Hey, Brooks," I say, after taking a sip of my water. "I have a weird noise in my car. I'm going to have to make an appointment."

"What kind of noise?" Bridger jumps in, frowning at me.

"Just a … noise. I don't know. A rattle? A … squeak?"

"Which is it?" Brooks asks as Bridger continues to frown. What the heck?

"Guys, I'm no mechanic," I remind them. "It's just a noise that wasn't there before."

"I don't want you driving an unsafe car," Bridger

183

says, making me shake my head. Good God, what is it with these overprotective men?

"It's not unsafe. It's just a sound. No warning lights are on or anything. Calm down, Chief."

Bee spews out her water with laughter, Blake's head whips up to stare at me, and everyone else is cackling as Bridger glowers down at me.

"Excuse us," he says, taking my hand and pulling me from the room. I can still hear the others laughing. I have to practically jog to keep up with him as he pulls me into an office and shuts the door, pinning me to it with his lower body leaning against me. One hand is pressed to the door, and the other is cupping my jaw and neck and part of my face because his hands are huge, and his brown eyes are on fire.

"Holy crap," I whisper.

"I said *no chief.*" But then his mouth is on mine, and he's kissing me like there's no tomorrow. When he comes up for air, he tips his forehead against mine, breathing raggedly, his thumb brushing over my cheek. "Call me that again, and I won't let you come for a week, Dani. I'm not kidding."

I gulp. For a *week*?

"But it caused *this*, and I like it."

"No. I won't tell you again."

My eyes are pinned to his lips.

"Fuck, I want to sink inside you so bad, but this is not the time or place. Let's go."

Before I know what's happening, he's opened the door and is dragging me back to the table. There's still so much laughter in everyone's eyes, Birdie looks bored, and I'm saved from any further questions because Beckett's holding up his phone, and it looks like their parents are on video call.

"Is that Dani?" Mama asks with a big smile. Their names are Brandon and Becca, hence, the Double B Ranch, but they always told us kids to call them Mama and Papa, and so I always have. Mama Blackwell is the only mother I've ever known. "Oh, you look wonderful, darling."

"Hi, guys," I reply with a wave and take my seat. "I'm crashing Sunday dinner."

"Well, now I'm extra homesick," Papa says with a wink.

They moved to Florida a few years ago, ready to retire from ranch life, and Mama loves Disney, so it made sense for them to be down there.

But I know that everyone misses them.

"Grandma, we rode the horses today," Birdie says, taking over the conversation. "And I got to play with the puppies, but they're going to find homes soon. And there are baby goats."

"Well, that sounds like a fun day," Mama says with a soft smile. "Did you help feed the cows?"

"Yep, and I got eggs from the chickens."

Bridger's hand covers mine, but I smile up at him. I'm fine.

I glance back to the phone, and I can plainly see that Mama notices where Bridger's hand is, but she doesn't say anything about it.

We make small talk as we finish eating, laughing at some of Blake's stories from the ER. I might be biased, but I think Blake is one of the best doctors there is.

Suddenly, I notice that Birdie gets a weird look on her face.

"Are you okay, baby girl?" I ask her softly, but Bridger hears me and turns his attention to his daughter.

"I'm just tired," Birdie says and leans back in her chair.

Bridger crooks his finger at her. "Come sit on my lap, peanut."

Not needing to be told twice, Birdie walks around the table as Bridger scoots back a little and pulls her into his lap. Birdie leans on his chest, as though they've sat just like this since she was a baby, which I'm sure they have, and it makes my chest squeeze.

He kisses Birdie's head and pats her back rhythmically as she settles in for a snuggle.

"I have news," Mama says, catching our attention. "Your father and I will be there in a few weeks. It'll be time for apple picking and going to the pumpkin patch, and you know how I love that. Plus, Birdie's old enough to really enjoy it, and I want to enjoy it with her."

"Great," Bee says, clapping her hands. "And you can see my shop."

"We can't wait to see it, honey," Papa says. "Get some Westerns in for me, yeah?"

"I can do that," Bee replies.

"Don't worry, Beck, we won't take over the farmhouse."

"This is your home," Beckett says. "Of course, you'll stay here."

"No, it's *your* home," Mama reminds him. "And we'll be staying at a place in town. We found the cutest bungalow, and this way we don't have to do as much driving."

"If you change your mind, just let me know," Beck replies.

"Dani, I'd like to have lunch with you and your sisters when I'm there," Mama says. "With Bee, of course. A day out with all my girls."

"That sounds fabulous." Bee and I share a smile. "We'll absolutely be down for that. You name the time and place and we'll make it happen."

"What about the boys?" Brooks asks, crossing his arms over his chest. "What are we, chopped liver?"

"No, darling boy, we'll get lunch, too. Oh, I'm so excited to see my kids," Mama says with tears in her eyes. "You all be good. We love you."

"Love you," everyone replies, waving and blowing kisses, and then they're gone.

The way the Blackwells grew up versus the way my family did, is as different as it gets. Polar opposites. I'm not used to family dinners together. I mean, sure, I get together with Holden and my sisters a few times a year to eat and talk, but we don't do this every week.

It's actually nice.

"Back to your car," Brooks says beside me. "Just drop it by any time this week and I'll work it in. It's probably nothing to worry about."

"Thanks. I'll do that. I appreciate it, Brooks."

I glance over to Birdie and see that she's fallen asleep in Bridger's arms. Without thinking twice, I reach over and brush my fingers through her soft brown hair.

"Sweet baby."

Bridger catches my hand in his and brings it up to his lips, kissing me softly.

"So." Blake's voice is calm and casual as he sips his drink. "Are we to assume that you two have made things official, since there's a whole lot of dreamy eyes and PDA happening over there?"

"So many dreamy eyes," Bee agrees with a snicker. "About damn time."

Bridger smirks at that and then gives me a bright smile.

"I haven't talked to Birdie, so I'm kind of glad she's asleep," he says softly. "But yeah, Dani's my girl."

"Aww, how sweet," Beckett says, giving Bridger shit, but then he smiles. "Good for you, guys. There's been something there since we were kids."

He's right. Bridger was always the one I'd seek out. He's the one I crushed so hard on. So the fact that we're together now fills me with hope and excitement, and let's face it, the sex is ... *wow*.

I feel better than I have in a long, long time. And as much as I've always felt like I was part of the Blackwell family, tonight was just the icing on the proverbial cake. Especially with Mama's easy acceptance of her son and me together. *It doesn't get better than this.*

We stayed to help with cleanup and then got Birdie in the car to head home. She's exhausted, the poor thing.

"She's been asleep pretty much since dinner," I say, glancing back to check on her. "What's going on with her, Bridge?"

He lets out a gusty breath and also checks on her in the rearview mirror. "We don't know for sure. This has been going on for a year, maybe a little more. She's just exhausted a lot. Sometimes she gets a stomachache. She's small for her age, but she's been growing like a weed through the summer, which made me feel better. She's actually been doing a lot better all around, but there are days like today when she's just beat."

I frown and look back at her once more. Her little bow lips are open, moving as she sleeps. Her cheeks are round, and her dark eyelashes fall against her skin, and she's the most beautiful, sweet thing.

I would hold her all day long if she were mine.

"Blake's put her through a ton of tests, but they've been inconclusive. It could be as simple as allergies, and he said she might grow out of it. This summer was a relief, since she's been so much better."

"Hopefully she's back to her old self tomorrow." I reach over and grab Bridger's hand, giving it a squeeze.

"Come home with us," he says as he kisses the back of my hand.

"I really should go home and get ready for the week. I

don't have much to do, but I'll be mad at myself if I leave it for the morning."

"You could come over when you're finished." He smiles over at me. "Late-night snuggles."

This man is a toucher. And I'm so here for it.

"Is that all you want to do?"

"Well, my bedroom door locks, and there are ways to keep you quiet." He lifts an eyebrow, and I laugh as his phone rings. "Fuck, that's work."

He lets go of my hand and accepts the call.

"Blackwell."

"We have another five-alarm fire," someone says through the speakers.

"Text me the address. I'm—shit, I'm thirty out. I have to take my daughter home."

"I'll send the info along. This one's been burning for a few hours before anyone saw, Chief."

I frown over at him. How could something burn that long without anyone seeing the smoke?

"Where the hell is it?" Bridger asks, obviously as confused as I am.

"It's a seasonal cabin on the other side of Lion Mountain," is the response.

"Fuck. I'll be there ASAP."

Bridger cuts off the call and blows out a breath.

"I have Birdie," I assure him. "Don't worry about her. I've got it."

He quickly glances my way before looking back at the road. "I have to bathe her, put her clothes out for school tomorrow, get her lunch made—"

"I've got it," I say again, my voice perfectly calm. "I can manage all those things, Bridge. Don't worry about us."

He takes my hand again and kisses it, harder, holding on tighter. "Thank you."

"Of course."

As soon as he parks, I run across to my house and gather clothes for tomorrow, a few toiletries, and make sure that Pickles has food and her box is scooped. I stop to give her some extra love and kisses.

"I'm sorry, baby, I have to go help Bridger and Birdie tonight. You keep an eye out here, okay?"

She blinks at me, obviously put out for being interrupted from her evening nap, and then less than fifteen minutes after getting here, I'm back out the door, rushing across the street.

I don't bother to knock and just walk in and see Bridger striding down the hallway, buttoning up the shirt of his uniform, and I have to take a split second to admire everything that's going on right there.

He's tall and broad-shouldered, with those colorful sleeve tattoos. I'm losing sight of the light smattering of dark hair on that chest as he buttons the shirt, and then when he opens his pants to tuck it in, I almost faint.

"Keep looking at me like that, sweetheart, and I'll be late. Too late."

"Like what?" I can't meet his eyes. I'm just watching his impressive hands as they tuck in that shirt and then fasten his pants.

The man's hips are something to write home about. I

know that there's a V under those clothes, and I have to lick my lips.

"For fuck's sake, Dani. You're killing me here."

Now my eyes climb to his, and I see the lust reflected back at me.

"Sorry. Not really sorry."

He barks out a laugh and shakes his head. "Birdie's in bed. She was too tired for the shower, so she'll get one tomorrow night. She'll probably sleep all the way through."

He steps to me and wraps his arm around the small of my back while tipping my face up to his with the other hand, and I wish he didn't have to go.

"Call me if you need me," he says softly before covering my mouth. The kiss is over way too quickly, and then he's out the door.

"Be careful," I whisper to no one.

Suddenly, the door opens again, and he pokes his head in. "Sleep in *my* bed. Not on Birdie's floor. Understood?"

I bite my lip and nod.

"Use your words."

I shiver every time he says that.

"I hear you."

He nods and then he's gone again, and I let out a long breath before I walk back to check on Birdie. Sure enough, she's asleep in her bed, so I gather my things and take them back to Bridger's bedroom, where I take a quick shower and change into my pajamas, then I go to the kitchen and make a lunch for Birdie for tomorrow.

My phone dings from the living room, and I run to check on it in case it's Bridger.

But it's my big brother instead.

> Holden: I know you're dating Bridger, D. You good?

Leave it to my brother to ask about my dating life via text.

> Me: Yep. Never happier.

> Holden: Good. Making sure I don't have to murder him. Love you.

> Me: Thanks, I think? Love you, too.

I've just turned off all the lights in the house, leaving just the entry light on for Bridger, and climbed into his bed when I hear little footsteps in the hallway.

"Daddy?"

"It's me, honey. Dani. Your daddy had to go to a fire."

Birdie starts to cry, and it breaks my heart, and then suddenly, she leans forward and throws up.

"Oh, gosh. Okay, we've got this."

When it seems there's a break, I rush her to the toilet so she can continue to throw up there, and then I realize that she managed to get it all over herself, so when she's finished, I simply help her strip down and put her in the shower.

"Just a quick one," I assure her. "We need to get you cleaned up, okay?"

"I want Daddy," she cries, knuckling the tears in her eyes as I help her get washed. I feel awful for her, and if I could take away how horrible she feels, I would do it in a heartbeat.

"I know you do, sweet girl. I do, too, if I'm being honest. But we can handle this. We've got this. Come on, let's get you dry and in some clean pajamas, and then you can get back in bed."

"Can I sleep in Daddy's bed?"

"You bet. You can sleep with me in your daddy's bed."

I manage to avoid the mess in the hallway and grab the little girl some clean clothes, get her dressed, and snuggled down in the bed. Then I clean up the vomit, make sure there's nothing she missed in the bathroom, and slide under the covers with her. She curls up to my side, snuggling me.

"You sleep." I kiss her forehead and push her hair off her face. "No more sickies, okay?"

"No more sickies."

Chapter Thirteen

BRIDGER

Goddamn, I'd like to punch the motherfucker who's decided to torch my town. The cabin was a complete loss by the time we got on the scene, so our main concern now is protecting the hundreds of evergreens from the sparks coming off the structure.

"Continue soaking that side," I tell my guys. "And get those walls pushed in."

As the structure collapses, we want it to fall inside of itself so the flames don't spread any farther. Our primary goal here is to keep it all contained.

"Where are the owners?" I ask Jones. We've worked together for years, and he's the best at pulling information.

"They live in Texas," he says. "I have a call out to them, but had to leave a message."

"Whoever did this didn't want us to find it quickly.

He could have lit this whole fucking mountain on fire, and there are homes just over that ridge."

Jones nods grimly as we watch the team use long poles to push the outside walls toward the inside of the house. There's a big plume of smoke, and flames dance high into the sky and then calm down again as the fire continues to smolder. Ash and smoke hang heavy in the air.

"He uses the same accelerant every time," Jones reminds me. "Always gas, always around the front door. He leaves the cans, for Christ's sake. He's not being exactly stealthy about it."

"No, but the fire is burning away any prints he might have left. I know we have to leave the investigation to the experts, but it's fucking annoying to be on the outside, cleaning up this asshole's messes."

"That's all we can do," Jones reminds me, patting me on the shoulder. "We need to make a statement to the media, Chief. Residents need to be vigilant because he's hit homes with people inside."

"I know." I pull my hand down my face. "We'll make a statement in the morning and make sure it's in all the media and on our socials. I want this asshole caught."

I can tell that the fire is losing its edge. It's calming down, and I don't have any more concerns about the surrounding trees and woods, but we'll keep dousing it to make sure no remaining embers creep away and start another fiasco.

This many fires in less than two weeks is unheard of in this town. We may have calls for small fires, but not usually a complete loss like this, not this many in such a short period of time. We take way more ambulance and accident calls than we do house fires.

Not that we can't handle them, but our community doesn't usually have to deal with it. I like keeping it that way. *Who the fuck is this guy? Why is he doing this? How do I catch him?*

When I turn, I see that Chase Wild's finishing up with his guys, bagging the gas cans that were left at the front door, taking down information.

There isn't much more they can do until the fire is cold.

"That fucker," Chase grumbles when I join him.

"My thoughts exactly. Any leads?"

He shakes his head, his mouth set in grim lines, as he watches the destroyed building. "He thought he was sly with this one."

"Keep an eye out at the ranch," I tell him, and his cold eyes turn to me. "I'll be telling Holden and my brother the same things. Obviously, this guy isn't sticking just to town, and this is the fourth fire in two weeks."

"All of the ranches have excellent security and cameras," he says.

"Yeah, well, maybe we up that security. I wish I could do that for every building in town. But I can't, so you have to get this guy under wraps."

"We're working on it." He nods once. "There's going to be a meeting this week with the concert people in charge of security for that show at our ranch. I'd like you there."

"I'll be there. Just text me the information. I'll be bringing Jones and a few others with me so we think of everything."

"Sounds good to me. There's nothing more I can do here tonight. I'll come back out tomorrow."

I nod, clap him on the back, and then return to my guys.

"We have this, Chief," Jones says. "Go home and get some sleep."

"I'll be in the office by nine," I reply. "I appreciate it."

I've been on the scene for four hours, and rather than wake the whole house up when I get home, I swing by the station to take a quick shower. It's after midnight when I get home.

Ready to climb into my bed and curl up around Dani, I let myself in quietly and toe off my shoes, set my keys and wallet on the table by the door, and then make my way down the hallway. But when I peek into Birdie's room, she's not in her bed.

With a frown, I cross to my room and find both of my girls fast asleep under the covers, and the scene sends a jolt through me so swift that it knocks me back a step. Birdie's on the edge of the mattress closest to the door, turned toward me, her little hands up by her chin as she sleeps.

Dani's in the middle of the bed, curled up around my daughter, hugging her close to her front. Her nose is in Birdie's hair, and seeing the two of them together like this makes me perfectly aware of two things.

One, I'm completely in love with Dani Lexington.

And two, I'm never letting her go.

As quietly as possible, I shed my uniform and pull on a T-shirt before I climb in on the other side of the bed and slip in behind my girls, wrapping an arm around them.

"She threw up," Dani whispers and then kisses Birdie's head, and I hug them both against me a little tighter. I hate that I wasn't here to take care of them. "But she's okay now. How are you?"

"I'm just fine, sweetheart." I kiss her hair and then brush her strands back, exposing her neck, and press a kiss there, too, breathing her in. "Go back to sleep."

She wiggles against me and sighs. "Okay."

God, this feels so fucking good. It feels right, having them together like this, tucked up against me where I can keep them safe.

I loved having Dani on the ranch with us today. Even with her meltdown, it was the best day that I've had in a long while. But I'm mad at myself for not anticipating that it might have been too much for Birdie.

After a few months of my daughter acting like a normal, healthy kid, it's easy to forget that there could be days like this, and I need to be more watchful. But I'm glad that Dani was here to help Birdie.

I gently kiss her neck once more, enjoying the way her soft skin feels against my lips, and then I lie back on the pillow and surrender to sleep.

Two days later, Birdie wakes up with the sniffles.

"Shit." School is a cesspool of germs, especially early on in the year like this, but I have the meeting regarding the Sidney Sterling benefit concert today, and I can't miss that. So, I do what any single dad would do in this situation.

I load my kid up with medication.

She doesn't have a fever, and once the children's cold medicine kicks in, she seems to be pretty normal, sitting at the island, eating her breakfast.

"How do you feel, peanut?"

"Better," she says. "My nose isn't running anymore. I don't want to miss school. We're doing D words today, and I'm taking in my stuffed dog, Ralph."

"I know. You can go to school, but if you start to feel worse, you need to tell Miss Dani, okay?"

"Okay."

"Do you like her, baby?"

"Miss Dani?" She pops a blueberry into her mouth. "Yeah, she's a good teacher."

"Do you like her when we're at home? When she spends time with us?"

Birdie nods and reaches for another blueberry. They're her favorite right now. "She's really nice, and she helped me when I was sick, and doesn't talk to me like I'm a baby."

I smile and take a sip of my coffee. "I like her, too. In fact, I'd like for Dani to spend a lot more time with us. What do you think about that?"

"Like, she can come over for dinner and stuff?"

"Sure, she can do that. What if sometimes she wants to stay the night like she did the other night when you got sick?"

She nods. "Yeah. She'll sleep in your bed?"

"Yes, baby, she'd sleep in my bed."

"Can we all sleep in your bed?"

I laugh at that. Birdie used to love to sleep in my bed with me, and she still does when she's sick like the other night, but I do not want to get back into that habit.

"You know that you're supposed to sleep in your room, in your big girl bed. But if you're ever sick or scared, you can always come to me. You know that."

"Okay. Does this mean that she's your girlfriend? Are you going to kiss and stuff?"

Surprised, I blink at my daughter. "How do you know about that?"

"Daddy." She rolls her eyes at me, and I suddenly flash forward to when she's a teenager. "I'm not a baby. Grown-ups kiss and stuff."

"I will probably kiss and cuddle with her. And you might see that sometimes." I swallow hard, suddenly uncomfortable with this conversation. "But that's because we care about each other."

"Okay."

It's as simple as that. She goes back to eating her breakfast and presses play on her tablet to watch her cartoon, not seeming concerned about anything else. But then, she hits pause again and looks stricken.

"What's wrong?" I ask her.

"What about Pickles? If Miss Dani stays here at night, Pickles will be alone and scared."

I laugh and walk around the island to kiss her head. "We'll bring Pickles, too."

"And she can sleep in *my* bed," she announces. "So she's not alone."

"I think that's a good idea. Now, finish your breakfast so we can get you to school."

Birdie seems to be feeling even more like herself when we reach the school, and I walk her to the door, where she hurries in without hardly giving me a second glance.

Dani's standing on the sidewalk, as usual, and she's smiling at me as I cross to her. I'm in my uniform today because I have to go to the office from here, and her gaze eats me up, from head to toe.

"Are you salivating, kitten?"

She laughs and doesn't flinch or try to pull away when I drag my knuckle down her cheek and then lean in to press my lips to hers, just for a moment.

"You have a big head," she says, and when I simply smirk at her, those eyes go wide and her cheeks burn up. "You know I didn't mean *that*."

"Later, I'll ask you to be more specific." I chuckle and take her hand in mine, threading our fingers together. "Birdie had a sniffle this morning, but I gave her some meds, and she seems to be better."

Dani frowns. "Oh, no. I'll keep an eye on her. Hopefully, the medicine lasts until the end of the school day. Poor little thing."

"Sometimes, it can lead to an asthma attack. Like I

said, she was fine just now. You'd never know anything was wrong, but she shouldn't run around at recess, just to be safe."

"I'll make sure she doesn't," Dani assures me. "Her inhaler is locked in my desk. I'll put it in my pocket and carry it on me today, just in case."

"Thank you." My eyes drift down to the crisp white button-down she's wearing, those black buttons undone at the top, revealing the top of her cleavage, and the only reason I can see that much is because I'm so much taller than she is. The shirt is tucked into black slacks that hug her curves in all the right places.

I know that Dani mentioned that she's self-conscious about her curves, but I wouldn't have her any other way. She fits against me like she was made for me. She's absolutely perfect.

"I should go in," she says, pulling me out of my reverie. "You must be working today."

"I am, but I'll have my phone on me, so if you need me, just reach out."

She smiles and nods. "I will, but we won't need you. We're good here. Have a good day at work."

"You, too." I lean in for one more kiss, and then I walk away toward my truck.

"Holy cow, girl, you and *Bridger*?"

I glance back to see another teacher talking to my girl. Dani's smiling wide and nodding, and pride fills my chest.

Day one of public affection was a success.

"We'll have medical tents set up," a man in a suit on the video call tells us.

We're in a conference room at the police station, with a large screen on the wall showing everyone in Seattle who is in on this call, as well as those of us in this room. It's a relief that everyone's taking this as seriously as I had hoped.

"With how many personnel to man those tents?" I ask him.

"There will be six tents with two doctors and four nurses in each one."

"Twelve doctors and twenty-four nurses," I mutter. "For ten thousand people."

"For a five-hour, at the max, event," someone else reminds me. "The concert will run about two hours, and we're factoring in ample time for people coming in and out."

"Where are these people going to park?" Jones asks. "We don't have public transportation in Bitterroot Valley, and the ranch is a twenty-minute drive from town."

"We'll be busing some of them in," comes the answer. "And the Wild family has assured us that they can clear out one of their pastures for some parking."

I shake my head and run my hand down my face. "Look, I love that Ms. Sterling wants to help our community and that she wants to put on a show for us.

We don't get opportunities like that here, and the town will go nuts. Hell, all of Montana will be clamoring to buy tickets when word gets out."

"We'll be controlling that, too. This concert is only open to this specific community and the surrounding areas."

I shake my head. "You guys, this is the age of social media. Do you think it won't spread like wildfire? This is Sidney Sterling we're talking about. The world can't get enough of her."

We spend the next hour going back and forth on logistics. I appreciate that they're bringing in plenty of medical and security help. They're doing everything for this concert so there's less burden on our community.

And yet, there are still logistics that sound impossible to me.

By the time we're finished, I'm still not convinced that the event will be pulled off without a hitch, but time will tell.

Just as I'm leaving the conference room, my phone rings, and I frown at Dani's name. She should be in class.

"Hey, sweetheart."

"Bridger, I need to let you know"—my heart starts to gallop—"that Birdie is okay now, but she did have an asthma attack and needed her inhaler. I've calmed her down."

Dani's voice sounds a little shaky, and I'm already hot-footing it to my truck.

"Okay, baby, take a breath." She does as I ask.

"It's in her file that I should call you, even if she's

okay. Do you want to come and get her, or let her finish the day?"

It's past lunchtime, with only a couple of hours of school left. "I'll come get her. I'm on my way right now."

"Okay, we're in the nurse's office. I have an aid taking care of the class right now, but I can't leave."

"I know. It's okay, Dani. I'll be there in less than ten minutes."

I should have kept Birdie home today. I knew this was a possibility, and she's been under the weather since Sunday night. Before I reach the school, I call my brother's office. Blake spends a lot of time in the ER these days, but he also works two days a week at a family practice, and this is one of the days he's there.

"Hey, Marsha, it's Bridger Blackwell. Birdie's having some asthma trouble today. Can Blake fit her in this afternoon?"

"Sure, he can squeeze her in, in about forty-five minutes. If you bring her on in, we'll get her roomed and he'll pop over to see you."

"Appreciate it. I'll bring her over as soon as I pick her up from school."

"See you soon."

After parking, I stride into the school and to the nurse's office, which is near the main office, and see that Birdie and Dani are sitting side by side, talking.

"I don't want to go home," Birdie says when she sees me, her little face screwed up in a scowl. "I'm fine now, Daddy, and I won't run anymore."

"You were running?"

Birdie looks guilty and sneaks a look at Dani, but she nods. "Miss Dani told me not to when I went outside, but we were playing tag, and I didn't want to sit out."

"I turned my back for five seconds to check on another student who fell," Dani says, shaking her head and looking so guilty, it makes me feel bad for her. I want to scoop her up and hold her, and I'll do that later.

First, I have to deal with Birdie.

"Hey, not your fault," I say to her as I press my hand to her shoulder. "Birdie, we're going to see Uncle Blake, just to make sure you're okay."

Birdie whines, but I pick her up, and she loops her arms around my neck. She's not feeling as good as she wants me to think she is if she's willing to let me carry her.

"I'll come check on her when I get home." Dani bites her lip, obviously worried. "I hate that I can't leave."

"It's only a couple of hours," I remind her and kiss her forehead. "We're okay. I'll text you."

Dani nods, and I carry Birdie out to the truck, secure her in the back seat, and then drive us over to the doctor's office.

"I want to be at school," she says with a pout.

"Yeah, well, I want you to feel better, and what I want is more important right now." I park in the lot, then help my girl out of her seat, and with her hand in mine, we walk inside.

"Hey, come on back," Marsha says with a smile, gesturing for us to come through the door to her left. "We have a room ready for you."

Sometimes it's convenient to be the brother of a doctor.

One of the nurses, Leslie, takes Birdie's blood pressure, checks her temperature, and takes all the vitals she needs, and then she smiles at us as she gathers her things to leave the room.

"Dr. Blackwell should be in soon. He's just wrapping up with another patient."

"Thanks, Leslie." I nod, and she leaves, and Birdie sighs as if this is the worst day of her life.

If she feels good enough to be this pouty, she's not doing too bad.

Less than a minute after Leslie leaves, the door opens, and Blake walks inside, giving Birdie a soft smile. He's in green scrubs and a white lab coat with his name embroidered over the chest. His stethoscope hangs around his neck. He looks tired as fuck.

"What's up with you, wee one?"

"Nothing," Birdie says and stubbornly folds her arms, and I scowl at my daughter.

"Just wanted to see me, huh?" Blake grins and squats in front of her. "I missed you, too, cupcake. How are you feeling, though?"

She shrugs, and I jump in.

"She woke up with the sniffles, but after I gave her the cold medicine, she seemed fine. She went to school, and at lunchtime, she was running around and had an asthma attack. Dani had her inhaler on her, though."

"Sniffles, huh?" Blake looks at the vitals that Leslie took. "Let's get a listen of your lungs, okay? Sit up here."

He helps her up onto the table with the strip of white paper along it, then tells her to breathe in and out while he moves his stethoscope around.

"You're a little congested in there," he says. "We'll do a breathing treatment before you go. Let's keep up with the cold meds every eight hours, too. She should be fine in a couple of days. I'll swing by and listen to her lungs to make sure there's nothing lingering. Until then, no running around. Hear me?"

"Okay," Birdie says with a long-suffering sigh. Blake pokes his head out the door and tells someone to bring him the nebulizer.

"Thanks," I tell my brother. "Appreciate it. She's been lethargic again."

"I saw that at dinner on Sunday." He sits on a stool and sighs, examining my kiddo. "She was such a little preemie, Bridger. The lungs may always be an annoyance for her. Let's get her recovered from this bug, see how she is for a week or two, and then we can run some more blood tests."

"I don't want any more needles," Birdie whines as Leslie bustles back in with the machine to give my daughter a breathing treatment.

"I'm sorry, cupcake," Blake says with a sigh. I know that Birdie's illness has weighed on him. He wants to help her so badly. "We're going to figure this out. Now, you know the drill. Hold the tube in your mouth, and take some deep breaths to get the medicine in your lungs."

The treatments always make her shaky for a while

after, but they really help when her poor lungs are working extra hard.

"How did Dani handle it?"

"She did great. I warned her this could happen this morning, and she carried the inhaler on her, just in case. I'm glad she did."

Blake nods. "I like you two together," he says, his voice low. "I think you're good for each other."

I run my hand through my hair, watching my daughter breathe with the machine. I doubt she can hear us over the noise of it. As much as I don't need affirmation about Dani from my brother, I like it. He knows. He's known for years that Dani has owned my heart.

"I think so, too."

Chapter Fourteen

DANI

I need to get home. I don't know how I kept it together for Birdie and Bridger this afternoon, because I was so freaking scared when she couldn't catch her breath. Her face was screwed up in fear, and my stomach was in my throat. I've seen asthma attacks before, of course, and I've been trained to handle them, but seeing a little girl you love struggle to breathe?

Terrifying.

I never want to relive that again, and from what Birdie told me after she'd calmed down, that wasn't even a bad asthma attack.

The thought makes me shiver and not in a good way.

Now that school's out, I rush home and quickly change into leggings and Bridger's T-shirt, then hurry across the street and knock on the door.

"Is she okay?" I ask, as soon as Bridger pulls the door open.

"Hello," he replies, his brown eyes warm as he wraps

his arm around my shoulders and leads me inside. "She's great. Come on in, we're making cookies."

I blink in surprise. "You're making cookies?"

"Sure. Doesn't that make everyone feel better? Come hang out with us." He winks at me as he closes the door, but before we cross to the kitchen, he pulls me against him and tips my chin up so he can kiss me softly. "Thanks for coming over."

"Wild horses couldn't have kept me away."

He grins and seems to want to say more, but I pull back and head for the kitchen, where I find Birdie standing on a stool, stirring batter in a bowl.

"Birdie, look who's here."

"Hi, Miss Dani," the little girl says with a grin. She looks perfectly fine. Her round cheeks are full of color, her dark hair is up in a ponytail, and she's wearing the cutest apron I've ever seen. "We're making peanut butter cookies."

"Yum, those sound delicious. I like your apron."

Birdie looks down at herself. "Daddy helped me tie-dye it."

I eye the pinks and purples and then turn to Bridger, raising an eyebrow. "Really?"

"Made a huge mess," Bridger confirms as he joins his daughter and takes over the mixing. His forearms bunch as he grips the wooden spoon, and holy Moses, that's a zing right to the vagina. "But it was fun. Right, peanut?"

"Yeah," Birdie agrees, nodding. "Can we make the balls now?"

"I think it's ready," Bridger confirms.

"How can I help?" I ask.

"You sit." My handsomer-than-should-be-legal boyfriend points at me with the business end of his spoon. "Just talk to us. We've got this covered."

"What happened at the doctor?" I ask, but then shake my head. "Unless that's none of my business, of course."

"Hey." I look up at Bridger, and he crooks his finger at me. "I changed my mind. Come here, sweetheart."

Jumping off the stool, I round the island, and he turns to face me.

"She's your business. I'm your business, just like you're ours, so ask anything you want. Got it?"

"Sure, but why did I have to come all the way over here for this?"

His lips twitch, and then he bends down and kisses me. Not a little peck, but a full-blown, erase-my-mind-of-all-rational-thought kiss. His tongue nudges against the seam of my mouth, and I open for him and wrap my arms around his neck, clinging to him.

"Grown-up kisses are *gross*." Birdie makes gagging noises, making us laugh as we pull apart, and I return to my stool. "Daddy said you're going to kiss in front of me, but not all the time, okay?"

My eyes whip to the man in question. He told her?

"And Birdie's very happy that you're going to be spending more time with us," Bridger agrees, smiling at me so sweetly, I want to climb over this island and go back to the kissing. "Right, peanut?"

"Yeah, you're his girlfriend. You can stay the night."

At that, I start to cough on my own spit, because I was *not* expecting that to come out of a five-year-old's mouth.

"And Pickles can stay, too. So she's not lonely," Birdie adds, so matter-of-factly, as if she's got it all sorted out.

She's the cutest ever.

Bridger slides a glass of water over to me, that smile still firmly in place, and as I raise the glass to my mouth, he bites his lower lip, as if he's trying to keep himself from laughing his butt off.

"Oh, this is funny, huh?"

He shakes his head, chuckling as he rolls peanut butter cookie balls between his palms and sets them on the cookie sheet. "You're adorable. You should have seen your face. Anyway, now that we have all of that cleared up, Birdie saw Blake, and she's got some sort of a bug. So, he gave her a breathing treatment and told her to lie low for a few days until it's gone. No more running around."

"I like to run around," Birdie says with a frown. "I'm good at it."

"You really are good at it," I agree. "But you can hold off for a few days, and then you'll be even better at it."

"Does this mean I can't go to dance class on Saturday?" Birdie asks her father, horror filling her brown eyes.

"Oh, you enrolled her? I'm so glad. I met Skyla, the owner, at Bee's shop the other day, and she was *so* nice. And seriously beautiful."

I frown down at my hands. I really shouldn't have mentioned the latter, but she really is so pretty.

"No one holds a candle to you, kitten."

I snort, and Bridger freezes, the fork in his hand pausing in the middle of helping Birdie to make criss-cross figures in the dough, and only his eyes lift to mine.

"Are you telling me that I haven't made it perfectly clear how gorgeous you are?"

And just like that, the man has me tongue-tied.

"You have made it clear that you find me attractive, yes. This is not a conversation to have in front of your daughter."

Birdie looks at me and then at her dad, and Bridger sets the fork down altogether, leans on the counter, and frowns at me.

Oh, jeez, I didn't mean to make him mad at me. My stomach sinks, and I wish I could erase the last three minutes of conversation entirely.

"I disagree," he replies. "I think it's important for my daughter to see that her dad thinks his woman is the most beautiful girl in the world. Because you are."

I feel my cheeks darken with embarrassment, and I simply shrug. "Thanks. Anyway, how exciting for dance. You must be so happy, Birdie."

Bridger's eyes narrow as he watches me, but he drops the subject and goes back to helping Birdie get the dough situated on the pan as the little girl tells me all about how ready she is for her new class.

Bridger slides the pan into the oven, and Birdie yawns.

"Can I go watch my tablet in my room?" she asks him.

"Sure. I'll let you know when the cookies are ready to eat."

"Okay!" She jumps off her stool and starts to run off, but Bridger stops her.

"Walk, peanut."

She slows down, walking calmly back to her room.

"I'm so glad that she's feeling okay. She scared me today."

Bridger marches around the island, and I turn on my stool, facing him as he reaches me. His face is so serious, so intense, that I put my hands on his chest and blink up at him.

"What's wrong?"

He frames my face in his hands and tips his head down so he can lean his forehead against mine. "It's really good to have you here, sweetheart. And you're wearing my shirt."

"Your clothes pretty much make up my whole wardrobe when I'm not at work these days."

He grins, and his hands slide back into my hair as his lips find mine, and my whole body goes from simmering to boiling with just that simple touch.

I grip his forearms as he steps closer, nudging his way between my knees, and my nipples are at full attention. Finally, he growls, palms my butt, and lifts me onto the countertop as if I weigh nothing at all. I let out a little gasp of surprise.

"I like being able to put you where I want you." His voice is raspy, and one hand is back in my hair now, gripping tightly. I love the slight tug against my scalp. "And I fucking love your hair. It's so soft, so thick, and it looks good wrapped around my fingers."

"Have I mentioned that you're good with your mouth?"

That has his lips tipping up in a sly grin, and I let out a breathy laugh.

"That, too, but you say the sexiest things."

"I can't help myself." He plants his lips on my fore-head. "And later, when it's dark and Birdie's asleep, and we're behind a locked door, I'm going to whisper all the sexy-as-fuck things that I'm going to do to you."

I don't suppress the shiver that runs through me with that comment.

"Yes, please."

"And you're going to do the same."

"Uh ..."

"You know I love your dirty mouth," he says, kissing down my cheek and over to my nose. "If you want to come, you'll use it."

"Well, when you use that kind of incentive, how can I argue?"

He laughs, and then I press my hand to his chest, pushing myself back.

"Wait. I have plans tonight."

His eyebrows climb in surprise. "You do?"

"Yeah, so we might have to take a rain check for dirty talk."

He braces his hands on either side of my hips, caging me in. "Who do you have plans with tonight, kitten?"

I lick my lips, watching his mouth. I *really* want it on me again.

"Dani."

"Yeah?"

"Who." He kisses my nose. "Do you." Kisses my cheek. "Have." Brushes his nose over my jaw. "Plans with?"

"If I don't tell you, will you keep doing that?"

"No." He pulls away.

"Well, that backfired." I reach for him, but he won't let me touch him. "Hey, come back. It's nothing bad. Don't withhold *you* from me, Bridge. I don't like that."

"Okay." He folds me against him, and this is much better. "Sorry, baby. I was playing with you and pushing your buttons. Now I know how far is too far."

"This is a way better method of getting me to talk." I nuzzle his chest with my nose. "I have a book club meeting at Billie's Books tonight. It's our first one."

He chuckles, and I can hear it vibrating through his breastbone. "First of all, I need to up my game if you're ditching dirty talk for book talk. What did you read for this meeting?"

"*Beyond the Thistles* by Samantha Young, and it was so good. Sexy with a little suspense, and it's set in Scotland, which only ups the sexy factor."

"Spicy books, then, huh?" He kisses the top of my head, and his hands are rubbing circles on my back. Maybe I shouldn't go to book club tonight.

"You know it. Anyway, it'll be fun. I probably won't get home until around nine, though."

"Just come over here when you're done. I'll go get Pickles, and she'll be here, too."

I tip my head back and rest my chin on his chest, watching him. "You mean I can have both book club *and* dirty talk? I don't have to choose?"

"I'd never make you choose." He kisses my nose as the oven timer dings. "Have fun with the girls talking about your smut, and then come home to me. Win-win."

"I will take you up on that offer." I kiss his chin before he pulls away to check the cookies in the oven. "I can make dinner before I go. Chicken noodle soup from scratch sounds good, and it's good for Birdie."

Bridger's gaze moves to the rain coming down outside, and he nods. "That actually sounds really good. I won't say no to that. Thanks."

"I just have to run home and get the ingredients. I already have everything. I'll pack an overnight bag and grab Pickles, too, if that's okay."

He turns to me, that smile still in place. "That's more than okay. I'll help."

After he transfers the cookies to a rack, he calls down the hallway.

"Hey, peanut?"

"Yeah?"

"I'm gonna help Dani grab some things from her house. I'll be right back, okay?"

"Okay," she calls back. "Bring Pickles."

Bridger shakes his head with a laugh. "Yes, ma'am."

"You're destined to be bossed around by women."

"I have no complaints with that," he replies as we

219

step out of the house. "As long as it's outside of the bedroom."

"Or the garage," I reply thoughtfully. "Or the kitchen."

"Point made, kitten." He takes my hand, leading me across the street. "Come on, let's get you back to my place, where you belong."

"My favorite part," Alex says, holding her hand up like she's swearing on the stand in a courtroom, "was when Walker was taking Sloane home from work, and she made him pull over, and they did it in the car, and he was like *holy shit, this is the best day ever.*"

Alex shimmies her shoulders, making us laugh.

"Walker was delicious, in a very alpha, grumpy, I-want-to-eat-him-up way," Bee agrees. "I'm so glad you recommended this author, Skyla, because now I have to go back and devour her backlist."

"You won't be disappointed," Skyla replies, that pretty Irish lilt in her voice. She's in some brown wide-leg denim pants and a green sweater that looks chic and casual at the same time, and her bright red hair is twisted into a long braid. She brought her massive dog, Riley, with her. He's curled up in a ball at her feet, sleeping soundly. "I'm just honored that you chose *my* author for the first month's book."

"This was a great way to start," I reply. I'd read the

book before, but I had no issue with reading it again so it would be at the forefront of my mind.

There are eight of us here tonight. In addition to Skyla, Bee, and Alex, Charlie's here, too. Now that wedding season is almost over, and her event planning business is starting to chill out just a tiny bit, Charlie has some time to read.

Summer and Polly Wild—sisters-in-law each married to a Wild brother—are here, and rounding out our group is Jackie Harmon, the owner of The Sugar Studio. She brought us little huckleberry tarts as a treat.

No one bakes like Jackie does.

"What should we read for next month?" Summer asks the group.

"Has anyone read mafia romance?" Alex asks, surprising me. She just laughs at my stunned look. "Oh, honey, I'll bring you over to the darker side."

"Mafia romance is delicious," Bee agrees. "Give me those *I will kill you without thinking twice, but I'm so obsessed with this girl, I'll burn the whole world to the ground for her* vibes. It's so hot."

"I'd love to try whatever you recommend," Skyla says, clearly excited at the prospect as everyone else agrees.

"I love a man who'd burn the world down for his girl," I admit. "So, let's do it."

We decide on an SJ Tilly read, *Nero*, for next month, and then spend an hour discussing authors, favorite reads and tropes, and, of course, the spicy scenes we love.

It's fun to talk about the books I adore with these

women. I hope we get more members as time goes on and we spread the word about our new club.

"Speaking of spice," Polly says, turning to me. "I hear you and Bridger have been extra cozy lately."

The whole room goes quiet as everyone turns to me.

"Who's Bridger?" Skyla asks, leaning over to Alex.

"The fire chief," Alex replies. "Super hot. Been our friend forever. They're just realizing that they've had feelings for each other for a long time. He's a single dad."

"Thanks for the recap," I tell my sister with a laugh. "But yeah, that sums it up."

"Oh, a friends-to-lovers, single-dad romance," Skyla says, leaning in. "We love those. So, is he good with his ... hose?"

"Oh, my God!" Billie exclaims, shaking her head. "No, we're not talking about my brother's anything."

"He's your brother?" Skyla demands with a laugh. "This just gets better. And aren't the two of you the best of mates?"

"Yes," I say, laughing with her. "Bee's the only girl out of five siblings."

"They're all sexy as fuck," Summer informs the newcomer. "It's gonna suck for Bee one day, when her sisters-in-law want to talk about how good her brothers are in bed."

"I can't believe we've gone from fictional sex to sex with my *brothers*. Gross." Bee shivers and then makes fake gagging noises.

"If you must know, Bridger *is* exceptional with his ... hose." I bust out laughing again at Bee's horrified expression, and then shake my head and hands both. "I'm kidding. Well, I'm not kidding, but I won't go into details."

"Ah, not fair," Polly says.

"Things are really good," I say instead. "He's kind and sweet, and he's a great dad."

"And he seems to be obsessed with you," Alex reminds me. "According to my sources."

"Sources that you won't divulge."

"Never." She flips her hair over her shoulder and takes a bite of her tart.

"I heard," Charlie adds, "that they were quite sweet at the drop-off line the other day. Or maybe that was today."

Was it today? This has been the longest day ever.

And it's not over yet.

"He likes me." I shrug and smile smugly. "And it's definitely reciprocated."

"I love this," Skyla says with a happy sigh as she reaches down to pet Riley between the ears. "I'm so happy that I found this group so soon after moving to town."

"And we're happy to have you," Bee replies. "Do you have any delicious, Irish brothers that might be single?"

Skyla's smile spreads. "You know, I might just."

"Well, bring them to town, friend," Charlie says with a wink. "We need more book boyfriend material."

Chapter Fifteen

BRIDGER

Kitten: *I'm headed your way now. Just leaving the bookstore.*

I grin and flick off the football game that I've had playing in the background.

Me: I can't wait to see you.

I'm glad that she went to her book club, but I'll be even happier when she's here and I have her all to myself.

I pad into Birdie's room to check on my daughter and smile when I see that she's sound asleep with Pickles curled up right next to her. I didn't have to do much convincing to get my girl into bed tonight because she was excited to have the cat with her. Not to mention, she's so tired. Lethargy has been one of her main symptoms for the past year anyway, but add on to that an illness and an asthma attack all in one day, and it's safe to say that Birdie will sleep like a rock tonight.

But I'll check on her several times anyway, just to be sure that she's okay.

The sound of a car door slamming comes from the front of the house, and I reach the front door at the same time as Dani.

"Hey," she says, keeping her voice low.

"Hey yourself." I pull her against me as I close the door behind her and frame her face so I can kiss the hell out of her. "Did you have fun?"

"It was so fun." She grins up at me. "I'm almost sad that we're only meeting once a month. How was everything here? Is Birdie still okay?"

"She's sleeping with Pickles," I inform her. "Go have a look. It's really cute."

Dani practically tiptoes down the hall, making me chuckle, and pokes her head in the door. When she backs out again, pulling the door not quite closed behind her, she has her bottom lip out.

"That's the cutest thing I've ever seen."

"Come on." I take her hand in mine and lead her farther down the hall to my bedroom. "I'm going to pamper you a bit tonight."

"Why?"

I blink and frown down at my girl. "Because I want to, sweetheart. I don't need a special occasion for it."

"Oh, well, okay then." She rubs her lips together nervously, and it makes me laugh as I take her shoulders in my hands.

"You're the only person I know who would look nervous in response to someone telling you they want to take care of you."

"That's not something that I'm used to." Her brows pinch together. "But it's nice when you do it."

Jesus. There's never a time when I forget what Dani went through as a girl, but there are moments when it kicks me in the stomach.

"Come on. Into the shower for you, and I'm going to pour you some wine. Are you hungry?"

"No, Jackie Harmon brought huckleberry tarts for everyone."

I give her a mock glare. "And you came home empty-handed?"

She smirks at me and toes off her shoes, then whips her shirt over her head, and my mouth goes fucking dry. Her tits are practically spilling out of her bra, and I want to get my hands on them.

"If you want treats, you have to join the book club." She unbuttons her jeans, and I have to turn away and focus on starting the shower, or else I'll boost her up against the wall and fuck her hard and fast, and that's not my plan for tonight. "And you have to read the books."

With the water on, I grab her a towel and place it on the warmer, and when I turn back to her, she's standing before me completely naked, and my cock is begging me to change plans for tonight.

Sorry, buddy.

"You're a walking wet dream, kitten."

She licks her lips and moves to fold her arms over her breasts, but I step forward and stop her, holding one wrist in one hand and using the backs of my fingers of the other to brush over one nipple.

"So fucking beautiful."

She sucks in a breath, and I let her go.

"Into the shower. Do you want red or white wine?"

"Neither," she says, watching me. "But some water would be good."

I nod and move to walk around her, but she catches my hand, and I stop, lifting a brow as I look down into her cobalt eyes.

"Thanks." Her lips tip up into a smile, and I know she knows the effect she's having on me.

My sweats are tented, for Christ's sake.

"You're welcome." After pressing a kiss to her forehead, I leave the bathroom and walk to the kitchen to get her a glass of water. After a brief check on Birdie to make sure she's still asleep, I return to my bedroom and set the water on the nightstand.

I showered after I put Birdie down, so I close and lock my door, and then undress and climb into bed, sitting against the headboard with the blankets over my lap as I check my social media and emails.

Before long, the water cuts off, and then soon after, my girl appears.

Still dewy from the shower, she turns off the light as she leaves the bathroom. The lamp next to me is the only light illuminating the bedroom as she walks, still nude, around the bed and climbs in on the other side, but she doesn't lie down or even sit next to me.

She takes the phone from my hands, sets it on the nightstand, and then, with that mischievous smile on her gorgeous face, Dani pulls the covers back and straddles me.

"Hi," she says, wrapping her arms around my neck. My dick's already rock-hard and ready for her. "This is the first time we've spent the night together since that first weekend."

"Too fucking long."

She leans in, but she doesn't kiss me. She presses her cheek to mine so sweetly that it makes my chest hurt. *This.* This is what I've missed. What I've needed every damn night. This beautiful girl in my arms.

My hands immediately rub up and down her back. I can't stop touching this woman. I can't get enough of her.

"I'm so glad you're here," I whisper into her ear as my hands glide down to cup the globes of her ass. "We have to be quiet tonight. Can you do that, sweetheart?"

"I can try."

I smile and kiss her neck and then shift us so that she's on her back and I'm looming over her.

"You have to do better than try." Lazily, I drag my lips down her neck to her collarbone. "Because I don't want any interruptions for a long while. I'm going to worship every fucking inch of you."

She sighs, her hands dive into my hair, and I pull a nipple between my lips, licking and nibbling on her. "Such an excellent mouth."

I smile against her smooth skin and then work my way farther south. I haven't had my mouth on her sweet pussy in weeks, and I'm about to rectify that right now.

She breaks out in goose bumps as I kiss down her stomach, my hand ahead of the game, already brushing through her wetness.

"Fuck, baby, you're so ready for me."

"Always." She sucks in a deep breath when I push one finger inside of her, arching into my touch. "Please, Bridger."

"You're soaked." I groan and kiss down her pubis, pressing my lips to her clit, before I pull my finger out of her and French-kiss her opening and pull those sexy fucking pussy lips into my mouth, and her back bows up off the bed. She squeaks, but I can tell that she's trying *so hard* to stay quiet.

"Bridger," she breathes, tugging and clawing at the bedsheets. "Oh, God."

"That's my girl," I murmur against her and press two fingers into her now, pushing my hips against the bed when she clamps around me. "Stay quiet, baby."

"Not easy."

My mouth is busy on her clit, my fingers working her over, and she's tugging on my hair, pulling me closer to her.

"You're so fucking delicious. Do you like it when I eat this pussy?"

"Yes."

"Tell me."

"I like it."

I bite the inside of her thigh. "You know what I want to hear."

"I love it when you eat my ... pussy."

"Good fucking girl." I reward her for that and hook my fingers up against that rough patch that will set her on fire and pull her clit into my mouth, working her over until I feel her muscles start to clench like a vise around my fingers.

She lets go of my hair, and I watch as she clamps her hand over her mouth, writhing as the first orgasm of the night wrenches through her. Her thighs press against me, and her upper body wants to twist away, so I reach up and hold her in place.

When she's coming down from her climax, I kiss her soft inner thighs and lick that crease where her leg meets her center, and then over to her hip.

"You're everything I've ever wanted in my life." I kiss that sensitive spot, on the underside of her breast, and she sighs. "Your body is a goddamn wonderland."

She starts to say something, but I cover her mouth with my hand.

"Every fucking inch of it," I insist. "Every dip and curve and valley. Did you know that you have two gorgeous dimples, right above your stellar ass?"

"Mmph pmmph."

I laugh and move my hand away.

"You'll have to be more specific. There are a lot of dimples on my backside."

I cock an eyebrow and then move closer to her face. "Well, now you've talked shit about my girl, and I don't like it when someone says anything like that about what's mine. So, you're going to have to pay for that."

Those stunning eyes widen, her eyes dilate a little more, and I can tell that that idea pleases her.

"Nothing to say now, I see." I kiss her chin, and my hand falls between her legs again, fingers brushing lightly over her clit, and she whimpers. "What do you want, sweetheart?"

"You."

I pull my hand away, and she frowns. "I want your cock inside of me."

"That's better, but it's not good enough to get you to come." Rubbing my nose along her jawline, I drag the tip of my cock through her soaking wet slit, and her fingernails dig into my shoulders. "You have to ask me."

"Please, Bridger."

"Please what, Dani?"

"Please."

I pull back from her, both my face and my cock, and wait. Dani licks her lips and looks down to where I'm holding the base of my dick, and her cheeks flush with need.

"Please fuck me." The last two words are a whisper. I push inside of her, bottoming out, and take her mouth with mine, and she wraps her arms and legs around me, holding me close.

"God." I bury my face in her neck, moving in and out of her in long, smooth strokes. "God, baby, you're incredible. You're so fucking amazing."

I take one of her hands and link our fingers together, kiss her hand, and then press it to the bed just above her head. Her other hand glides down to my ass, and I have space to look down to where we're joined together. *Fuck me*. I've never seen anything sexier than this.

"Touch your clit, kitten." She bites her lip, and with her eyes on mine, her hand moves from my ass to between us, and she presses her fingertips over that little nub, making her pull a sharp breath in through her nose. Her lips part into the sexiest *O*, and holy shit, this might have been a bad idea for my stamina. "That's it, baby. Ah, God, that makes you clench around me even tighter. Fucking hell."

She's so fucking tight, so *perfect*, that I can feel the orgasm building in me.

But she needs to come again first.

"Rub a little harder." I push in, pressing against her fingers with the base of my dick, and she groans. "Yes, baby, harder. Like that. God, you're incredible."

"Bridge," she gasps, and I feel it happening again, the quaking and clenching, and I know that she's so damn close. "Almost there."

I know what she needs. I lean in, pinning her hand right where it is, and whisper into her ear, "You are the sexiest damn woman I've ever fucking seen. I want you to come all over me, sweetheart. Let go. Let go, baby."

She bites my shoulder as the orgasm moves through her now, and I can't hold back anymore. I rock into her and push my release deep inside of her heat. Every time I'm with her I think it's the most intense orgasm of my life, but this is it.

Every muscle in my body is clenched from the ferociousness of coming inside of this woman.

"Christ," I mutter as I roll to my side, taking her with me, not willing to pull out of her yet.

"That's so much better than book sex," she says, obviously somewhat orgasm drunk.

"I hope so. Jesus, I fucking hope so." I grin at her and pull my fingers down her cheek. "You're so beautiful, Dani."

Her whole face softens, and she pulls my hand to her lips, pressing a sweet kiss to my palm. "So are you, Bridger."

"I want you to believe that when I say it. Don't brush me off, okay? Do you think I'd have a girlfriend who's anything less than fucking perfect?"

She snorts at that, but then leans in to rub her nose against mine. "Of course, you wouldn't."

"I like you here, in my bed. I'm going to keep you in it as much as possible. Birdie will be sad if she can't sleep with Pickles."

Now she giggles, and it makes me chuckle, too.

"I'll clean you up." I pull away and roll out of bed, headed for the bathroom.

"Oh, you don't have to. I can—"

"It's my mess. I'll clean it up."

I quickly rinse myself off and then wet a washcloth with warm water and return to her, thoroughly cleaning her, and then I toss the cloth into the laundry hamper.

"I'm putting pajamas on," she informs me as she crawls out of bed and pulls shorts and a tank out of her overnight bag.

I'll be making room for her clothes in my dresser as soon as possible.

"Good idea." After I've tugged on a T-shirt and my boxer briefs, I unlock the door and crack it open in case Birdie needs me, and then pull Dani into bed with me, and wrap myself around her. "Good night, kitten."

"'Night, Bridge."

"I'm *so* excited!" Birdie's practically bouncing in her seat. She's dressed in jeans and a Sidney Sterling T-shirt that matches Dani's. Birdie's hair is in braids, she's wearing boots, and she's vibrating with excitement.

It's concert day, and my girls are *ready.*

"I'm thrilled, too," Dani says, smiling back at Birdie. "I can't wait for her to sing "Life in the Slow Lane." And her whole new album is just so good."

They don't know it yet, but they're about to be even more excited. I hope there isn't any passing out.

"So, we're going early for parking, obviously," Dani says, turning to me. "But are you also being a bit of a workaholic, wanting to make sure the safety precautions are as they promised?"

"How do you know me so well already?" Pulling her hand up to my lips, I kiss her knuckles. "I'll just check in with everyone really quick. Remington called me and told me to park at the farmhouse with the rest of the family."

"That's nice of him," Dani says with a smile. "It's nice to know people."

Once we make our way onto the ranch, I deviate from the signs pointing to *Event Parking* and pull up behind the Wild family's farmhouse. There's already a line of cars here, all of them familiar.

"Holden's here," Dani says. "He and Millie must have come early, too. Oh, and Bee's here."

Everyone's here.

After I help Birdie out of the back, I guide the girls over to the shop that I know has been cleared out for this party.

"What's going on, Bridge?" Dani asks, frowning up at me. Birdie's walking between us, one hand in mine and one in Dani's.

"You'll see."

"You're here," Millie says, waving us in. "Just in time. This is so fun, I'm so glad that everyone came."

"No way," Dani whispers as Sidney Sterling, along with her husband and several other members of the Montgomery family walk into the shop, waving and smiling. "We get to *meet her*?"

"She wanted to hang with friends and family before the show," I tell Dani, leaning down to kiss her head. "Your brother's married to a Wild. And the Wild family is married to Sidney's family. So, here we are."

"Daddy," Birdie says with a shriek. "Oh, my gosh. Look!"

I pick my daughter up so she can see better, and Sidney must have heard her because she smiles our way and waves at my daughter, who is now suddenly shy and buries her face in my neck.

I shrug at Sidney but wave back at her, and she laughs.

Dani slips her hand into my free one, and we're sucked into the crowd of our friends and family, chatting and laughing.

And then *I* stop dead in my tracks because a man just walked in, and it's Leo Nash. The lead singer of Nash.

My favorite band of all time.

"Holy shit," I whisper, and Dani grins up at me.

"Weird, isn't it?"

"So damn weird."

"But also super cool." Dani kisses my shoulder, and I notice Holden watching us. "Hey, big brother."

"Hey." He pulls Dani in for a hug. "Do I need to kill him?"

"No." Dani laughs and smacks him gently on the arm. "We're good. I haven't seen you enough lately."

"We'll have dinner at the house," Holden replies. "All of us."

"We're in," I reply with a grin, and Holden narrows his eyes at me, making me laugh.

"Have you met Leo Nash yet?"

"Are you kidding? I was waiting for you. Let's go."

Thinking that Birdie might loosen up if we make our way to Sidney slowly, I follow Holden over to where Leo Nash is chatting with a group of guys.

"Leo," Rem says, pointing to us, "this is my brother-in-law, Holden Lexington, and our very good friend, Bridger Blackwell."

"Ah, I've heard about the fire chief," Leo says with a laugh as he comes to shake our hands. "You gave our safety crew a run for their money."

"Safety first," I remind him with a grin, shaking his hand. "I'm glad we got it all worked out."

"It's nice to meet you," Holden adds.

"Daddy," Birdie says, still a little shy, "can I go over with Holly and Daisy and Johnny?"

I glance over to where the Wild kids are hanging out together and set my girl down. "Sure, go have fun, baby girl."

She runs off, and I scan the building, looking for Dani. When I find her, she's with my sister and several of the Wild wives, along with her sisters, laughing with Sidney. She looks completely at home here, surrounded by her friends, and that sets me at ease.

"Hey, guys, I'm Keaton, Sid's ball and chain." The man who just joined us nods at each of us. "I'm going to hang out here, where there's less estrogen."

"Need a beer?" Leo asks him with a grin.

"No, I have to play tonight. Sid's pulling me up on stage."

"What do you play?" I ask him.

"Piano," he replies. "I never should have shown her that I can play. Whenever I'm at a show, she makes me join her. I'm not a performer."

"Sounds like you are now," Holden says with a chuckle.

"Excuse me, guys." Dani slips her hand into mine and presses herself against my side. "Can I steal my boyfriend, please?"

Fuck yes, you can have me any way you want me.

"You're being summoned," Keaton says, and with a nod, I follow Dani across the room.

"You don't want to miss this," she says, and she's right, because Sidney has just approached the kids, and she's squatting before them, hugging them and saying hello to all of them.

Sidney isn't in her concert costume yet. She's in leggings and a sweatshirt, but her makeup and hair are both done.

And my daughter has fucking stars in her eyes.

"Hi," Birdie says quietly. "You're my favorite."

"I am?" Sidney smiles and opens her arms, inviting my daughter in for a hug.

Thank God Dani has the bandwidth to be taking a video with her phone right now.

"Thank you," Sidney says and kisses Birdie's head. "I am so happy that I came here to hang out with all of you. Are you excited for the show?"

All of them jump up and down, telling her how they can't wait to hear Sidney sing, and it's really the cutest thing.

"Do you guys want some photos?" Dani asks them.

"Yes!"

Sidney takes turns posing with each of the kids, and then with them as a group.

"I brought presents for all of you, and I hope you like

the show. And I also hope I get to see you the next time I'm in town. Maybe we can ride horses together or something."

"You can ride our horses," Johnny, Remington's son, says with a nod. "Anytime you want."

When Sidney stands, she turns to us.

"Be sure to tag me on social media so I can share. Also, hello, handsome. I don't think we've met yet." She holds her hand out for me, and I shake it. This whole situation feels completely surreal.

"Bridger," I reply. "Nice to meet you."

"Oh, *you're* Bridger." Sidney turns to Dani and laughs. "My team was both impressed and irritated by your man."

Dani laughs with her and glances up my way. "He does have a tendency to dig his heels in to get what he wants."

"I'm right here, ladies."

Sidney laughs again, and then she's called over to chat with someone else.

"Did you like this surprise?" I ask Dani when we're alone.

"This was incredible." She rises on her tiptoes but is still too short to meet my lips, so I bend down to cover her mouth with mine. "Just like you."

Chapter Sixteen

DANI

This is, quite possibly, the best day of my life thus far.

Not only am I at a Sidney Sterling concert, which has been on my bucket list for eons but never thought I could afford the tickets, but said show is in my home town, and my boyfriend, who is *Bridger Blackwell*, is dancing with me.

I never thought any of those words would cross my mind in a sentence, let alone be true.

But, here we are. It's not even a dream. It's real.

Bridger seems to be content with the safety situation, and I have to admit, people are so happy to be here, there really hasn't been anything bad happening, that I've seen anyway. If there has been an incident, it was handled quickly and quietly, the rest of us none the wiser.

We're still with our group of friends and family, in a section near the stage that was roped off just for us, and I'm pretty sure this is what it feels like to be a VIP.

How am I supposed to settle for nosebleed seats after this?

"I can't see Birdie," I yell to Bridger, looking around our group.

"She's in front," he says. "Dancing with Daisy. I have eyes on her."

I nod, relieved, and then Sidney introduces her band, including her hot-as-Hades husband, Keaton Williams, before she sits on the stool next to his piano and starts to sing a slow song that I love, making googly eyes at her man the whole time. It's so romantic. And I do not miss the smug smile on Keaton's lips as he plays the piano.

Holy hotness, Batman.

Bridger wraps his arms around my shoulders from behind, swaying us back and forth with the music, and I melt back against him, my head leaning against his chest and my hands gripping his arms as he moves us in rhythm with the music.

Being in Bridger's arms is my favorite place to be. Nothing makes me feel more special or more cared for than when my man holds me against him.

"You're so fucking beautiful," Bridger says into my ear, sending tingles through me. "Your ass looks amazing in these jeans. I can't keep my hands off you."

I grin and look up at him. "The jeans worked, then?"

He nods, and when I look back to the stage, he plants his mouth by my ear again, and my panties are officially soaked.

"I saw the guy flirting with you when you went to get us drinks."

I frown. "There was no—"

"I saw him," he says again, perfectly calm, without a hint of jealousy. "But *I'm* the only one who gets to hold you and touch you. And it's such a fucking turn-on, knowing that you're all mine, sweetheart."

I have to take a deep breath to calm my hormones down because I'd like to pull him away and try to find a quiet spot to have my way with him, but I also wouldn't leave this show for anything in the world, so I just need to resign myself to being hot and bothered for the rest of the concert.

One of the things that I enjoy about going to shows like this is some of the people-watching. It makes me happy to see others so excited and having a good time, so I take a second to glance around at the crowd, smiling because so many of us are singing along with Sidney, and the happiness is contagious.

My eyes skim over a face that's all too familiar, and I freeze, but then a tall man walks in front of my line of vision, and when he's gone, so is the person I thought I saw.

No way.

I shake my head and turn back to the show. There's no way I saw that.

"What's wrong?" Bridger asks against my ear.

"Nothing." I shake my head, but he holds me closer.

"You went pale on me, sweetheart. What's wrong?"

I look up at him and cup his cheek. "I'm fine. I thought I saw someone, but I was mistaken. Honest."

He narrows his eyes, and for a minute, I think he'll

push a little, but then his gaze falls to my lips, and he's suddenly kissing me for all he's worth, here in the middle of this huge crowd amongst all of the people we love.

I guess my man has no issue with public displays of affection.

When the show's over, Bridger walks with us back to the Wild farmhouse, where Birdie and I will hang out with the others while Bridger helps with the traffic control back into town.

"That was the best concert I've ever been to," Bee says with a happy sigh as she leans against me and rests her head on my shoulder. I have Birdie in my lap, snoozing away, and Alex is sitting on the other side of me.

We're all wiped out, in the best way, talking about the show and waiting for traffic to thin so we can all go home.

"I'm glad to hear it," Sidney herself says as she walks into the room. She's already dressed in leggings and a T-shirt, her hair and makeup still done, and she collapses into a chair next to Erin. "It was the most fun I've had at a show in a long time."

"Don't you have VIP photos and stuff to do?" Erin asks her.

"I did them," Sidney responds with a happy sigh. "I did a bunch before the show, too. I snuck away to come hang out with you guys."

"We are the most fun," Blake replies with a laugh. "How can you do what you do? Obviously, you're in great shape, but you sang and danced for two solid hours, Sidney. What kind of training does that include?"

"When I was gearing up for the world tour," she begins, "I sang every single song in my catalog while running on the treadmill."

The whole room rumbles at that.

"You're kidding," Alex says.

"No, ma'am. I don't lip-sync, ever. Now, remember, there are some numbers that I'll sit on a stool and sing, and that is when I rest. Then, it's time to move again. It's rigorous. I have a specific diet and a nutritionist who goes on tour with us because I want to deliver the best show out there. I know that it's an investment, and I'd be mortified if anyone ever walked away disappointed."

"I don't see that happening," I reply. *Holy shit, am I talking to* Sidney Sterling? "Your concert has been on my bucket list for years, and this surpassed all my expectations."

"And that, right there," Sidney says as she points my way, "is why we do it. Your daughter is adorable, by the way."

I feel a pang in my heart as I brush my fingers over Birdie's dark hair. "Thank you, but she's not mine."

But, oh, how I wish she was. I don't think I could love this peanut more if she'd come from my body.

"She fits with you," Sidney says, and then is pulled into another conversation, and I feel my eyes fill with tears.

"She's right," Bee says softly next to me. "Birdie fits with you, and you fit with them."

I nod and take a deep breath.

"I know."

It's been back to regular life since the concert on Saturday night. Some of my kids were a little cranky today in school because they were still tired from the show, so we took it easy in class.

Now that school is out for the day, and all the kids have been picked up, I'm more than ready to go home and get comfortable. In the past couple of weeks, I've spent every night at Bridger's house, and Pickles hasn't been moved back to my rental.

I go back and forth to get clothes or things I need, but for all intents and purposes, I'm basically living with my boyfriend and his adorable daughter.

And I'm not sad about it.

In fact, it's the best thing that's ever happened to me. When Bridger's working, I pick Birdie up from her sitter and take her home with me. We have an evening routine down pat already. If Bridger's home, we cook dinner together and settle into a similar routine.

We make love every night.

I've never felt so cherished. Due to my hang-ups and trauma, I've never really been in a relationship before, certainly not one that feels so *right*. As if I was supposed to be here all along. I've never felt so comfortable in my own skin either, and I can attribute that to Bridger's attentive and loving nature. I feel ... safe.

There are a few other teachers leaving at the same time as me, and we smile and wave at each other, but it's raining, coming down in sheets, so we run for our respective cars.

However, once inside of mine, it won't start.

"Shoot." I try again, but it doesn't even try to turn over. With a deep sigh, I lean my head back on the headrest. I don't want to walk home in this downpour.

Suddenly, someone knocks on my window, and I open the door to find Stephen, a second-grade teacher, frowning at me.

"Won't start?" he asks.

"No. It's dead."

"Come on, I'll give you a lift."

"I have my snack tote with me today," I tell him.

"I have room. I'll get it for you." He gestures for me to follow him, waiting with his umbrella as I gather my things and then rush over to his SUV with him. He holds the door open for me as I sit inside, and then he rushes back to my car for the tote and back to his own, stowing it in the back, then walks around to the driver's side.

Stephen's a really nice guy. He's helped me out a lot since I came on staff, not to mention he's handsome. But he's never crossed the professional line with me, and I've always felt comfortable with him.

"Sorry about this," I say when he starts his vehicle.

"Don't be. I'm just sorry that your car is dead in the water."

"Yeah. I'll call Brooks when I get home to get a tow to his shop. I'm over on Pine Avenue."

"Got it," he says with a nod and pulls out of the parking space. "Did you go to the concert the other night?"

"I did. It was so great. How about you?"

"Yeah, I went with some friends. She puts on a great show. Were your kids a little grouchy today, or was it just mine?"

"No, it was definitely mine, too. They're probably still tired from all the excitement. Hang a left here, and then I'm three houses down on the left."

"Got it." He follows my directions and pulls into my driveway. "You go on up to the porch. I'll get your tote."

"You'll get soaked. I can do it."

"My mother would kill me if I let that happen." He offers me a lopsided smile, and I give in with a nod. "There. That wasn't so hard, was it?"

"Thanks, Stephen." With a chuckle, I climb out of his car and hurry over to the porch, watching as he opens the back of the car and grabs the tote, carrying it to me. "I appreciate it."

"It's my pleasure, really. If you need a ride to school tomorrow, just let me know. I'll give you my number."

"Oh, that would be great. Here, just let me ..." I pull my phone out of my pocket, unlock it, and pass it to Stephen, who adds his number to my contacts.

I also hear Bridger's door close and look over to see him walking toward us, his face not happy in the least.

"Stephen, do you know Bridger Blackwell?"

Stephen's head comes up with a frown, and then he must hear the other man approaching because he glances behind him and nods.

"I do. Hey, Bridger, I didn't realize you lived across the street."

"Yeah," my man says as he slips his arm around my shoulders, pulling me against him. "I do. What's going on here?"

"Oh, my car decided to die on the wettest day of the year, and Stephen gave me a ride home."

"Here you go, Dani. My number's in there." Stephen passes me my phone, smiling softly at me, and Bridger stiffens beside me. When I look up, his dark eyes are *furious.*

"In case I need another ride tomorrow."

"She won't," Bridger says, turning his attention back to Stephen. "But thanks for taking care of my girl today. I appreciate it."

He holds out his hand for Stephen to shake. The other man looks at me with a quizzical smile and then back at Bridger.

"Of course." He takes Bridger's hand, and I can see that Bridger's grip is *just* too tight. "Like I said, happy to help."

He pulls away, nods at me, and then walks down to his car, pulling out of my driveway.

"What was that?" I ask, frowning up at the angry man beside me. He's practically vibrating. "Why the dick-measuring contest?"

His eyebrow climbs. "Don't look now, sweetheart, but you just swore."

"Yeah, I'm kind of mad at you."

"*You're* mad at *me*?"

"Yes." I roll my eyes and unlock my door, walking inside. It smells a little musty, like it hasn't been lived in much.

Because it hasn't.

"You were rude to him, and there was no reason to be."

"I was perfectly calm. Trust me, I wanted to punch him in the face, so you should be pleased with how that all went down."

I set my things aside and prop my hands on my hips as I face him. "What? Why? He just gave me a ride home in the rain because my car died. He was totally nice to me."

Bridger's jaw tightens, and his hands flex into fists at his sides.

"Bridge, are you okay?"

"No." He shakes his head and walks slowly to me. "I'm *not* okay when another man drives you home, walks you to the door, and puts his motherfucking phone number in your goddamn contacts, Dani. There's nothing about that scenario that is in the vicinity of okay."

"Bridger." I sigh and close my eyes. My man is beyond jealous, and he has no reason to be. "I'm yours. You know that. I'm not interested in Stephen at all, even if I was single, which I'm not. He's just a friendly

249

coworker who saw that I had car trouble and helped me out. It was completely innocent."

"For you." He tips my chin up, finally touching me. "But I saw the look in his eyes when he looked at you, and it's not innocent for him."

"That doesn't matter," I insist. "My intentions are what matter here, and there aren't any intentions with that man. He's just a nice guy. End of story."

Bridger shakes his head and then his lips are on mine, hard and unrelenting, as his hands dive into my hair, holding me in place so he can plunder my mouth. With a groan, I lean into him, fisting my hands in the shirt at his sides, immediately ready for him.

I'm *always* ready for him.

I'm in a skirt today, and he bunches it up around my waist as he picks me up and carries me to the kitchen where he sets me at the edge of the countertop, and his fingers pull my panties aside, and then a finger slips through my already wet folds, making me groan.

"That's from you," I manage to say against his lips. "Only you."

"Damn right." He hits his knees, and his mouth is on me, sending me straight into a climax so hard and fast, I see stars. "This is mine, Dani. *Mine.* Fuck, do you have any idea how hot you are in this skirt? I've wanted to fuck you in it for weeks."

"I'll wear it more often." I groan and then gasp when he pushes his tongue inside of me. My thighs rest on his shoulders, and my ass is off the counter, in the air as he plunders me with that magical mouth, and all I can do is brace myself on the countertop with my hands. "Oh, God."

"My name is the only one you'll cry out when I'm fucking you, kitten. Do you understand me?"

He's so *intense.* As if he's proving a point, but he doesn't have to.

I already know.

I'm so in love with him, I can't see anyone else.

"Bridger." My hips are moving against his mouth, the sound of my desire for him loud and almost obscene in the complete quiet. "Inside me. Please."

He kisses my inner thigh, and then I'm in his arms again, and he's moving us to the couch, where he sets me down and starts taking off his clothes.

"Lie back," he says through gritted teeth.

"I'm still dressed—"

"Lie. The fuck. Back."

I've never seen this side to him before. This animalistic, out-of-control version of Bridger that intrigues me and has me on edge at the same time.

As he yanks off his clothes, I do what he wants, lying on my back on the cushions of the couch, still fully dressed.

When he's naked, he reaches under my skirt and pulls my panties off, tossing them over his shoulder, and then he crawls over me, nestles the head of his cock against my entrance, and pins me in his gaze.

"I'll remind you as often as it takes that you're mine." He thrusts inside me so hard, so deep, that I gasp with the twinge of pain, and then he starts to move, and it's absolutely amazing. "If you need a ride, you call *me*. If I'm not available, I'll find someone for you."

I swallow hard, my eyes pinned to his. I couldn't look away from him if I tried.

"Do you understand?"

I nod.

"Use your fucking words, sweetheart."

"I understand." I groan when he hits that perfect spot that lights me up inside. "I'm yours, Bridge. I promise."

My words ignite something in him because he suddenly buries his face in my neck and growls, and I can feel him start to come inside of me, and it sends me over on another wave of absolute bliss.

He's shuddering over me, inside of me, breathing hard, and I can't help but run my hands down his back, up his sides, soothing him.

"I'm yours," I keep repeating to him, whispering words of comfort. "Only yours."

Finally, he takes one long, deep breath and then rises up on his elbows, brushing my hair off my cheeks with his thumbs.

"Did I hurt you?" He gently kisses my swollen lips. "Was I too rough, baby?"

"No." Unable to stop touching him, I drag my fingertips down his cheek. "I loved it."

He cocks an eyebrow at that. "Yeah? What else do you love?"

My heart stutters. I've never told anyone but my siblings and Bee that I love them.

"I can start," he says, whispering against my cheek. "I love the sound of your name on my lips."

Oh, God.

"I love the way you smile at me when you first see me in the morning."

I can't help but tighten my grip on him. I feel tears fill my eyes, but he keeps talking, looking down at me.

"I love it when we're making dinner together and you hum while you cut the vegetables."

He kisses me softly.

"I love the way you are with my daughter, so funny and sweet. It always makes my chest hurt, watching the two of you together."

One tear slips down the side of my face, and he catches it with his thumb.

"Baby, I love the way I feel when I'm inside of you, and I love the way you make me feel when I'm with you."

This kiss is soft, and his tongue slips between my lips and brushes over mine, giving me goose bumps.

"I love you, Dani. I love everything about you."

Tears run unchecked now as I frame his gorgeous face in my hands. "I love you, too. So much. More than I thought possible."

"Thank God because otherwise, I was about to feel really stupid."

I laugh, and then he pulls us both up and rearranges us so I'm sitting in his lap. He brushes my hair back from my shoulder and then pulls his knuckles down my cheek.

"Say it again," he whispers.

"Which part?"

He narrows his eyes, and I chuckle as I lay my lips over his. "I love you, Bridger Blackwell. For a million reasons."

"Mostly because of my dick, though, right?"

I snort and then laugh outright, shaking my head. "Surprisingly, that ranks in the top three, but it's not at the top." I can't stop touching him. "I love how special you make me feel. And I love your daughter."

He takes a long, shaky breath.

"And then your ... dick."

He chuckles and then crushes his mouth to mine. "I can live with that."

Chapter Seventeen

BRIDGER

"I love tacos," Birdie announces as we join Holden and Millie in the kitchen.

The house they rent in town is small, but the weather has been nice enough today that they opened the door to the screened-in back patio, giving extra seating space for not only the Lexington family, but also for Millie, Birdie, and me.

"I think that just about everyone loves tacos," Holden says, offering his hand to my daughter for a high five. "And they were extra good tonight because you helped me chop the tomatoes."

Dani's on the patio, sharing margaritas with all three of her sisters, and I'm in the kitchen, nursing a beer, since we were able to walk over here for dinner, chatting with my two best friends as we finish cleaning up from dinner.

Holden and Millie got married early this year, after dancing around each other for the better part of a decade. They're two of my favorite people, and I'm glad that they finally ended up together.

"We've decided," Millie begins, "that we need to have family dinners more often. Everyone's so busy, and if we don't make time for it, we just never see anyone."

"Makes sense to me." I turn when all four girls on the patio start to cackle, and smile at Dani through the screen door. "Looks like it's a hit."

"They're just here for the margaritas," Holden says, but Millie shakes her head.

"No, they miss their big brother," she says and kisses his shoulder as she walks past him toward the patio. "I'm going out to chat. Come on, Birdie, come sit with the girls."

"Okay." Birdie jumps off her stool and follows Millie outside.

"Holden, it's time you and I had a talk." My voice is low because I want this to be a private conversation.

"I figured this was coming." He blows out a breath and crosses his arms over his chest. "I see how you look at my sister. It's as if she's the best thing you've ever seen in your life."

I send him a toothy grin. "She is. I'm in love with her, and I don't plan on ever letting her go. Hell, if I have my way, she'll be living with us before Christmas."

Holden's eyebrows climb into his hairline. "That's fast, buddy."

"Not fast enough. Hell, I'd marry her tomorrow if she'd say yes. And that'll be another conversation we'll have to have."

My friend sighs and drags his hand down his face, leaning back against the counter. "I've known you all of my life. Your family was always our safe place, Bridge. You're one of my closest friends, and I know the kind of man you are. If I had a problem with you and my sister together, I would have said something all those weeks ago when you came to me at the ranch. Scratch that," he says, reconsidering. "I would have beaten the hell out of you."

"You could have tried."

Holden rolls his eyes, and I smirk at him. "The point is, Dani's an adult. She can date who she wants."

"Yeah, but you're the only father figure she's ever had, man. You're the one who raised her, protected her. Loved her. The respectful thing to do is to have a conversation with you and tell you that I love her, and she's mine now."

His eyes darken at that. "Yours?"

"Are you going to stand there and tell me that Millie isn't yours?" I nod when his brows pull together in a frown. "Exactly. Your sister is mine. I'll make sure she never wants for anything, and that includes a safe place. I'm her safe place. Have been since she was little."

"I know. Bridger, what she and the others went through—"

"I know most of it and what I wasn't aware of, she's filling in the holes as bad moments come up. Which, you'll be happy to hear, aren't all that often."

His shoulders drop at that.

"She won't go near the chickens at the ranch, and she has a panic attack whenever they're mentioned."

He takes a swig of his beer and nods. "Yeah. And you know why?"

"I do. Fuck, Holden." I push my hand through my hair and pace away from him, and then back again. "Fuck."

"Listen, you're as much a brother to me as it gets. All of you are my family," Holden says as he sets his beer aside and crosses his arms over his chest again. "You know I'm not going to tell you to stay away from my girl. We already talked this out."

I nod, and when he reaches out to shake my hand, I don't hesitate to take it, and then pull him in for a hug.

"But like I told you before, you hurt her, and it's over for you. Family or not."

I grin at him. "I have a daughter, you know. I get it. I won't ever intentionally hurt her. I just want to love her, man."

"Are you guys ever going to come out here?" Dani calls to us. "Darby has something to tell all of us, and we need you guys."

Holden and I grab our beers and join the others on the patio.

I pull Dani out of her seat, take it, and then tug her into my lap, and she happily loops her arms around my shoulders.

"How precious," Charlie says, batting her eyelashes at us.

"What if I want to sit in your lap?" Birdie asks with a frown, and I do believe this is the first time that my daughter has shown any jealousy when it comes to Dani.

WHEN WE BURN

"Oh, you can sit—" Dani starts to get up, but I hold her firm against me and smile at my daughter. We need to set a precedent here.

"*Do* you want to sit in my lap, peanut?"

"No. But what if I did?"

I crook my finger at her, and she walks to my side. I brush my hand over her soft hair. "Then you just say so. Okay?"

"Okay."

Birdie runs back over to Alex, who was braiding her hair, and sits between her legs. Dani leans her head on my shoulder, and I plant my lips on her forehead, breathing her in.

"What's up, Darby?" Holden asks as he wraps an arm around his wife.

The eldest Lexington sister takes a deep breath and then says, "I'm moving."

There's shocked silence. I feel Dani stiffen in my arms, and she sits upright, staring at her sister.

"Like, across town?" Dani asks.

"No." Darby shakes her head. Holden's eyes have narrowed, and Millie links her fingers with his. "Look, you know that I love it here, and I love all of you, but there's got to be something better out there for me. I work my ass off and never get ahead. I never was good at making friends, and the men here are ridiculous. No offense, guys."

I grin at her, and Holden doesn't say anything at all.

"Holden and you girls have your lives figured out," Darby continues, pushing her hand through her dark

259

hair. Her blue eyes are shiny. "And I don't. I didn't go to college because ... well, we all know why."

Holden's hand tightens on his beer.

"I'm ready to figure my shit out, too. I'm going to vet school in Colorado. I have to do some prereqs first, but I want to work with animals."

"Oh, my God, that's amazing," Charlie says. "Darby, you'd be so good at that!"

"Vet school?" Alex asks with a frown. "With *animals*? The one thing we all avoid?"

"I'm over avoiding shit because the dumpster fire who sired us ruined everything in the world. Animals are awesome. They're better than people, and I'm going to help them. I'm through with being afraid. He's dead and gone, and it's time I live my life."

"Good for you," I say before I can hold the words in, and Darby's eyes, so much like her siblings', turn to me. "I know, I don't have a say here—"

"You're our family," Darby says, shaking her head.

"Thank you." Dani rubs my arm as I smile softly at her sister. "I think it's brave and badass of you to do this."

"Agreed," Holden says, and then clears his throat. "You know I'll pay for school. That's not a problem."

"I'm counting on it," Darby replies with a half laugh. "But even if you won't—"

"I will."

"I'll take out loans because I want to do this."

"When do you have to leave?" Dani asks. I can hear

the tears in her voice, and it makes me want to pull her to me.

"I'll start in January," Darby replies. "But I'll probably move down there in November, find housing, get a job. All the things. But, of course, I'll come home for Christmas. Did I mention I've already been accepted to the school?"

"Of course, you have," Alex says. "You're brilliant."

Holden stands and pulls his sister into his arms, hugging her close. "I'm so proud of you, sweet girl."

And just like that, Darby starts to cry in her brother's arms, and all three sisters surround them in a group hug.

Birdie looks at me with wide eyes, and I wink at her, letting her know that everything's okay, but my daughter still crosses to me and stands next to me.

"They're happy," I murmur to her.

"Oh, okay," Birdie whispers as she leans on my shoulder.

Millie and I share a look. She wipes a tear from her cheek, and then we nod and stand from our seats. I pick up Birdie and carry her inside.

"They need a minute," I tell my daughter as I set her on the stool at the island.

"I hate that they didn't have parents to lean on," Millie says, wiping her eyes, "but I love that they have each other."

"Darby's going to be awesome." I glance outside and see Holden wiping the tears from Darby's cheeks. "It's going to be scary, but she'll kick ass."

"I can't imagine starting college in my mid-thirties," Millie says, shaking her head. "That's incredible."

"It's not like we're old, you know."

"You are old," Birdie says as if she's breaking bad news to me, patting me on the shoulder, and Millie busts up laughing. "Sorry, Dad."

"Why are we sorry?" Dani asks as she walks through the door, wiping the last of her tears away.

"Dad's old," Birdie replies.

"Oh, I knew that."

I narrow my eyes on her. "Get over here."

With a sassy grin on her delectable lips, she saunters over to me. "Yes?"

Leaning in, I press my lips to her ear and whisper, "That's one less orgasm for you tonight."

"I have a secret for you," she says. "It was worth it."

We're absolutely, squarely into fall. Now that we're into the middle of October, all the trees are in the process of shedding their leaves. My parents will be here tonight for the next week so Mom can do all her favorite fall activities, and the weather will continue to get colder.

Brooks is finally finished fixing Dani's car, so I'm walking over to my brother's automotive garage to pick it up for her. I had the day off after a particularly grueling six straight days of work.

The arsonist struck again this week.

262

The motherfucker.

A bell dings when I push the door open and walk inside of my brother's business. It smells like motor oil and tires, and I grin at Brooks when his head pops up out of an engine.

"Hey," he calls out, wiping his hands on a rag.

"Bad time?"

"Nah, it's fine. You here for Dani's car?"

I nod and lean on the counter. Brooks is the oldest of us. He's in his late thirties and is built like a brick shithouse.

Whatever the hell that means.

We're all big guys. It's in the genes. But Brooks puts in extra hours in the gym, and it shows.

"How much do I owe you?" I ask him.

"Nothing." He shakes his head and takes a drink of water. "It was a cheap part, but it was a bitch tearing the engine apart to replace it."

"I'll pay you for your time, you know."

"Dude, you're my brother. I'm not taking your money. How is Dani, anyway?"

"I haven't seen her much over the last week or so, but she's good. She had a run-in with a parent last week. The mom of some kid came into her class and accused Dani of trying to force-feed the kid sugar. Apparently, the kid had never had sugar before and asked Dani for a snack from her snack closet, and she gave it to him. He discovered the beautiful world of sugar, and the mom was *not* happy."

"Did Dani get into trouble for that?"

"No, because the mom didn't put it in her son's paperwork that he's not allowed to have sweet treats. She just trusted him to know better."

"How did Dani do standing up for herself?" Brooks's eyes soften.

"She told the mom that if she had a problem with the snacks in her closet, maybe she should contribute to the stash so her son had things to eat during the day."

"Good going, Dani."

"Right? I was proud of her. Are you going to see Mom and Dad tonight?"

"Nah, I'll have a late night here tonight, but I'll catch up with them tomorrow. You?"

"I'll see what Dani wants to do."

Brooks grins at me. "She's just running the show now, huh?"

"It's considerate to take her wants and needs into consideration, you jerk face."

Brooks laughs and then passes me Dani's keys. "It's parked out front. I'll see you soon."

"Thanks, man."

Dani will be finished with school in just a little while, and given I haven't seen her much lately, I'm hoping that she votes to stay home. I thought I'd get some good takeout for my girls, watch a movie, and then after Birdie goes to bed, I'm going to fuck my woman senseless for most of the night.

It's a solid plan.

Chapter Eighteen

DANI

Today has sucked.

Badly.

It might have been the worst day of my teaching career so far, and while I know that six school years into said career isn't a lot, it's enough to know the worst day ever, and this was it.

It's Friday, and that's my only saving grace.

Because between *two* kids messing their pants, one kid deciding to be a cannibal and bite three students before I could stop her, and a parent who demanded to know why I'm not teaching her child multiplication—they're five, ma'am—I'm ready to forget that I'm a teacher at all.

"Are you excited to see your grandma and grandpa?" I ask Birdie as she slips her hand into mine, and we walk outside for after-school pickup.

"Yeah, we're going apple picking tomorrow," she

says. "And maybe even go to the punkin patch on Sunday."

"That'll be a fun weekend. Did you know that I know how to make apple butter?"

"You do?" Birdie grins up at me, her eyes going wide. "What is that, anyway?"

"It's something delicious to spread on toast or biscuits or just about anything. I'll make us some. Do you want to help?"

"Definitely."

She nods, making me smile, and now the day is starting to melt away, and even I'm looking forward to the weekend with Bridger and his family.

"Birdie!"

My hand tightens on Birdie's at the sound of that voice, and a chill runs down my back.

I wasn't wrong.

It was *her.*

Has she been in town since the concert?

"Birdie, oh, baby. It's so good to see you."

Angela's smiling at the girl at my side, who moves behind my legs and clings to me.

"Now, is that any way to greet your mama?" Angela looks up at me and plasters on a fake smile. "Hey, Dani. So good to see you. I'm picking Birdie up today."

"No." I shake my head firmly as adrenaline surges through me. *Over my dead freaking body, you bitch.* "You're not. You're not on the approved pickup list."

Angela scoffs at that. "I'm her mother. Of course, I

can pick her up. Come with me, baby. We're going to go have some fun."

She lunges for Birdie, who starts to cry, and I block Angela's way.

"You won't touch her," I say, catching Stephen's eye, and I call out to him. "Call the police."

He immediately pulls his phone out of his pocket, and I turn all my attention to the horrible woman in front of me. It should be illegal for her to still be pretty. Even as the nastiest girl in school, boys liked her. Seeing her is putting me in a bad headspace, and I can feel my shoulders stiffening.

Why her? Out of all of the women in the world, why did he have to sleep with her?

"Jesus, you're being so fucking dramatic." Angela rolls her eyes and tosses her perfectly curled blond hair over her shoulder. "Bridger knows that I'm picking her up."

"If that were true, he would have signed something with the office, and I would have been notified."

And he would have texted or called me.

"Give me my daughter."

"Not on this or any other day."

Her eyes narrow, and her mouth peels back in a sneer. "You stupid, fat, worthless piece of shit. Did you think that I wouldn't find out about you two? That my friends wouldn't see you and then call me so we could laugh about how fucking pathetic you are? Do you think he loves you? Fuck, no. You're a distraction. You probably begged him to let you spread your legs for him, didn't you?"

"What the *fuck* is going on?"

A crying Birdie is lifted into Bridger's arms, and she buries her face in his neck. Angela's eyes widen, and she takes a step back. She was obviously too focused on tearing me down to notice him walking up behind me.

At the same moment, a police car pulls up to us, the lights flashing. I recognize the cop as Rod DuVall, a guy I've known for a long time.

"She wouldn't let me have my baby," Angela says, as her eyes fill with tears. "I just want my daughter."

"No." Bridger's voice is ice cold. "You don't. You made that clear a long, long time ago."

Bridger turns to Rod.

"She's not allowed to see Birdie, let alone pick her up from school, and she knows it."

"We could call this attempted kidnapping," he says, and Angela's face goes white.

"I didn't do anything wrong." She licks her lips and then glares at me. "I fucking hate you. You stay away from my family, you hear me?"

"They're not your family," I say, speaking through the absolute rage that's boiling through me. "They're *mine*. And you'll never touch her again."

"Ma'am," Rod says, taking Angela's arm. "You have to come with me. Bridge, you need to get a restraining order."

"Consider it done," Bridger says with a nod.

I'm shaking as Rod leads Angela away.

"Thanks for calling the police," I say to Stephen, who's walked over to see if we're okay.

"Thank you," Bridger echoes, nodding at the other man.

"Of course. You handled that really well, Dani. Have a good weekend."

A small crowd has gathered, but they're dispersing now, and I am shaking like a freaking leaf from the adrenaline.

"I have to close down my classroom."

"We're with you," Bridger says, but first, he grips my chin and makes me look up at him for the first time. His brown eyes are full of anger and love and concern, and I bite my lip to keep from crying.

"Not here. Please."

He searches my face and then nods once, looping his free arm around my shoulders. "Let's get you finished up here so we can go home."

"Who was that lady?" Birdie asks, sniffling away the last of her tears. "She scared me."

"She's no one to worry about," Bridger assures her, kissing her cheek. "It's okay, peanut."

"She said mean things."

I take a shaky breath as we walk into my classroom. I'm just gathering my purse and coat, turning off the lights, when the principal, Miss Shephard, pokes her head in.

"I heard what happened. Dani, if you have time this weekend, would you please email me a statement so we have it on file?"

"Of course."

She smiles at me reassuringly. "I hear you did very well. Thank you."

When she's gone, I close and lock my classroom, and Bridger slings his arm around me again, kisses my temple, and I lean into his side, soaking in his warmth and strength.

"I love you so much, sweetheart."

Some of Angela's words roll through my mind, the way she'd intended for them to do, and I have to blink rapidly to keep the tears at bay.

"I know." I swallow hard. "I love you, too. Both of you."

I'm surprised when we get outside and Bridger leads me to my SUV.

"You picked it up for me?"

"Just came from the garage, yeah," he says as he helps Birdie get settled in the back seat. "Brooks says it's good to go."

"How much do I owe you for it?"

"Nothing."

I shake my head as I lower myself into the seat. "Bridger, I'm happy to pay for my car."

"He didn't charge me anything," he clarifies as he buckles himself in and then leans over to kiss me, right on the mouth. "But even if he had, you don't owe anything, kitten."

I can't argue with him right now. My mind is foggy from the craptastic day and the altercation with Angela, none of which I can talk about right now because we have little ears in the car, and she's been traumatized enough as it is.

The drive home takes less than five minutes, and then we file out of the car, and Bridger follows us into his house, where Pickles comes running to get some attention.

"Pickles," Birdie says, happy to see her favorite feline. "Come sit with me and I'll tell you all about school. It was *not* a good day."

Bridger's eyebrows climb as he looks over at me, and I nod in agreement with Birdie.

"Come here." He crooks a finger at me, and I walk right into his arms. He folds himself around me, and I cling to him. And then, to my surprise, I feel Birdie hug me from the side, and I reach down to hold her against me. "Family hug time."

"Oh, this is really nice."

Birdie lets go first and goes back to talking with Pickles.

"You have to call someone, Bridge," I whisper to him. "Right now. Because I don't know what her deal is, but she's in a mood, and—"

"I'll make a call as soon as I know that *you're* okay," he replies, clearly understanding who I'm referring to.

His ex-wife. The woman who's clearly been in town for weeks and just tried to take my kid.

"I'm okay." I square my shoulders and lift my chin, pulling away from him. I already miss his warmth and the safety of his arms, but I can go back there after we take care of some business.

I want to keep things as normal as possible for Birdie.

"Hey, pretty girl, your daddy has to make some calls, so why don't you and I go make a snack in the kitchen?"

"Can I have some yogurt?" she asks as we walk into the other room, and Bridger walks down the hall to the bedroom to make his call.

"Of course, you can. Do you want some granola and honey in it?"

"Yes, please."

Keeping myself busy is the best thing for me right now, because if I let myself think about what happened at the school, and what it means, or could mean, I'll make myself nuts.

Not to mention, Angela's mean girl antics were right on brand for her, and she sent me right back to being fifteen and completely unsure of myself. I'm shaking so badly that I have to try three times to get the lid off the yogurt.

"I got this," Bridger says, his big hand covering mine as he takes the container from me. "Go change and take a breath, sweetheart."

"I don't want her out of my sight," I whisper, unable to look up from the countertop. If I look him in the face, I'll cry.

I'm barely holding it together here.

"I'm right here," he reminds me. "Baby, I'm right here."

My nod is jerky, and then I walk down the hallway and close the bedroom door, leaning on it as I swallow through the fear and anger in my throat. I manage to get my skirt and sweater off and grab my leggings and one of Bridger's T-shirts out my drawer, but then I sit on the end of the bed, just in my underwear with the clothes in my hands, and stare blindly ahead.

Angela tried to take her. She's been gone for *years*, but she showed up today and wanted to take her.

Why?

Why now?

I knew that I saw her at that concert. When Bridger and I were dancing, and I was people-watching, I knew it was her that I saw, but then she was gone, and I thought I was seeing things.

This is my fault. I should have said something to Bridger, right then and there. At least then he would have known she was in town, and we all could have been on alert.

"Jesus, why didn't I say something?"

I hear the door close softly, and then Bridger's kneeling in front of me, pulling my hands away from my face and placing them on his chest before he cups my cheek.

"Say what to who, baby?"

"It's my fault." I'm shaking my head.

"Dani. Look at me."

My eyes find his, and he's not angry with me at all.

"Say what to who?" he asks again.

"When we were at the concert." I lick my lips, and I want to close my eyes again, but he's holding me firmly in place, keeping his gaze on mine. "I thought I saw her there. It was a split second, and I would have sworn I saw her in the crowd, but then she was gone, and I thought I was seeing things, and then we were dancing and kissing, and I didn't give it another thought, but I should have said something, because—"

"Breathe." He tips his forehead to my own and drags his hands up and down my arms. "Baby, there were more than ten thousand people at that event. It's likely she was there, but you didn't do anything wrong."

My eyes fill at that because it feels like I did do something wrong.

"You didn't. This is a free country, and Angela can come in and out of town as she pleases. And she does. This isn't the first time she's been around, but it *is* the first time that she's tried to see my daughter, and that pisses me off. It makes me irate that she scared Birdie and you. That you had to deal with her at all. She has no right to Birdie, at any time, and my attorney is filing a restraining order with the court right now, before they leave for the day. He assures me that after what she pulled at the school, it won't be denied."

"Good." My shoulders sag a little. "That's good. I'm sorry. Wait, where's Birdie?"

"My parents are here." He winces. "It's bad timing, but they just got to town and they wanted to see her, so they're hanging out with her right now while I check on you."

"You should go hang out with your family, Bridge. I'm okay. Actually, maybe I'll go to my place for a while and unwind a bit. I could use some alone time."

"No."

His voice is hard, and *now* he looks mad.

"What? Why not?"

"Because you're not alone, and you'll never be alone again. If you need to fall apart, you'll do it with me, and then we'll put the pieces back together as a team. If you're pissed or sad or hurt, you'll tell me and let me help you. I don't want you running away from me, kitten. I'm the one you always ran to before, and that's how it's going to be now."

Without another thought, I move into him, wrap my arms around his neck, and hug him so tightly that there isn't a millimeter of space between us.

"My mom asked to take Birdie out for dinner," he murmurs in my ear. "And I'm going to let her so you and I can talk."

"Bridge, I—"

"Let me do this. We both need it."

With a deep sigh, I nod, and he pulls back, wiping the tears off my cheeks I didn't even realize had fallen.

"You get dressed, and come out whenever you want."

"Okay." My voice is a whisper, and he kisses the top of my head so tenderly, it makes me swoon.

Once the door is closed behind him, I wiggle into the leggings and then pull his T-shirt over my head and tie it in a knot at my waist, then I walk out to the living room in time to see his parents pulling out of the driveway, and I join Bridger at the door, waving at them.

"Were they mad?" I ask as I wrap an arm around his waist.

"No, they completely understood, and they're

thrilled to have Birdie all to themselves." He lifts me in his arms, sits in the corner of the couch, and cuddles me to him. "Now, about what Angela said to you."

My head comes up. "Wait, you heard that?"

"Most of it."

"Look, it's nothing that she hasn't said to me before when we were kids."

"For fuck's sake."

"Well, that's not true. The last part about me begging you was new, but the rest—"

He growls, and I look up at him. He's so *mad* on my behalf that it makes me lean up and kiss his cheek.

"I know she's wrong." My voice is low but strong. "I know she is, babe, but for a minute, it stung."

"Don't tell me you believed her for even one fucking heartbeat."

"No, of course not. God, she doesn't know us. She doesn't know anything about us, including Birdie. And I'm telling you right now, I was ready to claw her fucking eyes out if she laid a finger on that little girl."

His lips twitch. "You're pissed."

"I'm *livid*. I'm not a violent person at all, but I wanted to hurt her almost as much as I wanted to protect Birdie. I would never let her do anything ..." My voice falters at that, and he pulls me to him, hugging me tightly.

"I know, sweetheart." He kisses my head and then my forehead. "Do you know how sexy it was to see you defending Birdie like that? You were so fucking fierce and strong, and I knew that Birdie was safe. I wasn't worried about that for a second. I was pissed off that Angela had the balls to try something like that."

"What would she have done?" I have to pull back to look up at him now. "What would Angela have done if she'd managed to get Birdie? She doesn't *want* her; she just wanted to fuck with me."

"You keep using the dirty words, which tells me you're still worked up."

"But that's what she did. She saw us at that concert or heard through the grapevine that we're together, and it made her mad enough to do this. Because I'm telling you right now, it wasn't about that little girl at all. It was about me."

"I know."

My eyes widen when he agrees so quickly. "You know?"

"I thought the same as soon as I saw what was going on. It's one of those *I-don't-want-them-but-I-don't-want-you-to-have-them* situations. I don't know, maybe things fell apart with the guy from New York, or maybe it's just a classic case of jealousy. Given that I don't give a rat's ass about her, I couldn't say, but I can guarantee you that she won't touch either of you again. I added your name to the restraining order."

I blink up at him. "You did?"

"Of course, I did. The attorney also added the school itself, the dance school, the ranch, and anywhere else I could think of where you and Birdie often frequent. She'll get bored with it and go away."

"You sound so sure."

"I am. She's a bully, remember? You stood up to her, and she'll leave town with her tail between her legs."

I blow out a gusty breath. "She never backed down from anyone else before, Bridge."

"Did you or anyone else stand up to her?"

I blink, thinking it over. "I guess not."

"Then trust me. Now, what else happened today?"

I frown up at him, not understanding, and then I bust out laughing.

"You know, I'd almost forgotten. It was just a monumentally bad day. From start to finish. But my super-sexy, smoke show of a boyfriend picked my car up for me, and he's snuggling me, so it's not all bad."

"There she is, my optimistic girl." He kisses me softly. "I think we can make it an even better day."

"Yeah? How's that?"

Before he can answer, his phone rings, and I recognize the ringtone for his job.

"I have to answer it," he says, closing his eyes.

"I know."

"Blackwell." His eyes narrow on me as he listens. "How in the hell did they manage that? You've got to be kidding me. Yeah, we're going to need ladders and climbing gear, and I'm on my way."

He hangs up and then leans back on the cushion and growls.

"Is someone hurt?"

"Someone fell between two old buildings downtown, and they're stuck."

I frown and blink into the middle of the room, trying to figure out how that's even possible.

"I don't know what that means."

"I'll take pictures." He turns my face back to his. "Baby, I don't want to leave you tonight."

"Someone's stuck," I remind him. "You have to go get them unstuck. I'll be fine here. Are your parents bringing Birdie back after dinner?"

"Yeah, they'll be back soon."

"Then Birdie and I will watch a movie and hang out. Don't worry about me."

He doesn't move me off his lap, and he doesn't say anything, and I can see the fight in his eyes.

"Hey." I take his face in my hands. "I knew what I was getting into when we started this. You have a demanding job, and sometimes it's going to interrupt us."

"It feels like it *always* interrupts us."

"And then you'll come home to me." I kiss him sweetly, and he groans as he leans into the kiss, taking it deeper, his hand drifting down to my ass where he grips my flesh with his fingertips. "When you get here, I'll be ready for you."

"I don't deserve you."

I laugh and kiss his chin. "Sure, you do."

Chapter Nineteen

BRIDGER

"Daddy, I want my own bucket," Birdie says with a frown. "I can carry it."

"You pick, we carry," I remind her. "You have an important job."

Snowline Orchard is a family-run apple orchard, nestled between Bitterroot Valley and our closest neighbor of Silver Springs. My parents have brought us here since we were kids, and even though they moved to Florida, Mom makes sure they come back every year to keep the tradition alive.

"Come on, baby girl," Mom says to Birdie, smiling as she takes her granddaughter's hand. "Come help your grandpa and me. We have to get a lot of apples for all the baking and canning we have planned."

"Miss Dani is going to let me help with apple butter," Birdie says, and I glance down at my girl and see her smile. Fuck me, that smile. It knocks me on my ass every time.

The fact that my *ex-fucking-wife* said such horrific things to her makes me want to punch a goddamn wall. She scared my daughter, hurt my woman, and, as far as I know, she's still in Bitterroot Valley, which only pisses me off more.

"Is that so?" Mom also glances back at Dani. "I want in on that action, sweetheart. I never could perfect my apple butter."

"Oh, it's an easy recipe."

"I still want it." Mama winks, and then she, my dad, and Birdie are off to hunt down a few baskets of apples.

We watch the three of them march away, into the heart of the orchard, and then I take Dani's hand in mine and lead her in the opposite direction.

"I think we're going the wrong way."

"Nope. I haven't had ten minutes alone with you, except at night, and I'm going to tuck you behind a tree and kiss the hell out of you. Did you wear those fucking jeans to torment me? To make me suffer, knowing that I can't touch you all damn day?"

She laughs as I tug her along, looking both ways to make sure we're not being watched, not that I really give two fucks. I then pin her against a tree and lean on the trunk just above her head.

"I didn't realize you were an ass man," she says. Her laughing eyes are pinned to my lips, and she's breathing a little hard. Her dark hair is tucked under a red beanie, and she's bundled in a thick flannel shirt, and she's so fucking adorable, I wish I could take her against this tree. "I thought you were a boob man."

"Did you just swear, kitten?" I lower my head so I can whisper in her ear. "I think you did."

"Don't change the subject." Her answer is breathy, and I love that she's already turned on. Her hands move from my chest, up around my neck, and those fingers dive into my hair.

"Am I an ass man?" I nip at her earlobe, making her gasp. "Fuck, with you, I'm an everything man. Every inch of your body does it for me, sweetheart. Your ass, your tits, hell, even your eyelashes make me weak in the knees."

"My eyelashes?" She snorts at that, and I grip her chin, tilting her face up to look at me.

"They're dark and thick, even when you don't wear any makeup, and when you sleep, they lay over your white skin so beautifully, it makes my heart catch. Every piece of you is fucking delectable, and I can't get enough."

She swallows, then licks her lips again.

"And now that you have me here, against this tree, what are you going to do with me?"

"Not even close to what I want to do to you." I kiss her forehead, then over to her temple. "But I'm going to kiss you until you can't remember your name and your pussy's so wet, you'll be begging for me."

"Already there, Chief."

I still, and when her eyes meet mine, they're full of mischief and humor, and I growl deep in my throat as I cup her face in my hand.

"Oh, kitten. You know better."

She bites her lower lip, and I tug it out of her teeth with the pad of my thumb and then rub the digit over her rosy skin, back and forth, watching as those gorgeous eyes of hers dilate.

"Now, you know that I don't want you to call me that."

She nods slightly.

"Use your words, baby."

"Yes, I know." Her voice is breathy, and the fact that this game turns her on is the only fucking aphrodisiac I need in my life.

"And that means that you get to be punished."

She swallows hard and moves to bite her lip again, but once again, I tug it free.

"And I know just the thing."

"You do?" The question is whispered.

"Oh, yeah. I do. You wore these jeans knowing that they would make me crazy. And this flannel shirt isn't even buttoned all the way to the top, so I can see the tank you're wearing beneath it. And if I slip my hand inside ..."

I do, and moan when I find her nipples already hard.

"That's what I thought. You're already turned the fuck on. Does taunting me do it for you, kitten?"

"It's fun." It's a confession, and she tips her head back and lets out a soft moan when I pinch her nipple a little harder. "God, that's good."

"And how are things down here?" I glance around and see that no one's around and then unbutton her jeans and slip my hand inside. Dani moans when I slip a finger through her folds. "Jesus fuck, sweetheart, you're soaked."

"Always," she says on a sigh. "You exist, and I'm wet. That's just how it seems to work."

"And I fucking love it." Her clit is hard under the pad of my finger, and I move my lips down to her throat. "I. Can't. Get. Enough of you."

She whimpers, and my finger leaves the hard nub, moving down to her entrance, and when it slips inside, that whimper turns into a moan.

"Shh."

"This isn't really a punishment," she says against my shoulder.

"Oh, yeah, it is. Because there are people twenty yards away, picking apples, and someone could walk up on us at any time."

She stiffens at that and tries to pull away, but I hold her in place.

"And I'm going to make you fucking come, right here and right now, and you can't make a sound. Do you hear me?"

"Yes. But how—"

I plant my thumb over her clit and push my finger in to my first knuckle, and whatever she was about to say flies right out of her head. She leans her face on my chest, grunting and moving against me, but not whimpering.

"Good girl," I croon into her ear and feel her tighten around my finger.

My girl loves being praised.

In less than thirty seconds, I have her worked up and

cresting over into oblivion. She bites my chest. It takes my breath away to see this beautiful woman fall apart like this.

Slipping my hand out of her pants, I lick my fingers clean, and then rebutton her pants and pull her into my arms.

"You haven't even kissed me yet."

With a laugh, I tip her face up to mine and settle my lips over hers, tasting the traces of the apple cider donut we shared when we got here and the pure lust moving through her.

"Better?" I smooth the hair off her face and tuck it behind her ear.

"Holy shit, Bridge." She swallows, leaning against my chest to keep her balance. Her gaze drops to my fly and the obvious bulge straining against it.

"Don't even say it," I growl and kiss her forehead. "You're not sucking me off right here, kitten."

"Seems only fair—"

"No." I laugh and take her hand in mine, linking our fingers. "I got what I wanted. I'm crazy about you. You know that, right?"

"Yeah." She sighs as I lead her away from our tree. "It's kind of wild, and I have to pinch myself sometimes to make sure that it's real."

"It's real, sweetheart."

"There you are, Daddy!" Birdie's running in our direction, her cheeks rosy from the cool air. "We got three big buckets full of apples. Grandma says that should be enough."

"Sounds like a lot of apples to me." I grin at my daughter and then at my parents, who are following her, loaded down with their goods.

"Bubba," Mom says to me, "we'd like to take Birdie back to the rental with us for the weekend. She wants to help me with my apple projects, and we thought we'd try to go to the pumpkin patch tomorrow."

"Yeah, Dad, can I?"

"I don't see why not. We'll swing by the house and pack you a bag."

When I glance over, I see Mom leaning in to say something to Dani, and my girl blushes and then nods and glances my way.

"We're happy for you," Dad says softly beside me. "Couldn't have handpicked someone better for you and our girl."

"She's the best," I agree, watching Mom fold Dani into a warm hug and then loop her arm around Dani's shoulders as they walk toward the checkout building so we can pay for our apples and head home.

"You need a foot rub."

Dani turns to me from where she's standing in the kitchen, washing apples.

"Me?"

"I'm not talking to Pickles, sweetheart."

She snorts at that and then shakes her head. "I have

to finish washing these apples, and then I need to do some laundry."

"Are you telling me that Birdie is out of the house for the next thirty-six hours, I'm not at work, and you're planning to fill that time with laundry?" I shake my head at her as I cross to her and turn off the tap. "The apples are clean. Let them drain. I want you to go sit on that couch and put your feet up."

She sighs, her shoulders droop, and then she smiles up at me.

"As long as you're the one giving me the foot rub."

"I don't know if you've missed it, but no one else is ever going to have his hands on you again."

She blinks at that and then simply saunters over to the couch, where she follows my orders and sits, peels off her socks, and wiggles her adorable toes.

After I get her settled in the corner of the couch, with her legs up on my lap, I start massaging the arches of her feet, and she groans.

"Oh, you're good at that."

"You're on your feet a lot."

"Most of the day," she confirms, watching me with relaxed eyes. "I'm used to it now. For that first year, I thought I was going to die. Being a teacher, especially to the littler kids, is a physical job."

"What made you decide to be a teacher?" I reach for the other foot and dig my thumb into her heel.

"I like kids," she says. "And I liked the idea of the schedule that being a teacher affords. You know, holidays

KRISTEN PROBY

and summers off, and there's good benefits and retire-
ment. It's a responsible job."

"A grown-up job." I chuckle and then rub up her
calf, making her moan.

"A stable job," she adds. "After all the crap my dad
handed out, I really wanted something stable. The rules,
the schedule, even the curriculum. There are no
surprises, you know? I don't love surprises."

"You just haven't had the good kind."

She shakes her head and then pulls her leg out of my
grasp and crawls over to straddle my lap, and my hands
immediately find purchase on her ass.

She really does have a stellar back end.

"Your job is nothing but surprises," she murmurs
against my lips and then moans deep in her throat as she's
the one to take the kiss much deeper. She grinds against
me, and I'm straining against the zipper of my jeans.

Suddenly, she shimmies back off my lap, falls to her
knees, and nudges my legs aside, nestling herself between
them.

"Off." She unfastens my pants, and I lift my hips so
she can work the denim, along with my boxer briefs, off,
then tosses them aside, and wraps her petite, magical
hands around my shaft, making me suck in a breath.

"You don't have ... ah, shit." She licks over the crown,
over the slit, and my skin tingles.

"You had me out of my mind in that orchard." She
licks the underside of my cock, up the vein there, and I
groan. "You made me come and drove me wild up against
that tree."

"And I'd do it again in a heartbeat."

She hums and opens wide, taking me into her mouth and sinking over me until I can feel the back of her throat before she moves back up again, her lips gripping me tightly.

"Christ, sweetheart."

"I wanted to do this there." She sinks over me again, this time loosening her jaw and relaxing her throat, taking me even deeper. Her eyes water, but she doesn't gag, and suddenly, my T-shirt is too tight, so I whip it over my head and toss it aside.

I want to pick her up and sink inside her, then fuck her until she's screaming. Especially because Birdie's not here, and she can be as loud as she needs to be.

But I'll let her control this and see where she takes it.

"It was about you, not me."

Those hot, lust-filled eyes narrow as she pulls back up, then swipes that fucking talented tongue around the tip.

"Now, it's about you."

"Shit, you look good with my cock on your lips."

She smiles, just a half smile, and then she starts to go to work. There are no more slow strokes up and down, no more gentle licks. My girl's hands tighten on my shaft, and she starts to suck.

I can't help it. My hands dive into her hair, and I hold on as she unleashes herself on me. I know she's sexy, she turns me on with every move she makes, but this pushes my need for her into a completely different stratosphere.

My hips can't help but move with her, and when she

moves one hand down to cup my balls, I start to lose my mind.

"Baby, I'm going to ... ah, fuck me, I'm gonna come. If you don't want—"

But she doesn't stop. If anything, this vixen works harder, and sucks every last drop down her throat, lapping at the last drops on the tip.

"You were saying?"

"Fuuuck." I laugh and brush her hair off her cheeks. I stand and pull her into my arms, marching for the bedroom. "You. Me. Bed. All fucking night."

Rolling over out of a dead sleep, I reach for Dani, who isn't in my arms the way she usually is when I wake up, and come up empty.

The bed is cool where she was, and a quick scan of the room tells me that she's not here.

She's also not in the bathroom.

After the energetic night we just had, I figured we'd both sleep until noon today.

Resigned to getting up, I pull on some sweats and pad out to the kitchen, then lean my shoulder against the wall, cross my arms over my chest, and take her in.

Not only is Dani in the kitchen, but she's wearing nothing but my T-shirt. Her hair's up in a twist on her head, and her hips move back and forth in time with the song playing on her phone, which is on the island.

I didn't plan on her. I didn't plan on opening up myself or my daughter to anyone, ever. We were doing just fine by ourselves.

But I also didn't plan on Dani moving back home and stealing the breath from my lungs. Yeah, I've wanted her for a long time, but I didn't think I'd have her.

And now that she's here, I'm never letting her go.

She spins to grab an oven mitt, and when she sees me standing here, she doesn't startle.

She smiles.

My kitten fucking smiles.

"Hey." She licks her finger, watching me as I push away from the wall and stalk toward her. "I was hungry."

"I am, too." My eyes move from her head to her bare toes and back again. "What do you have on under my shirt, sweetheart?"

Dani smirks and turns to pull something out of the oven, bending over, giving me a view of her gorgeous little pussy.

"I made a quiche," she says, and tries to turn, but I'm right behind her, and I press her back to my front. "I thought you were hungry."

"I am." Wrapping my arms around her waist, I lower my lips to her neck and press a damp kiss there, grinning when goose bumps rise on her flesh. "I'm fucking starving."

"This only has to cool for about ten minutes."

"Hmm. I might need just a little longer than that."

"Quiche isn't good cold." She moans and tips her

head back against my shoulder as my hands dive under the shirt, over her warm skin. "Bridger."

"I have something else in mind for breakfast."

I pick her up and carry her around to the other side of the island and set her down.

"Are you going to eat my pussy?"

My whole body jerks. My cock is unbearably hard. My eyes narrow on her smirking, beautiful face.

"You know I love your dirty mouth."

She bites her lip and spreads her legs in an invitation that literally *no man* could pass up.

"Yeah, kitten, I'm going to eat your fucking pussy for breakfast." I squat in front of her and lick her, one long swipe from her entrance to her clit, making her moan and grab the back of my head. I move my face back and forth, and she cries out my name as her thighs want to lock around my head. "I'm fucking obsessed with your cunt. I can't get enough of it. I could eat it and nothing else for the rest of my life, and die a happy man."

"Holy fuck, you're good at that." My eyes fly to hers, as aroused by her filthy mouth as I am by her body. "*Chief.*"

I pull away and bite the inside of her thigh. "Oh, I see. You woke up with your sassy pants on."

"I'm not wearing any pants at all." She bats those sexy-as-hell eyelashes at me as I stand, then lean in to kiss her lips.

"Do you taste yourself?"

"Yeah."

"Do you like that?"

"I do."

"Say it. Say, *I like the way my pussy tastes on your mouth, Bridger.*"

She swallows, reaching down to grab my cock, and I let her stroke it, up and down.

"I *love* the way my pussy tastes on your mouth, Chief."

I growl and take her mouth again as she chuckles against me.

"I like the punishments," she whispers against my lips. "Does it really make you mad?"

"It's unsettling, but no. It doesn't make me mad, baby."

She guides me to her opening, and I can't resist pushing inside, bottoming out as her legs wrap around my hips, tugging me closer.

"You're so damn snug and perfect."

I rock into her, press my thumb to her clit, and grin when she starts to clamp around me, and just as she's about to come, I pull out and take my thumb away, making her gasp.

"*Bridger.*"

"You wanted the punishment," I remind her. "One orgasm for every time you've called me chief, and you're at two today, so we'll be edging you for a while."

"Fuck," she mutters, making me laugh.

Rather than pushing back inside her, I squat again and French-kiss her, inhaling her delectable scent, lapping at her tender, most intimate place. Licking at her clit, I press a finger inside of her pussy and feel the tremors there.

Dani moans.

"Ah, baby. You have the prettiest little pussy."

"Bridger." Her hand fists in my hair, but she doesn't pull me to her. She's holding on, the way I was yesterday. "Please."

"That's it. Ask me for it."

"Please let me come."

I press against her clit harder, crook my finger to brush over her G-spot, and when she starts to shake, I pull away.

"Arrgh, Bridger!"

"I told you." I kiss the inside of her thigh. "Call me Chief, and there are consequences."

"What can I call you, then? Daddy's out."

I narrow my eyes at her, but I actually don't hate that one.

"No." She shakes her head. "Birdie calls you that. There's an ick factor there."

"Point taken."

Her hand is combing through my hair, and I stand and push inside of her once again, making both of us groan.

"God, nothing feels like you do." I cup her face, and she takes my thumb into her mouth. "You're so fucking beautiful. So perfect for me, sweetheart."

"Swoony," she whispers, her eyelids lowering halfway as I fuck her here on this island. "I love your body. Your muscles. The way you watch me when we're like this."

"Like what?" I kiss her chin. "How do I watch you?"

"Like you love me."

"Baby." I cover her mouth with mine and sink into her, still moving in and out of her, even harder now. "I love you so much I ache with it."

Tears form in the corners of her eyes, and I feel that buildup happening inside of her again, and this time, there will be no stopping it.

"Come for me, Dani."

She groans, bites my lip, and clenches around me.

"Yes, baby. That's it."

"God, love," she pants, gripping me so tightly she'll leave marks.

"I'm going to come, and you better go with me." My words are rough against her lips, and then we're both flying, soaring through the orgasm of the goddamn year.

"Holy moly." She drags her hand down my face. "Wow."

"Yeah." I grin and kiss her cheek. "Wow."

"We're good at the kitchen sex."

"A man's gotta eat."

Chapter Twenty

DANI

"Okay, we're going to measure the sugar," I say to Birdie, who's standing on her stool, her adorable apron tied around her middle, ready to help. "We need four whole cups."

"That's not enough sugar," she says, making Mama Blackwell laugh.

"She's got such a sweet tooth," Mama says as she washes out a bowl for us to reuse. "Just like her grandma."

"I admit, so do I. We try to limit the amount of sugar that we keep in this house, otherwise, I'd eat it all. Good job, Birdie."

"These apples are nice and soft," Mama says, stirring the mixture on the stovetop.

I'm doing this in batches, to keep it more manageable. We have one batch already jarred, one on the stove, and another that Birdie is currently mixing with a wooden spoon.

"Am I okay to take these off the heat?" Mama asks.

"Of course, thanks."

"Where did you get this recipe, Dani?" she asks as she turns off the burner and moves the pot.

"I found it online," I admit with a shrug. "I wanted to make some a few years ago and stumbled upon this recipe, and I have to say, it works."

"And how did you learn to can?"

"Video tutorials online."

I turn to find Mama watching me with sad eyes.

"What?"

"If I'd known you wanted to learn, I would have taught you and your sisters when you were teenagers."

"You taught us a lot as it was. If it wasn't for you, I wouldn't know how to sew a button or clean a toilet or iron my slacks. I wouldn't know how to get a stain out of the carpet or what to do for a bee sting. You taught us so much, and you're the mother of my heart."

Mama blinks and folds me in for a hug, holding on tight.

Birdie's swinging her hips back and forth in time with the Sidney Sterling song playing on the Bluetooth speaker that Bridger bought for me, since he knows I like to have music on in the kitchen, and Mama and I take a minute to dance with her, making her giggle.

"We loved it when Sidney sang this song at the concert, didn't we?"

"It was *so good*, Grandma."

"I bet it was," Mama says and kisses Birdie's head. "Your dad told me you guys had fun, and he sent me the

297

photos of you with Sidney. It looked like she was really nice."

"She gave us T-shirts and posters that she signed," Birdie informs her grandmother while I transfer the latest apple mixture to a pot for the stove.

"I'm glad you had fun," Mama says, and then her arm is draped over my shoulders, and she's hugging me to her side. "I'm glad you *all* had fun."

"We really did."

"You know, I love this."

I frown over at her. "Making apple butter?"

"Well, yes, I enjoy being in the kitchen, but I love being here, with both of you. Seeing you with Birdie and Bridger." She kisses my cheek, and it makes my heart swell. I know where Bridger gets his love language. It's from his mom. "You make a beautiful family."

I wrinkle my nose, mostly so I don't start to cry.

"I love them," I whisper, staring down into the pot of apples. "More than anything."

"Anyone with eyes in their head can see that, my sweet girl."

"And you don't mind?" I look into her eyes, needing to see her reaction to that question. "You've known me and my family all of my life, and if I'm not—"

"Hey." She pats my cheek and shakes her head, smiling at me. "Yes, I've known you your whole life, and I know what a lovely, good-hearted, strong, wonderful woman you are. I couldn't handpick someone better for my boy than you, Dani. I love you so much."

Maybe the tears are going to come anyway.

"I love you, too."

"Why are you crying?" Birdie asks, making me chuckle and brush at the tears on my cheeks.

"Because I'm happy. That's all. Are you ready to help me put these other apples into jars?"

"Yes, but when do we get to eat it?"

Mama reaches for a fresh batch of jars. "When we're finished working, we reward ourselves with a treat. We have to earn it."

"I've earned an extra treat," Birdie says, making me smile.

"You're my treat," I inform her and kiss the top of her head.

When I turn around, I find Bridger leaning against the wall, his arms crossed over his chest, watching us with a soft smile on that gorgeous face.

"I didn't know you were there."

"I know." He saunters over and leans down to kiss me before planting his lips by my ear. "You're *my* treat, kitten."

"Heard that, did you?"

"I heard a lot."

"It snowed!"

It's Sunday morning, and Birdie has just jumped on the bed, waking Bridger and me up.

"Get up! Get up! There's snow outside!"

"You're killing me, peanut," Bridger growls. "I got home at three this morning."

But Birdie doesn't answer. She just runs off, and I drag my hands down my face.

"First snow of the year. Did you have to drive home in it?" Reaching over, I drag my hand down Bridger's arm, over that colorful ink, enjoying his warmth.

"Yeah." He stretches, then reaches out for me and tugs me against him, so I snuggle down and rest my head on his chest. "It won't stay long. It's only early November."

I sigh and breathe him in. "How do you feel about pancakes with the apple butter we made last month?"

How has it already been a month since we went to the apple orchard? Time is flying by. Before long, the holidays will be here.

"I feel very fondly about that idea." He kisses my head, then tips my chin up so he can place a kiss on my lips. "Thank you."

"It's just breakfast."

"One that I don't have to cook, so I'm grateful."

My phone buzzes on the table behind me, and I frown. "I have no idea who could be messaging me at this time of the day."

"Check it." He kisses me again, sending a thrill down my spine, and I turn to get my phone.

Bridger's hand is planted on my ass. It makes me smirk.

He really is an ass man.

"It's your sister."

And she sent it to our book club group of me, Alex, Bee, Skyla, and Millie. We like to chat about what we're reading, even when we're not at the book club.

> Bee: SOS! I repeat, SOS!

> Alex: What's wrong?

> Skyla: Are you okay?

> Me: We're here.

I feel Bridger shift behind me, spooning me, and his breath on my shoulder as he reads along with me.

"You have a book group text?"

"Of course, we do."

He snickers.

> Bee: I need help. Psychological help. I went on a date last night, and … FFS.

"Do I need to kill someone?" Bridger asks.

"I think if that were the case, she'd be calling you for help. This is just girl talk, love."

"Hmm." He kisses my shoulder and then rolls away. "I'm going to make sure Birdie hasn't decided to go outside and take a snow bath."

"Good idea."

> Millie: Everyone come to the coffee shop and we'll discuss these current events like the dignified women we are.

Alex: I can be there in an hour.

Skyla: Me, too, if I can bring Riley. If not, I'll need a little more time.

Millie: Bring him. He's always welcome here.

Me: I can also be there in an hour. Can't wait to hear all about it.

Bee: Thank God. See you all soon.

I hurry into the bathroom to brush my teeth, take care of business, and tie my hair up on top of my head. Then, I change out of my pajamas and into black leggings, a T-shirt, and one of Bridger's zip hoodies before I hurry out to the kitchen to get breakfast made.

"Hello, my loves," I say when I see the two most important people in my life curled up on the couch together, with a fire in the fireplace, watching it snow. "It's pretty outside."

"Are you making pancakes with the apple butter?" Birdie asks.

"Yes, ma'am. And then I have to run over to Bitterroot Valley Coffee Co. for a bit." I move into the kitchen, but I can still see them as I pull out a mixing bowl and the pancake mix from the pantry. "Bee wants to talk to us in person."

"Girl talk," Bridger says, smiling down at his daughter. Birdie grins and snuggles down against him.

It doesn't take long at all to get the pancakes made and some bacon cooked up, and then the three of us sit at the island, scarfing it all down.

"That apple butter is stupidly good," Bridger says. "Mom was excited to make it with you."

Honestly, the day that Birdie, Mama, and I made the apple butter, right here in this kitchen, was one of the best days I've had in a long time.

"I enjoyed that." I wipe my face and set my empty plate in the sink. "I hate to eat and run, but—"

"Go." Bridger stands and pulls me to him, folding me into his big arms. "I'll clean up, don't even worry. Have a good chat. Let me know if I need to cause any bodily harm to anyone on my sister's behalf."

I snort and hug him back, then kiss his chest.

"I'm sure it's fine, but I'll let you know."

"And drive safe out there. It's slick."

"Oh, I'm going to walk."

Bridger frowns down at me. "It's twenty degrees outside."

"I have boots and a coat. It's eight blocks away, love." I walk over to Birdie and kiss her head, rubbing her little back. "Do you need anything, pumpkin?"

I started calling her that around Halloween, when we carved the pumpkins for the front porch.

"Nope." She smiles up at me. "Have a fun girl talk."

"Okay." I pull on my boots and mittens and pull a hat over my head, then zip up a winter coat and wave at them. "See you in a bit."

"Be. Careful." Bridger narrows his eyes at me, and I chuckle.

"Yes, Chief."

When he makes a move like he's going to run at me, I squeal and hightail it out the door, still laughing when I hit the sidewalk. I glance back to the window and see my man standing there, grinning at me, and I give him a little wave.

God, I love him.

I didn't know I could love someone so fiercely, so completely, the way I do Bridger Blackwell. I've always cared about him—I even had a crush on him—but that was absolutely nothing compared to how I've grown to feel about him since that night this past summer on my driveway.

He's protective and sweet and strong. His work ethic is incredible. I have so much respect for him as a human being, and the way he loves his daughter makes me swoon every day. He's the best daddy.

The snow is already starting to melt off the sidewalks as I make my way downtown, and when I walk into the coffee shop, I have to shed some layers because it isn't quite as cold as I expected.

"Am I the last one here?"

"You are," Alex says, looping her arm through mine as she kisses me on the cheek. "How's my little sister?"

"Two freaking minutes," I remind her with a laugh. "You're only *two minutes* older than me."

But she just grins at me, and I hug her back.

"I'm great. I want to hear all about Bee's date." It's

quiet in the coffee shop this morning, likely because of the snow, and Bee's bookstore is closed on Sunday.

"Gather 'round," Millie says, passing me an iced coffee. I love this woman and her ninja memory.

"Can I love on Riley?" I ask Skyla. "I know he's a working dog, so I thought I should ask."

"Of course," Skyla says, and then she says something to the dog, I assume to let him know that he can be petted. "He'll love it."

"Hello, beautiful boy," I croon to him, and scratch him between the ears. I may not have a lot of experience with animals, but I like them. "You're so handsome."

I glance up and notice the look of apprehension on my sister's face. Alex has always had the hardest time with animals. Where our father used water to torment me, it was animals for Alex, and it's something she's never gotten over.

"Hey," I say softly, getting her attention. "It's okay."

She nods, and then the five of us sit around the table.

"Okay," Skyla says, bumping her shoulder against Bee's. "Spill it. Who, what, where, and did he rail you all night long?"

"Irish people say *rail*?" I ask, blinking in surprise.

"I've lived in the US for a long time." Skyla winks one moss-green eye at me, and we return our attention to Bee.

"So, this guy came into the bookstore yesterday. He was a tourist from somewhere. Canada? No, Europe somewhere because he had an accent."

We laugh at that. "Quite a difference in geography there, but okay," Alex says.

"Anyway, he was kind of nerdy, with glasses, but also tall and broad, with muscles for days, but he wasn't really my type."

"Tall with muscles for days isn't your type?" I ask. "Come on, Bee, aren't your standards a little high?"

"No, I just mean, in general, he wasn't really my type. Looks wise. I know that's superficial, but—"

"You're amongst friends," Skyla says. "I have to admit, if I didn't know better, I'd think you were talking about my brother, but he left yesterday afternoon."

"Not him, then, but we get so many tourists here, from all over the world." Bee takes a breath. "So, this guy was nice. He asked me out to dinner, and I've been so consumed with my shop over the last few months that I decided that I should get out there and date. Even if it's just one date, you know?"

We all nod in encouragement.

"He took me to Ciao, the Italian place for dinner. Which, by the way, *yum*."

"So good," I agree.

"Oh, I have to try that," Skyla says. "Go on."

Bee takes a long, deep breath, and then in one run-on sentence, says, "And then I went back to his hotel with him, and he fucked me six ways to Sunday all night long, and I didn't know my body was capable of that, and holy shit, I need an ice pack for my vag."

We all stare at her for about four seconds, and then we bust up cackling like loons.

"Holy shit, you had me scared there for a second," Millie says, wiping a tear from her eye.

"Me, too. I thought I was going to have to tell Bridger he had to beat someone up."

"I want more details," Alex says, leaning closer against the table. "First of all, you were safe, right?"

"Of course." Bee nods and sips her coffee. "He wrapped it up, and I'm on birth control."

"Good," Skyla says, squeezing Bee's hand. "And he was obviously nice to you."

"He was *so nice*. Made sure I came first. Checked in with me to make sure I was okay. He did all the right things. But—" She bites her lip, narrows her eyes, and stares off into the distance.

"But what?" I ask her.

"I'm not sure. Something, but I don't know."

"Did you get his number?" Millie asks. "Or did he ask for yours?"

"No. And he was gone when I woke up this morning. That's why I sent the SOS."

We're all silent again, pondering this news.

"Did that hurt your feelings?" Skyla asks with a soft voice.

"A little bit, yeah. Don't get me wrong, we didn't make any promises at all. We had a good conversation at dinner, which he paid for, by the way. And the sex was great, like I said." She nibbles on her lip, pondering it. "So, I guess this was my first one-night stand with a hot stranger."

"What was his name?"

Bee's cheeks darken at Alex's question.

"YOU DIDN'T GET HIS NAME?" I demand, completely shocked. "I don't know who you are. This is *not* my best friend."

"I don't remember if I asked him his name, and it just never ... came up."

"One-night stand with a hot, possibly European stranger," Millie says. "Wow. If my husband wasn't the sexiest man on earth, I might be jealous."

"I'm totally jealous," Alex says.

I reach over and take Bee's hand in mine, giving it a squeeze. "Are you okay?"

She nods slowly. "Yeah, I am. I'm pretty sure I'm okay. I kind of wish I knew his name, though."

"This way, it's more mysterious," Skyla offers. "It's an experience that you'll never forget and one that most people don't get to have. If you think about it, it's rather romantic, and that's the truth of it."

Bee's smile spreads over her lips. "Yeah, it was romantic. And seriously hot."

My phone starts to ring with an incoming FaceTime call, and when I see that it's Bridger, I accept.

"Hey," I say, and then smile bigger when Birdie's sweet face comes into view. "What are you up to, pumpkin?"

"There's a *lot* of snow up at the resort," she says. "We want to go sledding. Come with us, okay?"

"Cutest ever," Alex mutters into her coffee.

"Heck yes, we should go sledding. I'm almost done here, so I'll see you soon, okay?"

"Daddy! She said yes!"

"I heard." Bridger takes the phone and grins at me. "Everything okay there?"

"Everything is great, and no, I'm not going to tell you about it."

"As long as she's safe, that's all I care about."

I glance up at Bee, who just smiles at me. "Yeah, she's safe. I'll see you in a few. I need to change before we head out."

"I'll bring her home," Alex says loudly so Bridger can hear.

"Thanks, Alex. See you soon. Love you, kitten."

"I love you, too."

I hang up and then look up into four sets of happy, smug eyes.

"What?"

"You two might be the cutest *ever*," Bee says. "You're so good for my brother and Birdie. They adore you."

"It's been really fun to watch," Alex agrees.

"And is it me, or are you more confident than you were just a few months ago?" Millie asks, and the others nod.

"Even I see it," Skyla adds, "and I'm new to this group. Love looks beautiful on you, Dani."

I take a deep breath and blink away the happy tears that want to come.

"It feels good, too."

Chapter Twenty-One

BRIDGER

"I'm here," Dani says as she walks through the door. Alex is right behind her, and Birdie immediately runs to Dani's twin to give her a hug.

"Hey there, cutest little girl in the world," Alex says as she squats down in front of my daughter. "How are you? How's school?"

"Good." Birdie starts to tell Alex all about finding dead leaves for an art project, and I tug Dani into my arms for a kiss.

"Hey there, most beautiful woman in the world," I whisper against her lips, mirroring Alex's words and making my girl chuckle. "How are you?"

"I'm great. My boyfriend and his super adorable daughter are taking me sledding today."

"Really? That sounds fun." I smirk down at her and rub my nose over hers. "Bee's okay?"

"She's great." Dani's cheeks darken, and I narrow my

eyes at her. "No, she's *really* okay, if you get my meaning."

I blink, and then I feel nauseous. "Jesus, I don't want to know."

"No." She laughs and pats me on the cheek. "You really don't want to know. But yay, Bee. I have to go across the street to get my snow gear."

"You know, you really need to just move in with me and let the rental go."

I didn't mean to blurt it out like that. I'd planned to ask her during a quiet moment, when it's just the two of us, but the words just slipped out.

And her jaw drops.

And she steps out of my arms, which really pisses me off.

"Forget I said anything."

"No." She shakes her head and takes my hand in hers. "I'm not going to forget it."

She licks her lips and glances over to make sure that Alex and Birdie are still busy.

"Bridger, are you sure?"

"Never been more positive of anything. You practically live here as it is. Pickles has been here for months. Most of your clothes are in our bedroom. Jesus, I've called it *our* bedroom for forever, because that's what it is. There's no need for you to keep the rental because I plan to keep you here, with us, forever."

"Okay, that was swoony," I hear Alex say. "If you don't snatch him up, I will."

"But, Birdie," Dani begins, and I turn to my daughter, who's listening carefully.

"Hey, peanut, what do you think about Dani living with us?"

"I thought she already did." Birdie frowns at Dani. "You don't live here? You sleep with my daddy, and Pickles sleeps with me."

"Sounds like you live here," Alex says, rocking back on her heels, a smile on her face. "Besides, this house is *way* nicer than the other one. And it has these two in it."

"You can't argue with that logic." I take Dani's face in my hands. "We love you, and we want you here. And that goes for your things, too."

She leans into me, rests her forehead on my chest, and when I tip her chin up, she has tears in her eyes. "That's a good idea."

"Yeah?" I feel like I just won the lottery. "Awesome."

"My lease is up at the end of next month. It was only for six months, so I won't renew it, and that gives us time to move everything over."

"Aww. So sweet. Okay, I have to go." Alex waves at us. "Have fun sledding, okay? Tell me all about it later, Birdie."

"I will."

It's amazing the difference a couple thousand feet difference in altitude will make. Most of the snow in town was starting to melt, but up here on the ski mountain, there's a few feet accumulated, perfect for sledding.

"Bee texted me," Dani says from the passenger seat. "She said she and your brothers are coming up, too."

"I sent them a message, in case they were up for it. All of them jumped at it. Even Beckett, which surprised me."

"Why's that?"

"He's been married to the ranch lately. I know he's stressed out, but he won't ask for help. It'll do him good to let loose for a while today."

We park near the Snow Ghost pub, and once I get Birdie's hat and gloves on her, we take the sleds out of the bed of the truck and trudge over to the area they've marked off for sledding.

We aren't the only ones up here.

"How many runs have you taken?" I ask Blake and Brooks, who are laughing about something as we approach. The snow is still falling up here, and it's damn cold, but it feels good.

"None yet. We're waiting for the peanut," Blake says, smiling at Birdie. "How do you feel today, cupcake?"

"Good. I want to sled."

"The princess has spoken," Brooks says.

"Where's Beck?" I ask.

"Not here yet," Bee says as she steps over to us, a hot beverage in her hands. "He said he'll be here in a little while."

"Why are you drinking that when we're about to sled?" I ask her.

"*You're* about to sled. I'm going to watch." Bee grins.

The woman grew up on a ranch, but you'd never know it. She's all about fashion and anything that keeps her clean and off a horse.

She's a girly girl.

And there's nothing wrong with that.

"Hold my purse," Dani says, passing it to Bee, who slings it across her body. "Let's do this!"

Dani grabs a sled, takes Birdie by the hand, and leads her over to the hill.

All four of us stand side by side, watching as my girls sit on the sled and then belly laugh as they fly down the snow.

"That's cute."

I turn at the sound of Beck's voice and smile. "There he is. Yeah, it's fucking cute."

"I'm going with them," Brooks says, and we all, except for Bee, follow suit.

For the next hour, we play in the snow. We throw snowballs. We make snow angels.

We laugh.

God, we laugh a whole lot.

"Smile," Dani says, holding her phone up to get a picture of Birdie and me sitting on the sled. "Got it."

Finally, Birdie looks up at me and says, "I need hot chocolate."

"I think we all do," Dani says. "Let's go to the lodge and have some. What do you think?"

With nods all around, we make our way to the parking lot to shed some layers and put the sleds in the trucks, and then walk up to the pub where we order a round of hot chocolates and then take our drinks to a lounge with views of the snow and the mountains.

Dani, Bee, and Birdie have settled on a couch, cuddled up together, talking and drinking their hot chocolate.

And the sight of Birdie snuggled up to Dani makes my heart ache in a great way.

"So, what's up with you, man?" Brooks asks Beckett. "I'm surprised you came up here."

"I'm swamped." He rubs his hand over the back of his neck. Beck is built like the rest of us. Well past six feet, with the Blackwell dark hair and eyes. He's the only brother with a beard, but it works for him. "I've had machinery issues, a sick cow, a coyote got into my chickens—"

I glance over to make sure Dani didn't hear about the chickens, but she didn't. She's braiding Birdie's hair for her.

"On the guest side of things, the first people who stayed in cabin number four put a hole in the wall," Beck continues.

"What the fuck?" I ask.

"Renters, man," Brooks says, shaking his head. "Vacationers are assholes."

"Not all of them," Blake points out. "But yeah, a lot of them. Shit, I'm sorry, Beck."

"It's just been one thing after another, so when you called to come up here, I said fuck it. I needed an afternoon away."

"You need to hire more help," Brooks points out. "You need a property manager for the rentals."

"Agreed," I add.

"I'm working on it." Beck scowls down into his hot chocolate. "I have some feelers out for someone. I might hire a local company to help me out until I can find someone to live on-site."

"The sooner the better," Blake agrees.

"You really need to get out more," I say. "Maybe actually date someone."

I'm met with dead silence, and then my asshole brothers laugh at me.

"You know," Blake says with a grin, "I remember saying something similar to *you* a couple of years ago, and you told me to go fuck myself. That you didn't need anyone because you had Birdie."

"I believed that." I shrug. "I was happy. And now, I'm happier."

"You're whipped," Brooks says.

"Totally and gratefully." I grin. "I mean, she's beautiful. She's smart as fuck, and she's damn good with my kid. What more could I ask for?"

"Dani's great," Blake agrees. "We've loved her and her sisters forever."

"Yeah, man," Beck adds. "No one's saying you shouldn't be with her. She's been good for you. It's just funny as hell because you were solidly a bachelor after the shit that Angela pulled."

"You mean, the shit she's still pulling?"

Brooks pulls in a breath and cracks his neck. "Yeah, tell us what's going on there."

I tell them about what happened last month at the school, and by the time I've finished, all three of them look like they'd like to punch someone.

"What a bitch," Beck says. "What's her deal? She's been gone a long time."

"Isn't it obvious?" Blake asks. "She's jealous. Found out about Dani and decided everyone had to pay for that."

"Bingo," I say, pointing at my brother. "So far, she hasn't done anything else, but I've heard she's still in town."

"She is," Brooks says, shifting in his chair. "She came into my shop and asked if I'd look at her car for her, on the house, since she's family."

I stare at him for ten seconds. "What the fuck? What did you tell her?"

"I told her she's no family of mine, and she could go somewhere else."

Beckett holds his hand out for a fist bump.

"She's delusional." I look to Blake. "Could she be certifiable? Like, literally crazy?"

Blake shakes his head. "Maybe. I'm not a psychologist. We've known for a long time that she's a narcissist. After Birdie was born so fucking small, Angela didn't even want to stay in the NICU with her. All she was worried about was herself."

The reminder still makes me so fucking angry. I didn't understand what in the hell was wrong with my ex-wife, how she could be so heartless and callous when it came to our infant. At first, I wondered if it was post-partum depression, but as time went on, we realized that she just didn't care if Birdie lived or died.

She didn't care about her name. I'm the one who named her. And I'm the one who sat with that baby, held her when I could, day and night, for two fucking months until I could take her home.

"Well, let's hope that she gets tired of this game soon and goes away," I say with a sigh. "And let's get Beckett a life that doesn't revolve around cows."

"Fuck you," my brother says with a laugh. "Just because you're all messy in love doesn't mean the rest of us need to be."

"I'm not messy."

"Hey, love," Dani calls out to get my attention. It seems she's settled on *love* as my nickname, which doesn't bother me at all and is way better than Chief.

"Yeah?"

"Who was it that bought that house out on the highway that's been abandoned for like a million years? Jerry somebody?"

"Jerry Klein," I reply.

"Thanks, I couldn't remember." Then she goes back to talking to Bee. Birdie is asleep, curled up at Dani's side.

"Thanks, *love*," Blake says.

"Fuck you."

My brothers are smirking, and I grin and shake my head. "She wanted to call me Chief, and I didn't like it."

"Why not? You are the chief," Beck points out.

"Because it's my job. The guys who work for me call me that. People all over town call me that. Not my girl."

"I guess it would be weird if a woman I was involved with called me Doc," Blake says, thinking it over.

"Exactly. You get it. Like, can you imagine? You're in bed, and she's all, *'Faster, Doc.'*" Blake shivers, and we all laugh.

"Fuck, point taken," Blake says.

I stand and walk over to check on my girls and grin when Dani leans over to kiss Birdie on the head.

"You guys okay?"

"Your daughter is exhausted," Bee says, and her eyes are full of concern when she looks up at me.

"She did a lot this afternoon."

Bee frowns and looks down at Birdie. "I know, but it feels like more than that."

Blake hears us and walks over to press his hand to Birdie's forehead and checks her pulse. "She's just sleeping. Wore herself out."

"Heck, I could use a nap," Dani murmurs, but she's also watching Birdie closely.

"Call me if you need me," Blake says, patting me on the shoulder before walking out. Brooks and Beck wave at us from the doorway.

"Come on." I lift Birdie into my arms and kiss her cheek. "Let's go home."

"Daddy?" Her voice is soft with sleep. "Can we have pizza for dinner?"

"Are you awake enough for pizza?"

"I just need a little sleep, but I'm hungry."

"How about homemade pizza?" Dani asks her. "Does that sound good?"

"Yeah." Birdie curls up against my chest and goes back to sleep.

"Do you want to join us?" I ask my sister, and to my surprise, she nods.

"I want to keep an eye on this one," Bee says, nodding to her niece. "And Dani makes the best home-made pizza, so it's totally for selfish reasons."

"Then let's go home and eat."

Chapter Twenty-Two

DANI

"**O**kay, guys, did you get your hand traced?" I'm walking around my classroom, guiding my students through an art project for Thanksgiving. It's the standard, trace the hand and turn it into a turkey craft. One that's been done for generations.

And, since it's a half day of school today because tomorrow is Thanksgiving, we're having fun.

"Good job, Ariel," I say, patting a little blond-haired girl on the shoulder.

We only have a half hour left of classtime today, and that's about how long it takes for my kids to glue their projects together.

"I hope you all have a good long weekend," I say to my class. "Have lots of fun, okay?"

The bell rings, and the kids gather their bags and papers and coats and start to file out of my classroom.

A little boy named Mason approaches me with pink cheeks and shy, downcast eyes.

"Hey, Mason. Do you need something?"

"Um, Miss Dani? Could I maybe take some food home with me?"

And just like that, my heart breaks for this little boy. He's so thin, and more times than not, his clothes are dirty. His parents didn't come to parent-teacher conferences, and he rides the bus to and from school, so I've never met them.

It's pretty plain to see that Mason has a rough life at home, even if that means neglect.

And I completely relate to him.

"Of course, you can. Let's go shopping in the closet, shall we?"

He nods and slips his sweet little hand into mine as we walk to the treat cabinet. For ten minutes, we fill a reusable bag that I keep on hand, just for these occasions, and he chooses some soups and other nonperishable meals that he can heat up at home, along with some snacks.

I want to take him home with me and feed him anything he wants.

"Thank you," he says with a smile before he leaves to catch his bus.

With a sigh, I turn to find Birdie still sitting at her desk. Bridger's been working extra hours this week because one of his guys just welcomed a new baby and is on paternity leave. Needless to say, Birdie and I haven't seen much of him lately, and we miss him.

"Are you about ready to go home, pumpkin?" I rub Birdie's back soothingly.

"I guess."

"What's wrong, honey? Are you feeling okay?"

"I miss Daddy."

I squat beside her and kiss her cheek. "I know you do. I do, too. I have an idea. Your dad and his guys have been working extra hard this week, right?"

She nods, watching me.

"What if you and I go home and make them something super delicious for dinner, and then we take it to them at the fire station?"

Birdie's eyes brighten at the idea. "Okay."

"Let's FaceTime your dad right now, to make sure it's okay with him. What do you think?"

"Yes. Let's do it."

I walk to my desk and gesture for Birdie to follow me, and we sit in my chair, my sweet girl in my lap, and Face-Time Bridger.

He answers on the second ring.

"Hey, it's my girls. Is school finished already?"

"Hi, Daddy," Birdie says and blows him a kiss.

"Hi, peanut. Did you have a good day?"

"Yeah, we made a turkey out of our hand. It was weird."

Bridger laughs. "You still do that?"

"We do," I confirm. "Hey, Birdie and I have a question. Would it be okay if she and I make a ton of food for you and your guys for dinner and bring it by later? If something comes up and there's an emergency, just let me know, but otherwise, would that be okay?"

"Are you kidding me?" He looks exhausted as he sighs. "Nothing would be better than seeing you two. We'd love that, and thanks for letting me know. We won't cook anything."

"Good. Are there any allergies or anything I need to know about?"

"Nope. We'll eat anything, and lots of it. There are eight of us here today."

"Awesome. Birdie and I better get to work, then. I'll text you when we're on our way."

"I love you guys," Bridger says to both of us. "I can't wait to see you."

"We love you, too, Daddy," Birdie says, and we both blow him another kiss before I end the call and slip my phone into my purse.

"It's settled, then. Let's go make some delicious food for everyone, shall we?"

"Yes! Can we make lasagna? With bread and salad and stuff?"

"I think that's a great idea. Absolutely. Come on, let's go to the store and then get to work."

Less than an hour later, we're standing in the kitchen, assembling a lasagna and getting it ready for the oven.

"It's going to be *so delicious*," Birdie says.

"I think so, too. Now, while this bakes, let's you and I grab a little lunch. What do you say?"

"Yeah, I'm hungry."

After I get Birdie set up with some scrambled eggs, toast, and fruit, I make myself a quick sandwich and then get to work on the garlic bread. Of course, then I decide to be extra and make a cake.

Because everyone needs dessert.

Finally, when I have two pans of lasagna, three loaves of garlic bread, a huge green salad, and a chocolate cake wrapped up and secure in my car—after many trips back and forth—I text my man.

> **Me:** Your dinner is ready. Is this still okay?

> **My Love:** We're all excited. Ready when you are.

"Come on, pumpkin, we're heading over to see your dad."

Birdie comes running down the hall from her room, ready to go, and I shoot off one last text.

> **Me:** There's a lot here. We could use some help with it when we get there.

Once Birdie is secure in her seat, I head out, driving over to the fire station across town. When I pull into the parking lot, I'm stunned to find eight firefighters waiting for us. Bridger's smile lights me up inside.

"Hey," I say, climbing out of the car as Birdie jumps out, too.

"We're here to help," Bridger says as he wraps his arm

around my waist and kisses me before he lifts Birdie into his arms, hugging her close.

The others are already pulling things out of the back of the SUV and heading inside with it.

"This smells good."

"I'm freaking starving."

I grin at Bridger. "This is fun. We'll have to do it more often."

"You'll spoil my guys," he says as he leads us inside, his fingers laced with mine, palm to palm, and it feels so good to be close to him.

"And *my* guy, so it's totally worth it."

Birdie is already flirting with one of the men who's helping her scoop up a small slice of lasagna for herself while everyone else digs in.

But Bridger hasn't left my side.

"Don't you want to eat?" I ask him, enjoying the way it feels to be tucked up against his side, his hand on my hip. I've missed him just as much as his daughter has.

"I will. There's plenty. But I haven't seen you awake in days, so I'd rather just stand here, holding you for as long as I can."

I turn fully into him and wrap my arms around him, holding on tight. "Do you still have tomorrow off?"

"Yeah. Tomorrow and Friday, back at it Saturday."

"At least we get you for two whole days." I grin up at him, and he bends down to kiss me softly.

No one comments. They all act like they don't even see us.

"Hey, Diego, are you and Birdie okay? I need to talk to Dani in my office for a minute."

"Sure, we are." The man, so big and tanned with tons of tattoos, grins at Birdie, who, if I'm not mistaken, just batted her eyelashes at him. "You wanna hang with me for a bit, beautiful?"

"Yeah." Birdie nods, and I can't help but smirk.

"We'll be back," Bridger says as he takes my hand and leads me down a hallway to his office, then closes and locks the door.

"Did you see your daughter flirting with that guy?"

"What?" He stops dead in his tracks. "What the fuck are you talking about?"

"Nothing. Forget I said anything. What's up? What do we need to talk about?"

But he doesn't answer me with words. He frames my face in his hands, backs me against the wall, and kisses me, setting my entire body on fire. His mouth feels like heaven, and then he licks my lips, and I open for him, and he sinks into me, letting out a soft moan that I feel all the way to my core.

I grip his sides, my hands fisted in his shirt, and then his hands are on my ass and he's carrying me across the room to his desk. The door is locked, the blinds pulled, and Bridger is on a mission.

"I'm hungry for you," he growls against my neck as his fingers dive into the waistband of my leggings, tugging them down over my hips, to my ankles, where they get stuck at my shoes. With a chuckle, I toe off the shoes, and Bridger manages to get my bottoms all the way off. Then he's spreading me wide and kneeling before me. "This is the only thing I want to eat right now."

"Holy cow." My hand dives into his hair and holds on as he lowers his face and licks me along my entire slit.

"Fuck, babe, you're so wet. So fucking beautiful."

He's lapping at me as if he's starving, and I have to cover my mouth with my hand so I don't make too much noise.

What is it with this man making me crazy where I can't make noise?

"Bridge." I'm panting, reaching for him. "Please, I need you inside of me. Please."

"God, I love it when you ask me for it." He plants a wet kiss on my inner thigh, then stands and unfastens his pants, unleashes his already hard cock, and immediately pushes inside of me, filling me up and making me groan. "There's nothing like this. Nothing in the world makes me feel like you do."

"Nothing," I echo. He pushes in and presses against my clit, making me clench around him. His face is in my neck, his mouth on me, licking and nibbling, as he moves quickly, in and out of me in the most delicious rhythm. "God, I love it."

"Love what, kitten?"

I grin, secretly loving this game. "When you fuck me like this. With your big, hard—" I gasp because his thumb is pressed to my clit, making all the words in my head disintegrate.

"Go on."

"Cock."

"That's right." He crushes his mouth to mine now, and cups his hand around my ass, pulling me even tighter against him, and I can't take it. My muscles start to clench even tighter around him. "Come on me, sweetheart."

"Bridge." I can't catch my breath. "Shit."

"Yes, my love. Let go."

I couldn't stop it if I wanted to, and Bridger bites my shoulder and lets go with me, following me over with a climax that shudders through him.

"Fuck," he whispers. "I'll never look at this desk the same way again."

I lean my face into his chest and let out a little laugh. "Well, that was fun. I've missed you. Missed this. You didn't wake me up when you got home last night."

"You were sleeping so well." He kisses my cheek and down to my chin. "And you had to work this morning."

"Always wake me up." I cup his face. "Always. We need this."

"Agreed." He kisses me so tenderly, so softly that my heart catches before he pulls out of me and reaches for a box of tissues to clean us up.

When our clothes are righted, Bridger tugs me to him again.

"I don't want to say goodbye yet. Come out and eat with me."

"Okay. I'd like that." He opens the door of his office and leads me down the hallway. "Has the arsonist stopped his shenanigans? You haven't mentioned it in a while."

Bridger blows out a breath and runs his hand through his hair. "I don't trust it, and I don't want to jinx it by saying too much, but there hasn't been any activity in a while."

"That's good."

When we walk back into the small kitchen and eating area for the firefighters, we find Birdie sitting *on* the table, with a big plate of chocolate cake on her lap.

"Whoa," I say, stepping forward. "Who gave you that huge piece of cake?"

"Him." She points to Diego, the guy she was flirting with earlier, and I narrow my eyes at him.

"She's a master at getting what she wants," he says, with his hands up. "I just do her bidding."

"Yeah, well, that's way too much cake." I take the plate from her and don't miss the way her face falls as I cut it into thirds and give her back her share. Then I send Bridger a horrified look. "I'm so sorry. That wasn't my place, and I should have checked with you."

"Bull." He kisses my lips and then walks over to the pan of lasagna where he dishes us both a helping. "Don't second-guess us now, kitten."

Pressing my lips together, I sit next to my guy at the table, and we dig into our food as Birdie eats her cake.

I'm so glad we did this today. I needed time with Bridger, even if he hadn't swept me back to his office. I just enjoy being near him.

"This is really good. Birdie, did you make this?"

"Yep," the little girl says. "But Miss Dani helped."

I wink at Bridger and notice that most of the other

firefighters have finished their food and have dispersed to other places.

"Will you be home late again tonight?" I ask Bridger.

"My shift ends at ten," he says and reaches over to tuck my hair behind my ear. "So, unless something catastrophic happens, not too late."

"I'll wait up." I take his hand and kiss his palm. "And tomorrow, we're all going to Ryan Wild's for Thanksgiving. Like, all three families."

"Yep." Bridger grabs the empty plate from his daughter. "It's going to be a shit ton of people, but luckily, Ryan's a billionaire and built a huge house, so there's room."

"I should be baking today to take something over."

Bridger frowns and shakes his head. "No. Stupidly rich, remember? Ryan's having it all catered, and they won't forget anything. He doesn't want anyone to have to do any of the work. It'll be nice."

"It'll be overwhelming." I shrug a shoulder. "But yes, it'll be nice. Well, Birdie, should we get home and start settling in for the night?"

"Okay." Birdie crawls into her dad's lap and gives him a hug. "I love you, Daddy."

"I love you, too, peanut. Be good tonight, okay?"

"I will."

He walks us out to the car and makes sure Birdie gets secured into her seat before he opens the driver's door for me. Before I can get in, he cups my face and kisses me sweetly.

"Thank you for this. I really needed it. All of it."

Grinning, I rub a circle on his chest. "Me, too. It was my pleasure. I'll see you in a few hours."

I get in and start the car, waving to Bridger as he shoves his hands into his pockets and watches us pull away.

I've just pulled out onto the street when I see who I'm sure is Angela coming in the opposite direction, and she's signaling to turn into the fire station.

I quickly shoot Bridger a text.

> Me: Just saw Angela turning into your parking lot. Heads-up.

Biting my lip, I do my best to set that aside and get us home safely.

His text comes in immediately.

> My Love: Thank you. I got this, don't worry. I love you.

Chapter Twenty-Three

BRIDGER

Seeing my girls today, after the longest work week I've had for a while, was the best. Taking Dani into my office and sinking inside of her? Nothing beats that. It was a fantastic couple of hours.

And then Dani's text came through.

I'm swinging from *best day ever* to *you have got to be fucking kidding me* in the span of two minutes.

So, it's no surprise when the outdoor doorbell rings, and one of my guys calls out to me.

"Hey, Chief, there's someone here for you."

Walking down the hallway, I shift my shoulders and concentrate on keeping my face impassive and my body loose.

I won't let her know that she gets to me. That's what she wants.

"Bridger!" Angela's face brightens with a wide smile, and she opens her arms, as if she wants a hug, and I shove my hands into my pockets.

"Hello, Angela. What's up?"

She sticks her lower lip out in a pout. God, did I ever think she was cute? For fuck's sake.

"Can we talk in private, please?"

It feels disloyal to take her to my office when, less than an hour ago, I was making love to the woman of my dreams in there, so instead, I lead Angela into a conference room and close the door behind us.

Before I can evade, Angela's hands are gliding up my back, and she's plastered herself to me, and I push her away.

"Don't touch me." My voice is even, but I'm so fucking pissed off, I want to throw her ass out of here.

"Oh, please. The sex between us was always good, honey, and you know it. We did some fun shit. Remember that time—"

"We're not here to walk down memory lane. What do you want?"

She lets out a gusty breath, and then to my utter entertainment, tears fill her eyes.

"Oh, Bridger. I just miss my baby so much." She swallows hard and brushes daintily at a tear. "I made a huge mistake when I left the two of you. I know that now, and I've come to apologize and get my family back."

"We were never a family."

"Don't say that." She shakes her head and covers her mouth. "You don't mean that."

"I do mean it." I cross my arms over my chest and wait. Angela breaks down into more tears and theatrically brushes them aside before lowering into a chair.

"I know I deserve the cold shoulder. I was horrible to you. I know that."

"Do you know it?" I tilt my head to the side, watching her. Watching the calculation move through her hard, calculating eyes. "Leaving me in the NICU by myself with a tiny baby. Leaving me at home with her, to take care of her, while you did what and who knows what? That's just the tip of the iceberg."

"I've changed."

I bark out a laugh at that. "No, you haven't. What, did Mister New York dump you?"

A sneer moves over her mouth, and I know that I've hit the nail on the head.

"Ah, there it is. Well, you're not welcome at my house."

"Don't tell me that you're actually into Dani Lexington." She scoffs at that and then lets out a laugh, pushing her long blond hair back over her shoulder. "Come on, Bridger. She's so ... *plain*. Such a fucking doormat, and she's—"

"One. More. Word." I let the anger show on my face now as I glare at her. "Say one more word about her, and you'll be sorry."

"Right. I'll say you tried to assault me in here."

My stomach rolls with nausea.

"There are cameras in this room." I point to two corners. "Do you think I'm stupid enough to be alone with you without it being recorded? Now, what do you want? I won't ask you again."

She blows out a breath, no sign of tears in sight, and pushes her hands through her hair.

"Are you sure I can't have *you*?"

"Let me make this perfectly crystal clear." I lower myself and get within a foot of her face. "There will never be a time or a circumstance where I would want you in Birdie's or my lives. You'll never touch me. You'll never so much as breathe near me after this."

"I need money, Bridger."

At that, I stand back up and laugh.

"I tried to get my car fixed, but Brooks wouldn't help me because you've turned your whole family against me."

"You did that all on your own." Jesus, she's a piece of work.

"Look, I don't want to stay in this shitty little town." She stands and walks across the room to the other side of the table and sets her hands on her hips. "My parents sold the hardware store, and they're going to spend every dime of that money, traveling and God knows what. They're not going to leave anything to me. There's no reason for me to be here. If you'll give me some money, I'll go, and you'll never hear from me again."

I want to laugh.

I want to rage.

Instead, I nod slowly, as if I'm actually considering this. "For the rest of Birdie's life, you'll stay away if I give you money?"

"Yes, I swear it."

"How much do you think I should give you?"

"One million dollars." Her face is perfectly serious. "And buy me a new car."

I continue to nod, and she gets bolder.

"Come on, I know you can get the money. Beckett could take out a loan against the ranch, or hell, one of your good friends is a billionaire. Ask Ryan Wild. I don't care who you get it from, just pay me, and I'll go away."

"And if I refuse?"

There's so much coldness in her eyes.

"I hear Dani's renting the house across from yours."

My hands fist in my pockets.

"It sure would be a shame if something happened to her."

"You're so fucking stupid, Angela." I start to laugh and enjoy the look of pure shock that crosses her face. "How did you think that you could show up here and make demands? How did you think that you could ask for anything from me?"

"I'm Birdie's mother!"

"You're nothing." I don't hold back the disgust anymore. "You're no one. You signed away your rights to *my* daughter years ago. Without hesitation. Without a flicker of emotion. You have no more claim to her than you do a stranger on the street."

She huffs out a breath, and I continue.

"In addition, there is a restraining order that prevents you from going anywhere near Birdie *or* Dani so you don't try to pull any of your shit the way you did at the school. In fact, that order covers this fire station, and with one phone call, I could have you in jail."

"Like restraining orders do anything," she mutters.

"I don't give a shit where you go, where you live, or what you do," I continue. "But you won't come near my kid or my girl, or I'll have you arrested."

"You'd have the mother of your child *arrested*?"

"Without a second fucking thought." I shake my head at her again. "Go away, Angela. Go find a life that makes you happy, and leave us alone."

"Wait, you're not giving me any money?"

I blink at her and then look at the ceiling. "Did you not hear anything I just said?"

"I thought you were just lecturing me. I figured on that. Mr. Goody-two-shoes who never does anything wrong was sure to give me a firm talking to, but I need that money, Bridger."

"And I need you gone."

"Bridger!"

"No." I point at her, my voice rising. "I'm not giving you a fucking dime. Ever. Get the fuck out of my building and out of my town."

I open the door and point for her to leave. She marches out, past me, and down the hall to the building entrance. As she opens the door, she pauses dramatically and turns back to me.

"This isn't over."

"It's been over for almost five years. Go fuck yourself, Angela."

After I make sure that she's pulled out of my parking lot, I call Chase Wild.

"Hey, Bridger," he says.

"Hey. I have a situation." I quickly tell him about Angela, remind him about what happened at the school, and then relay what just went down here. "I can give you the security footage from the conference room."

"Yeah, I'll take that. We'll drive by yours and Dani's houses regularly until we know Angela has left town."

"I appreciate that. I think she's all talk. She's so fucking horrible, so entitled and selfish, but as far as I know, she's never done anything violent in the past. She talks a big game."

"Still, we want to keep documentation on all of this. If she does go to your house, or anywhere else on the restraining order, we can pick her up."

"Thanks, man. I'll see you tomorrow, yeah?"

"Yep, we'll all be there. See you then."

Chase hangs up, and I walk into the area where my guys are.

"Did you see that woman who was just in here?"

They nod.

"Yeah, we know who she is, Chief."

"If she *ever* so much as sniffs around this place again, you call the cops. Got it?"

More nods.

"Got it."

Chapter Twenty-Four

DANI

"Dani?"

I've just walked past Birdie's room, and her little voice calls out to me.

"Hey, pumpkin." I push into her room and sit at the edge of the bed, smoothing her dark hair away from her sweet face. "You're supposed to be sleeping."

Pickles is purring at Birdie's hip, and I reach over to scratch her behind the ears.

"I know." Birdie yawns widely and holds my hand in hers. "Today was fun, taking Daddy and the others food."

"I thought so, too." *Especially in Bridger's office. Talk about hot.* The only thing that left a sour taste in my mouth was seeing Angela en route to see Bridger, too. He hasn't texted me about it, so I hope that means that nothing came of it. "Maybe that'll be something we do more often. Maybe once a month. Would you like that?"

"Yeah, it would be fun, and we can change the menu."

I grin at her. Sometimes, this little peanut is five going on thirty. "That sounds fun. I'm definitely down for that. What else is on your mind tonight?"

Typically, Birdie has no problem going to sleep at bedtime, so I wonder if something is bothering her.

"You live here. With me and Daddy and Pickles."

"Yes, I do. Are you sure that's okay with you?"

"I like it." She smiles at me, and I can't resist leaning in to kiss her little cheek.

"Good. I do, too. I love spending time with you and your daddy, but I also love it when you and I get time alone, like we have recently. Even though I miss your dad when he works so much, I love it that I get to be with you, you know?"

Birdie nods and releases my hand so she can reach down to pet Pickles.

"Yeah, me, too. Now, I don't have a bunch of different babysitters all the time, and I get to stay home with you when Daddy's working."

"Yeah, unless we decide to go somewhere. Do you still like being in my class? Because that's a lot of time together."

"I love school." Her eyes are starting to get droopy. "Our class is so much fun, and Ariel is my best friend."

The two little girls have become close, spending recess together and eating lunch together, as well. They're adorable.

"I like Ariel, too."

Birdie nods. "Ariel has a mommy *and* a daddy."

Ah, here we go.

"Yes, I've met them, and they're very nice people. Has Ariel told you about them?"

She nods again. "Sometimes, a kid can live with both their mommy and daddy, but sometimes they only live with one of them."

"Sometimes, yes."

"But I live with my dad and you. Together."

I press my lips together and nod, wanting to pull this sweet baby in for a big hug.

"So, does that make you my mommy?"

Oh, my heart.

"Well, I think that's a good question, sweetie. I love you so much, my whole body is bursting with it. You are such an incredible person, a wonderful little girl, and I'm so grateful that you're in my life. Do you know that I love you?"

"Of course." She frowns up at me, the immediate acceptance of my feelings humbling me. "You tell us all the time that you love us."

"Because I do, and I want to make sure you know it. That you never forget it. If we ever get to a place where you call me Mommy, it will make me the happiest person in the whole world. No one means more to me than you and your dad. I think we make a really great little family, don't we?"

"We're pretty much the best." I love her confidence so much.

Birdie yawns again and settles into her pillow.

"I'm sleepy."

"Go to sleep, sweetheart. You get to sleep in tomorrow. No school, remember?"

"Yeah. Good night."

"'Night, pumpkin."

I sit with her for a few moments longer, making sure that she's out cold before I leave her room, pulling the door most of the way shut behind me.

Talk about an arrow to the heart.

That little girl has managed to work her way into my heart and soul, and I don't think that I could love her any more if I'd given birth to her.

She's important to me. She's a *part* of me.

As I glance outside, I can see that the moon is out, and it's been a while since I laid on the driveway to watch the stars and do my meditation. I bundle up in warm clothes, complete with a Bitterroot Valley Fire Department hoodie of Bridger's, then wrap myself in a blanket and pad out to the driveway.

It's chilly, but I don't mind. The sky is clear, and there must be trillions of stars out this evening.

Lying on my back, I look up and watch a satellite make its way across the sky. The conversation with Birdie is still fresh in my mind. Am I her mommy? It feels like it, and not just because I take care of her so much, filling that physical role. I feel an attachment, a connection to Birdie that I never expected. I love her so fiercely; there isn't anything that I wouldn't do for her.

Staring up at the stars, I start my affirmations.

I am a good teacher.

343

I am a good person.
I am worthy of love.
I am a good partner to Bridger.

I take a long, deep breath, pulling in the crisp night air, and then exhale as I hear a vehicle turn onto the street.

The door shuts, and then there's footsteps, and Bridger's looking down at me.

"It's too cold out here, kitten."

"Nah, it's not bad. Come on, get under my blanket with me." I hold it open for him, and Bridger shakes his head.

"I won't have you getting sick. I have the next best thing." He reaches down and helps me onto my feet, and then he leads me through the house and out the back door, onto the deck, where he turns on a propane heater, sets it on the floor of the deck near the steps, and leads me to sit next to him. "You can look up if you want, but you'll do it while warm."

"I love the way you take care of me." Bridger wraps us both in the blanket, and I snuggle against his side. "So, what happened after I left?"

I'm not going to qualify that question with an *unless it's none of my business.*

It's absolutely my business.

Bridger sighs and hugs me tighter.

"It was nothing that I didn't expect. Actually, that's not true. I should say that I didn't *expect* any of it, but it didn't surprise me. First, she tried to seduce me—"

"She did what?"

I'm going to rip her hair out by the roots.

"When that didn't work, she tried to get me and Birdie back."

Now she has to lose her eyes. And her kneecaps.

"And when *that* didn't work, she asked me for one million dollars and a new car to keep her away."

I feel my mouth hang open, and then I pull away from Bridger to look him in the face. "For what? She has no legal right to Birdie."

"I reminded her of that. Hey." He cups my cheek and brushes his thumb over my lips. "I need to make something clear here. I don't want you to be uncertain or think that I could *ever*, in any way, want her—"

"Stop." I shake my head and move in to straddle his lap. Bridger plants his hands on my ass as I get settled, and then those glorious hands move up my back, making me want to purr. "I know that in the beginning of you and me, I was uncertain. I wasn't confident in myself, and I questioned what was going on between us, but those doubts are long gone, love."

"Thank Christ." He exhales and tips his forehead to mine. "You're all I see, Dani."

"Same." I kiss his nose softly. "I have a few things to say. First, you're not Angela's family. You're *mine*. If she wanted you, *really* wanted you, I'd fight her off. I'm not afraid of her. She's not my bully anymore, and as far as I'm concerned, she can fuck right off."

"I fucking love it when you get worked up," he growls.

"She isn't a threat to my relationship, but she *is* a

threat to the happiness of that sweet little girl in there, because if Angela really wanted to, she could make things pretty miserable and scary for her."

"Over my dead fucking body."

"We're on the same page there. So, no, I'm not worried about her. She was a surrogate for Birdie and nothing more. Bridger, I love Birdie so much. She and I had a really interesting talk tonight."

"Tell me, sweetheart." His hands are rubbing up and down my back, and he lifts one so he can drag his fingertips down my cheek. "What did she say?"

"She and I spend a lot of time together these days." I tell him about my talk with his daughter, about her questioning if I'm her mom, and the warmth in his eyes only grows with each word. "I don't think I could love her more if I'd given birth to her. She's my girl, and I love her so—"

He grips my face and kisses me, so deeply, so urgently, that it makes my toes curl. My fingers dive into his hair, and I open to him, kissing him back just as feverishly, breathing in his spicy scent.

"God, I fucking love you," he says against my lips. "You came into our lives, and you just fit so perfectly. Of course, Birdie wants to call you her mommy because you *are* in every way that counts, sweetheart."

"I know." I feel the first tear fall on my cheek. "I love it, and it scares me."

"Okay." He nods, brushing away my tears. "Let's talk about it. What scares you?"

346

"You know what I come from." The admission is a whisper. "Bridge, what if—"

"You are not him." He's ferocious now, so adamant and strong. "Not one single, precious molecule of you is him. You would never hurt Birdie."

"Of course not." I scowl at him and shake my head. "What I mean is, I don't know how to be a mom. Mine died when I was so young, and my dad ... well. I worry that I wouldn't be good enough for her."

"You listen to me." He frames my face once more, his dark eyes so intense, holding my own. "You're more than enough, for both of us. I hate to break it to you, but you've been doing pretty much everything a parent does for that little girl since school started. And she fucking adores you. When you're not here, she asks for you."

"Just like she does you when you're not here."

He nods, and a smile spreads over his impossibly handsome face. "Besides, you had a mom. You had *my* mom, and I see so much of her in you when you're with Birdie. I love our family, Dani. If Birdie wants to call you Mom, I have no issue with that at all because you're ours, until the last star falls out of that sky."

He points up, but I don't look. *Can't* look. Because his words ... his words have slayed me.

"You've been doing pretty much everything a parent does for that little girl since school started. And she fucking adores you. I love our family, kitten. If Birdie wants to call you Mom, I have no issue with that at all because you're ours, until the last star falls out of that sky."

Our family. Nothing has ever sounded so wonderful.

347

I can't look away from him at all.

"I love you so much, Bridger Blackwell."

It's been almost four months since the last time we were all at Ryan and Polly Wild's house for the summer pool party. This time, the pool is closed for the year, and we're all inside, in the biggest kitchen and dining room I've ever seen.

I needed just a minute to myself, so I walked over to the wall of glass that looks out to the mountains and the backyard, where the pool is.

So much has changed since I jumped into that godforsaken water that day. All the same people are here, but I don't feel the same at all.

I'm bolder.

Stronger.

And so in love, I'm almost stupid with it. I knew coming home was the right thing, but I hadn't expected to be this happy.

"Here you are," Bee says as she links her arm with mine. "You okay, buddy?"

"Oh, yeah, I just needed a second to take a breath. Can you believe I jumped into that pool a few months ago?"

"No. It scared the shit out of all of us. Why, are you thinking of doing it again?"

"Absolutely not." I shake my head with a laugh. "I

think one swim a decade is good enough for me. I draw the line at bathtubs and showers."

"Fair enough." Bee sighs as she also looks outside. "The mountains are pretty today."

"They're pretty every day. Any sign of your mystery man?"

"Nah. He's probably back in Scotland or England, or wherever he's from. It's fine. I've come to terms with it. I haven't slut-shamed myself too badly over it."

"There will be *none* of that." I frown over at her. "You didn't do anything wrong."

"I know." She chuckles. "I'm just being funny. I wouldn't say no to a repeat, though. A girl could get addicted to that."

"I know." My smile is smug, and Bee giggles.

"He's watching you right now, you know."

"Your brother?"

"Better be my brother, or he'll kill someone. Of course, my brother."

I look over my shoulder, and sure enough. My man is standing with my brother, and they're talking about something serious, if the looks on their faces are any indication.

"I wonder what they're talking about," I ask Bee.

"Might be cows, might be fire, might be marriage." She shrugs, and my eyes bulge out of my head.

"*Marriage*?"

"Sure. For all intents and purposes, Holden is your dad, babe. If Bridger wants to marry you, he needs to talk to your brother."

I hadn't even thought about marriage. I mean, sure, someday, but it wasn't really on my radar.

And we don't know that that's what they're talking about now, so I need to cool my jets.

Just as we're wrapping up, ready to head out, Bridger and Chase both get phone calls at the same time.

"We've gotta go, sweetheart," Bridger says to me just as Chase looks up and nods to Summer. "I have to go to work."

"What?" I frown up at him. "Why?"

"Because the goddamn ski resort is on fire."

Chapter Twenty-Five

BRIDGER

"I'm so damn sorry." I've got my girls in the truck, and we're headed to the house in town. I need to drop them off and change into my uniform, grab my gear bag, and then meet my men up on the mountain. They'll bring any tools that I need from the fire station. "We were supposed to spend our first Thanksgiving together, and—"

"Stop," Dani says, reaching over to take my hand in hers. She lifts it to her lips and kisses me sweetly. "We're fine. Aren't we, Birdie?"

"We're fine," Birdie echoes, making me chuckle.

"Actually, Birdie, would you like to come over to the other house with me, and we'll start packing? You can play in my makeup and stuff."

"Yes! Can I try on the makeup, too?"

"Sure, why not." Dani shrugs as if it's no big deal. "It's bath night anyway. It'll wash off."

351

I love how chill she is with Birdie. Dani's not afraid of a mess and enjoys having fun with my girl.

It's sexy as fuck.

"Do you think?" Dani whispers to me, and I nod my head, reading her mind.

"Probably." *Yeah, it's probably the motherfucking arsonist.*

"I wonder how bad it is," she says.

"I should hear soon. I'm sorry, but it's going to be a quick drop-off—"

"Hey, this isn't my first rodeo with the chief," Dani reminds me. "Stop feeling so guilty. This is your *job*. I'm not mad or disappointed or upset at you. I promise."

My chest loosens at her reassurance, and I smile over at her. "Thanks, kitten."

"Of course."

Ten minutes after I drop the girls off at home, I'm headed back out and up to the resort. The police have already done a good job of blocking off traffic up the mountain to anyone but first responders, and there's been a steady stream of civilian traffic coming down.

It's bad enough to evacuate.

"Shit," I mutter, and once I'm on the scene, I park and hurry over to where Rhodes, the chief of police, is, along with some of my senior guys. "What have we got?"

I can see the smoke and some of the flames coming up from the Snow Ghost, but then another fire catches my eye, and I realize that the condos are on fire, as well.

"We have four individual blazes," Jones says, pointing. "The pub, the condos, the main lodge, and the ski rental cabin."

"Fuck," I growl.

"We have surrounding area teams on the way," Rhodes says. "My guys are evacuating everyone, not just the condos and the lodge, but also the surrounding homes, just in case this gets out of hand."

"Excellent." I nod at him and turn to Jones. "Let's get these fires out."

Suddenly, there's an explosion that makes my ears ring and my chest tighten.

"Gas stove in the pub," someone says. "Had to be."

"Get those lines shut off," I yell, and run off to do my job. The fire is loud and spreading too fast. The smoke is thick, making it hard to see well, and I pull on my mask so I don't inhale too much soot.

The motherfucker wanted the entire village to go up in flames, and he might get his goddamn wish.

For the next few hours, we work fast. More engines and crews show up to help us, spreading out over the entire resort to make sure the fires don't spread to nearby homes and other buildings. The fires have been too hot for us to get inside, but we have tall ladders that can shoot the water from above, and that seems to be the most effective, particularly on Snow Ghost Pub.

"We need medical," I hear in my radio and feel my chest tighten. "Northeast corner of the condos, near run three."

"One of us?" I ask.

"No, I think we just found the goddamn arsonist."

I take off at a sprint. I'm at least a half a mile from there, but it'll be faster to run through the plowed parking lot than to weave my vehicle through, and it would just be in the way.

I'm shouting orders in my radio, calling for an ambulance and police presence, and when I turn the corner and take in the scene before me, nausea rolls through me.

"Jesus Christ, warn a guy."

"I didn't want to say this on the goddamn radio," Martinez says, shaking his head. "He's bleeding fast."

Martinez and I jump into action, stopping the blood pouring from his leg. He probably nicked the artery, and if we don't staunch the bleeding, he'll die before we get him into an ambulance.

"Damon Evans." Martinez shakes his head as we work on him. "The guy who applies for a job with us every fucking quarter, is passed up, but keeps coming back. This motherfucker has been torching our town."

"Made everyone pay," Evans whispers. "Passed me up, but I'll make them pay."

"Shut up," Martinez says. "Or I'll let you bleed."

"Go for a walk." I shove Martinez out of the way as more medics approach. "Go. Clear your head."

He doesn't argue with me, and I can't blame him for his outburst. I'm fucking pissed as hell, but we have a job to do.

"It's because of you that I'm missing the rest of my Thanksgiving with my family," I tell him, and watch as he smirks. "You think that's funny?"

"Should've given me a fucking job."

I lean in so only he can hear me. "You weren't good enough for this job. You're a fuckup, Damon. You couldn't pass the physical tests, and you couldn't pass the psych. No matter how many times you applied, you were never going to be chosen."

"You're a motherfucking asshole," he growls.

"Yeah, but I haven't tried to torch my whole town."

"I should have set your house on fire," he spits out. "I was going there next, and then I had to fall and get fucking caught."

What the actual fuck? Did he seriously just threaten to hurt my family? I want to put a fist through this guy's face, but I rein in my anger.

We've caught him.

The girls aren't in danger.

This madman will be put away and won't be able to harm anyone else.

We've got him.

"I think you should stop fucking talking right about now, asshole."

Chapter Twenty-Six

DANI

"I'm gonna need a dumpster brought in for all of this junk." I blow out a breath, eyeing my kitchen. Almost everything I have is old, second or third hand-me-downs, and Bridger has nicer stuff than I do, so I don't really have to take any of this over there.

In fact, it'll mostly just be the rest of my clothes and bathroom stuff, a few personal things, and that's about it. I'll donate the furniture.

I glance over to where Birdie's sitting on the couch, with my makeup bag in her lap, but she doesn't look terribly enthused about looking through it.

"How are you doing, pumpkin?"

She looks up at me, and I set the old dishes on the counter and hurry over to her. Something's not right.

"I don't feel so good." She shakes her head mournfully, and I kneel in front of her and brush my hand down her long hair.

"Okay, what do you need? Should we go home?"

"Yeah, I wanna go home. Okay?"

"You got it."

I don't even bother to turn off any lights or anything. I just lock the door behind me and, carrying my sweet girl, hurry across the street and get us inside and to the couch, where she immediately relaxes and snuggles into a blanket.

"Does that feel better?"

"Yeah." She looks a little pale, so I check her temperature, but she doesn't feel hot.

"Baby, does your tummy hurt?"

"No."

"Does it feel like you want to throw up?"

"I don't know." She starts to cry big, sad tears, and my heart aches for her, so I sit with her and stroke her hair softly. "Why do I always feel bad?"

"I wish with my whole heart that we knew." I kiss her head and murmur to her how special she is. "You're so sweet, pumpkin. I'm so sorry."

She takes a long, deep breath. "Maybe we could make cookies?"

My eyebrows climb. "You're feeling better?"

"A little. Maybe if we make cookies, I won't think about feeling bad."

Ah, distraction. I've used it myself often.

"We can do that. But, why don't you lie here while I make the dough, and then you can help me get it in the oven if you're feeling well enough?"

She nods, and I get her settled by herself on the couch, tucked in with the TV remote, and then I get to work in the kitchen, assembling the dough for simple snickerdoodles.

Birdie likes to roll the balls of dough in the cinnamon sugar before they go on the cookie sheets.

When I glance up to ask Birdie to come help me, I see that she's fallen asleep, so I leave her be and continue with the cookies. When the third tray is in the oven, Birdie wakes up and moans.

"Hey, baby." I hurry over to her, and when I touch her hair, it's wet with sweat, but she still doesn't feel hot. "Honey, how do you feel?"

"Icky." She swallows hard, like she's trying not to throw up, so I run and get a big bowl, just in case. "Why is the room moving?"

"Are you dizzy?"

"Yeah."

I take a deep breath. She's never been this bad when I've been alone with her. I can't call Bridger because he's in the middle of a huge fire, so I grab my phone and call the only other person I know who can help me.

"Hello?" Blake says.

"Hey, it's Dani. Blake, I'm sorry to bother you, but Birdie isn't okay. Bridger's still gone, and—"

"I'm on my way," he says. "Be there in less than ten, okay?"

"Thank you so much." Relief washes through me as he hangs up the phone, and I turn to my little girl. "Uncle Blake is gonna come help us out. I don't like that you're so sick."

"I don't like it either," she says, her voice so achingly small. "Will you hold me?"

"Of course, honey." I sit next to her, and she scrambles into my lap and rests her little head against my chest.

Birdie's five, but she's small for her age. I know that she was a preemie and that she's still catching up to other kids her age, and that makes her feel all the more fragile.

I hear Blake's vehicle pull up, and he knocks once before opening the unlocked door, and he smiles at us as he steps inside, carrying a black case.

"You have an old-fashioned doctor's bag." I grin at him. "That's so cool."

Blake laughs and kneels in front of us. "Hey, cupcake. Did you miss me?"

"I always miss you," she says to him. "But I don't feel good."

Blake's brown eyes sober, and he sighs, watching her. "I can see that. Let's have a look."

He reaches into his bag and pulls out his stethoscope, a blood pressure cuff, and the many other tools that are usually in an exam room, and he gets to work. She stays on my lap, but he has her lean forward.

"You're breathing fast," he murmurs, his eyes closed as he listens to her lungs. "But you sound clear. Does it hurt to breathe?"

"No."

He looks in her mouth and her ears, and he takes her temperature several times.

"No fever."

The timer on the oven goes off, and I move Birdie off my lap so I can go take the cookies out of the oven.

After pulling that batch out, I put another pan in, set the timer, and then return to my baby.

"She sweated out during her nap," I tell him. "She said she doesn't have to throw up, but she's been dizzy."

He frowns, looking at her. "Why can't I figure you out, cupcake?"

"I have a question." He turns to me, listening, and I clear my throat. "I know I'm not a doctor—"

"I want to hear what you have to say. You live with her, Dani. Ask."

"Could she have celiac disease? I had a roommate in college who did, and her symptoms were mostly different, but I've been wondering about it."

Blake chews on his lip and looks back to Birdie.

"We haven't tested her for it, but we should. I didn't consider that it could be a gastrointestinal thing. I was thinking endocrine. We even considered cystic fibrosis and a primary immunodeficiency. We screened her for cancers right away, and thank fuck those were all negative. Celiac is not typical in kids, but our girl likes to be unique."

I smile at Birdie, who's dozing against the couch.

"Thanks for the idea." Blake stands and, to my surprise, pulls me into a hug. "Thank you for being so good to them, by the way."

"I love them." I snuggle against him, accepting the comfort he's offering, just for a moment. "And I want her to feel better."

"I do, too." He steps back and sighs, and then, to our horror, Birdie wakes up, leans over, and tosses her Thanksgiving dinner onto the floor.

"So much for using the bowl," I mutter, as Birdie starts to cry, and Blake and I spur into action, cleaning up and stripping Birdie down, because she managed to get it all over herself, the blankets, *everywhere.* "I love that you never do anything halfway," I say to her.

"If you're gonna do it," Blake agrees, "do it big."

Blake puts the blankets in the laundry as I get Birdie in the shower, and when I'm drying her off and putting her in clean pajamas, I can hear the carpet-cleaning machine going in the living room.

"Wow, Doctor Blake cleans carpets." I kiss her on the forehead, and Birdie finally smiles at me. "Are you starting to feel better, my love?"

"I'm tired." She yawns. "But I feel a little better."

"Good. Maybe you ate something bad, and you just had to get it out of there."

Screech.

Oh, God, the smoke alarm. Birdie and I run out to find smoke coming out of the oven.

"Oh, crap!"

Blake is already pulling the burned cookies out of the oven, and I hurry to open windows to help get the smoke out.

"We were a little distracted," Blake says with a laugh. "Oops."

"I shouldn't have put that last pan in there. This really stinks. It's just some cookies; it shouldn't smell this

bad." As annoyed as I feel about them, I'm thankful
Blake was here to help with Birdie. I'd still be cleaning up
vomit from the carpets and furniture if he wasn't here.

I hope Bridger is doing okay up on the mountain. It
must be terrible if Chase was called at the same time—

"Why are there lights outside?" Birdie asks, pointing
to the front window, and Blake and I turn to see what
she's looking at.

"You two stay here," Blake says as he marches for the
front door, but when he opens it, there's no mistaking
what's going on out there.

My rental is on fire.

"What the hell?" I reply as I march outside and down
to the sidewalk. There's a lone police car, and Rod's
standing nearby, speaking into his radio.

"The blaze has enveloped the whole house," he says,
and all I can do is stare, zoning him out.

Everything I own is in that house.

Sure, I was going to donate most of it, but it was
mine. My photos, my books, the dress I wore when Millie
and Holden got married. I hadn't pulled out the senti-
mental things yet.

Feeling a hand on my shoulder, I turn and find Blake
standing behind me, Birdie in his arms.

"I'm sorry, honey," he says.

"I guess we didn't just smell the cookies." I shake my
head, taking it in. "Blake, I didn't leave anything on. Just
the lights, but not the oven or anything over there."

"It's not your fault," he replies.

"Oh, God. Everyone's up at the resort, fighting the

fire up there." Frantically, I turn to Rod. "No one can come fight this."

"They're on their way down," he says grimly. "But it's going to take a little time. This house is a loss, but I hope they're down in time to make sure the other houses around it don't ignite."

I cover my mouth and shake my head.

What if Birdie and I had still been inside it? What happens if it spreads before they get here?

Chapter Twenty-Seven

BRIDGER

"The condos, the rental building, and the lodge are all out," Jones says as he gives me the status update. "The pub is the last still burning, but it was the most extensive. He probably started there first and then made his way from there. It's a hot fucker."

"And the surrounding homes and trees?"

"No damage," he replies. "The resort is a mess and will likely need to be leveled and rebuilt, but that's a problem for someone else."

I nod, but I feel sick. This will have a huge impact on our economy and on people's livelihoods. It could be devastating for some, and that asshole did it on purpose.

"Where is he?" Jones asks me.

"I assume he's at the hospital by now. Ambulance took him an hour ago."

Jones shakes his head. "What a twisted motherfucker.

He did all of this because he was throwing a goddamn fit?"

"That's the gist of it, yeah." I sigh and watch as our guys send more water into the pub. "All those homes, the families hurt, all of this just because he didn't get his way. Like a fucking toddler. Scratch that, my daughter didn't throw fits this bad when she was a toddler."

Jones sucks in a breath. "Yeah, well, I hope he doesn't claim insanity or some shit and get away with it."

"Me, too."

"Chief!" I turn when Martinez comes running over to us. "We have another call in town. One of the engines is on the way there now."

"Are you fucking kidding me?" I scowl at him. "Where?"

He rattles off the address, and sheer terror rolls through me.

"Isn't that your house, Chief?" Jones asks.

"No, it's across the street, but my whole world is in that house." I take off to my truck. "Handle the rest of this, Jones!"

"I got it, Chief!"

Dani and Birdie went over there to pack. Jesus fucking Christ, they're in the house.

I pick up the phone and call Dani, my heart hammering in my throat and blood rushing through my ears as I drive down the mountain toward town.

"This is Dani. Please leave a message—"

"Fuck!" I end the call and try again, but it just rings and rings and rings in my ear until her voicemail picks up again. "They have to be out of the house. They *have* to be out of that fucking house."

The road down to town is windy and treacherous, and add in the dark and it's not quick or easy, and that only fuels my frustration and panic because I can't get to my girls.

I can't get to them.

Finally, I turn onto the road that gets me back into town, and as I approach, I can see the flames from two blocks away, where I have to park because the road is blocked off for the engines and first responders.

My blood runs cold when I see the ambulance.

In the second dead run of the night, I sprint down the middle of the street toward the fire, scanning the faces for Dani, but I don't see her.

"Status," I bark at my man as I approach the engine.

"It's a loss, Chief. We're focusing on keeping the homes around it safe while it burns out."

"Was anyone inside?"

"Bridger!" And just like that, my heart starts to beat again. I turn in time to catch Dani, who launches herself in my arms, and I hug her close. "Oh, my God, Bridge, you're here."

"Hey, it's okay. I'm right here. Birdie?"

"She's okay," she assures me. "She's fine. She's with Blake at Holden and Millie's."

"And why are you here?"

She shakes her head, almost like she's in a daze. "Because I had to wait for you."

"No, Dani, you shouldn't be here. This whole block is evacuated. Come on, we're going to your brother's."

I lead her the few blocks to Holden's and then see the group of them on Holden's porch.

"I'm so sorry," she says over and over again, her face pressed to my neck as she clings to me. I nudge her head up so I can look in her face, and she looks like she's in shock. Her gorgeous face crumples, and the tears start to come. "I'm so sorry."

"Hey, sweetheart, you didn't do anything wrong."

"That's what we keep telling her," Millie says as she runs her hand down Dani's arm. "And she wouldn't come back here with us."

"Would someone please tell me what happened?"

Dani cries against my shoulder, hard sobs that break my fucking heart.

"I was there," Blake says. He's holding Birdie, who looks terrified, and I nod to the house.

"Daddy," Birdie cries, and almost launches herself into my arms.

"It's okay, peanut. I'm here." And even though I'm covered in soot, I won't stop Birdie from snuggling into my chest. "Let's go inside."

"Wait." Dani lifts her head, pointing behind me. "Don't you have to put out the fire?"

"I have men for that, kitten. They have it covered. You're my priority right now. Let's go inside. I want to know if my girls were ever in that fire."

"No," Dani says, shaking her head. "We were over

there for a while after you dropped us off, but Birdie
didn't feel well, so we went home."

Home.

"I left the lights on and everything over there because
she was really bad, and I didn't want to waste time
getting her where she's comfortable."

I kiss her head and breathe her in, not caring at all
that she smells like smoke. She's safe, and she's whole,
and that's all that matters. "Thank you."

"Dani called me because Birdie really felt unwell,"
Blake continues. "So I came to have a look. Cupcake
threw up, and that set us in motion of cleaning everything up, including the kiddo."

"So, we didn't hear the oven timer go off," Dani picks
up. "I was baking cookies for Birdie and burned the last
batch. But when I opened the windows, the smell was
way worse than it should have been."

"I saw the lights," Birdie chirps and points out the
window. "And then we saw the fire, and it was scary."

"I bet that was scary." I kiss Birdie on the cheek. "Are
you feeling okay, peanut?"

"Yeah. I feel better. I'm not dizzy anymore."

"You're breathing okay, with all of that smoke?"

Birdie nods, but I make a mental note to grab the
rescue inhaler and keep it on me for a few days, just in
case.

"By the time we noticed what was going on, the fire
was bad," Blake says. "I have no idea when it started or
who called 911. I didn't see any signs of anything when I
got to your place about an hour before."

"It's an old house," Holden says, his arm around Dani, holding her close. "I'm no fire chief, but it doesn't surprise me that it went up quickly."

"You're right."

"I swear, I didn't leave anything else on," Dani says, shaking her head and turning pleading eyes up to her brother. "Just the lights. I never turned on the oven or a curling iron or even the TV. I don't know how this could have happened."

"It wasn't your fault," Holden says, kissing her on the forehead.

"Mommy's sad," Birdie says to me, and we all quiet, turning our heads to her. "Don't cry, okay? I'm sorry I got sick and we had to go home. Maybe it's my fault."

Dani pulls away from her brother and takes Birdie from me, hugging her close.

"This is *not* your fault," Dani says to her as she kisses her cheek. "Don't you even think that."

Birdie takes Dani's face in her tiny little hands and looks into her eyes. "Don't cry, Mommy. It's just an accident."

"Well, damn," Millie mutters as Dani starts to cry for all new reasons, and I just pull them both into my arms because I don't know what else to do. "Might be the sweetest moment ever. I'm such a crier these days."

Millie sniffles, so Holden wraps his arm around her. Then there's a knock at the door, and Blake looks grateful to have something to do as he crosses the room to open it.

"Chase," Blake says and stands back to let the man in.

"I thought you might be down here. Shitter of a night," Chase says in greeting as he joins us in the living room. "We've made an arrest."

"Good, that fucker deserves it," I reply, shaking my head. "You arrested him at the hospital?"

"Arrested who?" Millie wants to know.

"The arsonist," I reply.

"Oh, you found him?" Dani demands. "Who is it?"

"Can I have the attention again?" Chase asks, waving a hand. "Thanks. Yes, the arsonist is in custody, still at the hospital. But that's not who I was referring to. We've made an arrest in regard to the fire across from your house, Bridge."

Dani marches right over to him. "Who?"

Chase's eyes move up from Dani's to mine, and he blows out a breath. "It was Angela, Bridge."

Dani gasps.

"What the fuck?" Blake asks as I set Birdie gently on the couch, and she cuddles into a blanket, and then I turn my attention back to Chase.

"Why?" Holden asks.

But I know.

"Because she was mad that I wouldn't give her any money to stay away from us," I reply. "And because she knew she'd destroy me if she hurt Dani."

"She set the fire and then went to the Wolf Den, had a couple of drinks, and started bragging about it." Chase shakes his head. "Brenda the bartender called us, and we arrested her."

"Jesus," Blake mutters.

Dani hasn't moved. Hasn't torn her gaze away from Chase. She's just staring at him.

"She almost hurt my baby," she finally says. "If we'd been over there, Birdie could have been hurt. So, I want you to promise me that that bitch is going to jail, and she's going to stay there, or I'm going to hurt her."

"I didn't hear that last part," Chase says and reaches out to squeeze her shoulder. "We have a strong case, Dani. She's in a whole lot of trouble."

"Not as much as she'll be in if she gets out," Dani mutters, turning to me, her eyes hot. "That. F—"

"Okay." I take her face in my hands and lean in to kiss her. I'm fucking furious, my blood is boiling, but I think Dani's pissed enough for everyone in this room. "Take a breath, sweetheart."

"I didn't realize my sister had such a violent streak in her," Holden says, and Millie smirks.

"No," Blake says, shaking his head. "That's a mama bear, and she'll gut you without hesitation."

"Damn right," Dani mutters as I fold her into my arms.

"See?" I kiss the top of her head. "It wasn't your fault at all. Thank God you brought Birdie home."

"Yeah."

"You're incredible, baby." I lift her chin and smile down at her. "I love you so much."

"I love you, too."

"Marry me."

The room goes still, and Dani frowns up at me. "What?"

"Yeah, I know, I'm the king at blurting shit out even though I've planned something romantic, but I don't want to waste another second. You're mine. We're never letting you go. Marry me."

"Yeah, marry us," Birdie says, jumping to her feet and bouncing on the couch. "So we can wear pretty dresses!"

I hear Blake and the others mumbling and chatting, but I only have eyes for my girl.

"What do you say?"

"You want to marry me, even with all of my baggage, and—"

"You're the best thing that's ever happened to us." I tip my forehead to hers. "You're the piece that fits so seamlessly, so effortlessly, it's as easy as breathing. You're exactly what we need and who we love, and I don't have a moment of hesitation about your past. I lived it alongside you for years, and you'll continue to heal from it because you're strong and amazing, and I'm in awe of you."

"Wow," I hear Millie say with a sigh.

"Holden already gave me his blessing to ask you," I add for good measure, and her eyes, already full of tears, widen.

"He did?"

"I did," her brother confirms. "I just want you to be happy."

Without looking at her brother, Dani smiles up at me, two tears breaking loose and falling down her cheeks. "You *do* make me really happy. Sometimes I don't know if I deserve to feel so good."

"Ah, kitten." I kiss the tip of her nose. "You deserve the world. Let me give it to you."

"Yes, Bridger Blackwell, I'll marry you."

"Yay!" Birdie wraps her little arms around our legs, hugging us close as the others applaud, and I grin down at my girl.

"Are you happy?" I ask her, and she nods. "Use your words."

She bites her lip, and I tug it free with my thumb.

"I'm really fucking happy."

Chapter Twenty-Eight

DANI

Christmas Eve

"I've never pulled a wedding together so fast in my entire career," Charlie says with a laugh. We're in the bridal suite at the Wild River Ranch Event Center, getting ready for the ceremony. I wasn't expecting a wedding this big, especially on such short notice. Not to mention, I never thought I'd be able to *afford* one.

It's been a crazy month. Both the arsonist and Angela are in jail, awaiting trial. The Sidney Sterling concert raised enough money to build houses for every family who lost their homes, and as soon as the snow melts in the spring, they'll be underway.

The ski resort is another story altogether, and no one really knows for sure what's going to happen up there, but no lives were lost on Thanksgiving night, and that's the most important thing.

"You guys." I swallow hard and turn to my girls. I'm so blessed with so many amazing women in my life, and this is just a few of them.

Bee, Alex, Charlie, and Darby are here with me. All of the Wild women have been in and out to check on us and then see to other preparations, making sure that everything goes off without a hitch.

Bridger's parents arrived two days ago, and they'll stay in town through New Year's Day.

I love that our whole family is here, and the fire station is working with a skeleton crew for a few hours so most of Bridger's guys can be here for him.

Unfortunately, Skyla is in Ireland to spend the holidays with her family, so she can't be here, but she's been a part of the shower and so much of the planning, and she called me just this morning to gush about how happy she is for me.

"There's already a *lot* of people out there," Millie says as she bustles in. She's dressed in the prettiest green dress that brings out the green in her eyes, and I sigh.

"You're so pretty, Mill."

"Aw, look who's drunk on love," Millie says with a wink and then kisses my cheek. "You're the one who's gorgeous. This dress is just *wow.*"

"Charlie found it." I turn to the mirror and grin. When I told Charlie what I wanted, my sister went on a hunt, and this was shipped to us from Alabama. Thankfully, it only needed minor alterations.

I wanted lace, and a lot of it. The bodice is form-fitting, showing off my cleavage, and the skirt smooths over my hips and then flares at my knees.

Charlie calls it a *mermaid* style, and the description fits.

My hair is up, and I said no to a veil. I want to see my man clearly as I make my way down the aisle to him. Instead, I have a pretty clip in my hair with crystals that sparkle in the light.

"Birdie, it's time for you to get dressed, baby," Bee says.

We were holding off on putting Birdie in her gorgeous white dress until the last minute because she's been scarfing down gluten-free chocolate cookies, thanks to Jackie Harmon.

Blake tested Birdie for celiac disease, and sure enough, she has it. It's been an adjustment in our kitchen at home and what we cook, as well as what we get for her when we go out, but this is something we can manage, and my baby girl is already feeling better.

There's a knock on the door, and Millie answers it, smiling when she sees her man. "Well, hello, husband. You look delicious."

Holden smirks as he walks in, dips his wife back to kiss her, and then scans the room for me.

And when he finds me, his blue eyes, so much like mine, soften.

"There's my girl."

"Hey." I do a little twirl and then laugh when Holden walks to me and kisses my cheek. "Don't make me cry. It took an hour to get my face like this."

"You're so fucking beautiful," he whispers, just for me. Holden has been my safe place since I was a baby. He was our mother *and* our father. Our protector. Our fierce warrior.

And he's never once let us down.

Suddenly, I realize that everyone is leaving the room, even Birdie.

"Ten minutes until you walk down the aisle," Charlie says with a wink, and then the door closes, and I'm alone with my brother.

"Thanks for walking me down the aisle. I know how much you love being the center of attention."

Holden laughs at that and then shrugs. "I'd do just about anything for you. You know that."

"Yeah. I know." I swallow hard, willing the tears to stay away. "You know, I don't think that any of us has ever really thanked you for stepping up the way you did."

"And you never will because you're mine, and protecting every one of you is what I was born to do."

Okay, maybe just one tear. My brother reaches up to catch it on his finger, then brushes his knuckles over my cheek.

"After all of the shit we went through as kids, you deserve this happiness, Dani. I see how you are with Bridger and Birdie, and it's damn satisfying to know that you're thriving. That you're loved, and you love them, too."

"More than anything."

He nods and pulls something out of his pocket. It's a

small box, with a red ribbon on the top. "Bridger sent me in here with this for you. A wedding day gift."

Accepting the box, I push open the lid and then sigh.

"Wow," I murmur, touching the diamond pendant with the tip of my finger. "He already gave me an incredible engagement ring. He didn't have to do this."

"He likes to spoil you, as he should. Want me to fasten it for you?"

"Yes, please." Holden picks up the necklace, and I turn and lift my hair out of the way for him. Once the clasp is fastened, I turn and look in the mirror. "I love things that sparkle."

My brother laughs at that. "Most women do, honey. Are you ready?"

"I'm ready." I gather my bouquet of red and white poinsettias, and Holden offers me his arm, then leads me out of the room.

"I love you," he murmurs as we reach the end of the aisle, and I take everything in. There are no fewer than ten huge Christmas trees, all decorated perfectly. Lights are strung, giving off a soft, Christmas glow.

And don't even get me started on the stunning garland.

It looks like Santa Claus threw up in here, and it's absolutely amazing.

"I love you more," I whisper to him, and then my eyes move up the aisle to where my love waits for me, and my heart feels like it's going to burst.

I didn't want to do a *first look* moment for the photographer before the ceremony. I wanted Bridger's first sight of me to be right now, when I'm on my brother's arm, walking down the aisle to him.

And when I see his eyes get shiny, I know it's totally worth it.

Bridger bites his lip and then brushes a tear away as Holden and I stop just a few steps away from him.

"Who gives this woman to this man?"

"I do," Holden replies, and then he kisses my cheek. He reaches out and shakes Bridger's hand before he sits next to Millie in the front row.

With Bridger's hand in mine, I face him, and in front of everyone we know and love, we exchange traditional vows that have me choking up.

"As long as we both shall live," I finish, my smile bright because I'm *so* ready for this next part.

"By the power vested in me by the state of Montana, I now pronounce you man and wife. You may kiss your bride, Chief."

Bridger grins, leans in, covers my mouth with his, and kisses me so long and slow that there are catcalls in the audience.

"I'm so desperately in love with you, Mrs. Blackwell," he whispers against my lips as the room erupts in applause.

"I love you, too, *Chief.*"

His eyebrow pops up at that, and a slow smile spreads over his lips, making my core tighten and my panties damp with anticipation. "Oh, kitten. You know better than that."

Epilogue

BECKETT BLACKWELL

Just when things start to look up at the ranch, something happens to fuck it all up. That seems to be the trend these days, and it's stressing me the fuck out.

"I'm going into town for one hour," I tell Brad, my ranch foreman. "I need just one damn hour, and then I'll be back."

"You got it, boss," Brad says with a nod. "I can handle it."

I peel off my gloves and toss them onto my desk. Grabbing my keys, I get into my truck and head for town. I want a coffee, and while I'm there, I'll check in on my baby sister. Between Bee and Millie, I'll get a laugh, and it'll make me forget about asshole vacationers and equipment that doesn't want to work like it should.

Equipment that's costing me too much fucking money.

"Not thinking about it." I shake my head as I drive

into Bitterroot Valley and then park in front of the coffee shop that's right next door to Billie's Books, my sister's place.

First, caffeine.

The bell over the door dings as I walk into the coffee shop, and Millie grins at me with a wave.

"Hey, Beck. How's it going?"

It's the shittiest day so far this week. But I don't say that. Instead, I nod and give her a grin. "It's all right. How are things in here?"

"Hopping," she replies and passes me the coffee that I didn't even have to order because she knows what I like. "Even though the resort burned down in November, there are still a lot of tourists in town for the holidays, and that seems to be extending into January."

Nodding, I tap my card to the screen, paying for my order. "Yeah, I'm full, too."

"How's the guest ranch doing?" she asks, leaning against the counter as she crosses her arms over her chest.

"It's both great and a pain in my ass." I sip my coffee, enjoying the way that first jolt hits my system. "I'll get it figured out with time."

"I know you will." Millie winks at me and then turns her attention to more customers. I walk across the room to where the coffee shop opens to the bookstore and stop cold at the vision in front of me.

She's a little thing, probably no taller than my chest, but at six foot five, most women are significantly shorter than I am. She's dainty, with fire-red hair and freckles on her flawless face. Her profile shows me a perfect nose and a strong chin, and she's reading the back of a book, swaying side to side as if she hears music in her head.

Before I can approach her, my phone rings, and I scowl at Brad's name.

"Beck here," I say, turning away to look out the window.

"Boss, we need you to come back out here." When he describes the shit show that's just gone down at my ranch, I sigh and hang my head.

One fucking hour. That's all I wanted.

"Be back in twenty."

I hang up and turn back to see if I can talk to the redheaded beauty, but she's gone. And I don't see her when I do a quick scan of the shop.

Not that I have time to date anyone.

With a shake of my head, I push out of the bookstore, frustrated all over again. Adding on to the ranch was meant to be beneficial to the farm and to me. *When will something go right in my fucking life?*

Turn the page for a PREVIEW of Beckett and Skyla's book, WHEN WE BREAK, coming in May 2025!

When We Break Preview

Chapter One

Skyla

"What are you doing right now?"

I pinch my phone between my ear and shoulder and open my car door, ushering Riley into the back seat. I had to buy a huge car for my huge dog.

"I'm on my way to an appointment," I inform my brother. "What are *you* doing right now?"

"I'm between meetings." I can hear the exhaustion in Connor's voice. "Thought I'd check in with you. Any news?"

"No." I start the engine and wait for my phone to connect to the car. "I haven't heard anything in months, and that's encouraging. You know, you don't have to call me every day to ask me if my stalker has found me."

"That's not the only reason I call, and you know it."

"But it's the first thing you ask me. Don't worry, I haven't dropped my guard, but it's been nice to have some peace and quiet."

"It's relieved I am that you feel safe there. That's what you wanted, that's what you got, and that's all that matters. I'll be in town next week."

I frown out the windscreen. "Really? Why's that?"

"A potential investment opportunity. And to check in on my favorite sister."

"Only sister," I remind him with a smile even though he can't see me. "Good, you'll be here for our spring recital. I'll save you a seat."

"Sky—"

"Ah, ah, ah. If you're coming to town, you'll watch my recital. No amount of money you have will get you out of it."

"Fine." He sighs heavily. "I'll watch the bleeding recital. But you'll owe me some meat pies in exchange."

"I can handle that. What day will you be here?"

"I'll know for sure in a day or so. I'll keep you posted."

"See that you do. I'd better go, but I'll talk to you later."

We end the call, and I drive Riley and me from our adorable house to the doctor's office on the edge of town.

When we walk inside, Riley is at my side in his handsome red service-dog harness, we're greeted with a smile.

"Hello, Skyla. I have you all checked in. You can have a seat, and someone will be out for you shortly."

"Thank you." With a nod, I lead Riley to the end of a row so he can lie down next to me.

I'm completely obsessed with Bitterroot Valley, which has mountains and a quaint downtown full of shops and restaurants that I love. With the sweet people who have welcomed me here. It couldn't be more different from New York City, which I also loved, but this small town has quickly become home in the eight months or so that I've lived here. I have friends and a feeling of belonging that I was afraid I wouldn't find outside my ballet family in New York.

But I've found it here, and I'm so grateful.

"Skyla."

The nurse grins and gestures for me to follow her. Riley is at my side, walking with me.

"How are you today?" she asks.

"I'm doing well. And how are you?"

"It's been a good day around here so far," she says with a wink. "Let's get some vitals on you."

After I've been weighed and my temperature and blood pressure are logged, the nurse hustles out, assuring me that Dr. Blackwell will be here shortly.

Riley lets out a huff from his spot on the floor.

"I hear you."

Not long after, Dr. Blackwell bustles into the room, holding his laptop. He smiles at me and then at my dog. He's a handsome man, that's for certain. He's a mountain next to me, but then, most men are. At five foot five and lean from years of dancing, I'm used to feeling petite. *Some take advantage of that.* But the doctor is also broad and muscular, with dark hair and dark, kind eyes. I'm sure most of his female patients flirt with him endlessly. There's no spark here for me, but he's certainly nice to look at while I'm here.

"Hello, you two," he says as he sits on the stool next to me and types on the keyboard.

"Hi, Dr. Blackwell."

"Just call me Blake. How's that ankle been feeling, Skyla?"

"Not normal," is my immediate reply, and he frowns over at me.

"Okay, can you be more specific?"

The usual frustration sets in. "It's not *normal*. Not how it was before it was injured."

Before it ended my bloody career.

"Well, that's not unusual. But you've done everything right. You did PT for longer than was necessary, and looking at this MRI from last week, the injury is completely healed. I would give you the clearance to dance right this minute if that's what you wanted to do."

"But I *can't*." I shake my head. "Of course, I don't plan to return to New York to resume my professional career. That's not possible. But even when I dance for pleasure in my studio, it's not the same. The range of motion, the force it can handle when I jeté—"

He lifts an eyebrow.

"When I leap or jump," I clarify, "and land on it. There's *no way* I'd be able to put in fourteen-hour practice and rehearsal days."

"And you don't have to," he reminds me gently. "It's

386

my understanding that such rigorous days aren't a part of your lifestyle anymore."

"But I should be able to if I had to." I lift my chin. "I hate that it doesn't feel normal."

Dr. Blackwell sets his computer aside and gives me his undivided attention.

"Skyla, ankle sprains are sometimes worse than fractures. They heal slowly, and occasionally, the full range of motion doesn't return. But you're a strong and gifted athlete, and I think that with time and practice, you'll feel more and more normal."

"Ankles are important in ballet," I mutter.

"I know." He nods and glances at Riley, who hasn't taken his eyes off the doctor. "Strength training, stretches —all the exercises you did in PT will help."

I nod, feeling defeated all over again. "That's all we can do?"

"I'm afraid so. Dancers' bodies take a beating, Skyla. I'm surprised you're not more beat up than this."

"You don't even want to see my feet." I laugh. "They're not pretty."

He chuckles, makes some notes in his computer, and then my appointment is finished. Riley and I leave the office and walk out to the car, and he jumps into his back seat.

I'm not quite ready to go home, so we stop at my new favorite place, Billie's Books. I've become good friends with the owner, Billie Blackwell, who happens to be Dr. Blackwell's sister. We share a love of romance books, and our monthly book club is the highlight of my schedule.

"Hey, girl." Bee waves as she rings up a customer's purchase. "That new Monica Murphy book is on the shelf there."

With a grin, I find the paperback and hug it to my chest. Monica Murphy is one of my favorites, and I've been waiting for this one. Of course, I have it on my e-reader, but I'm also a paperback collector.

I turned one of my guest rooms into a library. It might not be the size of Belle's in *Beauty and the Beast*, but it's mine, and I love filling it up.

Taking my purchase to the counter, I smile at my friend as she rings me up. Bee's a gorgeous girl with dark hair perfectly styled in long, beachy waves around her shoulders. She's in a smart gray suit today, and *as usual*, her makeup is perfect.

This woman knows fashion, and I love it.

"How's it going?" Bee asks.

"I'm better now that I have this beauty for my shelves." I swipe my card and shake my head when she offers me a bag. "Do you mind if I sit in one of your cozy chairs and read for a bit?"

"That's what the chairs are for," she reminds me. "Since it's quiet in here, I'm going to run next door for a coffee. Would you like one?"

"Just a black Earl Grey tea would be lovely. Thank you."

"You got it. Back in a few."

Riley and I settle in our favorite spot. The purple

388

chair is deep and cozy, and Bee added a dog bed next to it just for Riley. He turns in a circle and lies down, but he's still on alert.

"Good boy," I say to him and rub his head before I open the book and get sucked into this talented author's words.

Bee drops off the tea, then bustles back to work. I enjoy an hour by the window, reading and relaxing, until I finally decide to head over to the studio to prepare for my afternoon class. It was a good choice to come to Bitterroot Valley. I might not have full range of motion in my ankle, but I'm fully and strangely content. At peace.

So bloody thankful.

Get more information on WHEN WE BREAK here: https://www.kristenprobyauthor.com/when-we-break

Newsletter Sign Up

I hope you enjoyed reading this story as much as I enjoyed writing it! For upcoming book news, be sure to join my newsletter! I promise I will only send you news-filled mail, and none of the spam. You can sign up here:

https://mailchi.mp/kristenproby.com/newsletter-sign-up

Also by Kristen Proby:

Other Books by Kristen Proby

The Wilds of Montana Series
Wild for You - Remington & Erin
Chasing Wild - Chase & Summer
Wildest Dreams - Ryan & Polly
On the Wild Side - Brady & Abbi
She's a Wild One - Holden & Millie

The Blackwells of Montana
When We Burn - Bridger & Dani

Get more information on the series here: https://www.kristenprobyauthor.com/the-wilds-of-montana

Single in Seattle Series
The Secret - Vaughn & Olivia

The Scandal - Gray & Stella
The Score - Ike & Sophie
The Setup - Keaton & Sidney
The Stand-In - Drew & London

Check out the full series here: https://www.
kristenprobyauthor.com/single-in-seattle

Huckleberry Bay Series

Lighthouse Way
Fernhill Lane
Chapel Bend
Cherry Lane

The With Me In Seattle Series

Come Away With Me - Luke & Natalie
Under The Mistletoe With Me - Isaac & Stacy
Fight With Me - Nate & Jules
Play With Me - Will & Meg
Rock With Me - Leo & Sam
Safe With Me - Caleb & Brynna
Tied With Me - Matt & Nic
Breathe With Me - Mark & Meredith
Forever With Me - Dominic & Alecia
Stay With Me - Wyatt & Amelia
Indulge With Me
Love With Me - Jace & Joy

Dance With Me Levi & Starla
You Belong With Me - Archer & Elena
Dream With Me - Kane & Anastasia
Imagine With Me - Shawn & Lexi
Escape With Me - Keegan & Isabella
Flirt With Me - Hunter & Maeve
Take a Chance With Me - Cameron & Maggie

Check out the full series here: https://www.
kristenprobyauthor.com/with-me-in-seattle

The Big Sky Universe

Love Under the Big Sky
Loving Cara
Seducing Lauren
Falling for Jillian
Saving Grace

The Big Sky
Charming Hannah
Kissing Jenna
Waiting for Willa
Soaring With Fallon

Big Sky Royal
Enchanting Sebastian
Enticing Liam
Taunting Callum

Heroes of Big Sky
Honor
Courage
Shelter

Check out the full Big Sky universe here: https://
www.kristenprobyauthor.com/under-the-big-sky

Bayou Magic

Shadows
Spells
Serendipity

Check out the full series here: https://www.
kristenprobyauthor.com/bayou-magic

The Curse of the Blood Moon Series

Hallows End
Cauldrons Call
Salems Song

The Romancing Manhattan Series

All the Way
All it Takes
After All

Check out the full series here: https://www.
kristenprobyauthor.com/romancing-manhattan

The Boudreaux Series

Easy Love
Easy Charm
Easy Melody
Easy Kisses
Easy Magic
Easy Fortune
Easy Nights

Check out the full series here: https://www.
kristenprobyauthor.com/boudreaux

The Fusion Series

Listen to Me
Close to You
Blush for Me
The Beauty of Us
Savor You

Check out the full series here: https://www.
kristenprobyauthor.com/fusion

From 1001 Dark Nights

Nothing Without You: A Forever Yours/Big Sky Novella
By Monica Murphy

Check out the entire Crossover Collection here:
https://www.kristenprobyauthor.com/kristen-proby-crossover-collection

About the Author

Kristen Proby is a *New York Times*, *USA Today*, and *Wall Street Journal* bestselling author of over seventy published titles. She debuted in 2012, captivating fans with spicy contemporary romance about families and friends with plenty of swoony love. She also writes paranormal romance and suggests you keep the lights on while reading them.

When not under deadline, Kristen enjoys spending time with her husband and their fur babies, riding her bike, relaxing with embroidery, trying her hand at painting, and, of course, enjoying her beautiful home in the mountains of Montana.

Made in United States
North Haven, CT
18 February 2025

66014423R00248